Praise for Holly Brown's *This Is Not Over*

"*This Is Not Over* moves with the unstoppable force of a runaway train. You won't be able to look away as the shocking climax rushes toward you. This is storytelling at its best."

—Tess Gerritsen, *New York Times* bestselling author

"Intelligently crafted and rivetingly dark, this chilling tale of two women waging psychological warfare will hook you, capture you, and keep you reading as fast as you can. Timely, terrifying, and disturbingly believable."

—Hank Phillippi Ryan, author of *Say No More* and winner of the Agatha, Anthony, and Mary Higgins Clark Awards

"An intricately plotted and highly entertaining tale of she said, she said, *This Is Not Over* takes a phenomenon of our times—the home away from home vacation rental—and exposes its potential for wreaking havoc on a pair of ordinary lives. Holly Brown ratchets up the tension, twist by startling twist, as a homeowner and a vacationer refuse to let go of a minor dispute and insinuate themselves into each other's lives. Brown manages to plumb the depths of social class, drug addiction, and family discord, all against a backdrop of everyday terror that should leave millions of readers wondering, 'Whom did I tick off today?'"

—Jenny Milchman, *USA Today* bestselling author of *Cover of Snow, Ruin Falls,* and *As Night Falls*

"*This Is Not Over* is dark, twisting, and addictive. I devoured it in one sitting, absorbed by both the driving plot and the layered family psychology."

—Flynn Berry, author of *Under the Harrow*

"*This Is Not Over* is an absolutely riveting novel that starts with a situation that could happen to any of us, and slowly and masterfully escalates it into a crisis of character for two women that is both nail-bitingly suspenseful and full of insight into our collective humanity."

—Alice LaPlante, *New York Times*
bestselling author of *Turn of Mind*

"Holly Brown's *This Is Not Over* is a hypnotic, psychological thriller that had me hooked from the opening sentence. Cleverly paced and pulsating with tension, *This Is Not Over* is the heart-pounding account of two women who resort to desperate measures to protect what they love. With sharp wit and an eye for detail, Brown takes the reader on a wild ride right up to the mind-bending conclusion. I thought I knew what was going to happen and was I wrong—brilliant!"

—Heather Gudenkauf, *New York Times* bestselling
author of *The Weight of Silence* and *Not a Sound*

"Brown, a licensed mental-health professional, offers a compelling look at two women from very different walks of life who have more in common than they care to admit. It's clear that Brown uses her expertise to the hilt—characters all have textbook issues . . . in fact, they don't just have issues, they have a multiyear subscription!"

—*Booklist*

HOW
FAR
SHE'S
COME

ALSO BY HOLLY BROWN

This Is Not Over

Stay Gone (novella)

A Necessary End

Don't Try to Find Me

5/18

HOW FAR

a novel

SHE'S COME

HOLLY BROWN

WM

WILLIAM MORROW

An Imprint of HarperCollinsPublishers

P.S.™ is a trademark of HarperCollins Publishers.

HarperCollins books may be purchased for educational, business, or sales promotional use. For information, please email the Special Markets Department at SPsales@harpercollins.com.

FIRST EDITION

Designed by Diahann Sturge

Library of Congress Cataloging-in-Publication Data has been applied for.

ISBN 978-0-06-274992-5

18 19 20 21 22 LSC 10 9 8 7 6 5 4 3 2 1

For Darrend and Daisy, always

ACKNOWLEDGMENTS

Love and thanks to my friends and family, especially to my parents, who believed I could do anything, and to the other two legs of my tripod, Darrend and Daisy, who make me want to do it all.

I am so appreciative of my agent, Elisabeth Weed, and my editor, Carrie Feron, for standing by me and supporting my aims as a woman, a mother, and a thriller writer. This book has gone through multiple extensive rewrites in a relatively short time, and while at times it was hard to face down the pages again, I'm extremely pleased by how far it's come. Thanks for always pushing, Carrie, in the best way.

I'm very grateful to Lisa Sharkey at HarperCollins for lending her vast knowledge and expertise of the media world. She was great at figuring out how realistic details could also become exciting plot points. And she wasn't even assigned to my book; she was just that generous. Harper is full of tremendously dedicated and talented professionals, and I'm so glad I've gotten to work with Sharyn Rosenblum, Julie Paulauski, Kaitlin Harri, and Carolyn Coons. Thanks for being on my team!

This book is close to my heart because I have a little girl and I want her to grow up to know that her gifts are about so much more than her sexuality, and her power is equal to any male's. This is a unique cultural moment, and I'm proud that this novel can come out in its midst. We all bear responsibility for shaping a future where everyone can safely live up to their potential.

Me too.

HOW
FAR
SHE'S
COME

PROLOGUE

They're watching me, I know that. And I'm not talking about the viewers at home, though it's no coincidence that ratings are up.

If they killed once, they can kill again. No one's loyal to me. Conspiracies are real.

I can feel my knees buckling, about to give way. While the past two months have been a crash course in power and paranoia, the truth is, I don't have any real journalism training—or nearly enough life training—to stand up to . . . who? Who's the real puppet master? How deep does it go?

At least I have the diary.

I can do this. I will do this, because I have to. They need to be stopped.

This can't be the end of my story.

CHAPTER 1

Eight Weeks Earlier

Has he already seen me naked?

It's usually my first thought when I encounter a new male. This time, though, it's not about my professor or a stranger walking toward me on the street or the cashier or someone who was supposed to be my friend but it turns out really only tolerated me for Chase's sake and who might very well be posting anonymously behind my back. This time, I'm thinking it about billionaire Edwin Gordon, he of the ordinary name and the enormous wealth, who helms INN, the Independent News Network ("Because independent thinking is the only way out").

I almost didn't come here today, figuring the invitation was most likely a cruel joke. One of the internet trolls decided to get creative and was nearby filming, ready to expose me as I craned my neck, searching for the private jet that supposedly had me listed on the manifest. He was waiting to catch me in the act, guilty of the ultimate hubris: believing I'd been marked as special, that Edwin Gordon actually wanted to meet me. But I decided that I wasn't going to pass this up, on the off chance it was real. It wasn't until I was in the Lyft headed for the Palo Alto Airport that it occurred to me that humiliation might be one of the better scenarios. A pro-rape activist who'd targeted me online could be luring me to the airport to kidnap me and carry out his sick fantasies. It might not be a joke but a trap.

Four months ago, that would have seemed beyond paranoid. Four months ago, I didn't know that "pro-rape activists" existed.

For the most part, I don't need to worry about the trolls anymore. About being heckled or threatened. About being photographed or followed. About my phone being hacked and my private texts and photos made public. That's because I shut it all down. I let them run me off the internet in exchange for some peace of mind. It wasn't a fair deal, but it was the only thing on offer from the police, and while I don't really have peace yet, I'm a lot closer than I was.

But this is no joke. I'm really here, on a private plane as sumptuous as I imagine a suite at the Ritz-Carlton would be, not that I've ever been in a Ritz-Carlton. I'm a twenty-four-year-old recent college graduate, and granted, that college is Stanford, where silver-spoon kids have been on many private planes and in many Ritz-Carltons, but I'm not one of them. I was raised in Tulip, Montana, a small town two hours north of Missoula, where my father ran a grocery co-op frequented by ranchers and aging hippies. The mother I never knew must have thought it hilarious to name me Cheyenne, so I could spend the next however many years I'm on this planet telling people that I'm not actually from Wyoming but from a state nearly as underpopulated.

Yet none of those silver-spoon kids are here, on a silk couch, across from Edwin Gordon. My legs are crossed chastely—*has he already seen in between them?*—while Edwin has his shoes off, his navy-blue-striped shirt untucked and unwrinkled, and a bourbon in his hand. When asked by a flight attendant, I declined not only alcohol but water. I'm not sure I'll be able to keep anything down. I'm glad my long red hair is pulled back in a low ponytail, so I can't fidget with it.

Edwin is in his early forties, his dark hair silvered in a way that looks strategic and a ridged forehead that's supposed to signal he's eschewed Botox, though the rest of his tanned face is suspiciously boyish. He's not exactly handsome, but his level of power makes up the gap so that he's just about the most attractive man I've ever seen in the flesh.

Not that it matters, because I have a boyfriend, and everyone knows that, to his credit, Edwin dates women his own age or older. They're entrepreneurs and philanthropists and humanitarians whose accomplishments are matched only by their immaculately preserved beauty, as if they've been cryogenically frozen and revived moments before their latest public appearance.

Edwin smiles and says, "You want to know why you're here?"

I'm too nervous to smile back, sweating in the summer-weight light gray blazer and skirt I bought for interviews, of which I've had only three since last month's graduation. My GPA was a 2.9, and my major was sociology. Every time a prospective employer googles my name, autofill will suggest the search "Cheyenne Florian naked."

Yes, I definitely want to know why I'm here.

"You're my dream girl from when I was a twenty-something," Edwin says, and my green eyes widen in shock. Plenty of men hit on me—and worse—but this is *Edwin Gordon.* "I'm hoping that you'll speak at some point in this conversation. That would be what defines it as a conversation, as opposed to a monologue."

Then suddenly, the flattery wears off, and I get it. I want to ask if this plane is taking off or if I'm just a stopover. A quickie. I've been sexualized by strangers, without my consent or my intent, for months now.

"I'm going to get off now," I say. Then I turn red, realizing that my language itself was inadvertently sexualized. Minefields everywhere. I stand up. "Nice meeting you."

"Wait, what just happened?"

"Like you haven't seen the pictures. Maybe you saw the video that sparked it all, maybe not. But I'm not who people have made me out to be. I'm an actual flesh-and-blood human being and not anyone's fuckbot. So, nice meeting you."

I start to head for the door, pushing past the two men who could be most accurately described as goons and who are standing sentinel on either side of Edwin's couch.

Edwin gets up and makes a move as if to block me. I can't help it, I flinch. I never used to flinch when a man was in my path. These months have changed me, which makes me even madder.

Edwin steps back and raises his arms in the air, like he's a hostage. As if he knows anything about that. About having to restrict his movements out of fear. About making his world small. Making himself small. Wishing for invisibility.

"I'm sorry," he says in a low voice, "for the terrible things people have done to you."

I look at him and find that he does seem truly sorrowful. But as much as I never wanted to be a sex object, I never wanted to be an object of pity either.

"I want to help you turn it all around," he says. "To use what happened to you to make a difference."

"What are you saying, exactly?"

"I'm here to offer you a job. I watched your videos. All of them. I was following you for months before everything happened. Scouting you."

Honestly, this is one scenario that never crossed my mind.

"Could we sit down? I'm an old man. I've got bad knees." He smiles. "Please?"

I pause a few beats, just trying to push through the absurdity of all this. Besides, it never hurts to make 'em wait. Slowly, I nod.

We retake our seats. He's on his silk couch, I'm on mine. It's really a very feminine jet. Is it possible it's borrowed? Or maybe one of his many women decorated it.

Focus, Cheyenne.

"When I said you were my dream girl—bad leadoff, by the way, I apologize—that was when I was what would now be called a millennial, though I was Generation X. Not that it matters." He shakes his head, impatient with himself. Is Edwin Gordon actually nervous talking to me? I almost want to smile. "I believe that the under-thirty set hasn't changed that much in their tastes. I want that demographic for INN. But I think you'll appeal to all males, really, including the old-timers who remember Rita Hayworth. Right now, the elderly watch the news. Fox, especially, is watched by men over sixty. Based on the originality of their programming, MSNBC and CNN seem content to let news die a natural death along with its viewers, but I have other plans. INN's going to succeed by trying where no one else has."

"I thought INN was already successful."

"We're not making the money we could."

"I thought it was a passion project." I like challenging him. Keeping him on his toes, after I've spent so much time lately off-balance.

"In my experience, passion equals profit."

I'm oddly disappointed. I've never watched much television, choosing to get my information from a handful of fact-checking websites and trusted blogs until the past few months, when, in addition to shutting down, I've been tuning out. That means I've barely seen INN since it launched a year ago, but I've been rooting for it. Its stated mission resonates with me: context-rich journalism, a pursuit of the truth, and a nonpartisan commitment to the public good. Other networks are as beholden to special interests as the politicians themselves, but INN isn't beholden to anyone, because Edwin is its owner and only funder, putting principle above profit.

So much for that. I should have fact-checked INN's propaganda before this meeting.

"If I have to keep funneling my own money to stay in the game," he says, "I always will. Because this is the cause of my life. Because I'm a patriot, not in any partisan sense of the word. A well-informed electorate is the only thing that'll save this country, and INN is the only network that's really invested in creating that. I want those advertising dollars because that means that I'm getting to the demographic that can change the future."

"You think only millennial men can change the future?"

"I think millennial females have done all they can, and now the men need to get on board. I know you care about the direction of this country. That's why you made those videos, right?"

I used to care about the country. Lately, all I've cared about is myself, and staying safe.

"After all, you are the independent vlogger with the red-state name."

So he didn't just watch my videos; he read the comments. And that's before the one went viral. "I'm not a vlogger anymore."

"I was sad when you let those assholes run you out."

Let them? Like I had any choice. I give him a stony stare.

"I'm sorry. That came out wrong. I just meant I've missed your videos. I've missed your voice."

Our eyes meet. It's a loaded moment. An intimate moment.

"Then I realized that's where I come in. You went viral once, so you can do it again, on a much larger scale, with the INN machinery behind you. You'll be unstoppable."

A much larger scale. That sounds . . . terrifying.

"That video was an aberration," I say.

"No, it wasn't. I loved your videos. I loved that you weren't right or left. You're a true homegrown independent, Cheyenne, and that's what I'm looking for."

I'm my father's daughter. I believe ranchers and hippies should be able to talk politics, and everything else. I believe in solving problems through information and discourse. But that doesn't make me a broadcaster.

"I see some of Ty Fordham in you," he says.

I haven't watched much INN, but everyone knows about Ty Fordham. He's the Angry Independent, INN's biggest star, combining Sean Hannity's vitriol with Rachel Maddow's brains. "I'm not really very angry."

"You could have fooled me."

"Well, I wasn't, before."

He doesn't have to ask "before what?"

"You're not angry by nature, which is good. No one wants to see women truly angry. But they like to see fire. Did you ever watch Megyn Kelly at the height of her power, back when she was still on Fox? That was barely contained fury, right there. That's righteous indignation. There's an appetite for that sort of thing that you can fill."

"I'm not that righteously indignant anymore." When your energy is wrapped up in survival, outrage becomes a luxury.

"You sure know how to sell yourself, don't you?"

"I'm not the one doing the selling." He smiles. He likes my fire. I used to like it too.

"You're a natural, and a critical thinker. Everything else can be taught."

It's a good line, sure, but can it really be true?

"I know what I'm looking for, and I know what you've got. You're gorgeous, with a true independent streak. That's a devastating combination from where I'm sitting. This time around, you're not just going to withstand controversy; you're going to reap the benefits."

Last time, I had to retreat. It was the only way to feel safe. I didn't have a news organization behind me then, but still. "Do I need to be controversial?"

"You will be, because of how you look and because you've come out of nowhere. Right out of the gate, there will be the Tomi Lahren comparisons."

After my viral video, I endured plenty of those. Tomi Lahren vaulted to fame (or ignominy, depending on your perspective) straight out of college with her big blond hair and big boobs and conservative views, expressed in the most provocative and incendiary ways. Some call her the next Ann Coulter, others "White Power Barbie." She was referenced in a Jay-Z song, and not in a good way. But then, for Tomi, there seems to be no bad way. All press is good press.

"I'm nothing like her," I say.

"I know. If you were, you'd have capitalized on your video instead of pulling it. So we need to work on thickening your skin."

"I don't like being followed by strange men. I don't like being the object of their rape fantasies on Twitter. I don't like women calling me antifeminist, or a traitor. I don't like—"

"Learn to like it. It means you're part of the conversation. People are interested."

"I don't want that kind of interest."

In response to my raised voice, he drops his, scooting closer. "It's a platform. You did those vlogs for no other reason than because you cared. You were crying out for a mission, and I heard you. That's why I'm here."

It's harder to think now that I can smell his cologne, warm and earthy and a little bit spicy. Or maybe that's just him.

"You weren't ready for the barrage last time. This time, you will be. INN will protect you."

He's close enough to touch. "What would I be doing at INN?" I ask softly. We haven't gone anywhere, so there's no roar of engines to overcome. It's like no one else is here—not the flight attendants or the goons. It's just Edwin and me.

"You'd start out as a cross-show correspondent, which means you'd be everywhere. The viewers will get to know you, and that's just the beginning. There are no limits."

When everything went down four months ago, all I wanted was to be anonymous again. Now I'd be putting myself directly in the line of fire. But who could turn down a chance like this? Who doesn't want to be unlimited?

"Can you work hard?" he says. I nod. "Like I said, what you've got can't be taught. But you have a lot to learn. You'll need to take full ownership of a story, and then you'll be the network expert across the shows."

"What story?" I ask, a touch suspiciously.

"We'd need to figure that out."

"Would you be the one figuring it out with me?"

"No, that would be your supervising producer. We're going to take very good care of you, Cheyenne." That grin again. His teeth must be regularly whitened. He could be an anchor himself. "I'm not around all the time, but whenever I am, my door is open to you."

"Is there much security at INN?"

"It's tight. And if you need your own, I'm happy to provide it. But none of my other anchors have needed it, including Ty. With online trolls, it's all bark, no bite."

"That's not true. They hacked my phone. Speaking of which, do you really want a news correspondent with a bunch of naked pictures online?"

"Yes, I really do."

I get it: He doesn't think the pictures will hurt me; he wants to use them. They'll help lure more millennials.

I should be offended, yet strangely, I'm not. Edwin said that it's my turn to reap the benefits, and it's an enticing idea. I didn't like being silenced.

"I'll keep you safe, Cheyenne. You're not just going to be a star; you're going to be an influencer. You're going to change the world."

This is too heady. I need to talk to someone. My father, or Chase.

"Come to New York," Edwin says.

"When?"

"Now. I'll take you straight to the studio and show you around."

"So I'd have to move to New York. I mean, if I took the job."

"Yes."

"I have a boyfriend." As soon as it leaves my mouth, I realize how stupid it sounds. A boyfriend is not a mission. Chase has his own mission. He'd never give it up for me, and I'd never ask him to.

Edwin doesn't even dignify my comment.

"Let's go," I say.

CHAPTER 2

D ad, can you hear me?" I'm in a bathroom stall, and though no one else is in the room, I'm whispering. If anyone tries the locked outer handle, I can apologize and say it was an accident. Fumbling fingers, first-day jitters, though it's not really true; it's not a job yet, just the world's strangest job interview, more seduction than interrogation. It's like I have nothing to prove, already, and somehow, as the day has worn on, that's become scarier than the inverse. Edwin the Billionaire has already bought shares in my stock, and he's the one trying to demonstrate that INN is a sound investment. The whole thing is—well, surreal is an understatement. I have to invent a new word. Transreal.

That's why I need my dad, the most levelheaded, best man I could ever hope to know.

But first, I have to ask. "How are you feeling?" I always get slight butterflies before his answer.

"It's a good day," he says.

"No pain?"

"Not much. I'm breathing easy. Got the energy of a man only twice my age." He chuckles. He's had it rough and yet he's so appreciative of everything, and—he tells me often—most of all for me. His beautiful, brilliant daughter.

His words, not mine. But suddenly, they've been pretty much echoed by a mogul. I lean my head against the cool silver partition between stalls. It's just too much.

"And how's your day?"

Deep breath. "Well, you're not going to believe this. I still don't believe it, but . . ."

Even with no one around, I lower my voice further. It's superstition, a knock on wood. It's the same way I tell people that Dad's cancer is well controlled by the clinical trial.

I try to convey the initial conversation with Edwin, his offer, and the five-hour plane ride that followed where we were basically hanging out. Our conversation was wide-ranging, and included my experiences at Stanford and his (much earlier) at Yale, and then we relaxed into where we grew up, and after that it was places he'd traveled and where I want to travel, which is everywhere, a list I've never been able to even start because of my father (though of course I don't relay that part; Dad already feels guilty enough about how his illness has impacted my life). Edwin found my desire to experience everything to be a reasonable ambition, one that he intimated he could help me fulfill. Then the plane was landing, and I could have vomited with anticipation. What if I don't want to buy what he's selling? What if I do, desperately? Then there's the fact that New York is so much farther from Montana than California. Not to mention it's so much larger than Tulip or Palo Alto, the only places I've ever lived. So many people, so much danger.

"So you're dating your future boss?" Dad sounds bemused.

Or maybe he's just as thrown by all this as I am. As smart as he is, he's not exactly worldly. He's never been to New York City. I'm pretty sure he's never watched INN.

"It definitely wasn't a date."

"It doesn't sound like any job interview I've ever heard of. Is this really how things are done?"

"I have no idea how things are done."

"Do you have time to find out? Can you slow this down?"

I don't know what the rules are. I just know that Edwin is giving me the shot of all shots. "What if while I'm taking more time, he has a change of heart?"

"Then it wasn't meant to be." But he doesn't sound convinced.

"He says he sees something in me, Dad. He really thinks I can do this."

"You can do anything. The question is, do you want to do this? It's not like you've been talking about being on TV your whole life."

"I made those videos on my own. I mean, I was moved to do that." It could be that there really is a divine plan, and everything does happen for a reason, like those *über*-religious people used to say in the waiting room of the oncology center.

Growing up, I'd suspected a certain preordination of the nonreligious variety. In Tulip, everything had come easy to me. Effortlessly, I did well in school, both academically and athletically; I was popular with people my age and with authority figures. Everyone thought I'd go on to do something big, even though I never had a clear notion of what that would be. College was where I planned to figure it out. Life felt like a smooth conveyor belt, delivering me to Stanford. But once I arrived, I found out what I was really up against, and my faith was sorely tested.

I met people whose entire existences had been focused on getting into Stanford, who'd attended high schools where everyone shared that same goal. They were used to intense competition, while I'd gotten inured to being unparalleled (no one else from my high school had even applied to schools the caliber of Stanford). In my dorm, there was a guy who admitted, without shame, to doing something called "rednecking": his family moved from their Silicon Valley neighborhood to an uncompetitive school in Nowhere California so that he could become the valedictorian, and then they moved back to their multimillion-dollar house just in time for him to be an incoming college freshman. I was the only one who found that shocking.

At Stanford, I felt like a wet stray among the Westminster show dogs. I was woefully underprepared—not only for the academic material, though there was that, but also for the competition. Everyone seemed to fall into a rank and order immediately, and I was a marked woman. People could be scathing once they decided you didn't belong, that you'd stolen the spot from someone more qualified, and for the first time in my life, it was hard for me to find friends. While it might have been a matter of acquiring better study skills and applying myself, it felt like I simply wasn't good enough. All my life I'd been lulled into a false sense of security, and now the lie had been exposed.

I had no practice being an underdog. The only thing that buoyed me was Chase. He was a golden boy, and he didn't just like me for how I looked; it became much more than that.

I should call Chase. His start-up, Until, is a darling of Silicon Valley, which is where Edwin made his first billion, and Chase is the darling of Until. He's a unicorn, the rarest of the rare: a brilliant computer programmer who's also great with people. Chase knows how to handle himself around the rich and powerful, around anyone. He'd be much better for advice than Dad, honestly.

But somehow, I can't bring myself to call him.

"Did Edwin give you a tour?" Dad asks.

"Yes."

The newsroom is an ocean of workstations with no barriers between them, and when Edwin and I had first walked in, everyone had been talking on their phones. The hubbub was incredible. I have no idea how anyone hears themselves, or the person on the other end.

There are offices surrounding the newsroom that belong to the executive producers of each show and to the anchors. The broadcasting studios are on another floor.

As we walked through, people barely looked up at Edwin, they were so engrossed in their tasks. "At other cable news networks," Edwin explained, "shows are trying to scoop each other. Their staffs are often at each other's throats. Here, there's teamwork. We all rise and fall together. We fail or succeed together, as a network. So the staff shares leads and follows them down. There's openness and transparency, as there should be in other industries like, say, government."

It's a utopian ideal, but I think of what I learned at Stanford about people who are that intelligent and that driven. They're not built to pool their resources.

Edwin took out his cell and sent an email or a text or some form of alert, because within five minutes, everyone was hanging up their phones and filing into the glass-walled conference room abutting the newsroom. Edwin was shaking hands and slapping backs.

There were fifty or sixty staffers in a conference room meant to hold a quarter of that number. The whole scene looked like a fire hazard, some sort of disaster waiting to happen, or maybe that was just my anxiety talking. The enormity of the situation had hit me hard, and while I knew what Edwin thought of me, his staff was another matter. They were packed in, standing, with an air of blasé anticipation. Most didn't seem much older than me, but they were rumpled in a hip/intellectual way. They wore the right glasses.

How many of these people have seen me naked?

My fifteen minutes of fame were a while ago, but these are the type of people who would remember. The viral video, like all my vlogs, was basically an opinion piece with some research behind it; I've never claimed to be a journalist. I don't know if that works for or against me in their eyes.

"This is Cheyenne Florian," Edwin began, "and she's going to be a star. INN wants in." Oh, Lord. "I just sprang all this on Cheyenne this morning. I had her meet me at an airstrip, propositioned her, and flew her here. She's handled it with great aplomb, but if she looks a little shell-shocked, well, you know why, and you know who to blame." They all laughed, like they were familiar with Edwin's antics, as if this was how he got all his correspondents. I would have preferred if he'd used a different word than "propositioned."

"One of the things I like most about Cheyenne," Edwin continued, "one of the things I like most about anyone, is raw, untutored presence. I like a lack of calculation. All our on-air personalities radiate authenticity and integrity. They're not afraid to be emphatic and to take a position against dishonesty and corruption. I've kept Cheyenne a little off-kilter today because to me, that reveals character, and she gave it right back to me, which also reveals character." So the day's been an audition after all. "She's everything we value at INN. Cheyenne"—he turned to me—"would you like to say a few words?"

Another test. I forced myself to look out at the expectant faces. Some were more frankly evaluating than others, but not in a sexualized way. I detected no hostility, or even wariness. They must trust Edwin, and that helped me relax just the tiniest bit.

Time to picture all of them naked.

I started with a smile. "It's great to meet you. Since this is a place for people to be real, I'll tell you that I didn't major in broadcast journalism, but the future of this country is deeply important to me. I believe that facts are nonpartisan. I believe that independent and critical thinking is vital. I believe in INN's mission. If I get the chance to work alongside all of you, I'll be honored, I really will. Thank you."

It wasn't incredible oratory, but it was competently delivered. It was sincere. In my peripheral vision, I could see Edwin's approval. He stepped forward and said, "Cheyenne hasn't officially accepted my offer"—that grin again—"but I'm going to do my best to persuade her. Until her debut, I want absolute silence. Secrecy. Loyalty. You know, the usual." He turned serious. "I've got a plan, and there will be no leaks." He surveyed the room, making eye contact with various people in turn.

Then he clapped his hands together. "Meeting adjourned! Thanks for your time! And as Cheyenne walks around, she's going to be asking questions. Answer them, with total honesty. If she's going to be one of us, she needs to know what she's signing up for." That garnered the biggest laugh yet.

Edwin and I formed a sort of receiving line as everyone filed out. There were predominantly warm handshakes, words of welcome, and smiles, but was I imagining the glint of knowing in a few people's eyes, contempt in the eyes of others? That could spread through the office in a terrible contagion. Edwin talked about the controversy I'd generate outside INN, but what about inside? He'd asked for loyalty until my debut, but I wasn't sure what would come after that.

Edwin took me down a floor to the studios. As I looked around, my body hummed with excitement. I wanted this. I want this.

There were four fully built sets. Ty Fordham, Beth Linford (of *Truthiness*), and Khalif Turner (of *Outside INN*) each had their own, decorated in their individual styles. Khalif's had hip-hop letters and an overall bright energy, while Beth's was designed with softer colors and expensive tapestries that portrayed touchability, and Ty's was straight, bold lines and a lot of crimson, a reflection of the angry energy that has been resonating so strongly with viewers. The fourth studio was the most generic, what you'd see at a typical nightly news broadcast, and Edwin told me that it was used by various other anchors throughout the day, for shows like *The Media Is the Message* and the live call-in show *Breaking It Down*. What stood out on all the sets was the proliferation of American flags, with stars and stripes worked in throughout.

"Love of country is not a conservative value," Edwin said. "It's an American one."

"I agree, completely." Then I took another look around. "Do you have another studio?"

"No. This is it."

"So where are you broadcasting from now?"

"We're not," he said. "For twenty-four-hour news, you need a billion-dollar infrastructure. With citizen journalism, Twitter, YouTube, you name it, we've got images in real time. I don't want to pay to have correspondents stationed all around the world only to be scooped by a kid with an iPhone." He gestured with his hand. "Come on."

He led me into the empty control room for Ty's show. It was three bleacher-type rows overlooking the set. Built into the wall was a bank of televisions. At the moment, they were all tuned to the same program.

"That's what INN is showing right now," Edwin said. "It's *The Newsroom*. Have you seen it?" I shook my head. "It was on HBO from 2012 to 2014. Greatest TV show ever. Aaron Sorkin's best work.

"The first scene features a panel discussion, and there's an anchor who's strongly identified as independent—who's staunchly refused to reveal his political affiliations—and he comes unglued when he's pressed to say why America is the greatest country in the world. He decides to tell the truth. He says America's not the greatest country, that we lead in only three categories: number of incarcerated citizens per capita, number of adults who believe angels are real, and defense spending.

"But he knows—like I know—that America can lead again, with a clear moral compass and the right priorities. So he changes his mission, with the help of his ex-love, who also happens to be a bang-up producer." He grinned. "Sure, it's soapy, but the point is, news used to be about something other than profit. It supported democracy by providing accurate information to the electorate. We're talking Edward R. Murrow here, and Walter Cronkite. Those people were before your time, and my time, too, but I'm educating myself. I didn't major in broadcast journalism either."

"So Aaron Sorkin was talking about the importance of truth and integrity?" I asked.

"Yes."

"But wasn't *The Social Network* pretty much a fabrication? Like, Mark Zuckerberg didn't start Facebook to impress a girl. He was already in a relationship with Priscilla Chan, who became his wife."

Edwin waved a hand. "Semantics. I've never liked that movie. But I love *The Newsroom*."

I ask Dad now, "Have you seen *The Newsroom*?"

"Never heard of it."

"You've heard of Edward R. Murrow, though, right?"

"Name rings a bell. None of this is exactly my area of expertise, Chey."

"What do I do, Daddy?" I haven't called him Daddy in a while. Not since I had to take a year off from school because it looked like that was all we'd have left together.

"What's your gut telling you?"

"That I can't walk away. This kind of chance is never going to come around again."

"So that's fear talking?"

"I'm afraid to miss out. But I'm also afraid to expose myself. The blowback from one viral video is nothing compared to being on a major news network. Last time, they released my pictures." One of the worst parts of the whole nightmare had been when someone emailed those photos to my father. "I don't have any other skeletons in my closet, but who knows what else they can do? What they can make up?"

"And you'd be on your own in New York. You don't know anyone there."

"Edwin says he'll take care of me." Hearing how it sounds, I add quickly, "I mean, he'll make sure I'm taken care of. INN has top-notch security, and he said that if I need it, I can have someone assigned only to me."

"I can't lie. It worries me."

"It worries me too. But do I want to hide out my whole life? What if I can really do something great, like Edwin thinks?"

He's quiet, considering. "I guess you can live small and hope no one hurts you, or you can live big."

"Even if I'm living small, they can still hurt me. People get targeted for all kinds of reasons. This way, I'm targeting them too."

"I think you're trying to sell me."

I let out a shuddering breath. "I want to say yes, which scares the shit out of me."

"So say yes. Now's the time to take a chance. You just graduated. If you don't like it, you quit."

"I'd be signing a contract. I couldn't just quit."

"You can stick anything out for a year."

That's when someone tries the door.

"Just a second!" I yell. Then I say in a rapid whisper, "I'm about to go around the newsroom and talk to people one-on-one. What should I ask?"

"Make small talk where you don't have to pay attention to their answers. Then listen in on the person next to them, who doesn't think they're being heard. Soak it all in. Be sure it's where you want to be before you sign anything. Ask for more time if you need it."

Another knock. "One more second!"

"Listen," Dad says, "whatever happens, you'll keep going. I don't care what Aaron Sorkin thinks; I'll tell you why this is the greatest country in the world. The lenient bankruptcy laws. People go broke, and then they start a new business. They start again. Because this is the country that rewards risk-takers. You always get another chance. You're my brilliant, talented daughter. That's how I know you'll do the right thing. And if you need to, you'll start again."

"Thanks, Dad. I love you."

"Love you too."

I unlock the door. It's showtime.

CHAPTER 3

I t was meant to be just another think piece, like all my other videos, which got little attention. It never occurred to me I had the power to hurt people I'd never met, or could be hurt by them myself.

I sat on my bed and filmed myself talking, with my research materials nearby for handy reference. That day, I read from "A Probabilistic Framework for Modelling False Title IX 'Convictions' Under the Preponderance of the Evidence Standard." Hardly salacious, though lots of men later pointed out that my tight T-shirt could make any conclusion palatable.

Respected UCLA researcher John Villasenor had discovered that on college campuses, when the disciplinary councils for sexual assault used the "preponderance of the evidence" standard rather than the "beyond a reasonable doubt" standard of the legal system, as many as one in three accused were wrongfully convicted. One in three! While I understood and supported the aim of making the process more comfortable for the victims, that wasn't justice. There had to be a better way, for everyone involved. So I advocated a thoughtful, evidence-based reexamination of the system, with fairness for all.

The video hadn't felt radical, but afterward I was excoriated online by young women who wrote that they'd been sexually assaulted and then victimized by a legal system that put them on trial for their conduct. To do away with the college disciplinary route would be shortsighted and dangerous; it would leave women with no recourse but a justice system nearly as traumatic as the crime itself. I responded that I was very sorry about what had happened to them, and that both systems—legal and university—are in need of reform. I said that I was no journalist, it was an opinion piece, and I welcomed dissent. A few back-and-forths, and that was supposed to be the end of it.

Only it wasn't. The video was spreading, with the presumption that I was some sort of right-wing tool, sent to undermine women's rights. "She's the next generation," one person wrote, "the way she can sound reasonable, espousing conservative propaganda while looking like a porn star." There was an offshoot debate about whether my tits and lips were real.

Thousands of comments, too many to respond to, even if I'd wanted to. I stopped answering, hoping that if I took the high road and ceased to engage, it would die down, but instead it progressed from accusations of me being as red as my home state of Wyoming (though I'm from Montana), antifeminist, and a slave of the patriarchy to my being a whore. Then there were all the people saying I'd posted something inflammatory on purpose just to make a name for myself, that it was my attempt to be the next Tomi Lahren. My style might have been different, some said, not so overtly vitriolic, but that's what made me all the more dangerous.

My defenders added fuel to the fire. There were conservatives who felt they'd found their next pinup girl and were clearly making me the object of their masturbatory fantasies. They were only too happy to claim me as their own. Then I found out about the existence of "pro-rape activists," and when they voiced their support for me, I had to answer back.

Asserting my independence just meant that everyone was now against me. I'd gotten on the wrong side of some truly scary people, and I was treated to gleeful talk about how I needed to find out what it was really like to be raped. The scenarios were lengthy and detailed, sometimes with grisly supporting GIFs, my head superimposed on other women's bodies.

At that point, I turned off the Comments section, but they continued unabated all over the internet. "Viral" was all too accurate. I felt sick.

The controversy carried over into real life. I was booed walking into my classes. All over campus, there were whispers, stares, and averted eyes. A woman confronted me in a restaurant, yelling that men were raping right now, thinking they'd get away with it, because of me. I sat, frozen and horrified, before I scurried out. Someone took a video of it with their phone, and that went viral too.

Chase suggested I post an apology for my insensitivity, a recommendation that felt like a betrayal. He'd initially said it was my best work. Now he'd done an about-face. Apparently, a unicorn couldn't have a pariah for a girlfriend.

It was a tense time in our relationship. Chase said that he was just trying to protect me, but it felt like he wanted me to give in to the haters. I couldn't bear the idea of living in a society where people who disagree can threaten one another into submission. Whatever happened to free speech? I hadn't shouted fire in a movie theater. I hadn't shouted, "Free the rapists!" I'd been calling attention to a damaging over-correction, that in attempting to address mistreatment by the justice system, universities have perhaps unwittingly created another unjust system. Rape is a heinous and brutal crime that should be punished. Period. Convicting innocent people is unacceptable. Period.

But the reaction to the video forced me to see what I'd managed to avoid: that in my years at Stanford, I'd never made any true friends. I had pleasant acquaintances. And then there were Chase's friends, all of whom deserted me immediately. In the internet free-for-all, buried among all the other insults about me being a closet right-winger and a Tomi Lahren wanna-be and a self-hating antifeminist, was talk about how I'd used my looks to get ahead and that I'd "bamboozled poor Professor Trent" into giving me an A that I didn't deserve. One clever—anonymous—poster said, "Cheyenne's DDs are clearly a flotation device. Otherwise, she'd be underwater. The Stanford current is way too strong for a little girl from Bumfuck Montana."

Dad managed to talk me through it all, saying the video was something to be proud of and I should hold my head high. "They're jealous that you can think for yourself," he said. "Your job is to exercise your right to free speech and free thought and to outlast them. Bullies move on."

I was living by that advice until the thread on Tag. It existed just to post my whereabouts, in real time. Initially, it was followed by a few thousand people, then five thousand, then ten, and soon it seemed like wherever I was, someone was there, posting. Not that I could catch who it was; I just saw the photographic evidence. I was following the feed that was following me. It was a postmodern Orwellian nightmare. I was terrified. What if one of the guys decided to turn his rape fantasy into a reality? There were so many of them—those who wrote their porn with me as the star; those who "liked" it; those who might be inspired by it; those who said that would be what I deserve, and that hopefully my accuser would walk away, unpunished.

I reported it to Tag, but the social media site never responded. Meanwhile, I was turning into a hermit. "Are you sure you don't want to just apologize?" Chase asked.

This was no longer about my views. It wasn't even about the video. It was about power. Chase is a smart guy. Didn't he see that they weren't interested in a mea culpa? They wanted to keep me in a vise. Keep me in my place. Humiliate me. The ones who had initially defended me were some of the most vicious now.

In the beginning, there had been people who'd been genuinely wounded and offended, who thought that a call for justice for the accused would mean further injustice for the victims. I'd apologized to them already, no problem. But now, it had nothing to do with any position I'd taken. It wasn't even about the video itself. It was that I was on the radar of the type of people who eroticized and fetishized the violation of women. What sweet irony for them that the original video had, in their minds, been a plea for leniency toward rapists.

Sometimes when I was out, I felt trapped inside the male gaze, a fly in amber. Men didn't have the guts to approach me, but they were happy to stare. They made me their property without risk of rejection. Without any loss of control.

My clothes got baggier, but it didn't help. Their eyes were still crawling all over me. I was acting like I had something to hide.

One night, walking home from class, a bulky man began to call my name. I'd never seen him before, and while he wasn't overtly menacing, I had a feeling. Like he was one of them. A rape fantasist, or a follower. A troll posting my whereabouts, or a follower. Evil, with its followers. They knew where I was that evening, because school was the only place I went anymore. I was only a few months from graduation, and I couldn't let them scare me off. But every day and every night, it was a struggle to get myself to campus. So far, they didn't seem to know my home address, but it was only a matter of time.

That's what I felt, most acutely, when I heard my own name that night, when my blood ran cold: it's only a matter of time.

When I ran, he ran. I ducked into the library and hid in the stacks, watching for feet on the other side, afraid to breathe. *It's only a matter of time, and there are way more of them than there are of me.*

After that, I gave in. The police were close to useless. Their only advice was for me to get off-line. So I did. I canceled every social media account and pulled down every video I'd ever done. For a couple of weeks, it seemed to have worked. They'd beaten me into submission. They'd won. My own version of "Where's Waldo?" was dying on the vine, with so few sightings.

Then my phone was hacked, and the photos that had been meant only for Chase were leaked, and I didn't even go to my own graduation. I stayed in my pajamas all day, every day, trying to get every site posting the photos to take them down. Mostly, I was ignored, but even when I could get them to disappear from one site, they reappeared somewhere else like a dam continuously springing leaks that could never be plugged. Eventually, I gave up. Retracted my head like a turtle, and it's stayed down ever since. Some days, I have trouble making eye contact. Sometimes I stare at people defiantly, like, *Oh, yeah? Go on and say something.* They never do. Not to my face.

I still have a handle, @fuzzysocksonmyhead, so that I can monitor what's being said about me, for my own safety, trying to stay a step ahead. Without my online presence to feed it, the threatening memes have mostly fizzled out, so now I just have to accept that they're getting off on my photos, and on their own power. I picked that handle because it's from a silly song Dad and I used to dance to when I was little, and just typing it in is a form of comfort. My daddy's with me. It'll all be okay.

It's always been just the two of us. My mother was a radar blip, passing through town, possibly running from something or someone—Dad was never quite sure—and then she was waylaid by pregnancy. She disappeared before I could form memories. There are plenty of pictures of me as a baby, but none have my mother in them. Dad said that she held me so seldom and briefly that he never had time to grab the camera and capture a moment. But I got so lucky in the father lottery that I can't really gripe about a missing mother.

Except for that constant refrain—*Has he seen me naked?*—my life is almost normal again. I'm just a college graduate trying to get a job. I can't say my relationship with Chase is the same as it was before, that I trust him as completely as I once did. I used to think he'd always have my back, and he'll say that he always has, but I'm nowhere near as sure.

I know the world in a way that I didn't before. Of course I'd understood, abstractly, that there was hatred and cruelty. But now I know that I can be targeted mercilessly, and that maybe next time, there will be no shutting down, and no going back.

CHAPTER 4

E dwin's office is as impersonal as it is large. He has a phenom-
enal view of the city through floor-to-ceiling windows, and
a whole lot of square footage, but no photos or mementos
of any kind. His desk is bare, and his bookshelves mostly are,
too, though he has a bar in the corner that's fully stocked. "I
moonlight as a mixologist," he says.

I sit down on a white leather sectional, which has the same
feminine flair as the jet. I've been a little on edge all day, but
now it's intensified a hundredfold because I'm actually doing it.
I'm willing to take the sizable risk for a potentially monumental
reward. I'm going to say yes, with one condition.

Edwin's half sprawling, his part of the sectional perpendicu-
lar to mine, deep in his frost-colored Corpse Reviver. He asks
again if he can make me anything, it's so sad to drink alone.
Not now, I've got to stay sharp.

He's willing to blur his edges, though, unless he drinks so
much alcohol normally that the cocktail won't even affect him.
Or he's that confident about my answer. Or that unconcerned.

I can barely breathe, not knowing if this is just a clever negotiating strategy on his part. I'm completely out of my depth.

He hands me the contract. "Let me know if you have any
questions." He studies his phone as I read it through. Well,
more like skim it. The thing is enormous. I can't make him wait
while I scrutinize every line. His time is valuable. "It's pretty
simple. No stock options or revenue sharing. But it's a pretty
generous salary for right out of school. Most of the pages are
about confidentiality and proprietary interests. We don't want
you jumping to Fox News and telling them our trade secrets."
He smiles.

The pages are full of consequences if I breach the contract.
This must be what a noncompete clause looks like. I've heard
the term, but I've never actually seen any sort of contract before.

I never thought I'd be offered $180K for an entry-level job,
and that's just for the first year. There are raises, incentives, and
bonuses built in, based on performance, if I'm able to meet certain benchmarks, if I can do what Edwin thinks I can.

"Three years," I say, trying not to do a cartoonish gulp.

"Yep. It's standard."

Locked in for an eighth of my life to date. This could be
three years of abject humiliation. Or worse.

The flip side is, INN would be locked in too. Regardless of
performance, even if they decided to sack me, I'd be guaranteed a minimum of $600K over the next three years. What that
kind of money could buy in Tulip . . .

Not that I'm ever going to live there again, but still. Yes, I
want to make an impact on the world and have a mission, but
I'm an American. I can't deny the allure of cold hard cash.

I continue reading. "I'd have to pitch and produce news
stories?"

"Everyone on the team does that. This is boilerplate stuff, Cheyenne. It's to cover all the bases, ours and yours."

I assume he's telling the truth, but I have no way to know. I can't exactly ask to see the contracts of other people at the network. Can I?

Chase would know how to play hardball if someone really wants you. But I chose not to call him when I had the chance, and I don't think I could do it now.

I don't think I want to.

If Chase tells me to stall and do my homework, which he almost definitely will, then it gives me more time to think. But it gives Edwin more time to think too. He might talk to his staff and find out that they're less than thrilled to work alongside a woman with my internet footprint.

I can't risk this. I want it too much.

"If all goes well," Edwin says, "and you're the hit I think you'll be, then you get yourself a high-powered agent and you fight me for what you're worth. And if you don't like it here, we'll part ways. You can stick anything out for a few years, right?"

That's exactly what Dad said to me in the bathroom.

My heart drops. I've been surveilled before, and the last thing I want is to go back there, voluntarily.

I'm being paranoid. It's a holdover from the trolls. "Sticking it out" is a common expression. Edwin can obviously see my hesitation, and he's trying to reassure me. In a few years, if I want to, I walk.

Why does "three years" sound like so much more than "a few"?

"I feel like I should have a lawyer look this over," I say.

"Understandable. You have a lawyer?" I shake my head. "You can borrow one of mine."

I'm not sure if he's kidding. He takes another sip of his icy drink and returns his eyes to his phone. "I can give you twenty-four hours to review it."

Is that standard, too, or a high-pressure negotiating tactic? Is he allowed to rescind during those twenty-four hours?

I can feel the shift from when we first spoke on the plane, when I was about to stalk off and he had to woo me back. He has the power now, and he knows it. He sold me.

"It's a good deal," Edwin says.

"I believe you." I really don't think he's trying to screw me. He whisked me away from Palo Alto this morning and introduced me to his staff as the next big thing. He's clearly invested in developing my potential.

Still, you don't just sign your life away without having a lawyer look things over. But I don't know how I would find a lawyer experienced in these sorts of contracts on this short of notice, and if I could, it might not be someone whose advice can be trusted. It would be someone who has no stake in me. Not like Edwin, who wants to link our fortunes.

"I can understand your hesitation, given your past experiences. But what happened to you, that's what happens to everyone who goes viral. There's more negative than there is positive. That's what holds people's interest—their own worst natures."

"So the goal is for me to get reamed online?"

"No. The goal is for you to get viewers, and for me to get advertisers, and in the process, we change the direction of this country. You're how I get millennial males to eat their brussels sprouts."

I wish I could smile, but I'm suddenly paralyzed. "I'm scared, Edwin."

"Last time, you didn't get the upside. This time, trust me,

there's going to be a lot of upside. This time around, they're all going to wish they were you."

"The past is going to come back up. All the awful things people said about me will get recycled. Not to mention the pictures."

"Your first report will be on cyberbullying, and you won't be the whole story, don't worry, but we'll incorporate what happened to you. It humanizes you right from the start, and it lets us get out in front. Then when people attack you, they'll have proven your point. They'll be cliché."

"You think that'll deter them?"

He laughs. "Of course not. But it's all part of the plan. This isn't checkers; it's chess. Trust me, Cheyenne. I'm focused on the long game."

I do trust him, and I want this mission. I want to prove myself worthy of it, and to prove all my classmates wrong, the ones who've underestimated me, and all the trolls who insist on the binary, you're left or you're right, you're entirely pure or you're a slut and an opportunist. I want to try to make the world better—more informed and inclusive and kinder. That desire is greater than my fear.

"There's something you need to know," I say. "A clause of my own."

He puts his phone down beside him, but not his drink. He looks intrigued.

"My father has terminal cancer, and he has for a long time. I delayed Stanford for a year because the doctors said he didn't have much time left, but then I found this clinical trial, this experimental drug, and it worked. So I went to school for two years, and then the drug stopped working. I took a year off to be with him. I found another clinical trial, and that's been working ever since." I get that feeling in my chest and throat, the superstitious one that makes me want to find some wood in this steel-and-glass office and knock as hard as I can. "But if it stops working, then I have to be let out of my contract."

"To be his nurse?"

"No, to be his daughter," I say sharply.

Part of that sharpness is the realization that I'm not actually choosing to spend as much time as possible with him. If that was my main aim, I'd be back there right now. Instead, I'm about to take a demanding job in NYC for the next three years. I've been visiting him once a month, and I was planning to keep that up for the rest of my—well, his—life. Will I be able to do that if I take this job?

Maybe I can get him to move to New York to live with me. On almost $200K a year, I might be able to afford a two-bedroom.

There's no way. He belongs in Tulip in a way that I don't, despite all the affection I have for the place. Tulip should be a model for the rest of the country. But I don't fit there, and I didn't really fit in Palo Alto either. Will I belong in New York?

Edwin is watching me carefully, calibrating. It's the first wrench I've thrown into his plan.

"I'll call my lawyer," he says finally.

That was easier than I expected, so I might as well push it. "I have to fly back and see him regularly. So I need to be guaranteed one weekend off every month."

"After that, we're good to go? No more changes?"

"Nothing."

"And you'll sign tonight?"

"Yes."

His smile is huge. How many teeth does that man have? "You've got yourself a deal." I burst into astonished laughter.

"You're going to have that drink now, right? I'm thinking . . . Bee's Knees. You like gin? You like froth?"

I laugh again, a girlish tinkling sound of such delight that I wouldn't have recognized it as mine. I haven't laughed like that since childhood, maybe, or at least since before my father's diagnosis.

As soon as we've had our drink, I need to call Dad. And Chase. I have to break the news that we're about to become a long-distance couple. No, bicoastal. That's a much better way to put it.

He'll have to understand. No woman—no person—could turn this down, especially now that I'm getting my Montana clause. Maybe I could have pushed for two weekends a month to have time in both Tulip and Palo Alto, but at some point, Edwin was going to push back. Anyway, it's too late now. The lawyers are hard at work, and Edwin is already mixing drinks.

Chase gets ambition. I'll just call him and explain. No, I'll tell him in person later. It's three hours earlier in Palo Alto, and Edwin's private jet is going to take me back tonight.

But first things first. I really need that drink.

CHAPTER 5

I let myself in as quietly as possible. Chase is on the couch, his chest rising and falling at regular intervals, the TV showing an episode of *Game of Thrones* that I know he's already seen. I don't dare turn it off, for fear of waking him. After the longest, most exhilarating, and most exhausting day of my life, I should probably be eager to share the events with Chase, but, really, all I want is to rest and deal with any fallout tomorrow.

Lovely as our apartment is, it's still a studio, which means any noise can become clatter. We're walking distance to downtown Palo Alto, with a large living room, separate kitchen, and a very cool Murphy bed that pulls out of the wall, though I won't pull the bed down for the same reason I can't turn off the television. If I just curl up on the floor, I know I'll be asleep in 2.7 seconds flat.

Only Chase sits up.

"Chey?" he says, turning on the lamp beside the couch. His blond hair is adorably mussed, and he's blinking profusely. He is adorable, that's the thing. Everyone at school agreed with the (also adorable) statement: Chase is a catch.

It's my moment. I get to share my big news with the man I love. I clear my throat. Nothing comes out.

The thing is, I've always felt like Chase is too good for me. He was exceptional in a school full of the exceptional. He's cute and confident, yet still self-effacing. He makes an impression without rubbing his ample intelligence in anyone's face. He's principled, too, turning down Google, Apple, and Yahoo! in favor of Until, because of its mission: to stop crime before it happens, when it's just a thought in someone's mind.

Until has figured out how to detect subacute changes in brain-wave patterns when someone is thinking in a manner most likely to lead to certain forms of deviance. They don't yet have a working prototype, but they've got tons of funding. Until is cutting edge, civically minded, and likely to be worth billions, and Chase is on the ground floor, the inner circle, with abundant stock options to cash in.

Chase is amazing. He's always been the amazing one in our particular couple. Now I have my own billionaire believer and the chance to be the next big thing in service of something huge and important, a foot soldier for democracy itself. Edwin and I signed, toasted, and tethered.

I do have one nagging question, and I hope Chase doesn't give voice to it. Perhaps I didn't call him all day because I wanted it to remain unspoken. Because I wanted to sign on the dotted line. Because this is America, with its lenient bankruptcy laws and its love of risk-takers. Because in this country, we can fail spectacularly and start again. Because sometimes we succeed spectacularly too.

But if Edwin's offer is as good as it seems, why the rush? I should have been given adequate time to evaluate. Instead, he wanted to lock it—and me—down ASAP. Yes, that's flattering, but it's also a little concerning. What does he have to hide?

The thing is, I wanted to be locked in. When I woke up this morning, I had no prospects and no true direction. I had nothing but Chase. I was a black hole to his star.

Edwin sold me, and now I have to sell Chase.

I launch into the story with gusto, but as I get closer to the part about the signed contract, I start to falter. There's nothing standard or boilerplate in how it's all come together, that's for sure.

Chase and I are supposed to be partners in life. We've talked about getting married someday, sometimes while sober. We've been together for the past three years. Well, for much of those years. There was that long period of hooking up and denying we'd caught feelings, but while I was missing my junior year, living in Tulip and taking care of Dad, Chase told me that there was no one else he wanted to be with, not really. He was in love with me, and how could I not be in love back? This was Chase, and I'd caught him.

He lets me finish the story. Then he doesn't speak. It feels withholding, like he's saying, *You didn't want my opinion earlier, so you're not going to get it now.*

"What are you thinking?" I say, when I can't take it anymore.

"So Edwin Gordon thinks you're a natural." His tone is flat, devoid of any inflection at all.

"Yes."

"He doesn't care that you have no training, or experience."

"Right." I feel a little like he's cross-examining me, and I'm fast becoming a hostile witness. "He believes in me." As in, don't you, Chase?

"I just didn't see this coming."

I force a laugh. "Who could have? It's crazy."

"Yeah, it is." He's not laughing. "Do you really think you're ready for this?"

"I want it, so I've got to get ready."

"You've wanted it since when? Since breakfast?"

I fight back the defensiveness. He needs time to process, that's all. "I've always wanted to be part of something big, ever since I was a kid."

"How do you know INN is big?"

"It's the fastest-growing—the *only* growing—cable news network. Edwin's got a mission, and I—"

"So you know it because Edwin told you? You didn't think you should do any *independent* research?"

The way he emphasizes "independent" stings, like he's questioning my one bona fide.

"I'm just worried about you," he says. "The trolls practically destroyed you once. You think they're not going to try to do it again?"

"Edwin's got a plan."

He raises an eyebrow. "A plan to stop them?"

"A plan to use them. You don't go viral without controversy. This time, the trolls can be part of what gives me power, not what takes it away."

Chase bites his lip, visibly grappling with self-censorship. "This affects me, too, you know. When you hurt, I hurt."

"I get that, but I can't just cloister at home for the rest of my life."

"You don't have to make yourself a public figure either. When those pictures got out . . ." He trails off, and I'm pretty sure he's not only thinking of me. Even though he wasn't in the pictures, he was still embarrassed that all his colleagues had seen every part of his girlfriend.

"There are no more pictures," I say. "They're all out there."

"Then maybe pictures won't be their weapon of choice. I'm just saying, you went underground for a reason."

"And you want me to stay there."

"That's not what I'm saying."

"I can become a target whether I join INN or not. You don't control who's coming after you. You only control whether you hide or fight back. This time, INN's going to help me fight back."

"You know that because Edwin told you?"

"Because it's in their self-interest. And, yes, because Edwin told me."

He nods slowly. I can't tell if I've convinced him or he's just too tired to keep on with the conversation. Besides, the contract's been signed, and Chase doesn't pick losing battles.

"Well," he says, "it's done. We have to make the best of it. We've been long distance before."

He hasn't expressed his confidence in me, but at least he's not angry. Another guy could easily have been. All day, I've been focused entirely on what the opportunity could mean for me, without really thinking about what it means for us.

My instincts were right though. I couldn't have let him weigh in sooner. If I'd slowed down, I might have started to doubt myself. I could have decided to go back into the shadows again. In Chase's shadow.

"Do we have any champagne?" he asks, smiling. "We should celebrate!"

"Are you sure you're feeling festive? Like you said, this is a big change in your life, too, with no notice. I'm sorry about that. I just didn't feel like I could say no."

"You, of all people, should be aware that you can always say no."

"I mean, I didn't want to say no. But I never want to hurt you. So I can understand if you're in no mood to toast. It's late. We can just go to bed."

"No, we should celebrate. You made this happen, Cheyenne."

I'd like to think it was said with pride, but somehow, it hangs there in the room, a touch ominously. Then he's popping the cork.

CHAPTER 6

A sterile corporate apartment in Midtown isn't what I would have chosen, but it's close to the studio and has top-notch security, and since INN is picking up the tab, I can hardly complain. Edwin told me to consider it a signing bonus.

Due to start work tomorrow, I have a day to explore. I traverse SoHo and TriBeCa, and there are some appreciative stares, but mostly, everyone is on their way somewhere, preoccupied with their own lives. I'm just another pretty girl, which is how I like it. That Tag thread is played out. New Yorkers have too much going on to bother with me, not like in Palo Alto.

I stop in a few boutiques and pick out some accessories with way more style than any I've owned previously. Sharp edges, industrial chic, I don't even know what to call it. I'm normally a jeans-and-T-shirt girl. J.Crew. The Gap. I even have some Abercrombie left in my closet. The saleswomen try to talk me into whole outfits to go with the jewelry, but I haven't even seen a paycheck yet. I promise I'll be back.

Late that night while I'm lying in my antiseptic bed (white

sheets under a white duvet cover), Edwin texts to ask about my first day living in the city. That's what he calls it, the city, as if there's only one. I tell him about the shopping, and the freedom, and how the city is much easier to navigate than I expected, and sure, it's pulsing, but it's not overwhelming. It's on a grid, with a design to each neighborhood that makes intuitive sense, so that the whole island of Manhattan has a geometry that Palo Alto lacks. Maybe this is it, where I belong.

We text back and forth for a while, like old friends, and then he writes, Relish your anonymity. It'll soon be a thing of the past.

A shiver goes through me. Then he adds, almost like he can see my reaction: You'll be recognized, but the locals will be cool about it. They won't mob you. You'll just feel their eyes on you, like they're trying to place you, even if they've already placed you.

They must be used to celebrities in their midst. I
mean, not that I'm a celebrity.

Not yet. Sleep tight.

But what about the out-of-towners? I want to ask. *What will they do?*

I don't really want to go there, though, not this late at night, so close to dreaming. Instead I say good night, and then I try to reach Chase. He's the one I should be texting from my bed anyway.

Even though it's three hours earlier in California, he doesn't respond. I wonder how he feels being stuck so far away, doing his same old, while I embark on an adventure. He probably never expected me to be the one to strike out for parts unknown and leave him behind. I didn't either.

I finally drift off to sleep and dream of nothing at all.

IN THE MORNING, I walk the three blocks to INN's building, where I'm met in the lobby by my supervising producer, Albie. He gives off the air of having been in the trenches forever. In his fifties, with thinning sandy hair and abundant sun damage, in ill-fitting carpenter jeans and a stretched-out pocket T-shirt over his paunch, he started with the major networks thirty years ago and then worked for Fox, CNN, and MSNBC. He says he's politically agnostic, which might be the same as being an independent. There's something about his gruffness that inspires trust, and that's enough to make me like him, even though he hasn't smiled once yet. He's interested in one thing, and it's not *that* thing.

He takes me through the unromantic tasks first, like getting my badge and meeting INN's security staff. Reassuringly, the checkpoints and safeguards are extensive. While there's a whole private security team, I see police too. Albie explains that the NYPD are a fixture in the building and will always be in the studio for shows with a live audience.

That's where shit gets real. It's not hypothetical anymore; I'm actually going to be on TV. But Albie doesn't seem to notice I've gone rigid. Maybe the news business is about knowing what to react to, and what can be ignored.

Albie escorts me to his office. If the space is any indication of how thirty-year veterans are treated, it's a pretty brutal industry. There's nothing on the walls, which is something it has in common with Edwin's office, but that's where the similarity ends. Albie's is windowless and barely big enough to hold a desk and two chairs. The lighting is painfully fluorescent. Albie isn't even on the same floor as anyone else from INN. Has he done something really, really bad and been sent into exile? Am I his punishment?

"You'll be visiting all the pitch meetings later," Albie is saying. "Basically, you're going to camp out in the conference room and see what goes on behind the scenes for each show, one after the other. Just listen with a smart look on your face. Don't try to impress anyone. That can only end badly."

I've already realized Albie doesn't mince words, and there's no time for offense taking. "Will the anchors be there?" I ask.

I met them all briefly, after the contract had already been signed. They were nice to me (especially Beth, and even Ty), but because they were in hair and makeup or just generally rushing around, I hadn't been able to progress beyond small talk. I've spent plenty of time with them, though, over the past week, watching all their shows to make up for lost time. Now I'm much more prone to being starstruck.

"They'll be there," Albie answers, "and they're expecting you. I'm not sure about the rest of their staff. As you know, Edwin's billed you as the Second Coming, so be ready."

"Ready for what?" I'm hoping Albie is from the there-are-no-stupid-questions school.

"Let's just say, part of your job is to figure out your enemies."

I would have thought "competition" or at most "rivals," but "enemies"?

"Look, some people want you to succeed, some don't. Some are willing to keep an open mind, and some aren't. You have to figure out who's who. But know this: they're not always going to show themselves at once, and they don't all share the same playbook."

I wish I had a playbook. "I'm going to prove I deserve to be here."

"It's news. We're all proving ourselves all the time. Don't think it's ever going to stop. I've been at this thirty years, and look at this office."

"I was sort of wondering about that."

"I knew what I was getting into."

"Which is?"

He gives a half smile. I haven't seen a full one yet. "You brought me out of early retirement. I'm a hired gun. I don't work on any show, I'm just assigned to you."

So that might mean he knows as little about what's going on here as I do.

"Welcome to journalism boot camp." He opens his desk drawer and lifts out a large stack of books, placing it on the desk next to my elbow. "This is your curriculum: politics, business and economics, crime and the legal system, education. There's a short runway, and then you've got to fly. That means you'll need to be able to speak off the cuff and hold your own."

My chest tightens, but I try not to panic. I remind myself, *I was valedictorian.*

In Tulip.

"Read these books," Albie says, "and then you've got to watch every TV show on our network, going back to the beginning, which, lucky for you, is only fifteen months ago. See what stories they've followed, and the point of view. That's what you do in your off-hours."

I nod and swallow hard.

He looks directly into my eyes for the first time. "You live up to your potential, and we won't have any problems."

He must be an incredible journalist, because he's onto something I've never admitted to anyone: at Stanford, I gave up. Not entirely, of course. I graduated. But when I felt the intensity of the competition, I lost a lot of the fire I'd had throughout my life, the fire that Edwin said a female broadcaster needs. I need to get it back, quick.

Edwin believes in me, and Albie's here to help. Unlike Stanford, this is not a solo enterprise. As Edwin said, we all rise and fall together here.

But he didn't say anything about enemies.

The first staff meeting I attend inside the glass-walled conference room is for the call-in show *Breaking It Down*. Rayna and Quill, the married hosts, boast an encyclopedic knowledge of politics, as well as the ability to improv. I never met them on my tour, and it's a little intimidating to see them in the flesh.

Quill is handsome in the old-school, Waspy anchorman mold, and Rayna is darkly exotic. While they're both avowed independents, they often play devil's advocate to each other, like a sexy debate. Each takes the liberal position sometimes and the conservative at others. They're in pursuit of the truth, they remind viewers, wherever it's found, and they like a good fight. They give off the distinct impression that the heat follows them home and into the bedroom.

Albie had explained that Edwin was inspired by the early days of CNN, when they were making it up as they went along under the renegade billionaire Ted Turner, when it was seat-of-the-pants, groundbreaking journalism. I hadn't even known that there was a time before CNN was the establishment; I'd imagined CNN was born fully formed, not a baby but a baby boomer. One of the first shows on CNN had been a call-in, and *Breaking It Down* is Edwin's flagship.

According to Albie, when CNN launched in 1980, management brought aboard a bunch of recent grads from journalism school, paid them peanuts, called them videojournalists (VJs), and had them do anything and everything. They were thrown into the deep end of the pool where they'd either sink or swim. Now INN has its own VJs, and its own pool. Here's hoping I don't drown. From what Albie said, I have to make sure no one holds my head underwater.

Quill and Rayna introduce themselves to me and then introduce me to the staff. Of course I can't help thinking it (*How many of these people have seen me naked?*), but I remember Albie's advice. Any attempt at wit or charm could serve to confirm whatever negative impressions might have been generated when they googled me, so best just to smile around.

The welcome is pleasantly professional. Then the producers and the VJs are tossing out topics for discussion so quickly that I can barely keep up. Quill and Rayna ask for more information or clarification, taking notes, and then they decide what's in and what's out. No one seems especially happy when their pitch is chosen or wounded when it isn't. The train keeps moving.

The executive producer, Judd, stands at the whiteboard, tracking which pitches make the cut and where they'll be placed. I'm trying to glean basic information about how a show is put together. There are A, B, and C segments, which ranks how much time they'll be given, and Judd is doing some preliminary stacking, which means putting the segments in an order that will flow and hold the viewers' interest.

Judd looks to be in his midforties, while both associate producers appear to be in their early thirties. The VJs are my age or at most a few years older, and there are two male and two female, all of equal attractiveness, which is to say average. The women both have straight dark hair pulled back in low ponytails and wear little to no makeup. All are in jeans. They possess a fierce and demonstrable intelligence, speaking with a brisk authority whether they're delivering their own pitches, adding to someone else's, or critiquing. They've already forgotten I'm here.

I feel like all I need is one probing question or cutting insight. But Albie told me to stay quiet, and he should know. It could be that whatever I say, the people in this room thought it already. In high school.

Before adjourning, Rayna looks at me with a very slight smirk. "Do you have anything to add?" Her tone is mild, but there's a challenge in it. No, a presumption that I couldn't possibly have anything substantive to share.

Unfortunately, at this moment, it's true.

"I'm just taking it all in," I say. "Thank you so much for having me."

Is Rayna an enemy? Or is she merely sizing me up, as anyone in her position might do? A certain amount of testing is understandable.

I don't have enough information to reach a conclusion. I have to do what Albie said: keep my eyes and ears open. It's good training for my new profession.

Judd wraps it up, and the staff files out, all except Quill, Rayna, and me. The next staff meeting is going to start soon. Rayna has me on edge. Why aren't they leaving?

"How's it going so far?" Quill asks me with a smile.

"Pretty well. I'm lucky to have a mentor like Albie."

"A mentor," Rayna says icily. "How nice for you."

"Albie's been around forever," Quill says. "He's an institution."

"Frankly," Rayna says, "I'm surprised he wanted this assignment." She gives me an appraising look and seems to find me wanting. "But then, Albie's always liked a challenge."

"So do I," I say.

When are they going to leave?

Then I remember: The next pitch meeting is for *The Media Is the Message*, and Quill and Rayna are the temporarily fill-ins. The last anchors departed suddenly, with a lot of speculation but no confirmation, and the replacements haven't been named. That means another hour with Rayna.

I may need a new game plan. Saying little might not be enough, if she's going to try to undercut me with the staff. What would earn their respect, and hers? I have to stand up to her, subtly. I have to outfox her.

Shit. Can I take a bathroom break and text Albie?

Too late. A man walks in and introduces himself as Luke, the executive producer. He's in his thirties, not half bad–looking with tousled brown hair, in jeans and a plaid button-down shirt with rolled sleeves and ink stains on the pocket, which feels a little affected (who carries pens? or is the shirt legitimately that old?).

I'm wearing a loose silk blouse in impenetrable navy, but it's like Luke has X-ray vision. He's not even bothering to conceal his ogling. Quite the contrary. He wants me to feel it, a painful reminder of what caused me to retreat from social media, and from life, just a short time ago. I don't even have to ask whether he's already seen me naked.

You wouldn't think he could do that so brazenly in this post-Weinstein world, but he makes sure I'm the only one who sees it, and I'm the only one he's directing it toward. He's cordial and entirely professional with the rest of the women. That means I just have to prove myself, and he'll keep his eyes to himself.

Still, it's disappointing. When I'd followed my father's advice on the tour, listening in throughout the newsroom, I hadn't picked up on any sexualized interactions. Women were toiling alongside men, their equals, and that's what I'd wanted to be a part of. I didn't realize I had to earn the right to have men look at my face and not my chest, that I wasn't guaranteed basic respect. Does Luke do this to all women in the beginning, or is it reserved for those of us who haven't been to journalism school, who've been handpicked by Edwin, or who look like me?

It's not the whole newsroom, I remind myself. It's one man, on one show. One rotten apple.

As the meeting begins, I ignore him and focus on what's going on around me. The tagline for *The Media* is "Follow the money." It's about the death of investigative journalism at the hands of not just corporate interests but also the government, which limits journalists' access based on how favorable or unfavorable of press they're receiving. The net result is that journalists are pressured to tell the stories the government wants out there, often by their own editors and news directors who have to play their own political game. *The Media* combats crony journalism and holds the media itself accountable for the stories it won't tell.

In the pitch meeting, the heft of the topics is a good reminder that this isn't about me; it's about the mission. What's a quick peek down my blouse and a smirk from Rayna compared to labor violations, veteran abuses, toxic waste, fracking, failed disaster relief, and mortgage scams? The show is exposing cover-ups and cozy relationships between corporations, government, and the media. Many of the pitches seem to be based on leads from obscure blogs, or at least, they're obscure to me. From what I can intuit, the VJs spend a lot of time following random internet links, like tributaries searching for the river.

I begin to see that I don't have to worry about Rayna, not in this meeting. In the eyes of the staff, I'm not the interloper. They seem close-knit and wary of the stand-in anchors. I have a sense they're still loyal to those who came before. They might even think Quill and Rayna overthrew their less telegenic pre-decessors.

The staff members continually reference the past and which stories the old anchors would have pursued, and in what way. Quill and Rayna adopt a deferential manner, in stark contrast with the meeting before, where they were holding court. They seem a little afraid to challenge anyone, as if they might have a mutiny on their hands.

So much for the campfire Kumbaya portrait Edwin had painted.

Given how Rayna treated me in the last meeting, I can't help but feel a touch of schadenfreude. I do feel sorry for Quill though. He seems like a good guy.

Everyone's incredibly dialed in, including Luke. I can feel that he's one of them, hardworking and well liked. I might have misinterpreted him earlier. What used to be outright paranoia after the viral video has softened into heightened awareness. I'm hoping the vigilance will serve me well as a reporter, that it'll be like a Spidey sense.

As the meeting breaks up, Luke dawdles. When it's down to the two of us, he asks, in an unmistakably lecherous tone, "So how was it for you, Cheyenne?"

"It's a great day," I say, as brightly as I can, with zero flir-tation in my tone. Luke's no Professor Trent; he's one of the enemies Albie warned me about.

"Glad to hear it." He smiles. "Look forward to seeing you around."

I'm left at the conference room table, fuming, yet knowing that the fear is not far behind. It's a sequence I became accus-tomed to not so long ago.

Two meetings, two enemies.

But whatever I'm feeling, I can't let it show. I'm on display, surrounded by glass. Exposed. Even though no one seems to be looking in from the newsroom—they're all involved in their computer screens, or their phones, or conversations with one another—they could turn this way at any moment, and when they do, they'll see whatever they want in me. It doesn't have to be true. I've learned that sometimes people prefer their fictions.

But I have to remember that glass is two-way, and I can see out too. I can observe, and I can make notes, and I can use whatever I find.

Like right now, I see Rayna and Luke in a corner, his lips close to her ear. It's a marked departure from how Rayna was treated during the meeting by Luke's staff. They part quickly, and neither looks back at me. Yet I wonder if I'm part of what unites them. The enemy of my enemy is my friend. They both tried to humiliate me today. Different styles, same intent. Same motive?

I'm feeling a bit jagged for the next meeting. But the show is *Truthiness with Beth Linford*, and Beth couldn't be kinder. "Cheyenne, come sit next to me," she says, patting the seat beside her. "I'm so excited you're here."

Beth is in her early fifties with shoulder-length hair that's impossibly straight, dark, and glossy, almost like a very expensive wig. She has more wrinkles than you'd expect on a TV personality, but it works for her. She's also softer and curvier than the average female broadcaster, attractive without the pinched face that comes from chasing youth. Her métier is interviewing. On her show, she comes across as genuinely worried about the future of the country in a way that could best be described as maternal. That's until she goes for a guest's jugular. There's an involving tension as you watch each interview, not knowing when—or with whom—she might snap. Beth doesn't suffer fools, that's for sure.

During the pitch meeting, though, she couldn't be more lovely, and it trickles down to her associate producers and VJs. Everyone is smiling at me with genuine warmth. They include me in the discussion, asking what I think about the various pitches with true curiosity. I'm trying hard to follow Albie's advice about saying as little as possible. It's tough, but I manage to pull it off with various jokes about being here to gather intel and needing to remain impartial and independent. It's an easy crowd, quick to laughter. No one pins me down.

Beth's EP is the hardass in the room, the taskmaster who refocuses the group when they're drifting off into small talk and laughter. Beth's response to every pitch is a smile and one of two phrases: either "Tell me more" or "Think on that some more."

Watching Beth, just feeling her energy in the room, activates a yearning I haven't felt in so long. It's the desire to be mothered. While I used to like that my father never brought women home and that I got all his attention, as I grew older, I sometimes felt what had been lost: a female perspective, a feminine nurturance, a shared understanding. I also became more conscious of what my father must have been missing: adult companionship, intimate connection, partnership. He claims he missed out on nothing, that he has a full life with more than enough friends. Some, I suspect, are friends with benefits. Still, I wouldn't have minded a stepmom like Beth.

I wish the meeting would go on and on, but it's time for Khalif. He's incredibly handsome, his skin darkest ebony, offset by the crisp white button-down shirts he wears for every broadcast. His smile is beautiful, a reward. He's soft-spoken, so much so that I've found myself leaning into the TV screen during his show. Yet his monologues are often full of quiet, quivering rage.

His show takes the "non-Eurocentric" perspective. I've read that he has the smallest audience, but it's devoted, as well as distinctive: it's composed of people who don't watch any of the other shows on INN, or other news networks. So in that sense, Khalif is quite valuable.

He's just as soft-spoken in the pitch meeting as he is on-air. I notice that his staff has the only black VJs. The intellect in the room is staggering, as everyone has a deep grasp of politics and history, complemented by a dizzying array of pop culture references, from myriad cultures.

Khalif is the only anchor I've heard turn down stories because they're not in keeping with the show's integrity. His sorrowful disappointment is evident as he shakes his head, and the staff member behind the rejected pitch appears chastened.

"I'm really sorry," she says.

"No, no," Khalif answers. "Don't apologize. Just remember, for the future: that's a story for Ty Fordham."

As in, Ty will do what Khalif won't touch. Nothing is beneath Ty.

Speak of the devil . . .

"So you saved the best for last," Ty Fordham deadpans. I don't think he's actually kidding, in that he appears to be surrounded by a vapor of ego. The network adds to the mist. I've heard multiple times in other pitch meetings, "I think Ty's doing that one," and then it gets dropped. The message is that if Ty wants it, it's his. It was only said as an insult by Khalif.

Ty is in his standard outfit: expensive gray suit, light blue shirt, no tie. His skin is more mottled than it appears on TV (they must put some heavy makeup on him), but he's also better-looking. On the air, he's full of kinetic energy, fueled by an outrage that can verge on the manic. In person, he's very still, mesmerizing in a different way. His light brown hair is heavily gelled, his lips are full, and his blue eyes are piercing.

In each pitch meeting, the tone has been set by the anchor—or anchors, in the case of Rayna and Quill—and with Ty, it's one of detachment. He takes notes on a yellow pad, rarely looking up. His staff is sharp and savvy, though his EP is a total sycophant named Rich. "Ty?" he asks often, with a simpering smile. "How's this one sit with you, buddy?" You would hope someone would outgrow that kind of sucking up by the time they're in their fifties.

Ty never asks for additional information. He judges entirely on the pitch as presented, with either "Yes" or "Next." It means that his staff delivers the most succinct, informative, and persuasive pitches of any that I've seen today. It also means that Ty's on-air wild-man persona is shtick. I guess Edwin is okay with less authenticity if it equals higher ratings.

Regardless of the verdict, Ty doesn't smile or frown; his expression never changes. It's a lot more "Next" than "Yes." A producer named Graham delivers more pitches than anyone, and his hit rate is higher too. He's short and nerdy, but in such an extreme way that it seems like shtick, too, like he's this close to a pocket protector. As he talks, he waggles fuzzy black caterpillar eyebrows. He's the only one who didn't say hi to me; I never even earned a glance.

The meeting ends abruptly, with everyone exiting the conference room as the EP babbles about what a great job they all did. I'm exhausted as I approach my workstation for the first time. I should be glad that my appearance seemed irrelevant. I don't want to be objectified, but I hate admitting this particular truth even to myself: that the whole time I kept waiting for the kind of additional attention that generally comes from how I look. Other than with Luke, it never came.

It's my dirty secret. I walk into a room and I'm stuck being noticed, and usually I don't want it, but I look for it. When it doesn't happen, it can be like I've ceased to exist. What do I have without that? I didn't set out to flirt with any professors, and I never intentionally tried to elevate my grades; I never meant to lead Professor Trent on, and I still feel ashamed of how I screwed that whole situation up. While I want to be judged on my nonphysical merits only, I'm afraid of what will happen when I am.

The newsroom is a large space with a high level of ambient noise. Each show has its own pod: a cluster of low-walled cubicles where the VJs and producers work alongside one another. My workstation is cordoned off, a pod unto itself. I'm surrounded by brilliance, yet clearly set apart, largely unnoticed.

Scratch that. Someone noticed. Resting on my keyboard is a large manila envelope with my name on it. Inside is a stack of papers, with a typed letter on top.

Dear Cheyenne,

I wanted to extend my congratulations. You might not have meant to, but you beat out many, many others. You're in a coveted position, but don't confuse that with enviable. What you need is an education, and that's where this diary comes in.

It's important to take your education very seriously.

Those who don't learn from the past are doomed to repeat it. They're doomed to have it repeated on them.

Of course your story isn't going to be the same as the one you're about to read, and even if you think you know hers, there's a whole lot more to it. Anyone can edit a Wikipedia page, after all. Read carefully and stay alert for similarities, because no matter how far you think you've come, how far you think women have come, there's still a long way to go. That's the story you're part of. The history. The herstory. Think now about how you want it all to end.

You've become a member of an exclusive sorority. It might not feel like it. At times, it might feel more like a fraternity party that you've crashed. And while there may be plenty of women around, that doesn't mean they know what you're going through. It doesn't mean they want to see you succeed.

I do.

That's all. No signature.

I look around, hoping someone is looking back at me. But, no, I'm all alone.

CHAPTER 7

I don't feel safe reading the diary in the newsroom. Perhaps it's because the purported feminist who's left it for me, the one who's supposedly rooting from the sidelines, has chosen to remain anonymous, like so many internet trolls before her. Or him. I don't know the identity of this person, or their intentions. So I have to proceed with caution.

Back in my apartment, I reread the letter, searching for clues. The envelope doesn't contain the whole diary, just one photocopied entry dated July 1, 1991. Is the author of the letter the same as the author of the diary? Could it be from, say, Beth and it's about when she was just starting out in journalism? The timeline seems right.

But if that's the case, Beth could have given me her diary outright. There'd be no need for the cloak-and-dagger.

Is it from one of my known enemies, Rayna or Luke? Or perhaps it's Rayna and Luke together, and that's what their little powwow was about. Or it could be another enemy altogether, one operating from a very different playbook. This might be someone's idea of a joke.

Whoever it is has access to INN. The envelope wasn't mailed. They want me to know they can get to me.

There's that paranoia again. Maybe I should just take the diary at face value. Someone has something to teach me, and I do have a lot to learn. That, or I could throw it away, unread. I have a whole curriculum to study and back episodes to watch.

But as I cross the room to toss it in the trash, my curiosity gets the better of me. I'm a journalist now, and this is from a source. If I don't read it, I'll never know whose diary it was. Even if it is from an enemy, I could still learn a lot. People aren't always in control of their messages.

I've come to fear the anonymous. If you have something important to say, announce yourself. Getting sucked into this could be a very bad idea.

Against my better judgment (or perhaps with the instincts of an intrepid reporter), I pick up the pages. The diary entry is college-ruled, the handwriting a girlish cursive.

July 1, 1991

Every day, I've been killing myself, trying to get my reads just right. My delivery needs to be flawless, every time, to prove that I deserve to be at Morning Sunrise, that I should be the one saying, "Back to you, Scott and Trish!" I have to prove that Dennis Graver was right to choose me. After all, what were the odds that the head of the network news division would be in Pittsburgh, of all places, for a business trip, and would turn on the TV and see me anchoring, just as he was scouting for a replacement for a morning show newsreader? Slim, right?

I never want to get sent back down to the minor leagues. I'll do anything to keep that from happening.

I got a new perm the week before I came to New York. It was like a security blanket. I remember when I got the first one in high school, that it was the equivalent of losing 25 pounds, and when I returned to school in September, everyone treated me like a new person. A beautiful person. I've never looked back.

If you don't count the terror and the stalking and all the rest, I've been lucky a lot: graduating from college with a great reel that led to a small-market anchoring job and then not even two years later, along comes Dennis Graver.

I've never liked the word "ambition." It sounds so venal, and I'm not about money. Yes, I'd like to live well, just like anybody, but more than that, I want to do something really well. Corny as it might sound,

I want to connect with millions of viewers. I want to help them start their day in a good mood. In a world where the news is often scary, you want it to be told to you by a friend. I try to be that friend.

I hope Mom was watching today, or taped it. I was telling a story about this Finnish company called Radiolinja that had just launched a mobile phone. The slogan was "So Finns can talk more." It seems kind of crazy that people can't wait until they get home, or get to a pay phone, or a car phone even. The mobile phone looks like a behemoth cordless, with a really prominent antenna. My script had me turn to the anchors and ask, "What do you think? Will Americans be walking down the street someday with phones glued to their ears?"

"They have enough trouble watching where they're going now," Scott said. "Imagine walking down Fifth Avenue in the future, where everyone's got a mobile phone."

"Oh, Scott," Trish said. "You always think the worst."

That's when I ad-libbed: "Let's just see how it goes for the Finns. They can be our guinea pigs."

Scott let out this genuinely delighted laugh. It was my first time contributing anything other than the initial prefab question, and it seemed like he really liked what he heard. Trish chimed in just a beat later.

The rest of the show went by in this fizzy rush, and I have to admit, I made a point of lingering by the corner of the set. I'm only a few weeks in so I'm sure this is going to change, but so far, I'm kind of an island, the only one of my kind, and no one's really been talking to me—not the producers or writers and not Trish and Scott themselves. I overheard someone making a mean joke about how newsreaders are like trained monkeys, so I guess they don't realize how much is involved in reading your copy well. As if a monkey could have pulled off an ad-lib like mine!

So I was waiting there after the show, thinking someone was going to compliment me, or maybe invite me out for lunch or happy hour. Getting Scott to laugh had to mean something. Out of the corner of my eye, I saw Scott and Trish finishing up their conversation.

Then Trish was headed right for me.

I froze. I didn't know if I should make eye contact or smile. Should I be the first to speak, or should I wait?

I went for a vague smile with my eyes slightly averted, like in submission, and that's why I'm not entirely sure what happened next. Maybe Trish stumbled as she rounded the corner. But when she said, "Excuse me," it was almost a growl, so different from her usual dulcet tones on-air. Like it wasn't actually an "excuse me" but a "get out of my way." Like Trish was marking her territory.

That can't be it though. Trish is the coanchor, and I'm just the newsreader. Every day, out on the street in front of the building, the autograph seekers mob her; I'm an afterthought.

But then, who predicted that Deborah Norville would unseat Jane Pauley? And no one expected Deborah Norville to tank and be replaced by Katie Couric. If a shake-up like that can happen, then no one can feel totally safe.

I decided to celebrate. I pulled my hair back in a scrunchie and washed the heavy makeup from my face and changed out of the newsreader pastels into a fluorescent pink blouse, miniskirt, and pink jelly sandals. I was a woman about town.

I wandered around in search of a place where I wouldn't feel conspicuous eating alone and settled myself at a restaurant bar. Through the bottles of expensive liquor, I could see the mirrored reflection of the bustling eatery at my back.

"Could I buy you a drink?"

The man who'd sidled up beside me smelled as expensive as his suit looked. It was a complicated scent, not one I necessarily liked. R.G. used to wear Davidoff Cool Water, clean and oceanic. I'd bury my head in his neck and think, This is what a man is supposed to smell like.

The guy beside me was no R.G. He looked more than ten years older than me, with craggy features. He probably thought I was just off a bus from Iowa or something, and he could take me back to his place for some afternoon delight.

"No, thanks," I said, meaning to reject the drink, and everything else.

He nodded, taking it in stride. Instead of retreating,

he signaled for the bartender and named a whiskey I'd never heard of, neat. I tried not to look at him, either directly or in the bar mirror, but I could feel that he was still attending to me in some peripheral way. I shifted on my stool, uncomfortable. Any sort of pursuit raises my hackles, since Lyndon.

He tapped a cigarette from a very sleek pack. "Mind if I smoke?"

"I do. It makes my hair stink."

"You've got a lot of hair. I get it." He took the cigarette out of his mouth and laid it down on the bar. His drink arrived, and he didn't thank the bartender, just took a sip. He gave me a sideways look. "You're good, you know."

"Excuse me?"

"On TV. You're a big improvement over that last woman."

"You spend a lot of time watching morning shows?" I asked.

"I have to." He took another sip, and then he slid me a card that had been concealed in his palm the whole time. His name is York Diamond, and he's an agent. "I know talent when I see it."

York Diamond. I'd never heard a phonier name in my life. He'd lured me into the conversation under false pretenses. Looking to get laid seemed honorable by comparison.

How likely was it that he just happened to notice me from across the restaurant, dressed down as I was, my hair back? New York has plenty of curly-haired women. I'm not that distinctive. He had to be looking for me.

He must have followed me from the studio, like I'm prey.

Not again.

I stood up and went to grab my purse from the floor, banging my head on the bar on the way back up. I fished around in my wallet, grabbing bills. Too much money was fine, as long as I didn't have to wait for my check.

"Sorry, I didn't mean to upset you," York—or whatever his real name is—said, but his voice held no remorse.

"You didn't upset me." I wouldn't give him the satisfaction. "I just have somewhere I need to be."

I went outside to the humid, honking, assaulting

boulevard. As I raised my arm to hail a cab, I realized it was trembling. My whole body was. That happens sometimes when I'm at the news desk, when nerves get the best of me, but somehow, I can always control it then. I can confine it to my lower body, beneath the desk. But standing there on the street, I couldn't control it at all. It was like my body remembered everything I went through. It was saying, Never again.

CHAPTER 8

E ven someone with as little investigative experience as I have can figure out within a minute whose diary it is. Plug in a few keywords (*Morning Sunrise*, 1991, newsreader) and I've got a name: Elyse Rohrbach. Since the anonymous letter mentioned Wikipedia, that must be where they want me to start.

Honestly, the diary feels like a relic. Sure, I know what it's like to look over your shoulder, but beyond that, Elyse and I have very little in common. I might be a fish out of water, but I'm not all gosh-gee-willikers like Elyse. And sure, Elyse and I both want to impact the world, but Elyse thought she could do it by reading the news with the right intonations. My role at INN is going to be a whole lot more than that.

Article | Talk　　　　　Read | Edit | View history

Morning Sunrise

From Wikipedia, the free encyclopedia

Morning Sunrise was an American morning television show. It debuted on September 24, 1981, and was canceled at the end of 1991. It was filmed in New York City and aired from 7 a.m. to 9 a.m. in all U.S. time zones (live in the Eastern time zone and on tape delay everywhere else).

History

Throughout its history, *Morning Sunrise* lagged in the ratings behind *The Today Show* and *Good Morning America* . . .

Notable On-Air Staff

The first anchors were Martin Breyer and Hillary Stein.

The last anchors were Scott Field and Elyse Rohrbach, though Elyse's tenure was brief due to the brutal attack . . .

Controversy, and the Demise of *Morning Sunrise*

Elyse Rohrbach began as a newsreader in 1991, known for her blond curls and sunny disposition, hailed by Tom Shales of the *Washington Post* as "the next big thing" . . .

. . . a rivalry that both denied . . .

. . . sexual harassment . . .

. . . alcoholism and domestic violence . . .

It came to light at the trial that . . .

The show was subsequently canceled with the following public statement . . .

Article | Talk   Read | Edit | View history

Elyse Rohrbach

From Wikipedia, the free encyclopedia

Elyse Marie Rohrbach was a newsreader at *Morning Sunrise* who made headlines after a brutal attack that galvanized the movement to pass antistalking legislation in the state of New York . . .

Early Years

She was born March 15, 1966, in Stanton, Pennsylvania, to an accountant father and a stay-home mother . . .

College Years

She attended Pennsylvania State University. She majored in journalism. Fellow students describe her as friendly but inaccessible—"hard to know" was a common phrase . . .

She was an on-air anchor at the campus television station for all four years. She has said that she was grateful for her time there as she gained varied experience . . .

That was where her "long stalking nightmare," as she termed it, began . . .

Broadcasting Experience

Shortly after graduating from college, she was given a job in Pittsburgh. Her boss has said that he knew she "was destined for great things" and was "unsurprised" when she left for a national market . . .

She was recruited by Dennis Graver to be the newsreader at *Morning Sunrise*, which he later stated was "a mistake, given her baggage" . . .

There was reportedly on-set tension from the start . . .

. . . fear and threats . . .

. . . jockeying for position . . .

. . . sexual harassment, which he denied . . .

. . . some blamed Elyse herself . . .

The Attack

On August 23, 1991, Elyse Rohrbach was attacked . . .

Questions remain as to what really happened leading up to the attack. Could the network have done more to prevent it? Were the right people on trial?

The trial itself was described as a "media circus" and, by some, a "miscarriage of justice" . . .

It's believed to have directly led to the cancellation of *Morning Sunrise* . . .

Holy shit. I can't believe I hadn't heard of Elyse Rohrbach before. I suppose that's a sign of how little I really know about broadcasting history. The letter's right, I do have a ton to learn.

Based on the number of revisions and the vociferous comments in the Wikipedia Talk section, Elyse continues to spark controversy. Two people have been embroiled in an editorial war, their iterations flipping back and forth several times a year, each wanting their version to prevail.

If these photocopied pages really are from Elyse's original diary, presumably with more to come, it could put many of the questions to rest. Unless it raises more.

Like who's R.G.? I couldn't find anyone in either Wikipedia

page whose initials corresponded to Elyse's past love. There's a mystery here. There are breadcrumbs.

Or red herrings.

If this is someone's attempt to distract me, it's working. I should be reading through my curriculum, not Wikipedia.

What I went through was bad, but naked photos being released is nothing compared to what Elyse experienced. Of course, my anonymous "friend" might be trying to tell me that naked photos are nothing compared to what I'm about to experience.

Even if the intent is to make sure I avoid Elyse's fate, it's hard to see how the diary could help me do that. There were no cell phones in 1991, let alone social media. It was an entirely different world. I have Edwin in my corner, and all INN's resources. Right now, I'm in an incredibly secure apartment building, paid for by the company. I can sleep well.

Only that night, I don't. It's hard to shake off what happened to Elyse, and why someone wants me thinking about what happened to her, and whether and how times have changed.

IN THE MORNING, as I'm applying concealer to the dark circles under my eyes, Albie texts to say we should meet in Edwin's office.

"Edwin's out this week," he says, upon my arrival, and if he knows more than that, he's not telling. I do my best to contain my disappointment, reminding myself that Edwin's the head of the network, a globe-trotting billionaire. I can't expect him to hold my hand through this. But another text exchange would be nice. "Let's get to work."

I appreciate how single-minded Albie is. I don't feel any pressure to make him like me, since he doesn't seem to feel that pressure on his end. He has a job to do, and so do I. There's no bullshit and no subtext. Once I adjust to the fact that he isn't inclined to fill in a silence with idle chatter, he's an easy person to cloister with for fourteen hours a day.

Edwin's office is on the fifty-first floor, above the newsroom and the studios. Every day, I take the elevator straight there. Occasionally, I ride up or down with staffers who smile and ask generically, "How's it going?," and I smile back with an equally generic "Good," and then we both train our eyes on the ascending or descending numbers. I don't know what's being said in my absence, which of my videos they've watched and with what degree of snideness, and of course there are the pictures, but if I start to worry about all that, I lose focus, which I can't afford, so best to just go up and down.

The sequestration continues for days, just Albie and me in Edwin's office.

Today, I'm being schooled in vocal delivery. Apparently, I've never known how to breathe correctly. I should avoid milk products before going on air and drink lots of water. Most important, I have to relax the tension in my body since it will show up in my voice, pitching it higher. "The last thing you want is to be shrill," Albie says. "For women, that's the kiss of death."

We work on intonation and pacing until ten that night, when Albie sends me home and I fall into bed, fully dressed.

The next morning, I'm given a script of my first story.

Shit. I'm appearing on *The Media Is the Message*, with Quill and Rayna.

As I start to read through the script, my chest tightens. It's like what Elyse said in her diary: my body remembers what I've been through. I don't know who wrote my lines, how he or she could understand so viscerally what I felt after the viral video, but it's perfect. Perfectly awful to relive it, but perfect for the viewer at home. Edwin was right. It answers the critics before they've even spoken. Someone at INN is capable of true empathy, so that's heartening. But because it's so real, in front of the camera, in front of Albie, I'm mortified to find there are tears in my eyes.

"Emotion suppressed is always more effective than emotion fully expressed," he says.

One more time, without feeling.

I manage not to cry, but now I'm tripping over the words.

"Just keep going," he tells me. "Recovery is everything."

Again and again and again, until all the feeling has been wrung out of it, until I've been inoculated against my own experience.

"Don't be so wooden," he says.

I nod, refusing to despair as I take it from the top. This is boot camp. I'm paying my dues.

"Again, but don't seem so rehearsed."

Rehearse exhaustively, but don't seem rehearsed. Got it.

When I finally sit down, I've never been this tired. I've never tried this hard at anything. Edwin said I was a natural, but where the hell is he?

"This is where everyone starts," Albie says. He's not looking at me, but he must be able to sense how dispirited I am. "You'll get there. Down the line, you'll be doing breaking news, not just tape. For now, just remember, we have multiple takes. We have editing. We'll get you there."

The TV descends from the ceiling, and as we watch, I realize I wasn't nearly as bad as I'd feared. There are usable moments. There are *good* moments.

"Next week, you're coming off the bench."

It's too soon. I need more time. I can't possibly . . .

"You start with *Media Is the Message*, and you work your way up to Ty. I've told him to take it easy on you. Edwin has too." He shrugs in a way that shows even Edwin doesn't control Ty.

"What's the rush?"

He shrugs again. "Ask Edwin."

I'm tempted to do it, to go ahead and text Edwin, but he's the guy, and the boss; he should make the move. And whatever his expectation is, I want to meet it.

Albie and I work through the weekend. He gives me feedback, and he never leads with praise; it has to be earned. I'm okay with that. When I get it, the feeling is indescribable. It's beyond pride. It's hope. It's the buoyant feeling that I can be plucked from obscurity and actually pull this off, less than two weeks later.

"This isn't a montage," Albie says. "I'm not Mr. Miyagi. You're not going to wax my cars and secretly learn the art of karate." I have no idea what he means. "*Karate Kid*?" I shake my head. Now he shakes his. "Jesus. I'm tutoring an infant." I smile, and he does, too, blink-and-you'd-miss-it briefly. "What I mean is, everything I do is transparent. Now do it again."

By the end of the night, we're both yawning and stretching, having grown loose with each other. As we're packing it in, I can't help asking. "Edwin talked to you about me owning a story that I'd report on across all the shows?"

"I told him you're nowhere near ready for that."

I know he's right, but I've got this feeling. It must be what people call "a fire in the belly." Put me in, Coach.

He must see it in me because he says again, "You're nowhere near ready for that. I do think you've got something, a quality.

But don't start believing your own press." As he's heading for the door, he turns around. "Have you been doing what I told you? Keeping your eyes and ears open?"

"I know who a few of my enemies are. Should I name names?"

"No. You should keep score."

I'm not sure what he means. I feel like he's implying more than he's telling, and that hurts a little. I'd thought he was in my corner, absolutely, and now I've got a twinge of doubt. He might have no allegiance to me at all. I could be nothing but a paycheck to him, a way to supplement his 401(k) postretirement.

"Listen," he says, "sexism is real, and it's alive. The newsroom is full of women these days, and they're going up higher than they have before. You all can get a seat at the table without much trouble. But no one wants women at the head of it, especially other women."

Maybe Albie is the one who left me the diary. He's telling me women haven't come as far as we think, and that I shouldn't get uppity. He's trying to keep me in line.

He must misread my expression, because he looks genuinely irritated for the first time as he says, "You think you know better than me? Look at the industry. The top echelon of news—the top echelon of business, period—is still primarily occupied by men. Who heads networks? Who heads network divisions?" He pauses. "Still not convinced? Think Hillary Clinton."

"It was a change election. People were angry, and they wanted the outsider. They didn't like Hillary's personality."

"Oh, right. She was too shrill." He rolls his eyes. "Hillary Clinton was more prepared to govern than any candidate EVER. And you know who won? A man with no political experience, born with a silver spoon and no connection to the common man. No, that's not true. He screwed over the common man. Walked over him. We're talking about a man who cares so little for the public good that he was proud he didn't pay his workers or his taxes. Not that he released his taxes. The electorate forgave him his bullying and bad temperament and Twitter rants; they forgave him his admiration for fascist dictators; they forgave him for groping and disrespecting women. Because subconsciously, much of this country—men *and* women— didn't want to be told what to do by a woman."

I'm proof that Albie is wrong. I grew up believing I could do anything, and look where I am. "What does any of this have to do with me?"

"You, Cheyenne, want power. I can see it in you. You never knew your own ambition before, but you want this. You want to go all the way. You're going to recognize that yourself soon enough, and then they're all going to see it, that you're not content to just stand there and look pretty and take orders, that you've got honest-to-God ambition. Then—what do they say in reality TV?—it's on. So watch your back."

And I thought I was the paranoid one.

Elyse talked about the shame of ambition.

It's Albie. It has to be. He's the feminist.

"Let's speed this up," I say. "Hand over the whole diary. Or better yet, just give me the *CliffsNotes*. Tell me what Wikipedia doesn't know. I have too much else to read."

"What?"

I search his face. He's genuinely mystified. "Nothing."

"I'll see you tomorrow."

The door shuts behind him. I sit down, reeling from the long day, and from all the ground left to cover, and from the talk with Albie. But I have a job to do, and this time, I'm going to keep my fire burning.

I hear Albie talking in the hall. It's always deserted around Edwin's office, so at first, I assume he's on his cell phone. Then I hear a woman's voice. It's the kind of voice I would love to have. It's mellifluous, calm, and commanding all at once.

Albie sounds muffled, his words indistinct, but the woman is like a fork tine against expensive crystal. It rings out: "Take her in the right direction, fast."

Could she be talking about me? If she is, wouldn't she lower the volume? *That* is a woman with vocal training. She must know I'm still in the office.

Or she wants to be overheard.

I yank the door open, but too late. The hall is empty. It's almost like I imagined the whole exchange in the delirium of overexertion, except for the scent. It's a man's cologne, clean and simple. Oceanic, like the one that Elyse said R.G. used to wear.

CHAPTER 9

I know you'll be amazing today, Edwin texts, minutes before my debut on *The Media Is the Message*.

That's all I get? Every day I half expected (well, hoped) that he would check in, just to ask how I'm doing, how it's going, but there was nothing. He's such a *guy*: he wooed me hard-core, and then after I said yes, he dropped me into a shark tank with the likes of Rayna and Luke and ghosted me. Sure, I'm in good hands with Albie, but still. Some part of me assumed Edwin would redeem himself today, that he'd be here to cheer me on.

I'm being ridiculous. I need to stop acting like a jilted lover. Edwin is a busy, successful man who doesn't owe me anything. He already gave me this golden opportunity. Then he disappeared.

I don't understand how he can run a network like this, not showing his face for this long. INN doesn't look like his highest priority, and it's television. Appearances matter.

What's he off doing, anyway? *Who* is he off doing?

Not my concern. I have a job to do, and I have to be amazing. That's what Edwin expects.

I'm standing to the side of the set, the generically patriotic one that features a long anchor desk that is faintly, almost subliminally tattooed with stars and stripes. There's a more informal area where four blue chairs are arranged around a rug that matches the anchor desk pattern. Behind the desk are Quill and Rayna.

Rayna, my enemy. But what can she really do to me in front of all these people?

I guess I'm about to find out.

I'm waiting for my cue. Albie is in the control room, and he'll speak through the earpiece I'm wearing. There are two cameras, and therefore, two camera operators, a stage manager, and the dreaded Luke. I can see engineers and editors both beside Albie and packed into the bleachers behind him. While the producers are evenly split among male and female, the crew today is entirely male. I've been so consumed with thoughts of my impending performance that it took me extralong to think it: *How many of these guys have seen me naked?*

With what I'm wearing, they're practically seeing me naked now. The wardrobe stylist put me in a nearly nude sheath dress truncated four inches above my knees, and then pinned back the bodice so it fits like a corset. But no cleavage. I was told that's a directive straight from Edwin. So he's communicating with someone at INN, just not me. But it is about me, which means he still cares.

My red hair was teased out and then brushed; the makeup is understated lips and a heavy eye. Everything's calculated and calibrated—only the suggestion of sex, but no one's missing that signal.

It's not that I don't recognize myself, exactly. It's that at once,

I'm both more sophisticated and trashier than I've ever been. I've been transformed into a newsy sex symbol, which is just what Edwin wanted. I'm bait to reel in the male millennials.

"Are you ready?" Shit. It's Luke. Despite how successfully I've avoided him since the pitch meeting, he is the EP of the show, which means there's no avoiding him now. His eyes are crawling all over me.

"I'm ready," I tell him. Say it and hope it'll become true. Right now, it's an alternative fact.

His eyes flick over me quickly, up and down. And then up again and down again, slower this time. This dress leaves nothing to the imagination, and still, I see his running wild, because he wants me to.

"I'll be in the control room," Luke says. "You remember how to work the equipment, right?"

His use of the word "equipment" is not accidental. I have no broadcast journalism experience, and I'm dressed like a high-end call girl, so he's treating me like one.

"I've got this," I say.

"A pro already." He grins wolfishly. "We'll let you know when to assume the position."

His double entendres could not be more obvious. But I'll play dumb. Let him underestimate me.

He forces his eyes upward to my face, as if with difficulty. "You'll want to stick to your script, to the word."

It's insulting, this reminder that I'm here for my body and not my mind, like I'm their little Broadcast Barbie. Dress me, wind me up, have me totter around on stilettos, and get those millennials jacking off.

I happen to glance around the room at that moment, and I see two men clustered together, their eyes on my body, leering.

When they get caught, they immediately go back to work. They must have thought they could steal an ogle while I was otherwise occupied by Luke. Hell, he might have told them they could. I can't entirely blame them. I'm so conspicuous in this outfit, like all my assets are on the outside.

But I know better, and so does Edwin, and Albie is becoming a believer too. I'll show them all.

The Media Is the Message is pretaped, unlike the other shows, which was why it was chosen for my network debut. Albie has assured me that I'm going to be edited within an inch of my life; I just have to give them enough footage and the crew can work miracles. I won't fail, even if some people on staff would love to see that. But I want to nail this in as few takes as possible, because fuck Luke, and fuck those cameramen too.

I have a few minutes to listen and admire Quill and Rayna before my entrance. Following the money makes for good TV. It's similar to how Fox once stole audiences from CNN and MSNBC: with an eye toward showmanship and entertainment, with outrage on behalf of the American people. INN is siphoning viewers of every political stripe, and attracting new ones who are hungry for transparency in opaque times.

Now it's my turn to join the conversation. My first stand-up! I wish I wasn't a part of the story I'm about to tell, as the idea of showing vulnerability right out of the gate is a bit frightening, but if Edwin thinks it's the right move, I have to trust him. He is the mastermind behind this whole network, after all.

I start with statistics about the percentage of social media users who reportedly experience cyberbullying, and then I catalogue the response of major sites. "Facebook and Twitter have been showing slow improvement in reacting to complaints, with increased content-blocking and banning of users. But one site,

Tag, is consistently rated as the worst offender, with responses ranging from ineffectual to nonexistent." I briefly detail a few specific cases, with images on the touch screen, then go on to trace the corporate ownership of Tag, and the many settled lawsuits against its parent company for its hostile work environment, with rampant accusations of discrimination and harassment. The implication is: meanness, bigotry, and cruelty flow downhill. They're big business, too, as Tag is growing far faster than all other social media sites, in part by plugging its "anticensorship" bent, which I proceed to demonstrate is being used as a dog whistle to racists, bigots, misogynists, and cyberbullies.

The report is going well, but now I need to move from the macro to the micro level, from the larger culture to my own experience. I turn toward the touch screen, using it as an opportunity to take a deep breath.

The screen fills with a sample of the nastiness I lived through before I terminated my Tag account. Fortunately, I only have to read the last one aloud: "Future rape victim." My breath has sped up, and my stomach is clenched in another bodily memory of the past. I'd thought Albie and I had exorcised it through repetition, but it's been rekindled by the knowledge that this will be seen by millions. And some of those millions are trolls. Some could be right here in this city. *The* city.

But when I speak, my voice is strong. "This aggression was in response to a think-piece video I'd made while I was a senior at Stanford University. I questioned the procedures of college disciplinary tribunals on sexual assaults. I made the case that rape is a very real problem that deserves our best solutions. It deserves justice. And nearly a third of the time, those tribunals result in the innocent being found guilty. That's not justice for anyone.

"I stand by my right to question the system, despite what came afterward. Despite the ad hominem attacks and threats and insults. Despite the character assassination and the impugning of my motives. Despite the hacking of my phone, which led to my private photos being stolen and distributed all over the internet. Despite the Tag thread that allowed people to keep tabs on my whereabouts in real time, that abetted unwanted confrontations and stalking and intimidation, and that was not shut down despite my repeated complaints.

"I still believe in justice. I believe in free speech, and positions that are neither knee-jerk liberal nor knee-jerk conservative, but are evidence based. I believe in thoughtful exploration and consideration and facts. I believe in reforming systems that don't work as they should, for accusers or the accused. I believe in asking questions."

Another deep breath. Remember, suppressed emotion is always better.

"But at the time, I was in my last few months of college, and I was under incredible stress. I caved. At the recommendation of police, I took down my videos and shut down all my social media. Retreating was the only way to feel safe again. They broke me, and I thought I could heal only in silence.

"I've since realized that there are more important things than feeling safe. That's why I'm here. To shine light on the behavior of Tag, and the impact it has on ordinary people. Like Nicole Bertolucci." I touch the screen. "And Clayton White." I touch again. "And . . ." I continue the list, with photos, and then say, "These are just some of the Tag users who have killed themselves, allegedly after repeated harassment. They complained to the website, but those complaints went unanswered." I turn to Rayna and Quill. "Those lawsuits have yet to be settled."

I did it! I didn't merely get through; I killed it. This is the beginning. I have the backing of INN, and I won't be silenced again.

Then comes the walk from the touch screen to the round table area. That's where I stumble.

Not really. That is, I don't trip or anything. But Luke tells me, plainly, that it's not sexy enough. I'll need to do it again. I can't know if that's really to get the best cut for the viewers, or for his own benefit.

It's very different to hear Luke say, "Again," and "Again," and "Again," than it is to hear it from Albie. I know Albie is trying to improve me. Luke is likely doing it to humiliate me, and it's working. With each take, I'm thinking of those crew members who were watching and smirking at me. They have their game faces on now, but I can only imagine the impure thoughts they're having.

It's even worse because I'm coming off what is obviously a triumph (after all, Luke didn't have me redo the report itself), so I'm forced to face the possibility that the work won't matter. They'll still have their nasty thoughts about me, and I can't do anything to stop them. I can't do anything to stop Luke right now, who's leaning into the glass of the control room, practically fogging it up. Is he getting off on how I look or on the power of bullying, right after my topic was anti-bullying? I wish Edwin were here. He wouldn't stand for this. But because Edwin isn't here to witness, I can't tell him about it later. It would be my word against Luke's, and those aren't the kind of waves I want to make after my first stand-up.

Albie's saying nothing. If he disagrees with Luke—and he must, feminist that he is—he's not in a position to speak up.

He's just a freelancer, really. Edwin promised me protection, but right now, I have none.

On the eleventh try, Luke declares me good enough. Everyone explodes into applause. My face is on fire under the pancake makeup. I head for the bathroom and run my hands under cold water, fighting to calm down. There's another segment to get through, and I can't let this—can't let Luke—derail me. It was going so well. I can finish strong.

Returning to the set, I take my spot on a blue chair, the one designated for me, carefully placed so that the viewer at home will have the best vantage point on my crossed legs. My makeup gets a touch-up. Then it's time to film the segment with Quill and Rayna.

They lob questions, and my every answer is scripted. It's harder to sound natural in conversation than it was during the stand-up. We have to do it three times, and while Rayna's face is impassive, I can imagine the internal judgment.

I hear Albie in my ear: "Cross your legs." They're already crossed. "Again," he hisses. What he means is, do it conspicuously. Draw the viewers' eyes to my newly spray-tanned legs.

I want to ignore him, because it's borderline offensive, but I know it's not really Albie talking. Albie has shown no interest in any of my body parts in the time we've spent together. He's following orders—Luke's? Edwin's?—and I need to do the same.

Slowly. Sexy, like my walk. Oh God, don't let them make me do this eleven times.

Rayna's eyes narrow. She gets what's going on, and it's clear she doesn't like it. But it feels like she doesn't like me. Doesn't she know I would never choose this?

Maybe she doesn't, because she doesn't know me. She could believe what some people were saying online about me being like Tomi Lahren, and that my every move has been calculated to take me to this point, opposite her. Meanwhile, she's a real journalist, having cut her teeth in the White House press corps. Of course she resents my presence.

"Could you tell us more about your sources on this?" Rayna asks. "How did you get the documents about Tag's parent company and the discrimination complaints?"

It's a deviation from the script. I have no idea how to answer; I don't know how the story was constructed. I didn't even participate in telling my own side. It hadn't even occurred to me until that moment how strange that was: that I wasn't one of the sources. Really, I'm just a newsreader, like Elyse.

Quill jumps in to ask, "Have they requested anonymity?" He's trying to bail me out.

I don't want to lie. This is supposed to be the news.

Albie whispers in my ear, "We'll edit it out later. Just go ahead and say yes."

"Yes," I say, "they requested anonymity."

"You're new to INN," Quill says. So we're back on script. "What should our viewers know about you?"

"I grew up in Tulip, Montana. Fewer than a thousand people live there. There were plenty of differences between us, but we treated one another with respect, and we disagreed with heart. My father owns a co-op, and he sold everything from wagyu beef to seitan. I was arguing issues with progressives and conservatives before I knew what either of those was. Since I was eight years old I've believed that you're entitled to your own opinions but not your own facts. And I intend to tell the truth here at INN, no matter who it inflames. Because frankly,

I couldn't care less about sides. I've got a red-state name, but I'm not going to adhere to any color lines, and I'll always admit mistakes but I won't be silenced."

Quill and Rayna exchange a choreographed smile, like a marital seal of approval, and then they turn to the camera to say how happy they are to have me beside them.

I know I could have done better with the speech, and Luke agrees. I'm just glad there's no more walking. I can feel my delivery getting stronger, my conviction deepening, and the words becoming mine with each attempt. Then it's a wrap.

"You were great," Rayna says curtly, like it's the end of a conversation rather than the start.

"Everything I said was true," I tell her. What I mean is, *Learn what I'm really about; it's not what you seem to think.*

"I never said you were a liar." Her tone suggests she's said other things about me. I can fill in the blank (untalented, opportunist, manipulator, attention whore, or just plain whore . . .)

Not to mention, she tried to sabotage me.

Well, sort of. She knew it would get edited out. So she was sending me a message, a shot across the bow. But whose bow? Mine, or Edwin's? Edwin is, after all, the one pushing me, hard.

Rayna and Luke can think whatever they want. I killed it. That's all Edwin will see, and at the end of the day, he's the one who matters. Edwin, and all of America.

All of America. That's what I wanted, right? So why does the thought give me such a chill?

CHAPTER 10

July 3, 1991

York has had a bad impact on my routines for the last couple of days. Each morning, instead of walking to the subway, I'm reliant on the doorman to hail me a cab. He doesn't react like it's anything out of the ordinary, it's just his job. But for me, it feels like a defeat, that I'm back to needing men to watch out for me. This is a good neighborhood, the Upper East Side, close to Central Park. I shouldn't be afraid.

From the sanctity of the taxi's vinyl interior, I always scan the street. It's five a.m. and still mostly dark. There usually aren't many pedestrians, just a few joggers and dog walkers. I haven't laid eyes on York again, but my experience is changed just having met him. I know that you don't have to see people for them to see you.

A few more days without any sightings and I'll go back to taking the subway, maybe. I refuse to live in fear. But vigilance—that's been a regular feature of my mental landscape ever since college.

York is probably just who he says he is. He's an agent who wants to represent me. It should be flattering, not frightening.

But he knows where to find me, and there are probably more where he came from. Men who think they know me because I'm on their TV screen, who won't take no for an answer. They don't even ask the question; they just assume that I'm somehow theirs. The scariest part about being on a morning show is that everyone knows where it's filmed. Anyone could be lying in wait outside the studio, just beyond the metal barricades, amid all the I LOVE YOU, SCOTT AND TRISH! placards and signs.

This is what I signed up for. And really, how often

does anything truly bad happen to someone in the public eye?

An image comes immediately, unbidden: Rebecca Schaeffer, the curly-headed sitcom actress with the ready smile, was murdered in the doorway of her own home by a deranged fan. It happens. Stalkers can kill you.

I don't have a stalker, currently. York Diamond is an agent, that's all. I wish there was an easy way to verify that he is who he said. Maybe I could look in the Yellow Pages? I did a story about something called the World Wide Web that just launched, and supposedly, someday it will let people find out all sorts of information with a few keystrokes. I'm not sure how I feel about that. If I can find out about other people, couldn't they also find out about me?

When I arrived at the studio, it was still dark out. People hadn't started gathering out front yet to meet Trish, Scott, and Conrad, the meteorologist. The fact is, any one of those "fans" could have a gun. Anyone could push through the metal barricade, if they were so inclined. There are no police officers, no metal detectors, and the security is fairly minimal. Not that security could do much. With Rebecca Schaeffer, it was over in seconds.

I went inside, got my hair and makeup done, reviewed my copy, and did a great show. Scott even gave me a thumbs-up from over on his couch. On my way out of the building afterward, eight people wanted my autograph. That's not many compared to the throngs that were still waiting for Trish and Scott, holding placards with their names, not mine. But those eight people weren't just overflow from the others; they seemed excited to meet me. I'm gaining ground.

I finished signing, and then I paused, debating whether to go to the subway or take another cab. That's when someone grabbed my elbow. Without thinking, I yanked it away, and then I saw that the person doing the grabbing was Dennis Graver.

"Oh, sorry!" I said. "I just . . ." I was flustered, having treated the head of network news like a mugger.

He was unflappable, and impeccable, as always, in his expensive suit. "Glad I caught you before the holiday weekend," he said. "I'm headed to the Hamptons later, but how about lunch?"

Before I could answer, he had his hand on my back and was ushering me forward, into a waiting limousine. Who was I to say no, really?

Besides, I was grateful that he'd made my decision for me. Cab or subway—no, it would be a limo. It felt paternal, though he's only fifteen years older than me, and his manner isn't precisely fatherly. But then, he's not my dad; he's my boss.

He's not bad-looking—he's tall and confident, he has all his light brown hair—except for the port wine birthmark near his temple. If he were a woman, it might be better for him, since he could try to cover it with makeup. But maybe it's better that he's a man because even without flesh-colored camouflage, that birthmark doesn't hold him back at all.

The thought of concealing makeup makes me think of Dermablend, and its spokesperson, Marla Hanson, the model whose face was slashed with a razor blade after she refused the advances of her landlord.

I turned York down, and I imagine there will be other men in this town who I need to rebuff. There are men who'll get the wrong idea just seeing a woman on their TV screen, men who will nurse fantasies and try to make them come true, regardless of what the object of their affection actually wants.

I have to remember that Lyndon is back in State College, Pennsylvania. He didn't even bother me while I was in Pittsburgh, only when I was in his backyard. There's no way he's coming to New York.

Of course, if he couldn't find me in Pittsburgh, it's actually easier now. I've gone national. Besides, Lyndon isn't the only sicko in the world.

For lunch, Dennis took me to the same steakhouse where we went after the tryout, when he let me know that the network would be making an offer. That was one of the best nights of my life. Once again, Dennis didn't open the menu, and when the waiter came, he ordered for both of us. Also like last time, he added a bottle of red wine, with a slightly ostentatious French accent.

"I've got to tell you," he said, "I like what I've been seeing so far. There aren't that many times in my career when someone has delivered so big so soon."

The wine arrived, and I let him fill my glass. I don't normally drink, but it was almost a holiday.

"Morning shows are cutthroat, they really are."

Dennis held his glass up by the stem and contemplated the ruby liquid inside. "Viewers can be fickle. Even if you're on top, you're worried about who's coming up behind you. I tell you, if I hear Katie Fucking Couric's name one more time . . ." He smiled, but there was bitterness around the edges. "Her Q score is off the charts while she's home breastfeeding."

"What's a Q score?"

He laughed. "That's what I love about you, Elyse. It's all new. You're not jaded yet." He took a big swallow of wine. "A Q score is likability plus recognizability. Just between us, Scott's is significantly higher than Trish's."

"Oh?" I tried not to sound too interested.

"You're headed for big things, but you've got to be smart about it. You've got to be feminine but not in that wily way, if you know what I mean. Not like some females in this industry." His face darkened. "Don't be a manipulator, Elyse, okay? Not with me."

"I'm not a manipulator with anyone."

Apropos of nothing I could detect, he said, "You know I've got a son, right?"

I like kids. "How old is he?"

"Fifteen. My ex gives me shit all the time about my parenting. She says I act too much like his friend. But there are things he has to know. I keep telling him that it's not the same as it was when I was young, back when you just took a shot of penicillin or whatever. Now, you've got to worry about catching AIDS. Now sex can kill you. I tell him, he's got to wear his jimmy hat, every time. I try to use the kids' language, you know? You've got to wrap it up."

I just blinked at him in disbelief. Fortunately, the food arrived, and like last time, Dennis went silent for prime rib. He talks before, and he talks after, and in between, he inhales his food like someone might try to steal it from him.

When he was finished, he moved back to a more palatable topic. "With your looks and your personality, I think you'd be a perfect fit as a morning show host."

I couldn't help it, the smile just overtook my face. I don't want to knife Trish in the back, but I want a future too.

"It's too early to make any moves. You've got to ease into these things gradually. Think Katie Couric, how they gave her a bigger correspondent role for a whole year before she elbowed Deborah Norville out of the way." He poured another glass of wine for himself, and for me. I hadn't even noticed I'd finished the last one. "We have to be strategic. But just know that you're on my radar." He drank the entire glass in one swig. "Shall we go?"

I felt a little nervous, since drunk men can be aggressive, but Dennis remained a gentleman. He dropped me off at my apartment, and I've been in a state of exhilaration ever since. I'm too happy to even think about the hang-up I got earlier.

It was a wrong number, I know it was.

CHAPTER 11

I t's already happening," I tell Edwin.

"How about a drink?" he asks. He's hovering near the bar in his office, a smile on his face. There's a fresh scab on his chin, as if he's just cut himself shaving. Otherwise, he looks like he did the first time. His ease is as attractive as ever. He couldn't be any further from Dennis Graver if he tried. And I'm no Elyse. If Edwin started talking about penises, I'd be filing an HR complaint before dessert. I don't need to bat my eyelashes to succeed.

I'm happy to see Edwin, yes, but I've got a lot on my mind. Since my first TV appearance I've been at the center of a media frenzy. My segment has gotten millions of hits on YouTube, with over thirty thousand comments. More are positive than I'd dared to anticipate, particularly from people who experienced bullying themselves and were grateful that I was bringing attention to what Tag had done or, rather, not done. Then there are plenty about how hot I am, and others about how undeserving I am of the current opportunity, that it's only about the aforementioned hotness. I'd been ready for all the links to naked photos, and for cross-referencing to my viral video, which most declared boring. To my relief, the threats, the vitriol, and the chatter about rape have been minimal. So far.

Media blogs have gone crazy, too, since they didn't have any advance warning that INN was getting a new correspondent, let alone an "explosively attractive one." (Edwin loves the element of surprise.) The major networks, CNN, and Fox are all running with versions of the story "Who is Cheyenne Florian?" Some of their answers are none too flattering, citing my undistinguished Stanford career and hinting at an almost Machiavellian level of planning behind my overnight success. One journalist managed to excavate the comments that I'd turned off. Early on, when I was still trying to respond to people who seemed reasonable, I'd written, "I'm not a journalist," and that's become its own meme.

TV reporters have even shown up outside Dad's co-op, and when they found out he's not there much anymore, not since the cancer, they waited for him outside his house. He told them he's proud of his brilliant, talented daughter. End quote.

Every word from my introductory speech has been analyzed. Some accuse me of plagiarizing from Daniel Patrick Moynihan about not being entitled to your own facts; others argue back that it often goes unattributed, I wasn't pretending that I'd come up with it at the age of eight. My talk of color lines has drawn particular attention. Am I truly independent, or was that a dog whistle about race relations for the left, or for the right? Was the girl with the red-state name speaking in code to a hidden base, like the one that Trump really wound up having? What's my true agenda?

Most feminist sites have been just as critical. They think I'm rewinding the movement every time I cross my legs on camera (one blog counts leg crosses per segment). One called me "an IINO (Independent in Name Only), manufactured and market researched, a wet dream of a broadcast journalist for a dumbed-down, oversexed viewership, who sets us all back by a hundred years, and a hundred thousand brain cells, and she comes, completely accessorized, with her own nude portfolio." *Salon*, though, had a different take: "Cheyenne clearly had a personal investment and involvement in the story she was telling. Do we ask whether male correspondents have done all their own research and writing? I think you know the answer. Judged strictly on her performance, Cheyenne gets an A-."

I have to hope everyone on INN's staff reads *Salon*.

But I was ready for all that. What has my stomach churning is the hack. Another hack, after Edwin assured me that INN would keep me safe. "I had a secret social media account," I say, "and someone's gotten it shut down. I went to log in and—"

"You're welcome."

I stare at him. "You did that?"

"Your password was weak."

"You knew about @fuzzysocksonmyhead?"

"Sure. You think I don't do a background check before I make a job offer? I need to know that what you see is what you get. In your case, I couldn't be more pleased." He finishes mixing my drink. "An old-fashioned." He thrusts it into my hand and then settles on the couch opposite me. "A toast, to the newest media It Girl. You brought it." He clinks his glass against mine. I'm not clinking back.

"I said I didn't want a drink," I set it down on an end table. I flash on Dennis Graver ordering for Elyse. Making decisions for her without her input, but that was just a steak. What Edwin's done is much bigger than that. "I can't believe you shut down my account without talking to me first."

"My bad. I thought I'd mentioned it."

"Mentioned it? You should have asked." Then I get it. "So the rest wasn't a hack either. On Facebook, Twitter, and Instagram, and who knows where else. @theRealCheyenneFlorian is you."

"Not me. It's you. But behind every great woman is a crack PR team. They've watched all your vlogs and read through all the social media you pulled down." I don't even want to know how they got their hands on that. It means what's erased is never really erased. "They know your voice, and they're going to make sure everything stays on brand."

"This is not at all okay."

"What's not?"

It's frightening that he even has to ask that, that he looks genuinely surprised by my reaction. "Where do I start? It's not okay that you somehow got access to the material I'd already pulled down, or that you shut off the account I was actually using, or that you created this person, this brand, who's supposed to be me, all without so much as a conversation."

"You have more than enough on your plate. I knew the team would do a great job, and I didn't want you to have any additional stress."

"Don't worry your pretty little head, is that it?"

He grabs his phone and holds it out to me. "You've already got a million and a half followers on Facebook, and over a quarter of a million on Twitter and Instagram. Obviously you won't have an account on Tag. And we'll never compromise your safety because your photos will never be taken where you really are. If anything, this'll keep you safer. We'll throw any would-be stalkers off your scent."

Perhaps this is how the industry works. Decisions get made by the higher-ups, and you just have to toe the line.

He's saying I get to focus on the real work, which is what I want to do. And he's right, I don't have the time to handle my social media. It's not like I even enjoy doing it anymore.

Still, it's creepy to have a whole team of people impersonating me, without my consent.

I could ask Albie if this is just how things are done, if delegating social media to someone who can do it better is standard. But I'm not entirely sure I can trust his answer. Did he know this was going on and kept it from me? The fact is, Albie isn't really mine. His loyalty is to Edwin, and maybe to that woman in the hallway.

"I'm sorry," Edwin says. "I haven't done a very good job of keeping you in the loop. I wanted to minimize your stress so you could prepare for your debut. I meant to get rid of the noise so you can do what really matters, but you're right. I should have talked to you."

It was an oversight, an error in judgment. I have no reason not to trust him. As I scroll through his phone, I like everything @theRealCheyenneFlorian is saying. She's like me, only plugged into what I have no time for these days.

"If it's about my image and how I'm being presented to the world, I want to know about it," I say.

"From now on, you will. I'm going to give you a new dummy account with much higher security so that you can monitor social media. If you don't like anything you're seeing, let me know and we'll take it down. You're in control."

"Deal." I smile. I don't like being mad at Edwin. "Are you happy with how things are going?"

"Absolutely. You're blowing up the interwebs."

"A lot of the coverage is pretty negative."

"If it wasn't, no one would be talking. You need the back-lash to have the frontlash. Listen, you've got it. That thing that everyone wants. We're not making any excuses or any apologies. We're not trying to say you're anything you're not. We don't have to."

"I did cut the line." Something that is surely not escaping anyone's notice, outside or INN.

He makes a face of utter dismissal. "People learn on the job. Your performance was stellar. You're not just beautiful; you're a star, like I knew you would be."

My face warms. I'm thinking of Luke and all that footage to get my walk right. Then there's the slooooooow leg cross.

Even Chase mainly commented on how I looked, that he wished he was there right then so he could . . .

My face gets even hotter thinking of that. Phone sex is pretty new to me, though it might end up being essential since I'm not sure when Chase and I will be able to see each other, be-tween his work schedule and mine. He wanted to sext, but I couldn't help thinking in terms of privacy in case of another phone hack. Sure, Edwin has given me a cell upgrade that's supposed to be more secure, but nothing's impenetrable, if someone (or a band of someones) is determined enough.

I reach for my old-fashioned and take a sip.

"It can be overwhelming at first," Edwin says. "But this is go-ing just like I planned. We want them talking. There's nothing damaging for them to find, no dirt to dig up because you haven't compromised yourself in this corrupt industry. You made some videos with the best of intentions, and you took sexy photos for your longtime boyfriend. So what? It was inevitable that you'd go viral. You're the real deal. People want to look at you." He didn't say they want to listen to me. "They're just curious about where you came from, that's all. This country loves an origin story. You're the woman who delayed Stanford—twice—to take care of your dying father. Who didn't die! They're going to love that."

"I don't want them to love that. Is it out there?"

"Not yet, but it will be. You'll be the one to post about it on your social media."

"No. Leave my father out of it." I'm thinking of how someone got his email before, and what they might send him next.

"But he's—"

"I said no!"

We both look a little stunned. Then we both take a drink.

"Sorry," I say. "I'm just protective of him. There's a lot I'm willing to do for this job, but you need to let me draw some lines, okay?"

"Okay."

I need to calm down, that's all. This is going according to plan. Edwin's plan, our shared mission. I'll deliver him the millennials, and together we'll change the world.

"I like that you want to protect your father, but you really need to think about yourself," Edwin says. "Every time you're out, think of your image. Don't do anything unless you want to be seen doing it. Because you never know who's there, capturing it."

There's a knock on the door. Edwin opens it, but not far enough for me to see who's there. "Well, hello," he says, with a hint of flirtation.

"I thought I'd find you here," the woman says. It's a self-possessed voice, possibly the same one I heard in the hall the other night, though I can't be sure.

"Cheyenne and I are talking about how well everything's going."

"Cheyenne?" the woman trills. "The next big thing? I want to meet her!"

Edwin opens the door farther, and she walks in. Tall, wrinkle-less, and slim—forty, fifty? As with all of Edwin's women, it's hard to tell. Her hair is past her shoulders, in loose, lustrous curls. She moves with the willowy grace of Cate Blanchett, and she's in an unlined green silk maxi dress. She's smiling broadly at me, approaching with her hand outstretched. "I'm Daphne," she says. "It's an honor to meet you." The words seem over-blown, though the tone is sincere.

"You, too," I say, though I have no idea who Daphne even is. But her manner says that I should know. I feel a stab of jeal-ousy, which is silly. I have no claim on Edwin.

Daphne is the kind of woman who doesn't just sit; she drapes herself attractively across the couch, one arm along the back. Edwin sits beside her, but he doesn't lean back into the crook she's created. Despite the intimacy in their voices, they haven't touched each other at all.

"Sorry to interrupt," Daphne says. She glances at my glass, which has only the barest trace of liquor left in it. "Old-fashioned?"

"It just felt right," Edwin says. "It's almost lunchtime. Would you like one?"

Daphne shakes her head. "I've been out since last night. I missed you." She gives Edwin a look that's more shrewd than it is sexual. So she was out all night, with another man? I can't tell what's really going on here.

Daphne's gaze is back on me. Her features are pretty, but in a very basic way. She's cheerleader pretty, seasoned by the years.

She's intimidating, though that doesn't seem to be her intent. I just can't imagine what I could say that would be of interest to this high-end creature before me, who's still coming down from last night's dinner and drinks with a rich boyfriend or visiting dignitary or Jay-Z, who knows.

"I'm so glad Edwin was able to lure you to INN," Daphne says. "He showed me your videos, and I told him, yes, we have to get her."

"Thank you." The compliment adds to my confusion about who Daphne is. It's almost like she's the one who calls the shots.

I try to discreetly sniff at the air. Nothing. Whatever fragrance I smelled the other night, more like a man's cologne than a woman's perfume, is not currently emanating from Daphne.

"I've been where you are," Daphne says. "I was once an It Girl, and while a lot has changed—and I mean, *a lot*—some things haven't. Do you know what I'm saying?"

Is she the one who left me the diary?

"So," Edwin says, "I have an assignment for you."

CHAPTER 12

It's not just another night in the newsroom. Instead of being in their own pods, at their workstations, the staffers of all the shows are gathered together, watching the enormous wall of TV screens. While normally they would be tuned to Fox, CNN, and MSNBC, keeping an eye on the competition, right then every one is tuned to INN.

Ty's glowering. He's just detailed an exclusive pay-to-play mixer between heads of corporations and the heads of Senate committees. "And no one wants to tell the story of how our government really operates, how it's bought and paid for?" he bellows. "Every other network is too afraid that they'll lose access, that if they alienate the politicians, they'll get frozen out. So they tell stories the politicians want told; they're distributing the government's press releases like a bunch of lackeys. Not me.

"This is a story about access. It's about way too much access. What it's not about is partisanship. The elite on both sides of the aisle are having their legislation written for them by corporations while they line their own pockets and fill their reelection coffers. There were high-ranking Republicans and high-ranking Democrats in that room. They're pigs wallowing in the same muck, and the media is turning a blind eye. Well, I'm not blind. Don't you be either."

The screen goes to commercial, and everyone explodes into applause and whoops. As the high fiving and hugging commence, everyone keeps saying, "Only in!," and I think, *Only in America?* Then I get it: only INN. INN is the only news network that would do something like Ty just did. The pride borders on jingoistic, but it's also contagious.

Someone grabs me around the waist, spinning me around into an embrace. It's one of the male VJs, I can't recall his name or even his show. I hug him back, happy to ride the wave right along with the rest of them. I've been so separate, off in boot camp with Albie, but he told me to read at my workstation tonight. He must have known this was coming and saw the potential for bonding (and for ferreting out more enemies.)

"Come out with us," the VJ says into my ear.

Tired as I am, I can't turn down this chance. If they get to know the real me, we can push past so much of the bullshit. The way you reduce bigotry is to increase personal connection. I need to be humanized. I notice, with relief, that Luke is absent.

There's discussion about which bar, and then that archetypally nerdy producer of Ty's (I think his name is Graham?) enters the fray with his own suggestion. A few people exchange furtive incredulous glances. Someone says, "In the middle of *Times Square?*," and Graham nods assertively. Decision made.

Times Square makes sense geographically, since INN is less than ten blocks away, but it feels farther given the almost overwhelming crush of people, like trying to swim upstream. I've never experienced population density like this, have never been suffocated on a hot, humid night, floating in the swamp of humanity. I'm afraid to lose the caravan, afraid to drift away.

My fear escalates when I'm recognized, loudly. The New Yorkers tend to ignore me like Edwin said, especially since I generally dress down on my way to and from work, my hair scraped back in a bun, but the Times Square tourists are a different breed. They came here for sightings, and they want their selfies. They have questions. *What's it like to be an overnight sensation?* They're standing way too close, and maybe that's because everything's too close. The tall buildings and the neon and all those people . . . It's a paradox, how such magnitude can feel so claustrophobic.

I think of the diary, and of Rebecca Schaeffer and Marla Hanson, and gunshots and razor blades. I think of what can happen when you say no to a stranger. So I just keep saying yes. I'll take another picture, I'll answer another question. When you're surrounded, don't anger anyone. They all seem friendly, fortunately. No insults or threats. It's compliments, autographs, selfies, and small talk. It's like being in the reception line for a wedding that's not yours, only everyone mistakes you for the bride.

When I can finally extricate myself, I realize I've been left behind. I don't even remember the name of the bar. This was my chance to break through with my coworkers, and I've blown it.

I'm standing dead still in the middle of the pavement as everyone flows around me. I'm praying no one else will recognize me or want anything from me. I'm about to grab a cab and go home when Graham returns to rescue me.

"Come on," he says, his voice businesslike. He takes me by

the arm a bit roughly, but I'm grateful nonetheless. I eke out a thank-you that he seems not to hear.

He picked a piano bar. Framed in the front window, a man is playing a show tune I can't place while scads of the exuberantly drunk belt out the lyrics. Well, that makes sense. We're on Broadway.

The INN staff has already commandeered the farthest booths. Spirits are flowing and spirits are high. They're all shouting over one another. I pick up that some people knew a lot more than others about Ty's report, but the word got around today (to everyone but me) that something big was brewing and they all needed to tune in. Now they're trading war stories, times they were in the thick of a big get on an adrenaline rush better than sex. I'm aware of how little I have to contribute, but I'm here, and that's a start.

Despite my successful debut, I'm as invisible as I was during all the pitch meetings. Maybe they don't care about fame; they care about people who've earned their stripes. One broadcast just isn't enough.

I belly up to the bar for a drink. After five lonely minutes, the two brunette VJs from *Breaking It Down* elbow in on either side of me. While they're styled like twins with the same low ponytails and dark-rimmed glasses, pale skin and brown eyes, one is actually much prettier than the other. The prettier one reintroduces herself: "I'm Nan."

"I'm Belinda."

"I'm Cheyenne."

They laugh. "Yeah, we know," Belinda says. "We wanted to say we think you're doing a great job. The way we acted in the pitch meeting, that was just sucking up to Rayna. It was nothing personal against you."

"I know," I say. "How could it be personal? We just met." I decide to take a chance. "Does Rayna ever come out for drinks? I'd love to talk to her in a less formal setting."

They exchange a look. Then Nan gives me a don't-you-worry smile. "Just let some time pass. Rayna was a sorority girl once upon a time. She's still got that hazing mentality."

"Sorority." That word was used in the letter accompanying the diary. But it's hard to imagine that came from Nan. It sounds like it was written by someone much older, a feminist who'd been in the trenches, who was disappointed to see how little had changed with the passage of time.

Or maybe that's what someone wants me to think.

"So I just need to show her I can handle whatever she throws at me? That I'm here to stay?" I ask.

"Something like that," Belinda says.

Nan expertly grabs the bartender's attention, procures three shots, and places one in front of me. We knock them back in unison.

"Your social media is boss," Belinda says. "You do it yourself?"

I hesitate. I'm not sure whether it's a secret or not that Edwin has enlisted a PR team. "This is all new to me," I say. "I'm open to suggestions."

"You and Edwin have been having private meetings, huh?"

I feel myself stiffen slightly. That was the rumor about Professor Trent and me too. "Not many," I answer. It was true then, and it's true now.

Nan and Belinda look less than 100 percent convinced.

"I know that I jumped the queue," I say. "I don't blame anyone for, you know, not exactly welcoming me with open arms."

Nan laughs. "There's no queue."

"Good genes are as valid as hard work," Belinda confirms. "You use what you've got."

"And we're all about open arms." Nan laughs again and calls my attention to the other end of the bar, where a female VJ from *The Media Is the Message* is making out brazenly with a male VJ from *Breaking It Down*. "We sleep with the enemy."

"We work hard, and we stay late, and we have to burn off a little steam," Belinda says. "You go in the next day like nothing ever happened."

"Are there any actual couples, or is it all hookups?"

Belinda shakes her head. "No couples."

"My boyfriend's back in Palo Alto."

"Chase is hot," Belinda says to Nan.

I'm surprised. "You know him?"

"No, I just saw his picture earlier tonight. There was a piece on one of the blogs about conflicts of interest in journalism, who's dating who in the news media, and they put up a picture of you and Chase."

I'm confused. "What kind of conflict of interest?"

"He works for that start-up Until, right?" Belinda says. "There are rumors about that place. On AstroTurf, but still."

"What's AstroTurf?"

They both laugh, like my naiveté is charming. I don't appreciate the condescension, but it's better than standing alone, so obviously outside the circle.

"AstroTurf, as in, fake grassroots," Nan explains. "As in, all those websites that are made to look legitimate, to make it seem like there's a groundswell of support for some idea or initiative, but they're just shilling for the government, or corporations, or even those other news organizations that INN's already over-taken in the ratings after a year on the air."

"On AstroTurf, people are talking about my relationship with Chase?"

"Don't even worry about it," Belinda says. "I shouldn't have said anything. There's no point stressing about rumors."

"Though there are plenty of options here for stress relief." Nan glances around and smiles. "Everyone's totally cool. And discreet."

Belinda and Nan are so different than they seemed in the pitch meeting. There, they were sharp and intimidating, entirely on their game. Now they've become a couple of gossipy twenty-somethings.

"Chase and I are pretty serious," I say. "I'm not going to need any stress relief."

Nan and Belinda smile at each other, like, *That's what they all say.* I like that look about as much as I like the two of them.

"You know who's into you already?" Belinda says. "Graham."

"You could have fooled me." I look over to where Graham's currently surrounded by people laughing at whatever witticism he's just dished up. He's clearly the alpha; his stereotypical geekiness is intentional, an emblem.

"He's in line to be EP on Ty's show," Nan says.

"Also, he's good in bed," Belinda says. "Or out of bed. In the bathroom or the closet, wherever."

"He's got plenty of women to vouch for him." Nan laughs, and Belinda joins in.

Can Graham really be INN's resident lothario? Or is this part of Rayna's hazing, a practical joke being played so I'll hit on him?

I'm glad when other staffers come over to join our trio. There are more shots. I feel looser and freer. The topic is no longer news, and I'm talking to whoever's closest, animatedly. There's some flirting but nothing more. I'll call Chase for my stress relief later, after I get home.

Then Graham's there, grinding into me from behind, his voice in my ear. "Come with me."

I don't feel like I can resist, or even ask questions. He's that authoritative, and I'm that drunk.

Outside, we're barraged by people, noise, and neon, even at this hour, whatever hour it is. I've lost track. Graham points, and I follow his finger.

"Holy . . . ," I say, the next word dying on my lips.

I'm on the Jumbotron, larger than life. I'd felt silly at first when Edwin told me about the assignment, and even more so when a film crew was following me around the streets of Manhattan. There were multiple costume changes, with corresponding hair and makeup tweaks, but the footage they wound up using came right at the end, when I spun around in my trademark scuba dress, a cardigan thrown casually over my shoulder. The confident turn, that smile . . . I barely recognize that girl. No, that woman. That go-getter.

Writ large across the Jumbotron screen: *The next face of news, Cheyenne Florian.*

This is really happening. I'm fast approaching a million Facebook, Instagram, and Twitter followers. In the days since my debut, with INN refusing to leak where I'll be next, the ratings for all the shows have had a boost overall, but most important, among the desired advertising demographic of eighteen- to thirty-five-year-olds. Meaning, people are watching for me.

I'm the next face of news, and the current face of Times Square.

As if from far away, I hear Graham saying that it's going to run every hour, and that it'll be all over TV and social media. It's going to be a blitz. Edwin has gotten his millennials, and he intends to keep them.

People are pointing to me and pointing up. Then I'm signing autographs, taking pictures, and listening to congratulations, and unlike earlier, I'm reveling. I've arrived.

Graham stays nearby, like a bodyguard, which is funny because he couldn't be less physically imposing. But he seems proprietary, and I'm sure that Edwin engineered this moment. It must be why Graham insisted on a Times Square bar.

Nan and Belinda were telling the truth. Graham is a power player.

But then, so am I.

CHAPTER 13

'm startled by the knock on my office door. In part, it's that I'm not used to having an actual office, with an actual door. I wouldn't have thought one broadcast would be so handsomely rewarded. I'm on Albie's floor, far from the rest of the staff, though my office is twice the size of his.

I'm feeling a rush of optimism. It's the cumulative effect of Edwin's approval, the Jumbotron, and INN's ratings. On top of that, my evening with my colleagues went smoothly, with no hostile interactions or strange vibes at all. Plus, I've had a revelation. All the media talk about me being a closet conservative and a Tomi Lahren and having no business in the correspondent role is just a display of their own impotence; meanwhile, the attention keeps my star rising, even as their disparagement is an attempt for them to stay relevant. They want to ride my coattails. And while my social media is far from uniformly positive, it hasn't been overrun by people calling for my rape and dismemberment. It practically verges on the civil.

"Come in!" I call. Edwin opens the door, and I beam. It's

his first time stopping by. Then he angles his body and I see a young, pretty, very tall blonde, and my smile dims.

"There's someone I want you to meet," he says.

"I'm Reese Benson," the blonde says, smiling widely, like she can't even contain her excitement. "I'm your new assistant."

"Hi. Nice to meet you." I smile back, then look inquiringly (and pointedly) at Edwin. I thought Edwin was going to consult me about matters that directly impact me, and hiring an assistant certainly qualifies. I don't even know what I'm supposed to do with her. I've never been anyone's boss.

"The fan mail is picking up fast," Edwin says. "You'll need someone to help you handle that. Then there are all the tasks of daily life. She'll make sure you're not living on takeout and that your laundry's done. She'll be in charge of your social calendar." I don't do social; all I do is work. "She'll be your liaison with PR and the other departments. There are some functions we're going to need you to attend soon, so Reese will keep you on track with all that. She knows the city. She knows where you'll want to shop and where you'll want to be seen. She can recommend fun things to do in your rare off-hours. She'll be your sounding board."

Like a paid friend? Or a role model?

"Anything you need"—another grin from Reese—"I'll make it happen. In my last year at Columbia, I had an internship with CNN. I just graduated, and I'm all yours."

I hope my smile doesn't seem as forced as it is. I feel for Reese. It's not her fault that she's being sprung on me. Now I'm wondering if this is why I was given an office, so I could have tête-à-têtes with a Columbia grad. I'm fine with being schooled by Albie, but this is a whole different thing. Sure, Edwin's talking about takeout and laundry, but if it was only that, my assistant wouldn't be so pedigreed. *Take her in the right direction*, that's what Daphne (or whoever) said in the hallway. I want to know what's really going on here.

"Welcome," I say. "Could you just give Edwin and me a minute alone?" She'd said anything I need, and at the moment, what I need most is to confront Edwin.

"Sure. I'll just wait in the hall."

When she's stepped out, I crook a finger to summon Edwin toward me. It's a bold move with your boss, but I'm too annoyed to care.

"I thought we agreed that you were going to include me in major decisions," I say, just above a whisper.

"This is hardly a major decision."

"She's going to be my shadow!"

"Not if you don't want her to. She works for you. You decide how much distance you need."

"You didn't think I'd want a say in who works for me?"

He shakes his head slightly. "I can't include you in everything, Cheyenne. You don't have the time to spare."

It's true, but still. He and I have radically different ideas about what constitute major decisions, and that's worrisome. "Are you telling me the whole story?"

"She's here to assist, that's all. It's right in her job title."

"I wish you'd picked a different day. I've got a lot on my mind, preparing for Beth's show tonight." It's my first live broadcast, and now I have to babysit my assistant. Or my assistant will be babysitting me. "I could just send her home, right? Tell her to start tomorrow?"

"If that's the tone you want to set, you can."

Now I need to be trained in how to treat my employee. "It just feels like more work that I don't need."

"She's here to make your life easier. I meant it as a gift."

As usual, I can feel Edwin's sincerity, and it starts to wear me down. That, and his nearness. "People aren't gifts, Edwin," I say with a sigh.

"I'm not so sure about that." His smile is full of affection, and I feel myself blushing.

"Will you be around tonight for the broadcast?" I'm not sure if I'll be more nervous or less if he's hovering around the studio.

"I'll be watching you on TV."

I have no right to be even a little disappointed, and yet . . .

It's better this way. Chase is three thousand miles away, and Edwin needs to keep his professional distance, just like Reese.

I invite her back in. I sit behind my desk, and she sits in the chair opposite, managing to appear simultaneously relaxed and eager. It's clear she's much more comfortable in her role than I am in mine.

Her blond hair is pulled back, and her skin is clear, with just a hint of makeup, enough to say she spent some time but that she didn't really need to. She's in a sheath dress, nowhere near as tight as the one I'll wear tonight, and flats. With her height, she probably always is.

"Is it totally cheesy to tell you that you're even more beautiful in person?" Reese says.

"Thanks."

"But it's a little cheesy."

I smile and then hold my thumb and forefinger a half inch apart. She laughs. She seems so sweet and enthusiastic that I wish I didn't feel like I do. "I have to be honest. I'm a little tongue-tied right now. I didn't know you were coming."

"You thought I was starting a different day?"

"I didn't know I was getting an assistant."

"Oh. Well, surprise! It's a girl!" We both laugh. "I promise you, I'm going to make your life so easy. You won't have to worry about anything. You can focus on what you need to learn."

What does Reese think that is? "What's Edwin told you about my"—I hesitate—"background?"

"Everyone knows you don't have a journalism degree or any formal experience or training, but that just makes you more impressive. There aren't many people who could get a million followers in a day."

Those people aren't really following me; they're following @theRealCheyenneFlorian. From my new and improved dummy account, I've been following, too, and I have to admit, @theReal CheyenneFlorian has great taste. She's eating amazing food, shopping at awesome stores, and commenting intelligently on other people's news blogs. I wouldn't mind living her life.

"I need to go," I say. "My second broadcast is tonight, and Albie's waiting for me in the studio to rehearse." I feel like it would be polite to invite her, but I'm not sure I want any extra spectators.

"Do you have anything you want me to do? I could run and pick up something for you to eat or drink. I can stock your fridge and get started on the laundry." In response to my quizzical look, she adds, "Edwin gave me a key."

I know it's not really my apartment; it's INN's. But still, for Edwin to just give away a copy of my key is invasive, and after all I've been through in the past, the last thing I want is the threat of invasion. I would have thought he'd be more sensitive to that, but he's got a lot on his mind, and the reality is, I can't expect anyone to truly understand unless they've experienced it themselves.

"You won't need the key," I say, trying to keep my voice light. "I've got all that covered."

It's a full-service building, with laundry and grocery delivery, but more than that, there are cameras everywhere, and the doormen are fully trained with concealed weapons. No visitor gets through without being screened. I've been told other celebrities live there, but not which ones. I've never seen anyone I recognized, though many of the residents exude VIP vibes. We all avert our eyes and wait for the next elevator.

I don't want to be rude, and Reese is just so damned excited, so I let her accompany me to the studio. After a little while, I forget she's even there. This is high stakes, my first live broadcast, and I can't allow any distractions.

Albie starts with a daunting amount of feedback, but as I do take after take, he's falling silent. That's a good sign. He's running out of criticism. Finally, it's time to get to wardrobe.

I send Reese out to pick up a salad. I could use some sustenance, and also, I don't really want an observer when I'm crowbarred into my sheath dress. It's royal blue tonight.

While my hair is being put through its paces, Beth swings by to ask how I am and to wish me luck. She seems as genuine and maternal as she did in the pitch meeting. "I'll be gentle, don't worry." It's probably a reference to the piranha moments she has in some of her interviews. We share a smile, and then the next time we see each other is on-set.

I'm less nervous than I would have expected because Beth and I have an instant connection. Sure, I'm delivering lines from a script, but it feels like a real conversation, like we've known each other forever. Plus, there are no pervert directors on Beth's show; the staff and crew are almost entirely female. It's like everyone is pulling for me to succeed, like what Edwin had told me about INN is really true: that we all rise or fall together, and tonight, I'm being lifted.

I'm doing a follow-up to my first story about Tag, though it's broadened to include the rest of the social media sites. It's about the difference in their responsiveness when they receive complaints of bullying from a typical user and a celebrity user. The kinder level of discourse I've been experiencing this time around isn't because the world has evolved in the past four months and people have rediscovered empathy; it's that I'm now in another category. When INN alerts the social media sites about abusive threads, they're pulled immediately, as they were with Leslie Jones from *Saturday Night Live*. The response time is very different for ordinary citizens, even those who can demonstrate an egregious pattern of abuse.

The story is well researched, with proof that inaction on the part of social media companies is not about the occasional dropped ball but rather about systematic, programmatic decisions being made and implemented. Cutting off abusers is bad for business, and business trumps individual human rights, mental health, and personal safety.

The report hasn't been thrown together hastily since my first broadcast. It's been in the works for some time, because Edwin knew exactly how this would play out. I was part of a plan to entrap the social media companies. But I'm okay with that. It's in the public good, and that was one of the main reasons I joined INN.

The segment is proceeding so well that I barely need to glance at the teleprompter.

Until I do, and see that it's blank. My mind goes blank too.

I should know what I'm supposed to say; I've certainly practiced enough. Again and again and again, that's Albie's way.

Where is he? Why isn't he feeding me the next line?

From inside the booth, he can't see that the teleprompter is blank.

Beth gives a surreptitious glance and realizes what's happened. She says, "This story reminds me of . . ." She goes into an anecdotal ad-lib that gives me a chance to regroup.

I'm able to recite the rest from memory, and then we're headed to commercial. I exhale loudly. "Thank you so much," I say. "I was panicking for a second there."

"That stuff happens."

"Technical glitches?"

"Sabotage. There was a woman who used to stay in the makeup chair for an ungodly long time just to make sure I wouldn't get my fair share. Phony HR complaints. Rumors. Bad-mouthing to the higher-ups. And keep your drink in your hand at all times so no one spikes it."

She says it so casually, like it's common knowledge. I'm speechless.

"It's the cost of doing business."

I glance around the set, at all the seemingly supportive faces. One of them is a saboteur. I had hoped it stopped with Rayna and Luke.

"I want you to know," Beth says, "that I loved having you on my show tonight."

"I loved being here. It was like"—I'm mortified to realize there are tears in my eyes—"coming home."

"Good. INN is your home now."

This close up, I notice just how green Beth's eyes are. Not exactly the color of mine—Beth's are more verdant, a little more fake green—but then, people sometimes think I'm wearing colored contacts. That's a whole thread on social media.

"You need to be very mindful," Beth says, "because your looks will open doors, but they can close quickly. You're going to have to outsmart some very smart people. I'm a woman of a certain age, and that requires a different skill set entirely than the one I'm about to share with you."

I lean in.

"Young beautiful women used to play a certain game. They'd let men believe the ideas were theirs; they'd encourage men to think with their little heads, while the women used their big ones."

Like in Elyse's diary. "It's good that women don't have to do that anymore," I say.

"You don't have to, but you might want to consider it." I stare at her, surprised. "It's just a tool in the arsenal, one of many. Being able to match the tool to the job—not using a sledgehammer when a smile or a hint of cleavage will do—is the single most important form of intelligence for a woman who looks like you. It's the definition of working smarter, not harder."

I like that Beth is taking such an interest in me, but it's definitely not what I wanted to hear.

"I can tell you, those strategies are undervalued these days, but they're not antifeminist. Antifeminist is four years in an Ivy League school, being told you're just as good as any man, and then going and erasing another woman's teleprompter."

I look up toward the control room. Reese is sitting in the bleachers and gives a wave.

Beth probably doesn't mean Reese. INN is stacked with Ivy Leaguers.

They're everywhere.

CHAPTER 14

"H ot as shit . . . hot as shit . . . hot as shit," Reese says. She lays one letter after another on the desk. "Let's just call this the HAS pile." It turns out to be, by far, the largest pile of my fan mail.

On the one hand, I'm relieved. Although there are people who don't like me or "what I stand for" (whatever they think that is), no one has sounded too unhinged or threatening. On the other hand . . .

"So much for being taken seriously," I say. "I'm pretty much Broadcast Barbie."

"What do you think Megyn Kelly's piles looked like when she started? This is a good sign, Cheyenne. You're a woman in broadcast news. Even when you get letters from other women, they'll often ask where you got your shoes or give you a word of advice about your eye makeup. *Maybe* twenty-five percent of your mail is going to be about what you actually said, and that's on a good day."

"It seems so retrograde." So 1991.

"Yup." Reese smiles. "But you're here. You've got a three-year contract and a platform. People would kill for your level of exposure. They'd kill for this chance." She sounds inordinately sunny. But she doesn't know about the teleprompter.

Unless she does.

I like Reese. I hope that she'll turn out to be a friend. But for now, I need to keep my eyes open and my drinks in my hand. As Beth said, it's the cost of doing business. It's a small price to pay for a three-year contract and a platform. For a mission.

"So we'll just need to figure out what you want me to do with the different piles of letters, and with your emails," Reese is saying. "We can identify some broad categories, so I'll know what gets a form response, what you want to handle yourself, and where you want me to get creative. We need a system."

"There isn't just a standard way stuff is done?"

"All you stars have your preferences." Another smile. Reese is good at skirting the edges of sycophancy, lacing it with irony or good-natured envy but never seeming resentful.

I want Beth for a mother, but I really could use a friend. I have Chase and my dad, but it's not the same. They're not right here, for one thing. They don't know this business, for another, though Chase tends to think he knows something about everything.

"Do whatever's easiest for you," I say. She's here so I can focus on the important things like studying the old episodes of INN, reading my curriculum, and practicing scripts until my eyes cross. The PR team handles social media; Reese will handle the fans; and I can just do the real work.

"I'm on it." She goes back to the main pile and then holds up a manila envelope with my name on it. "This one looks internal." She starts to open it, but I tell her no, when she gets those, she can give them straight to me. I ignore the curiosity in her face, taking the envelope and sliding it inside one of my books from Albie. I smile, feigning nonchalance.

There's an awkward pause. I'm not volunteering, and Reese wants to ask but knows better.

She looks around the office. "We should decorate in here."

I appreciate the subject change. "Like put my diploma up?"

"No way! Unless it's an Emmy or Peabody or something huge, you don't want cred up on the walls. It reeks of insecurity. I mean, let's bring in some personality. We could go shopping together. Art, pillows, tapestries—a nice mix of high and low. Like, something from a SoHo gallery next to something from HomeGoods. Want to go this weekend?"

"I'm flying to Montana to see my dad."

"He's so awesome! I follow him on Twitter."

Dad's embraced social media in a big way. He live-tweeted Beth's show when I was on. I wish he'd lie low, knowing that trolls don't confine their hostility to their target; they radiate outward. But he says so far, everyone's playing nice. I've asked Edwin to make sure that INN monitors Dad's accounts and intervenes if necessary, and he agreed.

"My father's having more fun with this than I am," I say. As soon as I do, I regret it. It's too revealing when I don't yet know if I can trust Reese.

Reese assumes a sympathetic expression. "Oh, no! You looked like you were having a great time on Beth's show."

"I have a lot to learn, that's all. Khalif's up next, and then Ty." Just saying his name is anxiety-provoking. Not to mention that there are INN staffers who are not only rooting against me, like Rayna and Luke, but someone is actively engaged in sabotage.

"I can help," Reese says firmly. "You're an It Girl, and you're going to enjoy it. Fuck anyone who tries to stand in your way."

I get this feeling she knows what happened with the teleprompter, though I didn't tell her. It could be a rumor going around, people congratulating themselves on their hazing (that's the word Belinda and Nan used).

"There's always backbiting, Cheyenne. The male staff are thrilled to have someone new, young, and hot around, but some of the women—not so much. You want me to try to find out which ones really have it out for you so you can stay clear?"

"Or win them over."

Reese shakes her head. "Bad place to put your energy. But listen, I went to school with Belinda. She was a senior when I was a freshman, so that's a connection. I can make more of them. All I have to do is hang out and when I sense something, I let them think that I'm on their team instead of yours, that I'm pissed you got the big break."

"Are you?"

Reese smiles. "No way. You're my big break."

There's something refreshing about her naked ambition. Reese isn't going to bite the hand that feeds her, and right now, that hand belongs to me.

"Do it," I say. "Be my spy."

CHAPTER 15

Finally, the lives of the real Cheyenne Florian and @theReal CheyenneFlorian have converged.

I'm standing on the red carpet of one of the premier New York galas of the year, not ten feet away from Sarah Jessica Parker, fielding questions about what I'm wearing when what I'm wearing is a red couture Valentino gown, flamenco meets Park Avenue wedding, my hair in a chignon that took two hours to achieve by a professional, not to mention the eye makeup and bright red lips that took nearly that long. Chase is beside me, in a tux. He held my arm as we walked up the hundred steps to the museum, to this red carpet. It's not my version of a fairy tale, but I do, indeed, feel like a princess, and I wouldn't have imagined I'd like it this much.

Some of the celebrities on the red carpet are much less conventionally attired. Glow-in-the-dark dresses, superhero shapes (Rihanna is actually holding a John Galliano scepter), unusually placed cutouts, gold-encrusted pantsuits—it's dizzying. I missed the Met gala by a few months, so this is August hangover, but still, it's pretty spectacular. It's ostensibly to benefit those who don't have enough to eat, though really, it's to benefit those who want to be seen in their couture finery before Labor Day. Lady Gaga is here, subdued for her in what looks like a black lace unitard with dragon wings. There are at least four Kardashians. Tom Brady and Gisele, Chrissy Teigen and John Legend, George Clooney and Amal . . . and Chase and me. If the reporters find that bizarre, they hide it well.

Katy Perry, in some sort of ninja garb, approaches to say she's already a fan. The cameras flash away, recording the moment.

Chase introduces himself and says that he's representing Until. Representing? I fight my embarrassment, though Katy couldn't be nicer about it. She even asks questions about Until, and as Chase describes how he's going to make the world safer, stopping crimes before they happen when they're just a thought in someone's mind, Katy manages to look impressed. Maybe she really is. I always was. But right then, I'm frustrated. Can't he, just once, be eye candy?

I shouldn't complain, not even in my mind (it's occurred to me before that someday, courtesy of Until, Chase might be able to see every internal eye roll). He did fly in on incredibly short notice, and except for this moment, I've loved seeing him and having him steady me in such a disorienting setting.

The only bummer is that I had to cancel my trip to Tulip. Dad was supportive, as I knew he would be, but that only made me feel worse. I miss him, and it's not like I can go out any weekend. If he's just had his treatment, he'll be exhausted, and he doesn't like me to see him like that. So rescheduling for next weekend is out. It'll be at least two weeks before I can curl up on the couch next to him and watch a movie. I could use a dose of normalcy. Though I'm enjoying tonight, which couldn't be more abnormal.

Reese says I ought to get used to it, that I could easily become a regular on the New York social scene. It's not a world I'm eager to inhabit; the occasional visit is plenty. It's clear that Reese would want it all. But that doesn't make me uncomfortable anymore. Instead, it makes me appreciate my life more. As I'm looking around the gala, I'm thinking of all the things I can report back to Reese, imagining the vicarious pleasure she will take in every detail.

Then I remember: I need to actually capture this moment. I start snapping shots of the room and ask Chase to take some pics of me with celebrities. I jot some notes in my phone and send them off to my PR team, who'll then take the observations and turn them into social media magic.

Chase is watching, not saying a word. It could be that he's respecting my work, such as it is, but I sense a hint of judgment. After each of my appearances on INN, he's said all the right things. He expressed his pride. He sent flowers. He humble-brags on social media and retweets me (well, not the real me, but still, it's the thought that counts). Yet I can't help thinking that in his mind, I'm not a broadcaster, I just play one on TV.

That could be my own insecurity. Two successful appearances, ratings-wise, and I'm still waiting to be somehow certified legitimate. Edwin says the media will come around on me, that the leg-crossing counts will stop trending soon. I just need to break a big story, and he has one in the works.

During the cocktail hour, Chase and I camp out at a table in the museum's atrium. It looks like Van Gogh's *Starry Night*.

There's crystal-studded netting suspended from the dark ceiling, and kaleidoscopic pink and purple lights rove the room. "Beautiful, isn't it?" I say.

Chase makes a noncommittal noise. I've never seen him so determinedly unimpressed. When I accompany him to Silicon Valley parties, he points out heads of start-ups with little-boy energy.

Reese tutored me in the New York social circuit, highlighting central figures, so that I'll be able to say something reasonably intelligent. So far, the celebrities seem much more interested in me than the old money. I would have expected to be the one fawning, but no, they're all expressing their admiration. Maybe they're sucking up because they think that someday they'll need me. Crazy.

"You'll get your show," Kanye West tells me with a finger point. "Count on it."

At least Chase didn't tell Kanye about Until.

I polish off a glass of champagne, and a server appears with another on a tray. Chase becomes his usual personable self. I talk about Reese, and how much fun we had shopping for office decorations. It might be the champagne, but I feel myself starting to gush. The truth is, Reese is the kind of person I wish had respected me at Stanford. I know that Reese is paid to like me, but it's not necessarily an act. Just because you're paranoid doesn't mean that nobody's after you.

Chase looks a little bored, which is irritating. I've listened to him well past the point of interest before. It's just what you do for someone you love.

I take a long swig of champagne. That's when Chloë Sevigny comes up in an outfit that is understated and cool and outrageous at once, like a pirate marooned in Brooklyn. I make sure that Chase gets a picture as I tell her how much I loved *American Horror Story*.

"I know how it is in Hollywood," Chloë says, "the way directors can ask what you're doing afterward, and how you respond determines a lot of your future." Her back is partially turned to Chase. This is a women-only conversation. "What's it like over where you are?"

I laugh uncomfortably. "No one's asked me what I'm doing afterward."

"But what's the news network version of that?"

"I haven't encountered one so far." Luke doesn't count. Chloë's talking about a Dennis Graver, someone who wants to demonstrate power over women and stroke his ego in the process. That's not Edwin at all.

Chloë's the one to laugh now. "Playing it close to the vest, huh? Catch me at the next gala, and we'll talk." She disappears into the crowd.

"It's like I wasn't even here," Chase grumbles.

"She had other things on her mind." The conversation has pulled me out of the fantasy and into the real world. I've been too busy to even read the next installment of the diary, but it's at home, waiting for me. "When do you think we're sitting down for dinner? I'm starved."

"Maybe they want you to see how the kids feel." I look at him blankly. "You know, why you really should try to stop hunger." He takes his phone out of his pocket and appears instantly engrossed.

"Seriously? You have your phone on?"

"So do you."

"That's for work."

"I have important things going on too." He sends a quick text and turns the phone over.

"So was that about work?" I think of what Belinda (or maybe it was Nan) said about Until on the AstroTurf. I've been so pre-occupied that I haven't even looked up the rumor.

"No."

The curtness of his reply piques my interest. "Who was it then?"

I'm not going to drop it, and he can feel that. Finally, he admits, "Lydia. She wanted to know if I had time to hang out while I'm in town. I told her no."

"*Lydia Garber?* After what she did to me?"

Lydia graduated near the top of her class at Stanford and works for CNN as a producer's assistant. That, alone, seems an indictment of my rocket ride. She's the friend of Chase's I most wanted to like me, because she seemed both whip-smart and kind, with personal integrity. She was compassionate after all that happened with the viral video. So when she went on rec-ord against me last week, that one hurt. Her quote was about how I was far from the hardest worker and that the general feeling was that I knew how to use my looks to my advantage with professors, and one professor in particular.

She means Professor Trent, of course. I wouldn't have thought Lydia would have spread or believed that rumor.

I'm in a new Valentino, feeling the old shame. Yes, Professor Trent was the one asking me to stay after class to brainstorm my next paper and give me suggested study areas for the up-coming exams; I never solicited that. But I never said, *I don't need your help, I can do this on my own.* I went out for coffee with him that one time, and even though nothing happened and it was far from campus, of course it still got around. He was so nice, and everyone liked him so much. I did too. He was beloved, and I wasn't. They said I was manipulating him, like I was the one with the power, and maybe I was. I hadn't thought so, but if everyone else seemed so sure, it was hard not to doubt myself.

What makes the heat rise to my cheeks even now is that I could tell he was attracted to me, and I never said no. I didn't know I could, not without hurting his feelings, and not without fearing that a rejection could hurt my grade. I did need that A, and I was working for it, hard. But maybe I didn't really earn it. I needed his curve.

Chase swore he didn't know Lydia was going to be quoted, and that if he had known, he would have tried to stop her. I assumed it was the truth. But then, I also assumed he'd ended their friendship.

"Lydia's going to know where you were tonight," I say. "It'll be all over social media." Not just social media but actual media. This is a big event. The red carpet was live-streamed. "What's Lydia going to say about you now?"

"She knows I'm here to support you."

It doesn't exactly feel that way, with the way he's been plugging Until, but this isn't the place to discuss it. There's press everywhere.

He moves closer and kisses me lightly. "I'm happy to be here. I love you."

I don't want to be upset with him. But it chafes that he's still friends with Lydia, and meanwhile, he's got little tolerance for hearing about Reese, who has my back.

I have to remember that this is all new to him. He's not used to being on my arm rather than the other way around. I don't like that he talked about his start-up on the red carpet, but he's proud of it. I have INN; he has Until. There's finally parity between us.

He's not comfortable yet, but he'd better work on that. Because I'm not going anywhere.

CHAPTER 16

July 8, 1991

What an incredible day. Scott asked me out for coffee. There we were, in the red-boothed diner, and he was smiling at me in this friendly way, a way that I'd seen so many times before ON TELEVISION. The way he smiles at Trish.

"Tell me something about you that I won't find in a press release," he says.

My mind goes to Lyndon, of course, but I won't let it stay there. "I'll tell you a secret," I said. "My hair. It's not real."

He brightened at the whiff of a scoop. "It's a wig?"

"A perm, but no one ever guesses. This hair is my superpower."

"You're like Samson. I'll start calling you Sam."

We were sharing a conspiratorial smile when a fan—middle-aged with one of those obvious crunchy perms, maybe Ogilvie home—approached. Customers at other tables had been whispering to each other and either pointing to our booth or just eyeballing Scott since he arrived. But that first woman opened the floodgates. The line snaked through the middle of the restaurant, and waiters and waitresses had to slither around it, trays held aloft. Some asked for my autograph too.

Scott said, "Good idea. Get it now because she's going to be huge."

Afterward, he settled back in the booth. He talked a little about his kids, and about having to give up his job as a foreign correspondent so he wouldn't miss their whole childhoods. That's how he landed at Morning Sunrise.

He started laughing. "Hey, you tricked me! This was supposed to be me interviewing you."

"I like to be the one asking the questions."

"Yeah, I do too." He grinned. "Let's have a staring contest. Whoever blinks first has to share their deepest, darkest secret." He shifted forward, his blue eyes on mine.

I was about to laugh, then realized he was serious. I got serious too. It was this strangely intense moment, with our eyes locked, and I really wanted to win.

The longer it went on, the more erotic (and embarrassing) it started to feel. So I forced a laugh, looked away, and lost. Immediately, I was kind of scared. I didn't want to tell any secrets.

He said, "Don't feel bad. It was kind of a setup. I'm a master of that game. I beat my kids every time. Since I rigged it, you get to keep your secrets." He paused. "This time."

I think he was kidding—flirting, even—but still . . .

"What used to make Trish and me work was that she likes to talk more than she likes to listen," Scott said.

Used to?

"I like having you on-set. Fresh blood is important

in a morning show. But I feel like we're not using you to your best advantage yet. Dennis and I have discussed this."

!!!!

Then we started talking and laughing, trading anecdotes like old friends, and I don't know how much time passed. But when I looked up, I saw York Diamond standing by the cash register.

"What's wrong?" Scott asked.

I couldn't even speak. What I was thinking was, *Not again. I can't live this way, always looking over my shoulder, never feeling safe, knowing how little the police will do until he's actually done something, and outside of California, stalking is nothing.*

It's nothing when he shows up where I am, when he sends letter after letter, telling me I'm his, no matter what I do or where I go or who I'm with. When he spies on me and I feel dirty and hunted and afraid all the time.

I used to wonder how much more I had to take before I'd be taken seriously. The answer? Everything.

Maybe York was just in the neighborhood. Standing at the register, he wasn't even looking at me. I could believe he hadn't seen me, that he was waiting to be seated, like any other customer.

I really want to believe that.

The fact is, York was right about me. My ship is coming in.

I wish it wasn't at Trish's expense. I wish there was room at the top, or on the couch, for two women. Despite the way she brushed by me the other day, I do feel for her. She must know all the things that Dennis was telling me at lunch about the scrutiny the morning shows and the anchors face, and about her Q score. She has to be on edge, and it's hard to do your best under those circumstances.

If I were in Trish's place, I'd be under that same pressure. Would I fare any better?

I've handled pressure before, like, of the life-and-death variety. When Lyndon was stalking me, R.G. broke before I did.

R.G.'s desertion was one of the worst parts of the whole horrendous experience. I thought he loved me enough to weather anything, that we'd do it together. But he said it had become too much, and he broke up with me on the steps of the courthouse, which meant I had to walk in alone and take the stand and stare out at that lunatic with his sick, vacant eyes, seeing him mouth the words "I love you," my stomach roiling.

If I could face the wrath of a man who wrote letters in his own blood, who saw a restraining order as a betrayal and a challenge, if I could survive without the man I wanted to marry, then a ratings war is child's play.

At the end, R.G. told me, "I want to be your boyfriend, not your protector." But love is sometimes about protection. People don't get to choose if the one they love will be in danger.

I've told myself a million times that he's a coward and I'm better off without him. But I was never as close to anyone as I was to R.G. He was the only person with whom I could be truly vulnerable. Look how that turned out.

CHAPTER 17

'm in my office, reviewing my latest script, while Reese is on a Starbucks run. It still feels weird that I don't get my own lattes, but then, the photos from the gala are splashed everywhere. Raising my profile was the whole point of attending, yet I still covet anonymity. I suppose I want to have my latte and drink it too.

My mind keeps straying to the diary. Knowing what's going to befall Elyse, and knowing that someone out there thinks it has some correspondence to my life, is uncomfortable, to say the least.

I have to remember that the diary was written almost thirty years ago; there's nothing prescient about it. Elyse and I are very different people. R.G. and Chase are very different people. R.G. and Elyse didn't break up because she got successful; they broke up because she got stalked and R.G. crumbled. That's not Chase.

Chase did the opposite of leaving me on the courthouse steps. He flew across the country at a moment's notice to hold my hand on my first red carpet. Sure, it got rocky during the cocktail hour, but then dinner was great, and afterward, we took a walk along the Hudson. Not that I could walk far in three-inch heels, but still. We didn't want to go far, anyway, because after a few minutes of kissing, I couldn't wait to get his clothes off. It had been too long.

A picture of Chase and me kissing by the river showed up on Instagram. It could have been a fluke and someone happened upon us and decided to capture a romantic image, but it felt more likely that we'd been trailed. Kind of like what Elyse was talking about.

That diary entry was delivered before the gala, not after. Is it possible someone is writing the entries in real time as an elaborate hoax, trying to plant ideas and shape what's to come? That the person who wrote it is also the one who photographed Chase and me? It seems crazy but not impossible, and there's a lot of crazy in the world. There doesn't have to be a comprehensible motive. It could just be someone who likes torturing me. Give the would-be journalist a sham of a mystery to solve. Get me distracted and paranoid, fixating on women from the 1990s who've been terrorized and victimized, and soon, maybe I'll be victimized the same way.

I need to stop reading, that's all. Even if the person giving me the entries is trying to help, it's not.

I get a text from Edwin saying I should report to the newsroom, now. When I arrive, he's in the center, clapping his hands. "Everyone, gather round! Off the phones. Now, please!"

The staff streams over. My eyes should be trained on Edwin, but I'm watching to see who's watching me, just like when I was being tracked on Tag.

Not again.

Isn't that Elyse's catchphrase?

"I wanted to tell you all how impressed I am by the work you're doing," Edwin says. "You're changing the landscape of our politics and our society. Sure, Ty did that amazing piece on the pay-for-play reception, and no other media outlets ran with it, so that was a disappointment. But story by story, step by step, we're making it happen."

He lifts up his phone and begins to read: "'INN is the true definition of fair and balanced, and there's evidence that it's moving the needle. Other networks are forced to cover what they might otherwise choose not to. They're being shamed into more investigative work, knowing that if they don't cover certain stories, their own corporate affiliations and allegiances can very well wind up on display. INN is journalism for a new world order.'" He looks up, smiling, at the loud swell of applause. "What we do matters. We're putting all the other networks on notice: tell the truth, or else.

"On our very first day on the air, I made a statement directly to the camera. I pledged that I'd never allow INN to be beholden to special interests because that's the death of democracy.

"Well, the story that Cheyenne will soon break on Ty's show is the first in a series. It's about a huge threat to democracy: the documented collusion between government and a private corporation. It's going to do us proud. It's what INN is all about, and it wouldn't be possible without every last one of you."

Edwin said I was getting a big story, but a series?

"Thank you all. Class adjourned!"

No one laughs. The positive energy that was in the room has evaporated. I can't blame anyone for the tepid response. I've been here less than a month, and I'm going to have a series, on the highest-rated show on the network. Whoever didn't hate me before will hate me now.

Edwin exits the newsroom, either oblivious or unconcerned. I overhear one of Khalif's producers grumbling, "We know Ty is at the top of the food chain, but that's because INN devotes all the resources to keeping it that way." There's palpable resentment in the room, and I'm not sure if it's more about Edwin, Ty, or me, or if we've become lumped together in some sort of unholy trinity.

No one's talking to me or looking at me. Even Beth's team has huddled up, walled off. It's more distressing because I thought I'd begun to make some headway at the bar the other night.

I force myself to walk to the elevator at a normal pace; I don't want to give the appearance of fleeing. Edwin might not have to care how he looks, but I do.

Reese is waiting in my office. "Your latte's cold," she says.

"Edwin was making an announcement. Good news: I've got a series on Ty's show."

I assume that Reese is going to help me feel the appropriate level of excitement, but she remains unsmiling. "Congratulations."

"You don't seem happy."

"Neither do you."

I can't really argue with that.

"You could have texted me to say where you were," she says.

"Sorry," I say, though really, I shouldn't have to apologize. Reese is my assistant; it's not my job to make her feel included.

I would have liked to get her opinion about newsroom dynamics or even have sent her downstairs to do some reconnaissance for me. She's supposed to be my spy, though so far, she hasn't told me anything useful. I haven't questioned that, assuming that it's been hard for her to gain anyone's trust given her association with me, but now, with the way she's acting . . .

I don't have time for this bullshit. I'm in final rehearsals for Khalif's show tonight. All I can control is my performance.

I lose track of time as Albie and I perfect my delivery. Then I notice that Reese is no longer in the studio.

When she finally shows back up, it's with home-cooked miso salmon and asparagus. It must be her way of apologizing for her attitude earlier. Albie says he's going to run out and grab dinner for himself. Reese assures him there's plenty, but he insists, so it's just Reese and me eating together in the bleachers.

"Thanks for cooking," I say. "This is delicious." I wash down a bite with Red Bull. It might not be the best for my vocal cords, but I need to fortify myself before the broadcast.

"It was the least I could do, after earlier. Besides, I thought your kitchen needed christening."

She cooked in my apartment, after I explicitly told her the first day that she wouldn't need the key. What I meant was, I didn't want her using the key. Is it possible she misunderstood?

The timing seems suspect, like I might be eating her passive-aggression.

But I have to express myself delicately. Reese isn't just a subordinate, she might be a friend. She's also a subordinate who knows a lot more than I do, and who can help or hurt me with my colleagues downstairs. "I really appreciate you cooking, but in the future, maybe you could ask first."

"My apartment's in Brooklyn; yours is just blocks away. I wanted to surprise you. What's the big deal?"

"It's not a big deal. I just—"

"You don't trust me?" There's true hurt in Reese's eyes. "Is that why you didn't text me about Edwin's announcement?"

I put the fork down and reach out to touch Reese's arm. "I didn't mean to leave you out before." She hadn't even crossed my mind. "Next time, I'll make sure I include you."

"But you don't want me in your apartment either."

"I like my personal space, that's all." Reese looks unconvinced. "This is a hard environment to trust in. Someone erased the teleprompter when I was on Beth's show."

"I know. That was so lame."

"Do you have any idea who could have done it?"

"Belinda isn't psyched you're here, but I think that's just because of how stressed Rayna's been. Rayna's thinking you might be under consideration for the permanent coanchor spot on *Media Is the Message*."

So it's not just about hazing, like Belinda (or was it Nan?) said. Rayna thinks I might be a true threat. "I'm not ready to host anything."

"Edwin might disagree."

I wonder why Reese didn't tell me this bit of intel sooner. But then, it is speculation, not facts. She might have been waiting for confirmation. "From now on, could you tell me anything you hear, even if it's just a rumor?" Especially if it's a rumor. When I was growing up, Dad said that as long as you know the truth, that's all that matters. He said what you don't know can't hurt you. He was wrong.

"I'll tell you everything," Reese says. "You can trust me. I swear to you. We're friends, and I'd never betray a friend."

"I never would either."

After dinner, the evening moves quickly. Wardrobe, hair and makeup, a dry run on-set, and then it's live with Khalif.

The show goes off without a hitch. No teleprompter "malfunction" today. After his sign-off, Khalif holds my hands between his, looks into my eyes, and tells me what a beautiful job I did. I can feel myself glowing.

Reese says everyone is going out to their usual bar. I don't know where that is, but Reese does. I'm glad that this time, I'll have someone to talk to from go. "Are you sure I'm welcome?" I ask her. "They seemed pretty agitated in the newsroom after Edwin's announcement."

"You should come. The news cycle moves fast."

THE BAR FEELS like a good-natured parody, wallpapered in yellowed newspaper clippings. Edwin's not there, but it feels like it's in keeping with his meta sensibility. When Reese and I arrive, everyone's had more than a few. I don't feel the tension from earlier between the staffs of the other shows and Ty's show, or between them and me. It's like they're all one big happy incestuous family again. Unfortunately, the pervy uncle (i.e., Luke) is here tonight. I'll make sure to steer clear.

Reese is already taking a shot and laughing with some of the VJs. I follow her lead. No one's supereager to talk to me, but I don't feel like persona non grata either. After a few shots, I look around and realize Reese has disappeared. This time, it better not be to my apartment.

Graham takes her place. "You feel good about having your own series on Ty's show?" he asks, by way of greeting. He's not smiling. Even when he holds court and tells a story that has everyone in stitches, he's never laughing.

I'm transfixed by his heavy black Dukakis eyebrows. Now that's a reference I never would have made before my education at INN.

Nan and Belinda had told me that Graham is a boy wonder who'll soon be helming Ty's show. But for some reason I can't quite pinpoint, he makes my skin crawl. I wish I felt otherwise, because he'd surely be a valuable friend to have.

"I feel good," I say.

He studies me with no self-consciousness at all, as if I'm a painting on a wall. "You are beautiful," he says, matter-of-factly. He seems very sober, where I'm tipsy. I don't like that power imbalance. I look around for Reese, but she's still nowhere to be found. Really, no one is anywhere close to Graham and me, as if they all parted for him like the Red Sea.

"Beauty isn't enough," he says.

"I'm a hard worker too." I hear how inane it sounds, but I'm not exactly at the top of my game right now.

"This business takes a certain ruthlessness. Not everyone has that." He's visibly sizing me up. "Do you?"

"It's not the first word people use to describe me." He nods, as if I've told him something important.

"I've got a feeling you'll do what you have to. And you'll do it soon."

He is one creepy dude. How come Edwin doesn't see that?

"I'm writing your series. I'll be feeding you the perfect lines."

The ego on this guy . . .

"Ty will expect to hear them. You don't want to disappoint him. Or anyone else."

"No, I don't want to disappoint anyone." This must be what it feels like to be shaken down by the mob. I don't entirely know what's being asked of me, but my sense that jealous women are my biggest threat has just been turned on its head.

Where the fuck is Reese?

Graham slides a shot glass in front of me. "Here, have mine. You look like you could use another."

I remember Beth's advice: keep your drink in your hand. "I'm okay."

"You need anything, at any time, you just come to me."

My stomach tightens.

"Coming aboard at INN can be pretty overwhelming, and I know you've got some personal stuff going on." I stare at him. "Your father's sick, right? Still undergoing treatment, and you were supposed to visit him last weekend?"

I really, really hate the turn this is taking.

"I can make life easier for you. I don't know if anyone's clued you in, but I'm Edwin's right-hand man." As if to prove it, he squeezes my knee and leaves his hand there. "I'll tell you a secret. You know that motivational speech Edwin gave earlier? What he read off his phone? I wrote that." He has a self-satisfied expression on his face. "When Edwin needs the finest in AstroTurf, he comes to me."

"INN has its own AstroTurf?"

"Of course."

His hand hasn't moved. Graham is a deliberate man. If he's telling secrets, it's for a purpose. He's putting me on notice that he can plant stories wherever he wants and put his hands anywhere he wants, and he doesn't have to worry about me telling anyone. He's in charge.

It occurs to me that in the brief history of the #metoo movement, the giants falling have been primarily because of the past tense. Women speak up when they're out of the clutches of powerful, headline-grabbing men. But what happens to the woman still in the employ, and at the mercy, of the predator, when he's no one famous, just some middleman (or right-hand man) and no reporter picks up the story? Who protects her?

Who'll protect me? It's clear that Graham thinks the answer is no one. And he would know.

"Excuse me." I go to stand up. I'm a little unsteady on my feet, but it's not the alcohol.

"You look like you need to go home. I'll take you. Make sure you get there safely."

"No, I just need some fresh air."

"You shouldn't walk alone. You're a celebrity now."

If only Graham were lying about his place in the pecking order. Ty's show is the top of the INN hierarchy, and Graham is its unofficial head. I can see it in the way he moves, and the way people move out of the way for him. There's an undercurrent to this whole interaction, almost an undertow, like he knows I'll give in someday, whether I want to or not. Like he doesn't actually care what I want. Or maybe he does, like those pro-rape activists I ran afoul of after the viral video. If I don't want it, that only adds to their fun.

I glance at my phone. "That's Chase. My boyfriend."

He laughs. "Get it while you can."

I race out into the street, mind whirling.

What did that parting line of his mean? And where is Reese?

CHAPTER 18

'm in a state when I arrive back at my apartment building. It doesn't help that I'm waved over to the security desk and handed a manila envelope. "From INN," he says.

"Who brought that?" I ask.

"A courier."

I should have known that whoever's leaving me the diaries could also easily find out my address, but it's still disturbing. The building is secure, but what about right outside it? Rebecca Schaeffer was gunned down in her home. Marla Hanson was slashed in the street. And Elyse Rohrbach . . .

I shouldn't read it. I should go to bed. But I know I won't be able to sleep, and once inside my apartment, my curiosity lures me back. Again.

July 15, 1991

Today was the worst. Well, not the worst of my life, but my worst on <u>Morning Sunrise</u>. Sandy and Frieda have always been the friendliest toward me. Today, they did my hair and makeup in a conspicuous silence.

Finally, while Frieda was working on my eye shadow, laying the sparkly powder blue with lavender and pink above it, so that it would look, fittingly, like a sunrise, I couldn't take it anymore.

I pulled it out of them: Last night, I was featured on <u>A Current Affair</u>, getting into Dennis's limo, supposedly looking up at him and smiling in this flirty way, and then doing the same sort of smiling at Scott in the diner. Maureen O'Boyle, the host, said something about how the new newsreader is making a big impression.

That kind of notoriety can't be good for my career. Morning shows are not the stomping grounds of femme fatales; they're for good girls.

I can't believe my career could come to a grinding halt, all because of some stupid tabloid footage that must have been highly edited to create a false impression of me.

Footage. As in, someone following me around with a camera, filming without my knowledge or consent. It's an awful lot like stalking.

I started trembling all over, so much so that Sandy declared, "Finito. You're beautiful." She probably didn't feel safe having a curling iron near that head of mine.

My performance on the show was, as I said, my worst. It was all I could do to keep my voice from venturing into vibrato. I imagined people at home thinking that I was screwing up because of too many late nights with network execs and other people's husbands.

I feel like it's over, before it's really even begun.

Then there are the hang-ups. I can't even pretend it's a wrong number anymore.

I'm going to double-check the three locks on my door, put a chair under the jamb, and try my hardest to sleep.

Tomorrow has to be better.

CHAPTER 19

t's not like it's Page Six; it's TMZ," Reese says. "And the source is unnamed."

"An unnamed source who says I'm sleeping with Edwin! Who says that's why I'm about to get a series on the network's highest-rated show!"

It's first thing in the morning and Reese just showed me the TMZ piece on her phone. Reese is bright-eyed and ponytailed, with no mention of where she disappeared to the previous night. No apology for leaving me on my own, to be felt up by Graham. It's not like Reese would have wrestled him to the ground, but if she'd been there to witness, he probably wouldn't have acted that way.

I was up for hours after I got home. When I read Elyse's diary, I have to admit that a part of me wants to blame the victim. I want to think of how she brought what happened on herself, so that I can believe that I would never make the same mistakes. So that I can believe I'll stay safe.

I thought how if I had a diary and someone read an entry

about my conversation with Graham, they'd think about what I could have done differently. How I could have stood up for myself while still shutting him down, all without risking my professional life. There has to be a way to let him know that I'm not someone to be toyed with; I'm INN's hot property. No, I'm a human being. He has no right.

#neveragain. #metoo.

But hours passed, and I couldn't think of anything.

I feel demeaned and helpless, like after the viral video, only this could get a lot worse. None of those people had daily access to me, but Graham does. He's the one with the power.

Like Elyse, with Dennis.

No, I'm not like Elyse. I'm not going to cleavage my way through this, even if Beth said that was a legit strategy.

Maybe Beth is the friend sending the diary. If so, it's meant to be a road map, a how-to manual. It's about manipulating powerful men, using their vulnerability against them. Well, maybe vulnerability is the wrong word. It's more like susceptibility, with their cocks and their egos. It's not how I want to get ahead, but maybe it's the only smart move.

Just look how it turned out for Elyse.

A Current Affair for Elyse; TMZ for me. The timing of the latest diary entry and the events depicted feel more than coincidental. It could be from someone who wants me to know that she (or he) is authoring my story. TMZ was just reporting a tip, after all. Any insider could have called it in.

Any enemy.

What with Edwin's announcement the other day about my series, it could really be anyone.

"This isn't going to hurt you," Reese says. "There's no video and no photos, which means practically no one'll click on it anyway. We're talking about unverified gossip. What's going to happen is that no reputable media is going to run with the part about you sleeping with Edwin, but they will pick up that you've got your first series, and it's going to be big. People will be watching for you. They'll know that you're breaking news. You're A-list."

"But people will think I only got it because I'm sleeping with Edwin." Same as they thought I only got my grade by sleeping with Professor Trent, as if I couldn't possibly have earned it. I remember how even Chase had looked dubious, just for a hint of a second, when I told him before he rearranged his expression and said how proud he was of me.

"It's a little added intrigue. Trust me, this is good for you." She looks around, perhaps a touch dramatically, to confirm that the office door is closed. "I have a theory," she whispers, "that Edwin is the one who leaked it."

"Why would you think that?"

"It's a clever promotion for your story, and it makes him look like a stud. Two birds, one stone."

"Would he really do that?"

Reese stares at me. "He's a major player. In every way."

I have to admit, Edwin's certainly been willing to do unorthodox things so far. And they've all worked out, right? I'm at galas with Katy Perry and Chloë Sevigny. That's A-list by proxy.

"I'm going out with some friends tonight," Reese says. "Come with us. You need to blow off steam. Act your age."

I'm flattered to be invited, as it confirms that I'm more than just a boss to Reese, but I can't really say yes. "I have to be careful about my 'reputation.'" I do air quotes like it's a joke, but we both know it isn't.

"Wear a wig."

"Seriously? Do people do that?"

"All the time. I'll get one for you. I'll pick up some sunglasses too. Do you want to be a blonde or brunette?"

"Surprise me."

THAT NIGHT, I'M rocking a blond bob poolside on a rooftop bar in the Meatpacking District. There's literal AstroTurf under my feet, and I'm feeling no pain. Reese and her two friends from Columbia are hilarious, but that could just be the fact that I've had five drinks. I'm pretty sure no one's recognized me.

The view of the Manhattan skyline and the Hudson is spectacular as the sun goes down, and the music shifts from a chill vibe to club style. The crowd changes, too, from after work to partiers, younger and rowdier. Many of the women seem like underage supermodels in the making. Older men with the aura of wealth hang around, chatting them up, while the young bucks look none too pleased. Talking yields to dancing. Drinks are spilled, voices are raised, people are pushed. I'm about to tell Reese we should go home when she grabs my arm and says we've been invited to the VIP room.

It's dark, with expensive sumptuous couches and a hot tub, occupied by two men in their early forties. Edwin's age. They're both in suits with no ties. The handsome one has wild curly dark hair, made more striking when contrasted with his conservative attire. The other is blond, his hair lacquered neatly.

"This is Pietro, and this is Marco," Reese says.

Pietro—the attractive one—extends his hand. "Pleasure to meet you," he says, in unaccented English.

I don't know where Reese's friends went. I reach up to make sure my wig is on straight.

Reese yanks it off. "You don't need that here. Pietro knows who you are."

I yelp, belatedly, "Hey!" It's another boundary violation, like when Reese let herself into my apartment.

But then, Reese has had as much to drink as I have. I don't want to be angry at my only friend in New York.

With the way Pietro is looking at me, I can tell that, yes, he's already seen me naked, and he's hoping to do it again in the flesh.

There are bottles on a cart behind Marco. "Can I mix you anything?" he asks.

I think of Edwin and his penchant for the Prohibition era. I wish he were here.

I should be wishing for Chase. But since the gala he's seemed so far away, and it's not mere geography. I'm feeling more and more that he's another life. I was another girl.

It's not just since I started working at INN; it's really since the viral video. I've never truly forgiven him for how he responded, that he tried to be sympathetic, but as it went on, I could tell that he thought I was becoming complicit in my own victimization. He thought I could have stopped it sooner if I'd only been willing to cry uncle. Sometimes he even seemed to think he was a victim too. I'd tarnished his perfect image.

"I've been enjoying your reports," Pietro says.

You mean you've been enjoying my sexy walks and my leg crossing? "Thanks," I say.

"We met at the bar," Reese says. "When he randomly told me he was a fan of yours, I felt like I couldn't hold out on him. I had to let him meet you, especially since I knew he had the VIP room. We're safe in here."

"No pictures," I say.

"Of course not." Pietro gives me a reassuring smile. "I have to be discreet, too, in my line of work."

"He's a real estate magnate," Reese supplies.

He laughs. "Developer."

"Who hasn't heard of the Pietro Lorenzi Group?" Reese says. I haven't. "I'll have a vodka tonic," she tells Marco.

Reese is definitely into Pietro, whose attention is firmly on me.

I don't like that Reese used me to get here. But if I leave Reese behind, wouldn't that be kind of like what Reese did to me with Graham?

No, this is nothing like that. Reese wants to be left behind.

Still, that doesn't mean it's a good idea. Reese is awfully drunk.

"Have a seat," Pietro says, gesturing to a couch.

I sit on one, Pietro takes the other, but his seat is the one closest to me. Reese flops down next to Pietro. That means that after Marco delivers Reese her drink, he's beside me. But he's obviously a wingman. He's probably there to get Reese out of the way, when the moment presents itself. That's if I'm reading Pietro correctly.

"Of all the bars in all of Manhattan, what were the odds I'd run into you here?" he asks me.

"And that you'd happen to mention me to my friend." It feels a little too York Diamond for my taste.

"We were in the limo driving near Times Square, and I saw you on the Jumbotron. You were fresh on my mind."

"She's the new It Girl, all right," Reese says. It's not her usual buoyant tone. Meeting me might have been the price of admission, but she doesn't like being ignored. "She was just on the red carpet at the Hunger Gala. Her boyfriend, Chase, flew in for it."

The Chase mention is pathetically transparent. But now I don't have to find a way to work him into the conversation.

I don't have to do anything. I stand up. "I have a boyfriend, and a job I really care about, and I'm sure you're discreet about your own affairs, but I can't know how you're going to treat mine. So I really need to leave." I turn to Reese. "I'd feel better if you came too."

Reese gets to her feet reluctantly. It's like she's remembering that I'm her boss, which makes it akin to an order.

"I completely respect that," Pietro says, standing up too. "You're right, you have no reason to trust me. I'm a stranger. But I can tell you that I hate this culture we live in, where you have to polarize to succeed. You just have to be marginally loved more than you're hated, and they call that being It. I would never give the trolls ammunition." His brown eyes are kind. "I'm really happy that I got to meet you." When he offers his hand again, I want to take it.

What is it with me and older men lately?

I reposition the wig. Time to make my escape.

CHAPTER 20

There's a man here who'd like to see you," security informs me. "Chase Taylor. He's not on our list. Were you expecting him?"

No, I wasn't. It's Friday, and I'm going into my highest-pressure weekend at INN yet. Chase knows that. So what's he doing here?

The thing about surprises is that they limit your ability to refuse. They take away your choices.

"I'll be right down," I say.

I get to my feet, adjusting my purple corseted sheath dress, the one I wore for my second appearance on *The Media Is the Message*. It taped an hour ago. I never really relaxed, with Rayna and Luke present, but they'd both behaved cordially. Luke's eyes actually remained on my face, and Rayna remained on script. It was purely a stand-up, with no couch time, so there was no walking, which reduced Luke's capacity to debase me.

I couldn't really tell what either of them were thinking. Have they moved on to a new target, like bullies often do? Or is the hazing over, seeing as I've proven myself? Or are they employing more subterranean methods, like the diary entries? Rayna's at least forty, possibly older, so she's plenty familiar with Elyse's story.

I haven't told Chase about the diary entries. I haven't even told my father. With Chase, it's about his potential judgment; with Dad, it's about worry. Plus, reporters don't tell their daddies and their boyfriends about their sources.

I'm glad Reese isn't here so I don't have to do any introductions. Early this morning, she texted to say she had the hangover of her life, and she would come in if I really needed her, but if there wasn't much to be done, or if she could do it from home or over the weekend . . . I'd actually been a little relieved. I didn't feel good about Reese, Pietro, and the VIP room. Best to deal with that next week, after my debut on Ty's show. Reese is supposed to make my life easier, not add complications.

Chase is definitely a complication.

Stopping off in the restroom, I peer at myself in the mirror. My hair is utterly untouchable, and the heavy stage makeup has obliterated all traces of last night's drinking, but away from the camera and the studio lights, it's so smooth, so opaque, that I'm more android than human.

I fluff my hair. A little muss would help.

I descend in the elevator and exit the security gates into the high-ceilinged, marble-floored lobby. Chase is sitting on one of the couches, his back to me, scrolling through his phone, a small wheeled bag at his feet. When he sees me, he stands, but his smile looks forced. We embrace, which seems just as forced.

TMZ. That must be it. I'd thought about bringing it up so I could reassure him, but the truth is, I do feel an attraction to Edwin, and I've been feeling increasingly done with Chase. Easier to say nothing.

He looks good, as always. He's in a light blue shirt that matches his pale beautiful eyes, and a pair of expensive jeans. His blond hair is wavy, fixed in place by a forty-five-dollar product called hair wax that disappears without a trace once applied, so he can disavow such vanities.

"How long will you be here?" I ask him.

"I fly back on Sunday."

"I wish you'd picked another weekend. You know I have to work a lot to get ready for Ty's show. I have to stay focused."

"I could watch you work." He tries to say it like the idea just came to him, but he has never been a good liar.

Or maybe he has.

Conflict of interest. A series about the collusion between the government and a private corporation.

What Graham said about how I should get it while I can.

At seven A.M. tomorrow, I'll be handed a script, and I'm pretty sure it's going to be about Until.

"No," I say. "You can't watch me work."

"Show me around now then. I'd like to meet the cast of characters." His charm is fraying around the edges, threadbare. He must be under stress.

"No. It's a newsroom."

He moves closer to me and lowers his voice. "When we talk, I want to be able to picture your world and the people in it."

I wish I could believe him.

This is Chase. This is the man I've loved.

"Let's meet for dinner later," he says. "My treat."

"No, it's my treat." It occurs to me that this is the most I've ever said no to Chase in one conversation. In our whole relationship, practically. "You're the one who flew across the country. What are you craving?"

He snakes an arm around me. "I'm craving time alone with you. You think we can do anything about that?"

He's trying to manipulate me, I can feel it. "I'll text you where to meet."

It's a 5:15 reservation, and I arrive at the restaurant a few minutes early. Chase is already waiting outside the unmarked building. "This is the right place, then?" he says.

"I thought we could try something new together. It's dining in the dark."

"That's very retro of you."

"Retro?"

"Circa 2012. The one in San Francisco has already come and gone."

Retro's okay. The selling point of this restaurant is the concealment.

As we enter the building, Chase takes my hand. It would be too strong a statement, too early, if I pulled my hand away. "The servers are visually impaired," I whisper to him.

"So no three blind mice jokes," Chase whispers back. "Got it."

"I'm Freya," a statuesque woman says. She has multiple long blond braids all over her head and is wearing sunglasses. "Please turn off your cell phones and all other light sources. Your experience is about to begin."

We form a train. I put my hands on Freya's shoulders, and Chase puts his hands on mine, and we're led past the curtain into a truly pitch-dark room.

After a series of instructions that ends with "lower your bottom," we're settled at the table. "Feel around," Freya says. "Find your cutlery, though you're welcome to eat without them."

"That might limit the hand-holding," Chase says. "So bear that in mind when you make your choice."

Oh, I'll bear it in mind.

I can't hear any other diners, which makes me wonder if there are any. It is the early-bird special, but still. I wouldn't think a restaurant could exist with only one table occupied. I have no idea how large the room is, or how close we are to other people. I might not know when Freya is nearby, and when we can be overheard. I keep forgetting, I'm a celebrity now.

Has Freya recognized me? No, wait, she can't. She's blind.

She might have recognized the name, though, from the reservation, and this might have been a really bad idea.

"So you're doing the five-course tasting menu," Freya says. "Do you like to be told what you're about to eat, or would you like to try to guess?"

"Guess," Chase says, at the same time I answer, "Be told."

Freya laughs. "That happens all the time. You can't see each other's visual cues. You don't know when the other person is about to speak."

I blink repeatedly, having the sensation that I'm actually asleep right now. To be awake in absolute darkness creates a sense of hypervigilance, to which I'm already prone. I feel wired. Electrified.

"We'll guess," I relent.

"Would you like wine or a cocktail?"

This time, I wait and let Chase speak. I won't be dulling myself with alcohol. "Wine," he says. "Something that pairs well with what we're about to eat."

"I'll be back soon," Freya announces. There will probably be many such broadcasts, though I wouldn't actually be able to test the veracity. But it feels like Chase and I are alone, as if the air molecules have shifted.

He's groping across the table for my fingers. "It's nice to have an adventure with you," he says.

"I imagined it differently."

"Me too," he says, tenderly. His hand around mine is warm, and suddenly, there are tears in my eyes. "I want you to know—"

"I'm back!" Freya says gaily, and I jump. "I'm uncorking your wine." I wouldn't have recognized the sound. I'm discovering the inadequacy of my senses more than the opposite. "Now I'm pouring just a little into each of your glasses. I've put them right in front of you."

This was a mistake. I should be looking into Chase's eyes when I ask him if there's anything he'd like to tell me about Until, if he's ready to come clean.

This restaurant should come with hazard signs. Only go into the dark with people where there's no subtext, where everything's out in the open and aboveboard, where you can say whatever you feel, at any moment.

No wonder the San Francisco restaurant closed down.

I can feel that Freya is poised, waiting. Chase says, "The wine is perfect, thanks." I echo him, though it's gone untasted.

"Excellent," Freya says. "I'm pouring you full glasses now. I'll be back in a minute with your first course."

There's a new sound. It's fumbling and laughter. Another couple is being led into the darkness. Camouflaging noise would be great, but just one other couple doesn't qualify. We'll be able to hear one another in all the pauses.

I'm fairly certain that the other couple is already drunk, at five thirty, and they're raucous, enough to fill the entire restaurant. It seems somehow wrong, like the blackness should have a certain reverent quality.

"Someone's having fun." Chase says it lightly, but it also underscores that it's not us. "Are you happy to see me? I don't mean right this second, obviously. I mean, are you happy that I came?"

"I'm in kind of a strange head space, what with going live on Ty's show next week."

"Tell me about that." When I don't respond, he prompts, "Do you know what the story is going to be?"

"No. I'll find out tomorrow."

"They don't tell you anything in advance? You have no input into your scripts?"

At that moment, my nostrils are assaulted. The nearest I can decipher, it's onions, garlic, cabbage, and stinky cheese. Freya says, "On your left, I'm putting down a bowl of soup. It's pureed, so you can just pick it up and drink it."

Pick it up and drink it? I want to perform an exorcism on it.

"I'll be back in a little while," Freya says, presumably withdrawing. I can't know how much of our conversation she's been privy to. Being blind, she probably has extremely good hearing.

"This is delicious," Chase says.

I lift the bowl to my lips, and the aroma is nearly fecal. I hold it for a few seconds, how long it would presumably take to drink, and then set it back down.

"Are they still enjoying your performance? Your bosses, I mean. Edwin," he says. He infuses Edwin's name with contempt.

"About TMZ—"

"I should have heard it from you."

"It was bullshit. There was nothing to say. And if you have something to say, then be direct." I'm not really talking about

TMZ, because while Chase's jealousy sounds real, it can't be the main reason he's here.

"You're the one who needs to be direct. I'm the one who's trying to save our relationship."

Could that be true? I've been sitting here basting in my suspicions when, really, he came because he can feel he's losing me?

We're sitting in silence when Freya comes to take our bowls. "How was the soup?" she asks.

"Top-notch," Chase says. I murmur approval as well, though Freya can probably detect the lie, given the heft of my bowl.

"It was an emulsion of celeriac, leeks, and sunchokes. I'll be back soon with your next course."

Chase's voice is lower, and closer. He must be leaning toward me. "There are things you should know about Edwin," he says.

"Like what?"

"You want to see him in the best light because he discovered you, and I get that. Then there's all that fawning press about what a genius he is and how he's going to save television news and democracy. I get that you like being a part of something, but you have to think about what that something really is."

"And what is it, really?"

"Edwin made his billions in Silicon Valley, so people there know him pretty well. No one thinks he's a philanthropist."

"He doesn't claim to be a philanthropist."

"There's a rumor that Edwin started INN on a dare, and a lot of smart people, ones who've spent time with him, believe it."

So Chase is here to spread his own rumors. To plant doubt on the eve of my big story, the one that's most likely about Until. "Why are you really here, telling me this?"

"It's not in your interest to drink the Kool-Aid."

Or it's not in Chase's interest.

This is not an isolated moment in our relationship. This is a stance Chase has taken throughout, as if he's above everything, or at least, above me. He knows how the world works, and he's just trying to help me find my way. I'm used to being talked down to so subtly that it didn't register most of the time. But I felt it acutely after the viral video, when my pain grew inconvenient and he didn't think I was cleaning up my mess fast enough, when I truly understood that phrase about how when you stop living your life, the terrorists win. I now realize Chase would have been okay if I had never started living mine again, if I'd just continued living his.

Freya returns. She recommends eating the next course with our hands. "The texture is like a work of art."

I move my fingers slowly across the surface of the table, finding a linen napkin, the fabric just a little nubbly, and on top of it, I feel each fork tine and the slight serration of the bread knife. I try to calm my rage through each deliberate motion, because no one likes a shrill woman.

On my plate are a bunch of small objects, like tiny hot dogs, but more slippery. Eel, maybe. If it is eel, though, why does it have no smell?

"I'm refilling your wineglasses now."

Chase's wineglass, that is. My glass is still full. Should I warn Freya so it doesn't overflow?

No, somehow Freya knows, topping off Chase's and leaving mine alone. It's all very mystical, really.

"So what is this?" I ask Freya.

"Jellied bone marrow."

"I'm going to use my fork for this one," Chase says. Then

after a series of scraping sounds, he starts laughing. "It's like it's running away from me."

I pick one up and let it slide down my throat. It's more texture than taste. But it's not foul either. I eat the next one and realize I'm starving. Without Reese to get me lunch today, I forgot to eat.

"So what's going on at Until?" I say. Speak now or forever hold your peace.

"Are you asking as a girlfriend, or as a journalist?" he says.

"Is there anything I should know, as a girlfriend? Or as a journalist?"

The silence is deafening.

CHAPTER 21

July 17, 1991.

I don't need to read this. In fact, I know I shouldn't.

Chase is sleeping in the other room, in my bed. I'm sitting up on the couch at three in the morning. The diary has become a part of my insomnia, not the cure.

Another envelope was waiting in my apartment building at the security desk when Chase and I got back from dinner. Like last time, I was told it was from INN. Chase looked way too curious as to what was inside.

I wish there was someone I could talk to, but the only one I absolutely trust is Dad, and if he knew what's going on, he'd be having sleepless nights too. With his health, I can't risk that.

I hope I can trust Reese, but hope is not knowledge. Then there's Edwin, who I've barely seen this week. Where does he go? Off with Daphne? Or, if Chase's intimations have any validity, is it somewhere more sinister?

Googling "Edwin Gordon and Daphne" or "Independent News Network and Daphne" yields nothing. It would be helpful if I knew Daphne's last name or any other information, or if I had the training to do a real search.

It's possible there are no mysteries at all, that this is a wild goose chase meant to keep me sleep deprived and unraveling. I need to throw these pages out. I swore I'd never let anonymous people have this kind of power over me again.

Yet I can't walk away. I want to know the parts of the story I can't readily learn online; I want to know how Elyse felt each step of the way. Sick voyeurism, perhaps. Or maybe it's that I do believe that original letter that said Elyse and I are linked, that we're kindred spirits. That there's something Elyse can teach me. That there's something here in these pages that could one day save me.

July 17, 1991

Dennis says that the way to counteract A Current Affair is to let the viewers at home see more of me. Conveniently, Trish was chaperoning her kids' school field trip, so I stepped in.

"Break a leg, Sam," Scott whispered to me right before the show, and after flushing with pleasure at having a nickname, I felt myself going white. The show Rebecca Schaeffer had been on—her big break, where her stalker first saw her, the last that anyone would see her—was My Sister Sam.

Meanwhile, I was about to increase my exposure

to the world. Millions would be watching, and they would see me in a different, more personal way than they had so far from my newsreader chair. People are going to feel like they know me now, and that intimacy can backfire.

I pushed those thoughts and feelings as far down as I could. As Glinda the EP likes to say: "The red light goes on, and so do you." Since that's practically the only advice she's ever given me, I need to take it.

Fortunately, anchoring really was like riding a bike, and I was happy to flex my muscles. In the segments with Scott, I was careful about my sexual cues, just like Dennis (and my mother) told me. I showed myself to be a girl's girl, occasionally poking at Scott in that annoying-kid-sister way, taking a page from Katie Couric's book. We were having fun, which meant the viewers watching were too.

The cooking segment was the first one I tackled alone, and by then, I didn't feel the slightest nerves. I was making a fifteen-minute pasta primavera in a five-minute segment with the energetic chef du jour. "Now we're just going to turn down the heat," she said, giving the pan on its burner a final stir. She lifted up the lid from the counter, revealing a small piece of paper with large cut-out magazine letters. She kept talking, but I couldn't hear. I was reading those familiar words.

YOU'RE MINE

I tried not to show my panic. What I was thinking was: Lyndon. Not again.

I couldn't fathom how a psychopath like him could have known I was filling in for Trish today, and even if he did find out, how he could get on-set. But I couldn't let him screw this up.

The red light was on, and so was I.

I refocused on the chef, who was talking about her cookbook. "Every single recipe can be made in fifteen minutes or less," she said, "and you never sacrifice flavor. Here, try this." She put the pasta on a plate and offered it to me.

My stomach was in revolt, but I took a bite. "Mmm, delicious," I said, because you never say anything less. I gave the cookbook one more plug and sent it to commercial.

I looked around the set. There were multiple cameramen, the sound guys, one of them holding the boom mike, the director, the assistant directors, the producers . . . so many people. It's like the whole city has access. Could it be one of them, and not Lyndon? But that was Lyndon's MO, the ransom-type notes, the wording.

Maybe Lyndon asked some staffer to leave the note. He could have said he was my boyfriend, that it was a way of supporting me on my big day, reminding me that I'm loved.

No, no one would believe he was my boyfriend. He looks deranged.

So if someone did that "favor" for him, it would be because they wanted to help him hurt me.

The red light was off. My shoulders slumped, and the chef asked, "Is everything okay?" She spied the paper. "I assume that's for you?"

I forced a laugh. "They always prank the new girl." I picked up the paper and was about to ball it up when I noticed the letters on the other side. ALWAYS.

As in, YOU'RE MINE, ALWAYS.

As in, it doesn't matter where I go, I still belong to him.

It wasn't just his actions that were a nightmare;

it was dealing with law enforcement and the legal system and having to justify my own actions. "Why were you out so late alone?" a police officer would query, and I would look down, ashamed. So much judgment, as if I'd asked for all of it by putting myself on TV. And that was just the campus TV station.

I'll never forget being up on the stand, where my job was to make my terror plain, in front of my terrorizer. My terrorist. That's how the system works. You have to explain yourself all the time—why you wore that skirt, why you went here or there, who you kept company with, how much you had to drink. It had been far worse for Marla Hanson, with her destroyed face.

The more appalling the perpetrator's actions, the greater the victim's crime must have been, because otherwise, why would this have happened to her?

When it was time for the next segment, I took my place on the couch beside Scott so we could interview one of the stars of fall's most hotly anticipated new sitcom (according to the teleprompter). Conveniently, that sitcom is airing on this very network!

See, this is what happens to me when I'm stalked.

I get cynical. I monitor myself ceaselessly. Stalking changes how I walk, what I wear, which places I'll go, where I'll position myself (only at tables with full views of the room and an exit strategy). That's if I go out at all.

So many questions: Is it safer to be with someone, even someone I don't particularly like? Should I bother calling the police, when they're not going to do anything anyway? There's no one to trust. The world becomes ugly, and frightening. I am not myself.

No, I was not myself. Now, I am.

He cannot take this away from me. He cannot turn me into someone else ever again.

So I got through the rest of the show, and at the end, Scott gave me a big hug and hearty congratulations. Glinda shook my hand. Dennis called down to my dressing room to tell me that I had exceeded his already high expectations. It was a roaring success. I should be proud and happy.

But instead, I've been sitting in the dark, curtains drawn, writing by a small bedside lamp. That way, if anyone's watching my apartment window, they'll think I'm out. When the phone rings, I jump.

I let the answering machine pick up. "Elyse, it's Dennis. I just wanted to tell you again what an excellent job you did this morning."

I've got to get that.

Okay, I'm back. I scrambled to pick up the phone and found out he was in my neighborhood and wanted to stop by. He was slurring his words.

I don't really want Dennis in my apartment. That feels like a different sort of danger. What would my mother say?

But I can't say no. That could be career suicide.

Okay, Diary, I'm back again.

I'd turned on every light until the place was ablaze. When he came in, he asked if I had anything to drink, even though his face was ruddy and his birthmark looked positively inflamed, practically Gorbachevian. I lied and told him I have only water and soda.

I have to keep vodka around for emergencies so that if I have a man over, I can top off whatever I'm drinking and put myself in the mood. No, that's not exactly accurate. I don't get in the mood to have sex; I get in the mood to be sexy. I lose my self-consciousness, and I can give men what they want. It's funny because I always thought that men would be the ones with performance anxiety, but really, it's me.

No vodka tonight, that was for sure.

Dennis blinked in this exaggerated manner, almost a wince, as if he were a vampire and the light was painful. I sat far away from him on the couch in the loose clothes I'd put on, my hair still up in a scrunchie, the opposite of alluring. But he was looking at me like I was in a negligee, and he went on way too long about how America's going to fall in love with me. Then he flopped back against the couch like a dying fish. "I'm seeing someone, you know."

"I didn't know." But I was glad to hear it.

"I'm not sure if it's going to work out. I'm afraid she doesn't care about me. The real me. It's all about money and power."

He started to talk about his manipulative ex-wife, their ugly divorce, and the sense that she's turning his son against him while I made sympathetic noises.

"I'm good at my job, and I'm successful," he said, "but I've got this fear all the time. It tells me that if I let up for more than an hour or two, it'll all come crashing down."

"That sounds tough," I murmured.

"Everyone's trying to get power, or be with powerful people, and then you're there, and you've got to make decisions all the time. Big decisions, with big consequences. But you, Elyse, are the obvious decision. I'm going to make sure everyone sees in you what I do. I'm going to take care of you."

Maybe that's what did it, his choice of wording. I told him about the note under the lid, and about Lyndon.

"Have you called the police?" he asked.

"No."

"Good. That means we get to control this story."

It's not a story; it's my life. But he was off and running.

"I'll have a talk with the security staff, don't you worry. Heads will roll. I'll give you your own bodyguard. Meanwhile, there are a lot of ways to handle this. I'm going to come up with just the right one." He grinned. It was like he'd just done a line of coke.

"You don't ever need to worry again," he said, and I'm lying here at three a.m. trying my hardest to believe him.

CHAPTER 22

f what's in the Until story is true, it's worse than I could have imagined. But if Chase is right, and I'm just drinking the Kool-Aid . . .

I want to think Edwin's nothing like Dennis, but if you don't count the sexual harassment, there are some disturbing similarities. Elyse did what she was told, because she was supposedly getting what she wanted too. Meanwhile, her boss was manipulating her life for ratings and for ego strokes.

Edwin didn't even give me a heads-up as to the topic of my series. Elyse didn't ask questions, but I need to.

"What happens if I don't report this story?" I ask Albie.

"You'd have to take that up with Edwin."

"Before I do, I want you to tell me, hypothetically, based on thirty years of experience, what's likely to happen."

"I can't. Edwin's unpredictable."

"Chase is at my apartment right now. I need to confront him and see what he says."

"You do that and your career is over." Albie stands up and

moves so that he's behind the camera. It's the weekend, so we have the studio all to ourselves. INN is in reruns until Monday.

"Then, hypothetically, I want to talk to Edwin. Is he in his office?"

"No."

"Is he in New York?"

"I have no idea. He doesn't text me his itinerary."

I feel like Albie could at least be sympathetic. He could show some appreciation for the quandary I'm in. It's not likely, but it is possible that Chase doesn't know any of this about Until, and that he just happened to show up this weekend to fix our relationship. If that's the case and I go forward, he'd be devastated. He'd be losing his mission and me in one fell swoop.

But Chase isn't just an employee. He's not a cog; he's a unicorn. If this story is true, he has to have known.

"Did Graham contact Until for a quote on the story?" I ask.

"He's very thorough. He follows protocol."

"Does that mean he contacted Until?"

"Almost certainly."

I could try to reach Graham and confirm, but I don't even want to hear his voice if I can avoid it. What I know is this: Chase chose to work at Until rather than a more established tech company because he would be privy to everything, and Until was almost certainly contacted about this story, and Chase showed up unannounced the weekend he knew I was preparing.

What I don't know is whether Edwin handpicked this story for me *because* Chase is my boyfriend, if it was in the works before I was hired, if it was even part of the reason I was hired.

Edwin said he was playing chess, but that doesn't mean I want to be his pawn.

Albie releases a deep sigh. I can tell he hates the drama; he's about the work. "Let's shift the focus from Chase, shall we? This report will be the first in a series. A series, Cheyenne. You'll be on Ty's show, repeatedly, breaking news. That's Ty, the big cheese.

"Then let's talk about the story itself. It's an incredible piece of reporting. Well researched and sourced, as close to airtight as I've seen in a long time. Plus, it's important. It's in the public interest. It's what INN is about, and it's what you're about. It deserves to be told. So you have to decide if you're the one who gets the privilege of telling it."

I hate the idea that Edwin is manipulating me into the story, but what a story it is. If I decide not to do it, I might just be trading Edwin's manipulation for Chase's. Chase is here to work me over. He's been alternately romancing me and creating all sorts of opportunities where I can tell him about my series, so maybe the plan isn't for me to simply refuse the story, at which point it would be given to someone else. More likely the plan is for me to feel guilty and tell Chase what's in the story ahead of time. Perhaps Until would leak strategically and begin putting their own spin on the story. They could start the damage control ASAP.

It seems so far-fetched, and yet, people do strange things when their livelihoods are on the line. Chase has a lot invested in Until, and not just stock options.

Chase has been issuing numerous warnings about Edwin, and yes, Edwin has both patriotic and profit motives, but he's never pretended otherwise. He told me point-blank that he was going to use me to get the male millennials. Chase is the one trying to use our relationship against me, knowing it'll destroy the biggest opportunity I've ever had.

I'm not his errand girl. And if even half of what's in my script is true, if that's what he's mixed up in, then he and the rest of his cronies at Until deserve to have their company blown up.

"Let's do this," I say.

As we practice, my heart is pounding in my ears. It doesn't help that Chase is texting me messages of love interspersed with requests to come to the studio, to meet Albie, and to "see what I'm up to."

"Again," Albie says, "and you'd better do it a hell of a lot better. This isn't the time for cold feet."

"I'm trying here, but I'm torn. I know someone at INN is going to report this. I just don't know if it can be me."

"Get your head on straight, okay?" Albie stalks away.

I reach for my phone. Sorry to bother you on the weekend, I type. I didn't know who else might understand this dilemma I'm having, and I don't know why, but I get this feeling you would. I don't have your cell phone, which is why I'm emailing. If you have a few minutes, could you give me a call? My cell is . . .

When Beth calls late that night, after an entire day of demoralizing rehearsal, after dodging Chase's texts and then dodging his questions about my bad mood, I jump up. "It's work," I tell him. "I really need to take this."

I step out onto the balcony, shutting the door firmly behind me. I whisper, "Thank you so much for calling me back."

"Happy to help. What's up?"

I hesitate for just a second. I know very little about Beth. I don't even know whether she has a husband, or a wife, or kids, or a life. I don't know for sure that I can trust her, except that my gut already does. And if I can't trust my gut, what do I have?

"I'm sorry to bother you," I say, "but I could really use your advice, off the record."

"Sure. This is just between you and me."

I launch in, concluding with, "So either he's been lying to me all this time, or he just doesn't know what his company is really up to. If it's the latter, and he learns it from me, on TV, he'll be destroyed. But honestly? I really feel like it's the former, in which case he's not only a liar but he's involved in something that's—well, let's just call it what it is. It's evil. Or it's got a strong potential to unleash evil, and he's smart enough to know that."

"But perhaps arrogant enough to think he can control it."

"He could be that too."

"So in the best-case scenario, he's ignorant, or arrogant, or both. If that's the case and you break the story, can you live with that?"

I pause a long minute. "What does it say about me if I can?" I think of what Graham said about ruthlessness. I'd be his dream girl, the same as I was Edwin's twenty years ago.

"Sorry to answer a question with a question, but do you believe the public should hear this story?"

"Yes. That doesn't mean I have to be the one to break it. Albie didn't even want to talk about this, but I could just tell Edwin no, couldn't I?"

"The story will break regardless. You can't really protect Chase."

"If I tell him first, if I warn him—"

"Then you'd be out. You give up your career, and for what? Are you really going to end up married to this guy?"

No. However this goes down, I don't want to be with someone who liked me more when I had less.

"Edwin is giving you a gift," Beth says. "Refuse it, and you don't know when you'll get another. He's seeing how serious you are, and how committed you are to INN. If you fail, you could be sidelined."

"Then this isn't a gift. It's a loyalty test."

"It's both. So choose wisely."

CHAPTER 23

For once, Edwin's not drinking. He's also frowning. "Albie says you were struggling a lot this weekend. He's not sure you're emotionally ready for this." Am I imagining the disdain when he says "emotionally"?

I don't know if he's questioning my readiness for this particular story or for INN. But in either event, he might be right. I might not have the stomach for this. "Maybe we should postpone."

"You don't postpone a story like this. If we don't cover it now, we could get scooped."

"No other network would have the balls to touch it, right?"

"You need to get your head in the game."

"It was a rough weekend. Chase showed up—"

"I know." Even more pronounced disdain.

"I don't want to let you down, so if you want to give the story to someone else, like if Ty can read it off the teleprompter—"

"Don't tell me how to run my network, Cheyenne!" Edwin snaps as he strides around the office. "This was supposed to be yours. You were supposed to rise to the occasion."

If he's been planning this all along, that explains why my process has been so rushed. I'm being asked to throw away a relationship with the only man I've ever loved. I don't think I love him anymore, but Edwin doesn't know that. Or he does. He seems to know everything else.

Maybe Chase is really a good guy, like I always used to think, and I've been focusing on all his worst traits and on the negatives in our relationship. It's possible that I'm spinning our past and who he is, putting it all in the most dire light, so that I can sacrifice him to my ambition. To Edwin's ambition.

Now I'm mad too. "I was supposed to rise to the occasion of cutting my boyfriend's head off?"

"The head of the snake, you mean?"

The head? I've been focusing on what Chase knew, not on what he's done. What he may have initiated.

"Chase is high level at Until. I have it on good authority that he's been instrumental in designing Until's strategy. He's your unicorn, right?"

Before I shut down all my social media, there was an Instagram post: a picture of Chase with the caption "My unicorn." Is Edwin actually jealous?

He softens his tone. "We both know what you need to do, Cheyenne. In your heart, you know. And deep down, you want him to pay. For keeping you in the dark, for not being who he pretends to be. If you let him get away with it, Until could damage this entire country. You're a patriot. That's what I love about you."

I sink down on the couch. "I need to know something. An investigation this extensive takes a while. Is it part of why you chose me—because having me take down my boyfriend would be something you couldn't see on CNN or MSNBC?" It would be pure INN. Pure theater.

"It was a story we were pursuing. I didn't know if it would pan out. But it did, and now we're all agreed that it's the best possible direction for you."

Direction. That's what I overheard the woman in the hall saying to Albie.

Who's "we"? Ty? Albie? Daphne? Or could it be Beth? Beth did a good job of talking me into this. Could she have been the woman in the hall?

"Have you ever read an author who was willing to kill a beloved character with no warning?" Edwin asks. "No hint on the jacket cover. You're just reading along, and bam. He's dead."

What the hell is he talking about?

"That author has just broken the pact. Rewritten the rules. Once they do that, forever after, when you read that author, you're on your toes. You can't be sure what they'll do next." He comes and sits beside me. "That's what this series is for you. You tell the world about Until, and you've proven you're willing to do whatever it takes. Anyone who presumed to know what you're about or what you're capable of . . . well, this will show them." His eyes are on mine. "What do you think? Are you in, or are you out?"

It's a devil's bargain, I can feel it. But I want to say yes. Edwin's right. I am angry with Chase for lying to me, and underestimating me. I don't just want to show all our old classmates at Stanford what I can do. I want to show Chase too.

"If I need to, I'll reassign the story, but I'm telling you, it's your ticket."

So he's not going to sideline me. He'll just give my story

away. Even though I came in here suggesting it, the thought is a shard of glass. This is going to happen, either way. I don't want to see someone else get the glory. But I'm not sure I can take the heat.

"If someone else breaks it," I say slowly, "I can tell Chase that I chose not to report it. I don't control what the network does."

But would Chase make the same sacrifice for me?

Of course not.

The truth is, no matter what, I know in my heart that our relationship is over. I haven't trusted him for months, and even if I bowed out, he'd never trust me again. He belongs to my past, not my future.

But being this ruthless, it's just not me. Is it?

"Think about what Until has done, what we can stop them from doing," Edwin says. "Think about how high this goes. Don't you want to be a part of that?"

Finally, in a small voice, I say, "Yes."

"Could you say it once more, please, like you mean it?"

I look into his eyes. "Yes. I want to be a part of it."

"Good." He smiles. "Give it everything you have tonight, okay? You've got this." As I'm on my way out, he asks, "Could I give you a quick word of advice?" I nod, assuming it'll be about my performance. "You might need a new mentor."

He's going to fire Albie?

"Beth," he clarifies.

"What makes you think she's my mentor?"

"A little birdie."

It could have been Reese. She saw Beth coming in to check on me earlier today. It's hard to fully trust Reese after that Pietro nonsense.

That was about a guy, though, not about work. As far as I know, Reese has always been aboveboard at INN.

I contacted Beth through email, using her INN account. Was someone monitoring it? I've had the suspicion for a while about surveillance and always pushed it back down, labeled it paranoia, but Edwin seems awfully knowing.

"Beth's not my mentor," I say.

"That's good, because hers is not a career path you want to emulate. Do you know she used to be a blonde?"

"No." What's wrong with Beth's career path? I've never heard anyone cast aspersions on her before.

"A rose by any other name . . ." He smiles. "I'm just messing with you. Beth is amazing. I know. I hired her."

I don't have the bandwidth to figure out what he's saying. I just know that I don't like being messed with, or being told who my friends should be. That's a fight for another time though. I'm headed to the studio to meet Albie, where I need all the practice I can get.

The Until story is what's best for me. It's what's best for the country. So for the moment, my interests are Edwin's. But it might not always be that way. As much as I'm drawn to Edwin, because I am, I have to be more careful. Work smarter, not harder. That's what Beth said. Work the men as much as they're working you.

If Edwin doesn't like Beth giving advice, that's all the more reason for me to follow it.

Do this story, do it well, and then see where it can lead. INN isn't the only network. But everyone's got to start somewhere.

I head to the restroom to splash cold water on my face. I need to wake up more than I ever have in my life.

Opening the door, I see there's a woman stationed in front of the mirror, her hair pulled back tightly, items spread out all around one of the sink basins. "Excuse me," I say, about to withdraw and find another restroom.

"Hi, Cheyenne," the woman drawls. Without her shiny blond curls, without the evening dress, without her face on, Daphne is nearly unrecognizable.

This Daphne droops. Not like a basset hound but like a fifty-something-year-old woman who's never had work done.

I feel like I've caught her in a compromising position, but she smiles brightly and says, "Stay. I've been meaning to talk to you again. This is your big night, yes?"

"Yes."

Daphne is slowly, methodically—well, there's no other way to describe it—giving herself a facelift. She's applying what look like adhesive strips to her forehead, her cheekbones, and the area between her mouth and nose. As I watch, fascinated, the strips vanish, and the other Daphne appears, smooth and incandescent.

"You look like you've seen a ghost." She laughs. Then she indicates the strips on the counter. "Your mother probably uses them. If she doesn't, she should. I'll give you some to send to her."

"That won't be necessary."

"Your mother's as beautiful as you, huh? Some women have all the luck."

I don't correct her.

"You probably don't pay attention to every antiaging miracle that comes down the pike, and you shouldn't, since mostly they're bullshit. But as you can see, these are the real deal. What you just watched is the demonstration I did on QVC three years ago, what turned me from a millionaire into a billionaire." Daphne turns fully toward me. "Enough about me. So you've decided?"

"Decided what?"

"Love or career. Loyalty to Chase or to INN. Such intrigue!" She laughs. "I know what I'd choose."

"What's that?"

"I'm just going to keep you in the dark for now!" Her tone is playful, but it occurs to me that Edwin said that same phrase. Do they both know about the restaurant the other night? Could they know the actual conversation I had with Chase, where he disparaged Edwin? What else do they know?

I'm going to have to learn to cover my tracks. I don't like it, this Big Brother stuff, but life is about trade-offs. It's about trading up. Maybe I can use this to my advantage sometime. I can drop some false intel and see where it gets me. Two can play this game. Or three. Or more.

"I'm doing the story," I say.

Daphne nods, but her face betrays nothing. Maybe she can't emote with those strips holding her in place.

"Who are you?" I ask.

"I'm not your fairy godmother, if that's what you're thinking."

"That's not what I'm thinking."

"Touché," Daphne says, though it hadn't been meant as a riposte. "Maybe I'm Edwin's fairy godmother."

"An investor, so he doesn't have to shoulder all the risk?"

She shrugs, but she doesn't deny it.

"Are you his girlfriend?"

"I'm no girl, Cheyenne. I've earned every line on my face."

Then why does she try so hard to cover them up? To hoist them up is more accurate. But then, she's probably the face of . . . "What's your product called?"

"Stick It to 'Em."

"That's cheeky."

Daphne laughs. "Good pun! But you're right, I meant it to be cheeky. I hate the products that take themselves too seriously, the ones that are always talking about defying your age. If there's one thing I've learned, age will not be defied. When I say stick it to 'em, I don't mean the wrinkles; I mean the men." She winks. So she can move her face. She begins loading the rest of the strips into her purse.

I find myself lurking, waiting. It feels like something else is supposed to happen between us.

"I don't have any more advice for you. Unless it's this: stop looking for wisdom from women like me."

Is she talking about Beth?

"I don't mean to be harsh." Daphne's eyes are now glistening with compassion, and the change is so startling as to disorient. "I understand you, Cheyenne. I do. I didn't really have a mother myself, not the one I wanted, anyway, and when I was first starting out, I was casting around, looking for a mentor. But I didn't need one, and you don't either."

The smartest thing would be to trust no one: not Edwin, or Daphne, or Albie, or Beth, or Reese. Chase is already out of the picture.

Good thing I still have my dad, no matter what.

Unless . . .

I can't let myself go there. The treatments are working. Dad would tell me if anything changed. We've never lied to each other.

"Thank you," I say, "for the nonadvice."

"That one was a freebie. The next time," Daphne says, smiling, "it'll cost you."

CHAPTER 24

'm on INN's biggest stage, and despite the topic of the report, I can't deny the excitement.

There's Ty Fordham, behind his anchorman desk. *The* Ty Fordham! The Angry Independent! Sure, I sat in a pitch meeting with him, and occasionally I've seen him in the hall, but that was different. Here, he's a superstar.

Ty Fordham, the man whose fury is truly nonpartisan. During back episodes of INN, I've watched him sneer, "Don't get behind something because it's *progressive*; get behind it because it's *pragmatic*. Don't get behind something because it's *conservative*; get behind it because it *works*." This is the man who speaks in italics more than any human being *ever*. The man who's feminist because it's practical: "You don't weed out half the talent pool. There are far too many stupid people for that." The man who can actually pull off the parting line, "I'm biased toward the truth, and you should be too."

I've made peace with what I'm about to do, mostly. The

documents are indisputable. Until is a danger to the public. To the republic.

In my ear, Albie is counting down, "Three, two, one . . ."

This is my story. It's my moment.

"Good evening. I'm Cheyenne Florian. And this fellow"—I gesture to the photo of a young African American man on-screen beside me—"is Drake Dixon. His father is Bryan Dixon, the CEO of Trip Records, who donated millions to the president's campaign. Drake was convicted of various drug offenses and sentenced to six years in prison. After less than two months served, the president issued a pardon, and Drake Dixon was released.

"The pardon was in January. Less than three weeks later, Drake broke into a house that he says he thought was unoccupied. Startled and with a large amount of methamphetamine in his system, he killed the owner with an iron from the fireplace.

"INN has obtained a number of emails, among other documents, that have been authenticated and will be revealed in subsequent broadcasts. In this particular email"—it appears on the screen, with sections highlighted—"the president's chief of staff writes, 'Rape and murder rates have recently spiked, and while we've kept Drake Dixon from being much of a story so far, he could become the president's Willie Horton during the reelection campaign. We must begin to counter that ASAP. The president will establish himself as THE ultimate in law and order. The cornerstone of that will be Until.'

"To provide context, in the 1988 presidential election, Democratic Massachusetts governor Michael Dukakis was running against Republican George H. W. Bush. Willie Horton, an African American man convicted of murder, was furloughed from a Massachusetts state prison, and while on that furlough, he committed rape, assault, and armed robbery. The Republican attacks ads are infamous for their racist overtones, but they were also undeniably effective at the time, and of course, George H. W. Bush went on to win the presidency. Our current president's chief of staff apparently believes little has changed, and history could repeat itself, to the president's detriment. That's where Until comes in."

Don't think of Chase, don't think of Chase, don't think of Chase.

"Until is a surprising choice, since it's a technology start-up based in Silicon Valley, which has not always been the most receptive to the president. But Until is different." Dramatic pause as the screen changes to show the Until logo—a brain at the center, with happy scenes all around (children playing, an older couple on a bench looking out at the ocean, etc.). "By their own description, Until is 'not just a company, it's a force for good.' The stated aim? 'To create a safer future.'

"How do they create this future? By 'thought monitoring and impulse-control building,' using this wristband." The screen changes to a picture of a smiling person wearing a device the size of a large watch. "Until uses a process they call 'mapping,' where they claim to tell through changes in respiration and brain waves when deviant thoughts are occurring and which of these have the greatest probability to be operationalized. In other words, Until will attempt to stop crimes before they are committed, when they're simply ideas.

"It might sound like science fiction more than science. But according to these government documents, the device is close to ready." I show another highlighted page. "The government has a strong vested interest in getting it through beta testing and reaching the market, at which point the government plans to become the only customer. That's why $100 million has been essentially gifted to Until, in the form of research and development.

"In a nutshell, your tax dollars are paying the R&D for a private company that has never created anything before to rush a product to market that will exist for the exclusive use of the government, and that will, essentially, read minds.

"Now, you might say, 'It's not my mind they'd be reading; it's those of criminals.' Because the first people who would be signed up would be those who've been previously convicted of violent crimes. You can already look up whether sex offenders are living in your neighborhood; this is just the next level. It's in the public good, right?

"That's what the president is counting on. Look over here"—I wave my fingers in the air—"and you won't pay any attention to Drake Dixon. Look over here, and you won't pay attention to the civil rights violations involved in forcing anyone to submit to having their thoughts monitored, to their thoughts being treated as if they were behavior and then finding themselves surveilled as criminals before the act has been carried out. Look over here, and you won't worry that it's not really just going to be people who've previously been convicted of a crime; next, it could be anyone. No technology is foolproof, so it might not start out as you, but who knows where it will end up?

"More on that—much more—in our next report. Back to you, Ty."

"Thank you, Cheyenne." His brow is furrowed. "So you're saying that ordinary Americans could eventually be surveilled, and their thoughts monitored."

He wasn't supposed to say "eventually"; he was supposed to underscore that ordinary Americans *will* be surveilled, that

that's where this is all headed, as demonstrated in the next cache of documents.

We're live, so I have to go off script too. "It's imminent, as I'll show in tomorrow's report. None of us are immune."

"And how did you get these documents?"

"A whistleblower who works for the government approached INN," I say. "He's chosen to remain anonymous, but as I said, the documents have been authenticated."

Ty is supposed to invite me over to the couch now. But instead, he says, "Do you have reason to believe in the purity of this source's motives?"

Another bizarre ad-lib. I pause, hoping that Albie will come through my earpiece, as I have no idea how to respond. How can you vouch for the purity of anyone's motives? Ty is weakening the argument that I—that Graham—so painstakingly made.

"Yes," Albie says.

"Yes," I say.

"In the interest of full disclosure, you have, until recently, been romantically involved with an employee of Until."

He's back on script, sort of. The "until recently" implies that Chase and I are already over, which is not technically true.

It'll be over soon enough. Our relationship was an organism of a very particular ecosystem and couldn't survive outside the shared habitat of Palo Alto, where Chase is a unicorn and I'm just his girlfriend.

"Why have you chosen to report this story, despite the personal cost?" Ty asks.

"Because journalism is about the greater good. Our viewers and the country need to know."

"They certainly do." He turns to the camera. "This is not

an isolated instance. Rarely do we catch the perpetrators red-handed. Rarely can we follow the money all the way up to the president's chief of staff." He looks at me. "Thank you for bringing this to America's attention."

That's his level of outrage?

Where are the bulging eyes? Where's the absolute fury?

First he undermined the story with his invalidating improvisation, but this is worse. His refusal to be enraged sends a message to the viewers at home. Nothing to see here, folks.

I'm enraged enough for both of us. Despite the personal cost, I managed to kill, but Ty sabotaged me. Like Rayna did, only this is live, and can't be undone.

As the show goes to commercial, I storm off the set, waving Reese away. I take the elevator directly to Edwin's floor. His office is dark, the door locked. I'm breaking the story of INN's lifetime (short as that lifetime is), and he didn't stick around to see it.

I don't know what's really going on here, but I know one thing for sure: Ty undercut me.

It could be that he's a narcissist, and after his pay-to-play story flopped, he wasn't going to help me fare any better. But it's not just a jab at me; it's a jab at Edwin, too, who built this up in the newsroom for the whole staff. Edwin is deeply invested in this, and in me.

If that's true, then where is he?

I slide down to the floor, wanting to pound my head against the closed door. Edwin told me he's playing the long game. I'd assumed that game was for my benefit as well as his. But not only am I a pawn, I can't even see the board.

Doing the story seemed like the right move. It seemed like the only move.

An incoming text from Edwin: I knew you'd pull it off.

Did you know Ty was going to sabotage me?

He was playing the elder statesman. Makes the story
     more credible.

It didn't feel like that.

This isn't the time for paranoia. If not now, when? Go celebrate.
The thought of going to the bar where Graham can cop
a self-congratulatory feel is nauseating. But heading straight
back to my apartment after what should be a triumph seems
pathetic. And lonely. I've got no one.

No, that's never true.

"Hey, Cheyenne!" Dad's voice is strained, like he's trying to
sound happy to hear from me.

"What's wrong? Are you okay?" It's possible he got some bad
news about his health and hasn't wanted to distract me while I
was preparing. That would be so like him.

"In terms of the cancer, no news."

Which is good news. "Then why do you sound like that?"

He hesitates.

"You're scaring me. Just say it, please."

"You've been at INN a month. You've been with Chase for
years."

I can't believe what I'm hearing. I never thought I'd have to
defend my actions to my father. He saw the report where I laid
out all the evidence. "You've never liked Chase."

"That's not true."

"When he came to Tulip, you were pleasant but that's it. You didn't warm up to him, and now I get why. I see what you saw."

"He seemed a little high on himself, like he could stand to get knocked down a few pegs. But how could he not have a big head, with the way you treated him? The way you said everyone else treated him. This is more than a few pegs, Chey."

"As in, I was too hard on Chase?"

"He just works there."

Dad doesn't get it, and I don't have the heart to try to explain it to him. Not tonight.

"Did you ask him about any of this beforehand?"

"I couldn't! I'm a journalist. And of course he knew. Why else would he have done his surprise visit this weekend, of all weekends?"

Dad finally says, "If you're sure."

"I'm sure."

"Then you did a great job."

It feels cutting, though it wasn't meant to be. "I've got to go celebrate."

"Love you."

I hang up without answering, which I never do, because for years, I've been living with the fear that each time I talk to him could be the last.

I take the elevator down to the street, not even stopping at the newsroom, not wanting to look for congratulations that might be half-hearted at best. It's only a few blocks to my apartment, and usually, I change my clothes and cover my hair. I try not to be recognized. Tonight, I want some validation, some sign that what I do matters to real people.

Text after text comes in from Chase, protesting that none of it's true and demanding to know how I could have done this to him. You didn't even ask me, he says. Like I should have given up my career so he could lie to my face.

I'm determined to walk with my head held high, and I get appreciative glances from men, but they don't know who I am. They just see a pretty girl on a busy street. That's all anyone cares about.

Beth texts: No one could have done it better.

It sounds like a consolation. No one could have done it better, and no one will care. Ty as elder statesman? Bullshit. He was killing the story.

I'M TOSSING AND turning in bed when there's a knock at the door. I sit bolt upright. The doorman is supposed to call up to tell me I have a visitor. It could be a neighbor, but I don't know any of them. What neighbor knocks for the first time after midnight?

More knocking. Then a key turning in the lock.

I'm groping around on the nightstand, trying to find something heavy, realizing just how defenseless I am when I hear Reese's voice.

That's why the doorman didn't call up. Reese has a security clearance. Maybe she told him she wanted to surprise me. Another fucking surprise.

I fly into the living room. "You can't just come in here any time you want!"

"I was worried about you. You looked really upset leaving the studio. You didn't answer my texts."

"Because I want to be left alone! And I am upset. I'm upset that you're barging in. I'm upset that you got drunk off your ass at the club—"

"That's what people do at clubs!" Reese says.

"You used me. You wanted to be alone with Pyotr or what-ever the fuck—"

"Pietro."

"Pietro the real estate mogul—"

"Magnate."

"If you interrupt me one more time, I'm going to . . ." I look around my apartment madly. There's nothing on any surface that I can pick up and throw. It's barren. I have no life here. And I've detonated the life I had back in Palo Alto with Chase.

I sit on my couch, feeling like I need a good cry, but I can't do it in front of Reese. She works for me. I'm a boss now.

"I brought Patrón," she says.

I shake my head.

"I also brought red velvet cupcakes."

Tequila and cupcakes. I almost smile.

Reese takes the seat beside me, but not too close. "I've been wanting to apologize ever since that night. I was an asshole."

"So why didn't you apologize?"

"You were so busy working on this huge story. I didn't want to take up your time. And honestly, I didn't know you really cared. I mean, you're the talent. I'm just the peon."

"Don't say that. We're friends."

"I can tell." Reese smiles. "No, really, I can tell. Because it hurt you that I did such a shitty thing, and I'm sorry that I did, but I'm kind of glad to see that you care about our friendship. Because I do too. I never should have leveraged your fame like that."

"The fame thing is going to be fleeting, after tonight."

"You were awesome."

"It doesn't matter. Did you see Ty's nonreaction?"

Reese puts her hand over mine. "I'm sorry."

"So you think I'm right? You think it's dead?" I was hoping that I was off in my read of the situation, that maybe Edwin was telling the truth about Ty behaving like a grown-up instead of a tantruming child.

"I have no idea," Reese says. "This is a really unique story. But even if it goes nowhere, you have a three-year contract, and Edwin's practically in love with you."

"What makes you say that?"

"Everyone says that."

"Because of TMZ?"

"No, it's just kind of obvious. You should have seen the look on his face when he was talking about you during my job interview. Yes, he was the one doing the interviews for your personal assistant. You think he does that for everyone?" Reese goes over to the doorway where she'd dropped her paper bag full of goodies. "Enough work talk."

We eat our cupcakes. Reese tries to be entertaining, and while I can't muster much laughter, I appreciate the effort, and the company.

After she leaves, I don't even bother trying to sleep. I turn on the TV. INN is showing *Spotlight*. I'm not exactly in the mood for a movie about a sexual abuse cover-up, as hot as Mark Ruffalo is.

I'm traversing seven hundred stations when the phone rings. Two A.M. isn't when people call. It's when they text.

Wrong number? I think of Elyse and all those hang-ups.

I look at my cell and blanch. It's Graham. I didn't enter his number into my phone, so for his name and number to show up, he must have entered it himself.

What if the call is actually something about work? I have another Until report coming up tomorrow night. Maybe Graham is going to tell me he's revised the script.

He could have just texted that.

I don't answer, and Graham goes to voice mail. But he doesn't leave one. Instead, he calls back. I have the distinct feeling that he'll keep calling.

I could turn the phone off, sending him immediately to voice mail, but that could seem aggressive. Of course, this second call is aggressive. His hand on my leg was aggressive. But I can't anger him, not in the middle of the series he wrote, not when I'm still hoping to salvage things. Maybe he can get Ty back on my side. Or maybe Ty is already on my side; he's just playing it classy.

Hard to believe.

"Hello," I say, making my voice as groggy with sleep as I can.

"Just making sure you got home okay," he says.

"I'm fine. Thanks."

"I'm picturing you right now. The way you looked leaving the studio. You know that old saying, I hate to see you go but I love to watch you leave?" His voice is languid. I can only imagine what he looks like right now, where his hand is. That same hand that was on my leg a few days before. I rub at my thigh, like it can be wiped away.

"I'm tired, Graham. I'll see you tomorrow, okay?"

"You . . . are . . . really . . . beautiful." He's drawing out each word softly, as if in time with his strokes.

I know sometimes women being harassed blame themselves. They think about what signals they've sent, whether they invited the unwanted attention. They make it their fault.

I'm not doing that. I get exactly what this is. I get that I'm being violated, and that there's nothing I did to bring it on myself. But there's also nothing I can do to stop it. I can't even hang up. I need Graham in my corner.

He's so bold, calling the night of my big story. He must know he can get away with this. If I tell Edwin, if I tell anyone, it'll be my word against Graham's. I want to think Edwin and HR would support me, but I can't risk it. I have so much ahead of me, and so much to lose. That's what Graham—like all harassers—is gambling on.

It's my big night, and I've never been more insecure about my position at INN. Edwin could hire a new pretty girl, but Graham may be irreplaceable.

I squeeze my eyes shut, and endure.

CHAPTER 25

July 26, 1991

Today was a big day. My first cover of <u>People</u> magazine, and I hope it's not my last.

I know I should be excited, and I am, but I can't help feeling that it's not about my accomplishments. It's about human interest of the most prurient kind. Dennis offered <u>People</u> an exclusive of my pain. This isn't how I wanted to land the cover.

Dennis showed up in my dressing room this morning at the crack of dawn, before even Sandy and Frieda. He held up the magazine, cover facing outward. Vanna White has nothing on him.

I was sitting in my robe, but apparently, he was no longer concerned about the appearance of impropriety. A little while later, I understood why. It had been an incredibly effective PR maneuver, not just in the wider world but among the _Morning Sunrise_ staff as well. They were practically lined up down the hall, wanting to express their amazement at what a survivor I am. It was as if the chill I'd detected in my first month on the job had been a figment of my imagination, and the _Current Affair_ insinuations are bygones. First they fell in line to believe a nasty rumor, and then they'll fall in line to demonstrate how compassionate they are.

I don't want any of it. I hate that my past has been laid bare like this. It feels so cheap and opportunistic. And that cover is bringing it all back.

"Stalking Nightmare" was writ large beside my picture. I have to admit, they made me look beautiful—somber and a little bit haunted. Professional hair and makeup plus a two-hour photo shoot will do that for you. I hated that quote: "Your life doesn't feel like your own anymore."

Dennis was crowing about how well I did in the

218 · HOLLY BROWN

interview. I wondered if The Tank could hear from outside the door. That's what I'm calling my new bodyguard, for obvious reasons. He's a Dolph Lundgren type with a broad face and short-cropped blond hair, though I've never seen Dolph Lundgren in a suit.

The Tank probably sees women in jeopardy all the time. I'm an old story, a telemovie. I flash on Marla Hanson. Slashes on Marla Hanson.

"Women will relate to you, and men will want to protect you." Dennis handed me the magazine. "I want to see your face when you read the good news."

My hands tore at the pages. I found the article and skimmed it.

It was all there, in graphic detail:

The letters from Lyndon, at least once a day, sometimes as many as ten, saying we were kindred spirits. He wrote about dates. Not dates he wanted to take me on but dates we'd supposedly already had: where we'd gone, how I'd looked at him, what I'd said, how we'd "made love."

I'd tried to involve the police from early on. Lyndon was signing his real name and including his address. I thought that they could pay him a visit and tell him to stop sending the letters. But that wasn't how it worked; his civil rights trumped mine. Sending disturbing letters was only a crime in California. In the other states, you can harass people with impunity, so long as you don't make direct threats on their life. Lyndon's letters were invasive, but he never made an explicit threat. So he was protected, but I wasn't.

The police tried to make me feel better by telling me Lyndon was "mental" and lived with his mother. They said that these kinds of guys barely left their houses, and if Lyndon actually saw me in life, he'd run the other way.

Only they were wrong, because I knew Lyndon was watching me. He mentioned places I actually hung out, food I ordered, a purple scarf I bought, things that he couldn't have known unless he'd followed me. But somehow, I could never turn fast enough to catch him.

I didn't even know what he looked like. He was just out there, which was terrifying, so I stopped leaving my apartment, except to go to class and the TV studio.

I could feel that it was going to get worse. It was a

woman's intuition. Like how you know before you go to a certain party or walk down a certain street or get in a certain guy's car even though your gut is screaming no, but you don't want to hurt his feelings, you don't want to be impolite. You put yourself in danger, and afterward, you're kicking yourself. You're thinking, I knew better.

But with Lyndon, I wasn't going quietly. I was trying to put up a fight, and the police refused to hear me. They acted like I was making a big deal out of nothing. "Let him have his fantasy," a detective once told me.

The flowers came next. Lyndon must have spent every cent of his disability checks, because they were on my car and on my doorstep and delivered to the campus TV station. Big gaudy bouquets. People would ask, "New boyfriend?," and finally I had to tell them I had a stalker because it looked so weird that I was constantly throwing these bouquets into the trash. Also, I needed someone to walk me to my car every night.

The police advised me not to communicate with Lyndon. They said it was better to give him nothing, and eventually, he'd lose interest. Which is not at all how stalking operates. Stalkers are desperate for your attention. They'll do anything to get it.

I stopped following police advice. I wrote a letter back to Lyndon. I told him that I was flattered and I wished him all the best but that I had a boyfriend whom I loved. I asked him to please stop all contact.

There was a slim chance he'd actually listen. But more likely, I could smoke him out. I was sick of him being in the shadows. If he got mad enough to show himself, then the police would have to do something.

I started to get phone calls at all hours of the day and night. He never said a word. I changed my phone number, and the calls stopped for a while before starting up again. I never figured out how he got unlisted numbers.

I finally decided to consult an attorney instead of the police. She told me we should file a restraining order. Lyndon would be served a subpoena and ordered to appear in court, though she said he probably wouldn't show up. Well, she didn't know Lyndon. He

was there, early, with bells on. It was the first time
I ever saw him.

Lyndon was overweight, with black Coke-bottle
glasses that made him look like a raccoon. Behind
them, he blinked constantly, like he could never really bring the world into focus. I faced him down,
and I won. I was awarded the restraining order,
which meant he couldn't have any contact with me,
not even letters.

Now there were dead flowers on my car, on my
doorstep, at the station. The police said it was only a
violation of the restraining order if I could prove they
came from Lyndon. If I could prove it! As in, they
didn't intend to help. They'd washed their hands of
me. Meanwhile, Lyndon now knew the parameters,
and just how far he could go.

Since I didn't get any more letters, I had no idea
what he was thinking—if he still thought he loved
me, or if it had turned to hate. I no longer had
a window into his mind. I thought that's what I
wanted, but I was more terrified than ever.

Here's what I didn't tell the People writer:

About R.G.

That in some of Lyndon's letters, he was describing my sex with R.G., as if it had been with him. He knew specific noises and utterances. Was he peeping in the windows, hiding in the closet, bugging my room? I never found out. But by the time R.G. and I broke up, I'd stopped having sex with him. There wasn't enough vodka in the world to relax me.

I could feel Lyndon all around me, all the time. I could tell sometimes, when I came into my apartment, that the air was different. There was a slightly different smell, or the closet door was half closed when I knew I'd pulled it all the way shut. I kept mustard and mayo on the refrigerator door, and when I came back, they'd be on the main shelf. He was letting me know he'd been there but in a way that would sound ridiculous if I called the police. "Arrest him, he moved my condiments!"

The People writer and all the readers would probably have thought I was crazy too. That's why I had to keep it to myself.

For the first time in my life, I was depressed. Nothing brought me joy anymore. I felt as dead as those flowers.

Then the cut-out magazine notes started. They were left at the studio, under objects or taped to them. They'd say things like "You're mine. Always." I couldn't prove they came from Lyndon, and the police wouldn't even try.

My car window was broken, but nothing was taken. At the TV station, I was locked in the studio and had to pound on the door until someone let me out. I slipped on a patch of ice on my recently de-iced steps and got a concussion. But with no proof it was Lyndon, I just had to watch my back constantly. No one else was going to.

I didn't bother telling the police, so I didn't tell People either. I just told the woman who interviewed me that I got a job in Pittsburgh and headed out of town, and I never heard from Lyndon again. Dennis and I agreed that I wouldn't say anything about last week's note. Better to give the impression that it's all in the past. I'm a survivor.

The writer asked me what I wanted to tell Lyndon, in case he was reading this article. I said, "That he can never steal my life again. To all the stalkers out there: You can't love people you don't know. Even if we're in your living rooms, you don't know us."

She included the whole quote, but it was a gotcha moment. A twist.

"I see you got to the good news," Dennis said.

Lyndon was found dead by his mother eighteen months ago. It was ruled a suicide.

If it's not Lyndon, it's someone else who got into the studio and left me that note. Someone else who knew Lyndon's MO, who could use Lyndon's very words against me. If this is an intentional copycat—if someone in New York found out about my past and about the ransom notes—if he realized that by using my old stalker's methods, he could terrify me even more, then that would mean Someone Else isn't delusionally lovesick but truly sadistic.

That's hardly good news.

"You're shaking like a leaf," Dennis said.

"I'll be okay."

"You have to be willing to share yourself with the audience if you want to move up." He studied me. "Do you still want that?"

"Of course."

"Sitting in for Trish was the first step. Did you see that rave from Tom Shales?"

"Yes. You had it delivered to my apartment." I stared at him, as it dawned. "Didn't you?"

Someone Else delivered it. Someone Else knows where I live.

I have no en suite bathroom in my dressing room, and I had to dash down the hall to throw up. On my way back, everyone wanted a piece of me. I've been here a month, but I've just become a celebrity.

Scott stopped me to compliment my strength; even Trish got in on the act, wanting to tell me she'd had a stalker once. Scott rolled his eyes behind her back. Then he walked away, and there, at the end of the hallway, York Diamond was waiting. York didn't notice me, or pretended not to. Scott said to him, "Good to see you!," and backslapping ensued.

On the one hand, this means that York must be who he said he was. On the other hand, it means York has access to the set. I know that the security footage for that day has been reviewed and everyone's been cleared, but maybe York is a regular visitor so he didn't get flagged as suspicious.

With Lyndon dead, I have no choice but to speculate.

I was relieved to just be in my newsreader chair and not on the couch today. Though afterward, when all I wanted was to get home, I had more people approaching me for autographs than Trish and Scott did. Everyone seemed so friendly and nice and supportive, but I couldn't help thinking that it could be any one of them.

The Tank stayed next to me the whole time. His bulk communicates a clear message: <u>Why attack this little lady beside me when there are so many easier targets in the world?</u>

But he might not be able to deter someone who's truly crazy. So even as I did my best to smile and accept their compliments and sympathies, I wasn't really there. I was lost in frightening scenarios. Battery acid being thrown. Butcher knives wielded. Shots fired.

Then three women approached me together. I could tell they'd wanted to be last in line to have the most time. They said they were in a support group together, and it seemed like they'd been victimized in some

228 · HOLLY BROWN

way that they weren't specifying. They praised me for speaking out and held me up as a role model for their daughters. They said it's not just about the stalking but the double standards: how women have to be careful what they wear because then they're asking for leers and catcalls; how if you drink too much and someone has sex with you without your consent, it was your fault; how you can't walk around after dark without being afraid, and if you do get raped, then you brought it on yourself because you shouldn't have been out there alone.

I hadn't thought before how much stalking and rape victims have in common. I'd assumed that if you were actually attacked, then the police had to take you seriously; rape is a crime. But from what these women were saying, even those who've been violated suffer from scrutiny and judgment, just like I did. And they feel guilty and ashamed and terrified, just like I have. Like I do.

They were there to thank me but also to invite me to their group. They slipped a card into my hand. I could never go though. I'm on TV. I can't share with a roomful of strangers.

Just a country full of them.

I'm barricaded in my house now, and The Tank has gone home. I'm as afraid as I've ever been.

So this is going to be my life again.

But I'm getting what I want, right? I'm a celebrity.

CHAPTER 26

Cheyenne Florian is an anus licker who better shut the fuck up about the president. #greatman

Cheyenne wants child rapists on the street. #stupidcunt #TeamUntil

She needs to know what rape is really like. #rapefantasies #whatIddotoCheyenne

Just look at her legs. Don't listen to her mouth. #seenandnotheard #watchonmute

She's anti-American. #Communist

Talentless cum receptacle. What's she ever done? #greatman

I bet her cunt smells like old garbage.

After she fucks you, she bites your head off.
    #blackwidowCheyenne #worldsworstgirlfriend

What's the big deal? She's ugly. #getbronzer

Her father needs to go ahead and die already.

And that's just on the mainstream social media sites, where as fast as INN can get a thread or a comment removed, another one sprouts up. There's no head of the snake; there are thousands of heads, like Medusa, and they keep propagating, and, more frightening for me, migrating. INN is making it harder for them on the major sites, but there are thousands of angry fringe sites, communities, and message boards, too many to monitor, where they're congregating, spewing hate, and hatching plans. It's funny because if those guys actually met Chase, they'd hate his privileged ass, but as a concept, the idea of a woman turning against her guy at the same time that she's attacking the man holding the highest office in the land—it's too much for the sexist, misogynist, and pro-rape contingents to take.

I accept the drink Edwin offers even though I'm going on Ty's show again tonight. I need to settle my nerves somehow.

"I know it's brutal, what they're saying," he tells me. "But remember, they're a very small minority. A vocal minority, sure, but the mainstream media response is positive. They're not even talking about you but about the story, which is the whole point, right? They're insisting on answers. From the president of the United States! Journalists go their whole lives waiting for a moment like this."

He's right, I need to keep things in perspective. I took this job for the good I could do, and I'm doing it.

But perspective is hard to maintain when I'm this afraid. After the viral video, there were plenty of rape threats, but now it's whole websites devoted to me. On www.whatiddotocheyenne .com, there are long and detailed descriptions and enthusiastic back-and-forths about which implements they'd shove inside me and which they'd use to bludgeon me to death when they're done. The accompanying videos and GIFs are professional grade, like someone's really taking their time on the violence and the gore. There are discussion groups that have elements of reality, like including INN's address and suggesting ideas for how they'd get to me in a way that could cause maximum professional disruption and personal damage. Most are absurd, but then, a lot of people said that about the circus of the 2016 election. If they're obsessed and determined and they don't have much to lose, then anything becomes possible.

I'd been lulled into a false sense of security when it hadn't happened sooner. I'd been so smug about INN's ability to put pressure on the major sites, and so sure that the goodwill from my earlier reports on cyberbullying would form a protective shield around me. I thought people would continue to remember their higher selves, and that I was helping them do that.

I've been so stupid. People don't want to be their higher selves; they want to indulge their vitriol and feel powerful through their bullying rings. Of course this would happen again, and at a much greater intensity.

It's like with Elyse. There's always Someone Else. But unlike 1991, now they can find one another and form lynch mobs.

They band together and egg one another on to be more and more extreme. The natural endpoint is for someone to follow through, just like it was with Elyse.

"I'm thinking someone else should take over the story," I say. "Ty, maybe?" Meaning, a man. They don't write the same things about men. Male media personalities don't face the same type of danger.

"You can't let a bunch of misogynists win."

"This isn't about winning. It's about survival."

"A bunch of freaks on the internet aren't a credible threat, but I can see how it's scary to read some of that stuff."

I close my eyes. "I don't think I can handle this, Edwin."

"When's the last time a broadcast journalist was physically attacked in this country? The 1980s, when Dan Rather got mugged, maybe? And that was random. The guy didn't even know who Dan Rather was. Journalists get attacked in war zones. You planning to go to a war zone anytime soon?" He smiles at me.

I don't smile back. Has he really forgotten Elyse Rohrbach?

This is probably another part of his grand plan, what he hoped would happen all along when he hired me. I can take the viewers on a tour of the depths of fringe misogynist America. But I don't want to go, and he can't make me.

Only he already has.

There've been a few disturbing emails before, but now Reese is having trouble keeping up with the flood of filth to my inbox. According to INN's security team, none of it constitutes a direct threat. It makes me think of Elyse's diary, and how the restraining order just showed Lyndon how far he could go. Now the internet has shown them all how to walk that line, to terrify without consequence. I long for the days when my biggest worry was not being taken seriously by the viewers, when my hot-as-shit pile was too high. Now they're taking me seriously, all right.

But will the police, if the time comes?

"Stick to your guns, and it'll die down," Edwin says. "#strongwoman. That's what you are. You withstand the hate to get the love. And the money. And the power. That's how it works."

"Are you just capitalizing on that, or are you trying to change it?"

"You've already done two stories on bullying in social media. What do you think?"

I don't know anymore.

"Every strong woman feels weak from time to time. Every strong man too."

"Is that my latest tweet?"

He laughs. "I love that you can keep your sense of humor. That counts for a lot. But haven't you noticed the increased police presence in the building today?" I haven't. "An officer will be assigned to get you to and from INN, every morning and evening. If you go out, they'll patrol where you are."

"What about my dad?" He didn't choose any of this. Sure, he laughs it off for my benefit. He says they're cowards hiding behind a computer screen, and he's stockpiled plenty of artillery if anyone wants to come for him. But just the idea that someone could wish death on someone as wonderful as my father is too disgusting for words. I'm ashamed that I've brought him into this.

"No one would touch an old man."

"He's not an old man."

"Sorry. I didn't mean it like that." He comes and sits right beside me. "I'm going to tell you the truth."

What's he been telling me so far?

"You're working yourself up over nothing. Those groups can't touch you. You're a celebrity. You want to know who they can touch? Everyone else. Before you came to INN, when you googled yourself, the first thing that came up was your naked pictures. That's not true anymore. There's so much about you that all their bullshit gets buried. They want to disseminate false information or rumors about you? It never gains any traction. In a heartbeat, I can line up interviews for you with the top periodicals and TV newsmagazines in the country. We can get the cover of any magazine we want. We could get you *60 Minutes*. You can tell your story and drown them out."

"Why haven't you done that?"

"Right now, we're focusing on the work. Then we start on the media training to get you ready for that. Honestly, at the moment, we don't need it. We're keeping you exclusive to INN. People want to see you, they have to tune in."

While I don't care for his patronizing tone, he is reassuring me, a little.

"The other thing those groups do to people? They call and text you incessantly with cruel, disgusting, harassing messages. You had any of those?"

If you don't count Graham, then no.

"Your phone got hacked before and your pictures were stolen, but that's not going to happen now. They know better than to even try. They know you've got the toughest cybersecurity, plus the police will be on them immediately."

That wasn't true with Elyse. But then, she didn't call the police after she was a celebrity; she called them when she was on campus television.

Edwin's not done. "Those groups also love to come after your

family and friends. They barrage them with the same nastiness, or they trick them into giving up information that they can then use against you. They want your dirty laundry, and then they'll air it. But you, you don't really have family or friends, do you?"

I feel another welling of shame. I had friends in high school, but I dropped them when I went to Stanford. Any new friend I thought I met turned out to be, well, not. I don't have Chase anymore. Dad's an only child, and both my grandparents are dead. I'm not sure if I can count Reese. She's on Edwin's payroll.

"I have my father," I say, "and he's the most important person in the world to me. What about him?"

"Do you honestly think that if those groups try to call a bunch of people in Tulip and spread rumors about your father that it'll work? Or that if they call your father and tell him shit about you, he'll believe them?"

"No."

"See, the reason those groups air people's dirty laundry, and make sure that Google searches turn up rife with it, is because they're trying to limit prospects. Make you untouchable. Make you a liability to friends, so it's hard to keep old ones or make new ones. Make it hard for you to get a job or a place to live. You looking for a new job?"

"No."

"Good. Because INN's your home. What I'm really saying is, we keep you famous, we keep you safe. You get your own police detail. You get INN monitoring and scrubbing your social media. You get all our connections. Those groups are looking for easy targets and lives to ruin, and celebrities don't fit the bill. Right now, they can fantasize, but that's all. You walk away and who knows?"

Who knows indeed. So that's where all this truth telling has been leading. Just in case I'm a flight risk, he wants me to know that there's nowhere safe to run. I'd be at the mercy of the mobs.

Has this been part of his long game too?

I look at his face, and there's nothing threatening in it. He's just Edwin, who I've liked from that first day on the plane, and who I thought liked me. But he's shrewd, and he's cunning, and he never claimed to be otherwise.

"I want you on the air tonight," he says. "This is your series. INN needs you."

"I'm not sure I have it in me, Edwin."

"I'm sure that you do. But stay here and relax. I'll be back in a little bit." After he's exited, my head lolls against the back of the couch. I just need the quiet.

It doesn't last long. My phone is ringing. Chase's ring. Am I even allowed to talk to him when I'm still on the Until story?

I won't give anything away. It's time to end this once and for all.

"I got your texts," I say. They seemed tame compared to the vile things I've read over the past twenty-four hours.

"I shouldn't have said some of that stuff," Chase says. He sounds as tired as I feel. "You were ignoring me, and I just kept getting madder."

"I was ignoring you because you called me names."

"Come on, Chey. We both know I didn't start out that way. I didn't know how you could do something like that to me. How you could just set fire to everything I've been working for."

"If I hadn't done it, someone else at INN would have."

"That's a cop-out."

"INN has the documents. We have the proof."

"There's no proof."

"If you think that, then tune in tonight."

"You get what Edwin just did, right? He declared war on Silicon Valley. He turned against his own."

I glance toward the door. Edwin didn't say when he'd be back. "He's unbiased. That's what 'independent' means."

"He made all his money in tech. He's biting the hand that's fed him. Because he thinks the real money is in media, which is nuts anyway. You're working for a lunatic."

"INN is exposing the truth. We're telling the stories no one wants to tell but everyone should hear."

"OH MY GOD!" he explodes. "Is that a slogan for INN?"

"No, that's what I think." I need, so desperately, for it to be true, for all this to mean something. "We're the only ones acting in the public interest, working for an informed electorate."

"Oh, right. Edwin's going to galvanize the citizenry."

"He's trying to, at least. You're trying to surveil them."

"The thing about you, Cheyenne"—and now he's dripping with a simpering pity—"is that you're so suggestible."

"You just hate that I'm not taking your suggestions anymore. You flew out here to manipulate me, and it didn't work."

"Oh, right. I'm the manipulator. Everyone at school told me about you. They warned me that you were the world's biggest cocktease."

"I didn't sleep with any professors then, and I'm not sleeping with my boss now."

"Of course you're not. That's your trick. You make people think it's possible. You make them think they have a shot. That's what everyone sees when they look at you on-screen. Like you're almost accessible. It's Professor Trent writ large."

The low blow lands, and the shame floods in. "You know I never did anything with Professor Trent."

"My point exactly. He gave you all those advantages because he had hope. You never kill their hope, Cheyenne. That's not your style. And everyone told me. Even Lydia, who doesn't like to think badly about anyone. Now everyone, everywhere, knows what a fool I am. You've ruined me, Cheyenne." He sounds like he's about to cry.

It's always about him. It always will be.

I hang up.

It's for the best that Chase and I are over. He never really knew me anyway. Because if he had, he would have known that during that conversation, I was trying to convince myself as much as him. That I drank the Kool-Aid, but it's threatening to come back up.

I stand and straighten my clothes, not that it matters if they're wrinkled. My scuba dress will be pristine as always.

I THROW MYSELF into rehearsals, trying to think of nothing else, and then it's time. In Ty's studio, I await my cue. Graham walks right by, like he doesn't see me. He might not even remember last night's call. In the ferocity of the online onslaught, I'd practically forgotten myself.

I need to get through this. I can't give in to Graham, or Chase, or the trolls.

After Ty opens the show, welcoming viewers, he tosses it to me. "Thanks, Ty," I say, my heart galloping, yet my delivery is smooth, just as Albie and I practiced, again and again. "I'm happy to be here."

"Pivot," Albie says, "toward the camera. Now you're talking to the viewers at home."

I pivot in the way I've been taught, the one that gives my body the most flattering lines, and perform Graham's script as written. Not a single deviation, or a single stumble. I'm on an autopilot that's assured but not mechanical. I walk the viewers through another cache of documents, even more damning than the first. Until is toast. Chase is a liar.

"Pivot toward Ty," Albie says.

I do, and Ty says, "Have a seat. Let's talk some more."

It's time for my walk, on live TV. I'm haunted by the memory of Luke and all those takes, but I've put in a lot of practice since then.

The walk is a purposeful sashay. As I lower myself onto the couch, I don't even need Albie to tell me to cross my legs, slowly. I've got this. The one advantage to being targeted from outside is that Ty doesn't seem nearly as frightening inside.

Tonight, he does me the favor of getting incensed. Being associated with the scorch of his indignation is good for my brand, though it might be too little, too late.

He looks into the camera, and now he's the one flirting with the viewers, making them feel special (and superior) for tuning in. "Listen up. You want a country you can be proud of, just like I do. So I'm going to tell you what to do. Get angry at the right people. The right institutions. Government was designed to contain people's worst selves; instead, it's taken on the character of people's worst selves. The opposition party only opposes. But YOU can oppose too." His face is rapidly turning crimson. "WAKE UP, PEOPLE! DON'T LET THEM DROWN OUT YOUR VOICES LIKE THEY DROWN OUT THE TRUTH!"

It's practically a call to arms. And there I am, beside him. I've arrived. I wish it felt better. I wish it felt like anything at all, but I've gone numb.

Albie is effusive in my ear (well, as effusive as he gets), and even Ty gives me a nod and a "Good job." I'm sure there will be another celebration at the bar. Yet all I want is to get far away, to slow everything way down and really ponder. It's like I haven't been able to truly think for myself in weeks.

I sleepwalk my way to the elevator, and then down to the street, and since it's only ten o'clock, the avenue is busy enough to swallow me up. It's only once I'm outside that I remember I was supposed to have a police escort. I think about going back up, but I'm just so tired. All I want to do is get back to my apartment as quickly as I can, and when I glance around, no one seems to be lying in wait for me. No one's paying me any attention at all. Just to be safe, I'll hail a cab to go the few blocks home, and I won't forget my police escort again, because you never know.

I'm thinking all that as I make my way to the curb. That's when someone bumps into me, hard, and I'm flying into the street, with cars approaching.

Then there's a hand on my arm, yanking me back. Beth's hand.

"Are you okay?" she asks.

I look down in amazement as if to confirm that I'm still in one piece. "I—I think you just saved my life." I look around, and once again, no one is looking back. I don't recognize any-one. Maybe I tripped, or someone didn't even realize they'd bumped into me, or didn't care, and they kept going. It could have been an accident. It must have been.

"Thank you," I say. Then I really look at Beth and see that her face is tear-streaked; there are rivulets through her heavy stage makeup. "Are you okay?"

She doesn't answer. She's shaken up herself, but I'm not sure if it's because of what she just did for me or what came before, the reason she was crying.

"I'm here for you," I say. "It doesn't have to be a one-way street, you helping me." I realize just how much I'd like to help someone else.

"I can't pull you into this. Just keep going, Cheyenne. I'm really proud of you." Then she lifts her arm, hails a cab, and is gone.

It's only when I'm in my own cab that everything catches up with me, and I start to hyperventilate. I could have died. Someone might have tried to kill me.

And he (or she) had the chance because Edwin told me that I would have an officer assigned, yet no officer had introduced himself or followed me down to the street. It could have just been an oversight, but it might not have been.

These are crazy thoughts. Edwin doesn't want the future of INN to break a major story and then get run over in front of the building.

Unless he thinks that would make great news.

I'm really and truly losing it.

I should have asked Beth what she saw, who she saw. She's the only person who knows the truth. As soon as I can, I'll ask her. It's not the kind of thing you text.

The cabdriver is watching me in the mirror. "It's a panic attack," he says in a heavy New York accent. "You just gotta breathe, and you'll be okay."

He continues to monitor me in the mirror, and I think, *Has he seen me naked?*

Breathe. That's my only job right now.

The cabdriver doesn't engage me in conversation. The doorman doesn't either. By the time I'm letting myself into my apartment, all the adrenaline has fled my body and I'm on the verge of collapse.

I see a text from Dad, telling me what a great job I did, but it rings hollow after what he said last night. It's like he's snowing me, too, like I can't even trust my own father.

I fall into bed with all my makeup and my scuba dress on, and I'm out immediately.

I wake to my cell phone ringing. I grope for it and see the number.

I'd hoped that the other call had been a one-off. I'd hoped that my second good performance on Ty's show would have been an umbrella, and that Graham would have to see that I'm the real deal, I'm going places, and he has no choice but to back off and respect me.

Instead, I'm the one who has to respect him, or at least pretend to. Which means I have to answer.

"I didn't wake you, did I?" he asks.

"It's after two in the morning."

"Sorry. I lost track of time. I missed you at the bar tonight." He lets out a sigh. "I'm just lying here thinking about you."

If I say nothing, give him nothing, he'll have to move on to the next victim. No, he can move on to someone who wants his attention. According to Nan and Belinda, there are plenty of women who do. And yet, he keeps calling me.

"I'm imagining my hands on your zipper. It's a long zipper, from those beautiful shoulder blades on down to the small of your back. And that ass of yours. Oh God, oh shit, that ass . . ."

I say nothing, give him nothing, but I have the awful feeling that my lack of participation, my lack of consent, is part of what keeps him coming back.

CHAPTER 27

August 9, 1991

A lot's happened in a week. I'll try to catch you up, Diary.

I met a guy, B.N. He works on the show, and everyone likes him. He's always dressed really conservatively, with polo shirts and horn-rimmed glasses, and he has the most beautiful hazel eyes. His lips are nice too. He talks in this way that's shy and gentle. He often hesitates, like he's really considering what you've said and he's not just waiting you out so he can speak again, like so many of the producers do. But then, he's a writer.

It was kind of funny how it happened. I finally got invited to happy hour, only I was in a lousy mood, and B.N. turned it around for me. Everyone was trying to be nice and ask me all these questions, though nothing too personal, nothing that would touch on Lyndon, so it felt almost like a job interview. That's until I started talking to B.N.

Then that night, I got a bunch of hang-ups, and I don't know what came over me, the spirit of Dirty Harry, I guess, but I answered and said, "The police can see your number, you know." Whoever it was hung up, and I had to hope he believed the lie.

Then my whole body broke out in a cold sweat. Answering had been a mistake. I'd confirmed I was home, and Someone Else might assume that meant alone. He'd be right. The Tank had already left for the night. Dennis has shortened his hours (more on that later).

I was in a panic and I didn't know who to call, so I tried B.N. He didn't even mind that I woke him up. He just came right over, though I made it clear it was as a friend. I don't need any more men getting any more ideas.

It's five nights later, and he's still here. We talk for hours. The dark acts as a truth serum, and we can tell each other anything. He's let me know some things I had no idea about, like that Trish and Dennis had an affair that ended badly, and now he's determined to drive her out. B.N. said that Trish has been really ashamed and scared, and that she can be self-centered but she can also be kind (unlike Scott, who B.N. said is a chameleon who becomes like whoever he's around, and right now, with the contract negotiation, Scott is often with "that shark agent of his").

"York Diamond?" I asked fearfully.

"I don't know. Is that his name?"

We both made jokes about how phony it sounds, and then started coming up with other, equally phony names. I was laughing, but a part of me stayed scared the whole time.

It's still platonic, but I do have feelings for B.N., and I'm pretty sure he has some for me too.

So of course that's when R.G. shows up. When it rains, it pours.

And of course he looked good. Dark hair, light eyes,

athletic build, and that sexy smile aimed right at me. It's only the second time I've ever seen him in a suit. The other time was when he accompanied me to the courthouse.

He was with the autograph seekers outside the studio, and he hung back until they all left. Then he came up to me and introduced himself to The Tank, which nobody ever does. I learned The Tank doesn't shake hands.

Right there, in front of The Tank, he told me that he still loved me, that he'd never stopped, and the article brought it all back. He scribbled his number on the back of his business card and asked me to call so we could meet up and he could apologize properly. "Afterward, if you tell me you don't ever want to see me again, I'll respect that. But hear me out first, okay? Please."

I shouldn't have taken it, but I couldn't stop myself. He's R.G.

I haven't called though. I've been busy, between work and B.N. and Dennis telling me that the network won't pay for The Tank forever, that I need a safety plan. He sounded really cold, and I didn't understand what I'd done to lose my value so quickly. He'd seemed so high on me after the article.

B.N. confirmed that Dennis is just a dickhead, which helped, and then B.N. suggested a self-defense class. I thought it was a great idea, and so did Dennis, who later popped into my dressing room and told me his great idea: to film the classes. "It'll be ratings gold," he said. "It's all about female empowerment and keeping our viewers safe, with you as the surrogate. You're their everywoman." He snapped his fingers. "I've got the title. 'Safety First!: With Elyse.'"

It's a five-week class, which means a five-week segment, and I know that kind of exposure will be good for my career. But just like the article, it feels exploitative. Still, I am bringing awareness to violence against women, and they could learn some techniques that really could save their lives. That's the way I have to think of it.

Yet Dennis being on the set today made me feel dirty. Every time I look at him, I think of what he's doing to Trish. If that's not violence against women, what is? B.N. believes the best about everyone, but not Dennis. And I trust B.N. Night after night, he's in my bed, and he's never made any sort of move on me. He's a true friend, and someday, maybe he'll be more.

Dennis looked me over in my designer sweats, from head to toe, and told me pink is my color. Then he returned to his favorite theme—how much he's doing to advance my career, always coming up with ways to keep me front and center. I wanted to ask him, What about his promise to keep me safe? How does firing The Tank fit with that? But I needed to show him proper gratitude or he'd never shut up.

I have to make him feel important at all times, but never cross any lines. I know. I'll put the word out that I'm dating B.N. and let it get back to him.

I tried to forget about Dennis, which was hard since the gym was mirrored.

Val's my instructor, a woman with graying dark hair, wearing a loose belted outfit, like she's going to practice karate. She started the class by lying down on the mat and closing her eyes. I got a sinking feeling right away. A moment later, a man covered in a head-to-toe padded suit loomed over her. He put his hand over her mouth. Her eyes opened, and he told her not to scream. "I'm going to take what I want from you," he said. "If you make any noise, I'll have to hurt you. Don't make me hurt you. Nod if you understand." She nodded, and he removed his hand.

I felt like I'd stopped breathing. It was my worst fear, come to life.

He tried to pull her legs apart. "Don't resist me. You resist, I'll have to hurt you."

She stopped resisting. But as the assailant went to unzip his pants, Val rolled and kicked him in the eye. He fell backward, and she kicked him again, in the groin. She started on his head, kicking repeatedly, until he stopped moving, seemingly out cold.

Val stood up. A second later, the "attacker" stood up too. My heart was in my ears, in my throat, everywhere. No part of me registered it was a simulation.

Val pushed back a stray hair and looked right at me. "You're thinking, 'There's no way I could do that. If someone attacked me, I'd be paralyzed.' That's what every woman thinks at the beginning of this course. They all turn out to be wrong." Val walked slowly from one side of the mat to the other. She was speaking as if it were a roomful of women, and not just me.

"Notice that adrenaline you're feeling. Over the next five weeks, you'll learn that it's your best friend. Fight or flight, you've heard that expression before. That's inborn. Which means you're a warrior. You just don't know it yet." Val smiled briefly. Then she said, "Step on up here."

I wanted someone else to volunteer, but it was only me on the mats. Me, the surrogate for all the viewers. I needed to be brave.

Val said there's an "assaultable look," and it's not about what you're wearing. Victims tend to have an awkward gait, rather than a smooth one. But most significantly, they appear preoccupied. They're not paying attention to their surroundings. I needed to project strength, confidence, and awareness at all times.

As we practiced walking, I actually forgot about the cameras. I felt good, like there was really something I could do. I'm not just a sitting duck.

"Now, the next thing you need to know is that in cases of attempted rape," Val said, "the best policy is active resistance. Run away, or at least try to. Scream, 'Fire!,' not 'Help!' What doesn't work is pleading. You're not going to get him to feel sorry for you. Rape is about power and aggression; it's not about sex. He wants your fear. But he can't have it. You're using it. You're using it for motivation. You're using it to run, scream, kick, punch, jab, and elbow your way out of there."

I had never thought of fear as motivation, as something I could use. Well, I've got plenty of motivation stored up.

"Fight or flight," Val repeated. "In this case, it's flight whenever possible, then fight. Are you with me?"

I nodded.

"Say it. Flight, then fight!"

"Flight, then fight!"

"Scream it!"

"FLIGHT, THEN FIGHT!" This time, I felt like I'd rattled the walls. I felt powerful.

Without warning, the attacker sprang at me. I froze, and he wrestled me to the ground.

"Get off, get him off me," I sputtered, on the verge of tears. He'd exposed just how powerful I'm not.

What can happen at any time when I'm not paying attention, when I'm just living my life. He showed how vulnerable I'll always be.

The attacker let go, and Val was squatting beside me on the mat.

"What are you feeling?" she asked kindly.

"My heart is beating out of my chest. I felt like I was going to die. I mean, I know now how stupid that is, but it's like, my heart didn't know. It thought this was real."

"Perfect. That's just how we want you to feel."

"Scared? Powerless? Like I can't remember anything I'm supposed to do?"

"This time, he surprised you. Next time, you'll be ready."

"Because you'll tell me he's coming?"

"No. Because you're going to learn to be ready all the time. This is going to work itself into your subconscious, Elyse."

"This is what I always feared," I whispered.

"Good news," Val said, offering a hand. She pulled me to my feet. "Your biggest fear came to pass, and look at you. You're still standing."

blink back into the present. This entry was so different from the others. I felt like I lost myself for a while, like I was feeling her fear and then feeling her strength, like the person who gave this to me has to be a friend. Like Elyse herself is somehow my friend.

I could really use that right about now, between Beth having to yank me back to the curb and the continued online maelstrom and Graham turning me into a sex toy. Reese has made it clear she wants to be my friend, but get a few drinks in her and all bets seem to be off. Then there's Edwin. He's this strange amalgam of friend, boss, and captor. He's made it clear I can't get away easily, and not just because of my contract. I need his protection.

But where was he last night, when Beth had to save me?

I still don't know exactly what happened. It occurs to me that if someone really had pushed me, Beth would have stayed and insisted we call the police. So it must have been a freak accident. Celebrity or not, this city is dangerous.

I go back to Elyse's Wikipedia page the way I do after each entry, searching for any inconsistencies. While reading the diary entry, I was surprised to hear about Trish and Dennis having an affair, but now it's showing up on Wikipedia. I check to see when the page has been edited, and it's today.

By R.G.

Is that *the* R.G.—Elyse's ex-boyfriend—or just someone who knows about the diary and is sending me a message?

I go to the comments. People are questioning certain details, asking why sections are as long or as short as they are, just the type of specious debate typical of Wikipedia. Then I see, earlier tonight, that something was added by R.G.:

Which of the following three statements are true?

Lyndon gave Elyse a concussion.

Lyndon locked Elyse in her campus television studio.

Lyndon rearranged her condiments.

Okay, if there's a message here, what could it be? I reread the statements. All three are true, according to the diary.

So someone is trying to tell me that Elyse was lying, or crazy. Or that the diary is a fake. Or maybe they're telling me to look for R.G. Or that I'm nowhere close to safe.

CHAPTER 28

'm staring at the television, rapt. Edwin is beside me on the couch, his body unusually taut. Daphne's on the other couch, nearly supine, cocktail in hand. She's in a suit, as unwrinkled as her face, though I know the levers and pulleys involved in that illusion. I've seen behind the curtain, but only because Daphne wanted me to.

The president is in the Rose Garden. "Jim," he says, "first question."

"Everyone's talking about Until—"

The president interrupts. "Let me be clear. I'd never even heard of Until before this nonsense report. We're not talking about some huge government program. An R&D payment was made, which is not unusual, by the way, we do it all the time. I wasn't a part of any discussions because it wasn't a big deal. You know me by now: I'm only involved in big deals.

"Since then I've been briefed. I don't like what this is all about, and I'm pulling the funding. I'm investigating who was involved and why certain decisions were made, and we'll go forward from there." He looks around. "Barbara."

"So, to be clear, you're saying that prior to the INN story, you knew absolutely nothing about Until—"

"Correct." He chooses his next reporter. "Daniel."

"I'm not sure Barbara was finished."

The president smiles. "She's finished. Daniel, what's your question?"

"In the documents, there are a number of references to your reelection campaign and how Until is an attempt to bolster your image in advance. Were you aware of the potential for Willie Horton/Drake Dixon comparisons and the need to appear tough on crime?"

"I am tough on crime. People talk all the time in Washington. It's a town full of blather. If I paid attention to every single thing, I'd go crazy, and I'm the sanest person you'll ever meet. So when it comes to this company, this Until, I knew nothing. Now the media is trying to make it into something. But I'm moving on." He points. "Phil."

"The recent jobs report . . ."

As the journalists ask questions on multiple topics, never once returning to Until, I can feel anger radiating from Edwin. He turns off the television, and it's swallowed back up into the ceiling.

"Well," he says, "I wouldn't have expected anything less."

"We knew the president would deny it," Daphne says, her tone soothing.

"No, I meant from the media. They're going to let it drop. They're going to let him have the final word. He tells them to move on, and that's what they're going to do."

"They're talking about the Until story a lot," I venture. I

didn't put myself in the cross hairs of the woman-hating fringe for nothing. "Until is shutting its doors. We've stopped the collusion between the White House and a private company that would have harmed the American people."

"There'll be another Until," Edwin says, looking disgusted.

"Edwin's right." Daphne sets her drink down on a side table. "The media is happy to let this one drop. They did their thing for a news cycle, had all their pundits line up to form a united front, insisting that the president provide answers, and then they covered their own media firestorm. He denies everything, like they knew he would, and now they're done."

"Because it's INN," Edwin says.

"Yes," Daphne responds. "Because it's INN." Seeing my confusion, she adds, "They hate us, Cheyenne. We expose their hypocrisy at every turn, and this is payback."

"But we did the right thing." I look back and forth between them. "We did what the fourth estate is supposed to do. We uncovered a potential atrocity. We brought it to light and now Until is dead."

"It's about respect, Cheyenne. Don't you get that?" Edwin says. "They have five Washington correspondents, and we have one. We don't have the billion-dollar infrastructure, but we scooped them. We led the charge against the president, but they don't want to follow. They won't give us the satisfaction." He smashes his hand against an end table. "It's the country we're talking about here! Those petty motherfuckers!"

It's the failure in his own model. He wants to have his cake and eat it, too: attack the other networks but also get their backing. He bit the hand that feeds him, like Chase said.

"Well," Daphne says, unfazed by Edwin's outburst, "the good thing about the news is, there's always more of it."

Edwin turns to me. Turns on me. "You never believed in the story, did you?"

I chose INN over Chase, over my own safety, and Edwin is sitting here doubting me. "Of course I did, or I wouldn't have done it."

"Even the day of the first report, you were questioning it."

"You were on the fence until the very last minute," Daphne says.

"But I did everything I could to sell it!" Neither of them responds, which is clearly an indictment. "Ty didn't back me! He didn't even get mad."

"This isn't about Ty," Edwin says.

"You have to take responsibility," Daphne adds coldly.

So they've got their party line. This is my fault, not Ty's. After all, his value's been proven, while mine is still in question.

It's not fair. My job was to bring in the millennials, and I've done that. If the network can't get respect from CNN, MSNBC, or Fox, that's on Edwin. And Daphne, too, it looks like.

If it were just Edwin and me, I might be able to get him to understand. He's seen the error of his ways before and apologized. But I don't think he would with Daphne there. "I should get back to work," I say, standing up.

I'm almost to the door when Daphne asks, "You haven't heard from Beth, by any chance, have you?"

"No, I haven't. Why?"

"She hasn't come in today, or called, and no one's been able to reach her." Daphne waves a hand. "But I'm sure everything's fine. I just thought that since you two were close, she might have told you something."

"No," I say faintly, "nothing."

As I step out into the hall, I'm remembering Beth's last words to me: *I can't pull you into this.*

CHAPTER 29

B y the afternoon, the newsroom is swarming with police. They've set up a command center in the conference room. Because it's glass-walled, I can see Beth's staffers trying to hold themselves together through the interviews. The prevailing view is that INN is Beth's life, and the only thing that could keep her from work is unspeakable.

I might have been the last person to see Beth alive. She yanked me back from the brink, and now she's missing. Are the two related?

No, that doesn't make sense. Beth was already crying when I saw her. Meaning, something had happened before that.

I've been thinking more about what those three things on Wikipedia had in common, and it's that Elyse didn't tell the police about any of them because she either wouldn't be believed or there'd be nothing the police could do about it. In Palo Alto, after the viral video, the police had been sympathetic but useless. I'm hoping they can do more for Beth. Is the message from R.G. that I shouldn't trust the NYPD? If so, can I trust R.G.?

I can, if R.G. is Beth. Otherwise . . .

The newsroom is distraught and somber. Though Beth is a maternal figure to many, not just me, no one has met any of her family or friends. Everyone seems to be realizing, simultaneously, how little they know of her private life.

But the show must go on, and INN needs to find a fill-in for Beth tonight. It won't be me since I have the final installment of the Until story. I've been given an abridged script to practice. Edwin's prophecy has come to pass, and the coverage of the story on other networks and online has dwindled significantly since the press conference. The only way to revive interest would be to directly link the president to Until, but INN has gotten only as close as the chief of staff. While we can unveil more documents to show how deep the conspiracy goes, we can't demonstrate how high. We can't refute the president's claim that he was never told. So the final installment's been gutted, and with my current mental state, I can't say I'm sorry.

On the set of Ty's show, the atmosphere is tense. There's a miasmic cloud of anger coming from Ty before he's even on the air, which is unusual. The leadoff is the president's press conference, and Ty makes the point that just because there haven't yet been documents to connect the president to Until, that doesn't mean they won't emerge later. Even to my ears, it sounds face-saving. Worse, it sounds like a line from the administration: what I said might not be true yet, but just wait.

Only INN told the truth. That's what's infuriating. We scored a hit on the administration, and if the president doesn't know what his own chief of staff is doing, shouldn't that count for something?

It should, but it doesn't. I perform my truncated stand-up, knowing there will be no walk to the couch tonight, that I'm being shunted off-air as quickly as possible. I'm worse than garbage. I'm yesterday's news.

But Beth might be tomorrow's.

As I head for the bathroom, no one on the set will even look at me. Baby-faced Officer Mortimer is in conversation and doesn't seem to notice I'm leaving. They really gave me New York's finest.

I'm about to lock the outer door of the restroom when it flies open. My spine connects with the sink, and while I'm too dazed to react, Graham is the one locking the outer door.

Then he's grabbing me by the wrists and pushing me into a stall. "I knew we never should have trusted you," he hisses. "Not with something this big."

"Let go of me." I'm struggling, but he's strong for his size. Now he's slamming me into the wall. I have to position my legs around the toilet to avoid falling in the water. It would be laughable if it wasn't so terrifying. "It's not my fault."

"Of course it's your fault." His eyes are wide with amazement at my naiveté. "You put a spell on Edwin, and he gave you our best story. You can't carry something like that. You've got no gravitas. If it had been someone else, the president couldn't have—"

"The president couldn't have what? He's the president! And we're just INN!"

"You fucking bitch."

Now I begin to struggle even more furiously, but he holds firm. He grinds his face into mine, his tongue a weed whacker in my mouth. I bite down, and he yelps. Instead of letting go, though, he pushes harder against me. I can feel his erection, but I know this isn't about desire. Graham isn't afraid of reprisal for what he's about to do. The men are united against me, scapegoating me for the failure of the story.

Does Edwin want me to pay too? He said INN was my home; he said I couldn't afford to leave because it's not safe on the outside.

I've been fearing the wrong things. The wrong people. It's like those old horror movies: the calls are coming from inside the house.

Graham is holding both my wrists in one of his hands now—how can he be this strong?—and his other hand is reaching up my dress. "Just pretend I'm Edwin," he breathes into my hair. "Don't cry, Cheyenne. Edwin likes you. *Just not in that way.*"

Maybe he's not going to rape me; he's just going to humiliate me. Like Luke, with his roving eyes.

But Graham keeps going, rimming my underwear. I squirm so that his fingers can't get inside me. "I'm going to scream."

"Go ahead. Everything's soundproofed. People only hear what they want to hear."

I'm bone dry, and his fingers are jabbing into me. I let out a moan of pain.

"See? I knew you'd like that." His breath is hot and fetid. "Though even your boyfriend said you're a cocktease."

Surveillance. My phone is definitely tapped. Am I being watched too? If only that were true right now. But I can't rely on anyone else. I need to get myself out of here.

The diary comes back to me, the self-defense class. No pleading. No appealing to his humanity. It's active resistance. You run, or you fight.

It's the weirdest thing, like I can hear Elyse's voice, urging me forward, telling me that I can push through the fear, I can find my anger, and I can use it. Then I remember: *They've got me in these fucking stilettos.* I slam my foot down on top of his.

This time he doesn't just yelp, he howls. Most important, he releases me.

I beeline for the door. I don't hear him pursuing me, but I can't be too careful. I take off my stilettos, drop them, and run down the hall.

Officer Mortimer catches my arm. "What is it? What happened?"

I look back. The hall is empty. I'm not sure if Graham dashed the other way, toward the stairwell, or if he's hiding in the bathroom.

It is the ladies' room, which is incriminating, but Graham could find some excuse. He went in to check up on me, and I turned on him like some rabid animal. See, he's the one with the smashed foot. It would be my word against his. A scandal. Humiliation. Judgment. Everyone saying that I'm a liar or that I brought it on myself. I can only imagine the retreads of my video on rape tribunals. Of my naked photos. It wouldn't matter that I'd been in a monogamous relationship at the time, that I'd sent them to the man I loved, that I'd had the expectation of privacy, that they'd only gone public because of a hack. It would only matter that they were out there, and I'd be labeled. A slut, a whore, you name it. They would only be too happy to name me.

"Nothing," I say. "Could you take me home, please? Those shoes were killing me."

CHAPTER 30

I call out of work sick the next morning. I haven't slept all night. I keep seeing Graham's face close to mine, and feeling the sensation of being pushed up against the wall, his fingers like grappling hooks. Closing my eyes doesn't help. Opening them doesn't either.

I can't call the police now. They'll want to know why I didn't tell Officer Mortimer last night. Besides, there's a strong possibility that the NYPD would just collude with INN. Power sides with power, and at the moment, I haven't got any.

I checked myself for bruises, and there were none. There's no semen or other fluids, no physical evidence at all. Could Graham's attack have been calculated to ensure he'd leave no trace? Could he have done it before?

He told me to go ahead and scream. That people hear what they want. Translation: No one at INN is going to want to hear this about their golden boy. Or no one's going to care what happens to me after I botched that story, though I didn't botch it at all. INN had just reaped what it sowed, after building its audience on the disparagement of the rest of the media.

Speaking of which, CNN, MSNBC, or Fox would be all ears.

But with so many sexual harassment and assault claims coming down the pike about rich and powerful men, the viewers might be reaching their saturation point. Graham is small potatoes, just a producer, not a megastar. At home, people will weigh my story against those of the other women, considering the behavior along a continuum, assigning values: the demeaning calls I got from Graham are nothing compared to Weinstein's bullying, and being rammed against the wall unsuccessfully is little compared to a completed rape. What I've been through could be downplayed and dismissed, and that's if I'm believed at all. I can hear the speculation now about how after my hubristic failure to take down the president, I'm trying to extend my fifteen minutes of fame by any means necessary, that I got here on my looks and my sexuality, and then I want to cry rape when a man tries to follow through on the promise I've made.

I would have to go toe-to-toe against Graham in the court of public opinion. Surely what I did to Chase would come up, with all the attendant black-widow memes about how I mate and kill. To this point, Chase has made no public comments about me (probably at the advice of Until's counsel), but he could start talking at any time. I can just imagine all the joking tweets about how Until could have stopped Graham, when it was just an idea in his mind.

If I took my story to another network, what would INN do? I'd be fired immediately, unless sexual harassment provisions prevented that. But if I had to stay there in the midst of an investigation, I don't even want to think of the sort of attacks I'd face. For three years they own me. The damage they could inflict in that time is too awful to contemplate. I can just imagine Edwin and Daphne justifying it because of how I failed with the Until story, as if I ever stood a chance.

The only good thing about the series going out with a whimper rather than a bang is that it's dampening the internet furor against me. There's a lot of gloating about the president coming out on top. Fine, let them think they've won.

Maybe they have. I've never felt so defeated in my life.

Professor Trent tweeted: *@theRealCheyenneFlorian, close but no cigar. Better luck next time!*

I suppose it could look supportive. It will, to anyone who wants to see him in that light, which is everyone on campus. He's one of the most popular professors. Who wants to believe that he was sexually harassing me?

Even I didn't want to believe it, but now I can see. He's actually gloating about the story falling flat. And it's because after he groomed me all semester, abusing his power and making me feel like there was no way I could get an A without his direct assistance, he showed up at my apartment uninvited and I did what I should have done the whole time: I said no.

I don't know if the cigar is a Bill Clinton/Monica Lewinsky reference or not. If it is, it's probably because Professor Trent thinks Monica was the young femme fatale manipulating an older man. That's the narrative I bought into, the one that the rumormongers fed. I felt grateful for the A that I could have rightfully earned, and guilty that I'd turned him down after all his kindness. Sorry that I'd strung him along, when really, I'd told him that I had a boyfriend. When I'd never asked for his help. It was offered—freely, I thought, only it turned out that it actually came at a great cost to how I saw myself and my competence, and how the other students saw me.

> You okay? It was a rough night for everyone, with
> the story not turning out the way we'd hoped it
> would. We're all missing you here at INN!

The exclamation point is so unlike the Graham I know that I can't tell if he's making fun of me or if this is his warped expression of concern, his version of an apology, even.

This time, I can't tell myself he doesn't remember. He wouldn't have been drinking on the job. He attacked me stone-cold sober, unless you can be drunk on rage.

He failed. I fought back and got away. That might have to count as a win.

But he's still texting me; I'll have to keep seeing him, and working with him, and pretending that what happened didn't.

It beats the alternative. Beth might not have gotten away at all.

The police investigators gave a placeholder press conference about Beth that offered no real information, so on every network and on social media, speculation flourishes. I can't bear to watch INN's coverage. I don't want to see their spin, don't want to even see that logo. So instead, I watch the other networks, where there's a nearly vengeful focus on INN and how secretive it is. No one who's inside talks to those outside, and even the people who've left won't talk.

Won't, or can't?

I have a contract, and I ought to finally read it, since I'd rather walk away than be run out. Or disappear.

It's a daunting task, but it's blessedly absorbing. Term, Salary/ Rate of Pay, Re-assignability . . . that's all straightforward. Work for Hire—anything I create while I'm an employee of INN will belong to INN. I can't take any ideas with me, unless I keep them in my head. And off my phone, email, or wherever else INN might be looking. Good to know.

I'm troubled by a phrase in the Job Description/Duties section that I cruised right by that first day: "as reasonably may be required by Company." I don't want to think what Company considers reasonable.

Termination for Cause: A breach of agreement would include a refusal to perform assigned tasks, failure to comply with policies, conduct that hurts INN's reputation, insubordination, criminal conduct, and "ethical lapses." If they want me out, it shouldn't be hard for them to make it happen. But I have no escape hatch. Under Liquidated Damages, it says that if I quit in less than three years, they could fine me up to my salary, plus all that they've spent in training and developing me. Who knows how they'll tally it up.

But that's not the worst of the contract. Conflict resolutions have to be settled in arbitration, not in court, which means that INN will have home court advantage. Then there's an airtight noncompete clause, which would survive the termination of my employment. In the next section, Confidentiality, it says: "Employee may not reveal company business, trade secrets, terms of employment, general business conditions, current employees . . ." It goes on for a page and a half and ends with, "including the existence of this clause." As in, this is a gag order so complete that employees aren't even allowed to reveal that it exists. But it's not just current employees. The contract specifies that the gag is in effect "throughout the period of employment, and for a period of five years after termination of employment."

Five years, under penalty of a ten-million-dollar fine. That can't be standard in the industry, no matter what Edwin said. He's been lying to me from the start.

For now, I'll have to be careful about everything I say and write. I'm pretty sure I'm being spied on, given the things that Graham, Edwin, and even Daphne seem to know. I was so gullible, never even questioning the "gift" of this apartment.

I look up at the muted TV and see, "Who is Beth Linford?" I turn the sound back on. Though I missed the beginning, I get the gist. Nothing from Beth's résumé has checked out. There's no record of her at her stated alma mater; her previous employment can't be verified; no family is stepping forward to claim her as theirs. She appeared out of nowhere in 2001 after the September eleventh attacks, just turned up at an NYC news affiliate with tapes of incredible interviews with first responders and victims' families. She leveraged those tapes into a job, and from there, she worked her way up to INN.

I remember that strange comment from Edwin about how Beth used to be a blonde, about a rose by any other name.

So he knows who she really is. Does he also know what happened to her? Is he behind it?

CHAPTER 31

I get a call from my building security. INN's dropped off another courier package.

"Could you bring it up, please?" I say. I'm still in my pajamas, using my sick day to try to figure out my next move. Edwin wants me to think all the threats are on the outside, and that the only way to stay safe is to remain with INN. But the first key to self-protection is to quit believing him.

I answer the knock on my door. As I expected, it's a manila envelope. I have to hope that Beth is the one sending them, that she's somewhere, alive. The diaries could be a clue to a present crime, not just a past one.

August 13, 1991

B.N. is snoring away. Nothing happened again last night. Nothing, except I don't just want him as a bodyguard anymore.

But I know I can't be with him until I clear everything up with R.G., and maybe not even then. Maybe I need to wait until I figure out who's after me. Wait until I'm free. Otherwise, B.N. could do what R.G. did. He could decide I'm too much trouble, that he doesn't want to live this way when he could be with another woman and have it so much simpler. Because the truth is, even if I find out who Someone Else is, there can always be another Someone Else. That's if I'm successful, and I'm not yet ready to trade my dream for the safety of anonymity.

R.G. wanted to take me out somewhere nice, but I picked lunch at a deli. I didn't tell B.N. I was going. I got recognized by the waitress, who fawned all over me, and I was glad R.G. got to see what he missed out on, the good parts.

He did this long speech about all the stress he was under back in college but said he has no good excuse. He abandoned me in my hour of need, he said. All he wants is to make it up to me. He loves me with all he has.

I told him he doesn't have enough. Then I said I forgave him and that we both need to get on with our lives. It seemed like the easiest way to put a period on the end of our sentence.

He doesn't want to get on with his life.

"I'm in a relationship," I said. "Respect that."

He shook his head regretfully. "I can't."

"Then respect me. Respect what I'm saying."

"We're meant to be together."

That's when I got mad. Lyndon thought he knew better than I did too. I've had it with men trying to overrule me and make their desires mine. But I had to keep my voice down. People can recognize me. I stood up and spoke, low and definite. "I'm leaving now. Don't contact me again, please."

"I can't do that. I'm sorry. You still love me."

I reminded him that he told me if I never wanted to see him again, he'd listen. All he asked was that I hear him out, and I did that.

He shook his head again. "I didn't know how it would be to sit across from you. To feel what we had. What we still have. It's right here, between us." He stood up so we were eye to eye. "You feel it too."

I don't know what I feel. I just know what's good

for me, and he isn't it. I walked out of the deli and I tried my best not to look back.

It was unsettling, how insistent he was, and that I did feel some vestigial attraction sitting there across from him. But I'm trying not to think about it. I've got so much going on professionally. The first installment of "Safety First!: With Elyse" was a huge hit, just like Dennis said it would be. The reaction has been immediate and positive, with lots of kudos for the network and lots of attention for me. So many letters from women telling me their stories of victimization and how much my message of empowerment means to them. More photo shoots and interviews are being lined up. Dennis said that he'll tell them not to focus much on my past but on my bright future.

I started the morning feeling pretty good. No calls again last night; looking forward to my next self-defense class. I was getting a special bonus assignment, a reward for doing so well and for "Safety First!" connecting with viewers: an extra segment where I give women safety tips, on the couch with Trish and Dennis, working the tips into the conversation. There are the obvious ones, like "Trust your instincts" and "Scan your surroundings," but there's also "Don't be nice," reminding women that they don't need to make excuses for men who seem suspicious. My personal favorite is "Do something gross," like picking your nose if you think a man is watching you.

I was getting my hair and makeup done when Janelle knocked on the door. My happy mood evaporated as soon as I saw the bouquet of dead flowers in her hand.

"I'm so sorry," she said. "These were sitting on the floor outside of your dressing room. Should I call the police?"

"The police won't do anything," I said. "There's no card, there are no fingerprints on dead flowers, and there's no antistalking law in New York."

Someone got into the studio again; someone knows The Tank is gone. Or maybe it's someone who's on staff and therefore doesn't look suspicious on security footage.

Whoever left those flowers could have had them around for a while, waiting for the most opportune moment. They are dead, after all.

B.N. says that the staff is full of good people, but he could be fooled. He's way too easy on Trish, for example, saying that she's the sole breadwinner for her family, that she has a jerk of a husband and two little girls. We almost got into our first fight when he told me that. Like it's my fault she has a shitty life and slept with her boss. We're all responsible for our actions, aren't we? B.N. is just too good a person himself.

I know that York can get into the studio, and I rejected him the first time we met. I continue to reject him by not using his business card. Spurned men, even if they've only been spurned in their own mind, can be incredibly dangerous. York might look nothing like Lyndon, but they could have everything in common.

Had. They could have had everything in common. Lyndon is dead. Yet I'm living in fear, déjà vu all over again.

I'd been feeling so good about getting to be on the couch today with Scott and Trish, trying to empower women and convince them that they're in charge of their own lives. Is that why I received the flowers now? Is someone trying to throw me off before the segment, just like they left that note when I was cohosting for the first time?

Maybe this isn't about insanity at all. Maybe all this has been entirely strategic.

I burst into the hallway and found Janelle. "Is Trish here?" Sandy had griped that Trish was getting to the set later and later recently, that it was making Sandy's job harder. If Trish was early today, that would be a pretty big coincidence.

"She's here," Janelle said, "in her dressing room."

Trish could have left the note for me to find during the cooking segment. She wasn't there that day, but she could have done it the day before, or put someone else up to it. Trish could easily get my phone number. She's the person most threatened by me. My ascension could be her downfall, and I'm clearly on the rise.

Yes, it all makes sense. Trish has the motive, means, and opportunity.

Only it's backfired. I'm turning into America's sweetheart, and Trish is receding into irrelevance. She's getting what she deserves.

I'm not in any real danger after all, and I was about to give the best performance of my life on that couch with Scott and Trish. Like Val said, use the adrenaline. Anger is motivation too.

After Conrad did the weather and sent it back to me in the studio, my news reading was flawless. By the time I was on the couch with Trish and Scott, I was raring to go.

They were a tag team, alternating their questions for me. Trish stumbled a few times, her smile wobbly, and there was something about her manner, and her breath.

Trish had been drinking.

She really was unraveling, which could explain a lot but doesn't excuse anything.

Inside, I was calm, and ice-cold. Outwardly, I was projecting just what I needed to, confidence touched with vulnerability. "It can be scary, being a female," I said, "but women have a lot more power than they realize."

Once the segment had ended, I lingered on the couch an extra second. Scott gave me a high five. "Way to go, Sam!" he said. I thanked him, but my real focus was Trish, who was averting her eyes. More proof.

Trish started to get up, and I put a hand on her arm. She looked over in surprise, and perhaps a little fear. I liked thinking it was fear. She deserves a taste of her own medicine.

"I get it," I said softly. "I've figured it out."

Trish pulled her arm away. "I don't know what you're talking about."

"If you don't, then I apologize. If you do, then you're going to hell." Oh, she knew all right. She's not a very good actress.

Yes, it could be dangerous to put the coanchor on notice. But I'm a rising star, and Trish is on her way down, and out.

That was a twist I hadn't seen coming. I hadn't expected Elyse to turn into some kind of badass.

I still don't know who R.G. is, but B.N. has been easy enough to find.

When I check Wikipedia, there's nothing new from R.G. (or from his impersonator). But I have a feeling Elyse and I haven't seen the last of him.

CHAPTER 32

I t wasn't easy, getting myself to work today. But Graham kept texting and then Edwin joined in, and I wasn't making headway on any of the mysteries (not Elyse's, or Beth's, or my own). Hiding out at my apartment offers the illusion of safety, but if I truly want to protect myself, I have to go back and put a stop to this, whatever this is.

I jump at the knock on my office door. "Who is it?" I call, hoping I sound more grounded than I feel. I've given Reese some bullshit tasks to do just to keep her out and about. She's a reporter at heart, and I don't want to answer any questions right now.

"It's your humble foot servant." It's Albie, and he's decided to try stand-up comedy.

"Come in."

He shuts the door behind him, leaving Officer Mortimer in the hallway. Tongue-tied Officer Mortimer, who looks nineteen and flushes every time I speak to him.

"What's my next assignment?" I ask Albie.

"Just keep studying."

"So I don't have any appearances scheduled on any other shows?"

"Correct."

"Am I being punished?"

"Not that anyone's told me." Hardly the most reassuring answer.

"Could I stay under contract here at INN for the whole three years with them giving me nothing to do?" Being sidelined, like Beth said. But that was only supposed to happen if I refused the story or screwed it up. That's not how it went, and yet I'm still benched.

"You'd have to ask Edwin about that."

As in, Edwin has the power to do whatever he wants. "Now's when people are interested in me. By the time I'm a free agent in three years, no one will want me."

He nods.

It's infuriating. I'm not even sure I want this career, but I don't deserve to have it snatched away. I'm actually good.

"So I need to suck up to Edwin," I say.

"Among others."

Graham, is that what Albie's saying? I need to make nice with the man who sexually assaulted me?

I'm glaring at Albie, though it's not his fault. He doesn't know what Graham did to me.

Probably doesn't know.

He stands up. "I'll tell you as soon as the situation changes. In the meantime, do your homework."

Does he mean I should keep studying the curriculum, or does he mean my homework is to make it up to Edwin and Graham?

Wait, if my apartment is bugged and my phone definitely is, then my office could be too. "You're right," I say. "It was my fault."

"That's not what I—"

"No, I could have done more. I *will* do more. I'm going to make you all proud of me. You believed in me, all of you, and I let you down. It's not going to happen again."

Albie seems distinctly uncomfortable with my sudden change of heart. "Well," he says, "we'll talk soon."

Play the part, that's what Beth told me. Use their perceptions against them. They think they're so much smarter than I am, so I can feed that, and feed their egos. It's time to channel Elyse.

I might as well face what I've been dreading head on. Get out in front of it, so there's no element of surprise. No bumping into him in the hallway or having him pop into my office unannounced.

I call Graham's office and ask if he has a minute. "I'll be right up," he says.

He is, in record time, like he has his own private elevator. He's slightly out of breath.

As I watch him close the door behind him, even though I know Officer Mortimer is just outside, that this time, someone will hear me if I scream, my body remembers the other night. It remembers Graham's fury, and his threat, and his fingers, and his breath. It remembers being told that people only hear what they want to hear, and no one wants to hear me.

No, he's wrong. The world is changing. Think about Harvey Weinstein, Kevin Spacey, Matt Lauer, Louis C.K., all the producers and entertainers and broadcasters and politicians and moguls brought low.

But in those cases, there were multiple accusers, strength in numbers. Right now, I'm all alone.

My stomach's clenched, my limbs have gone cold, and my respiration has shallowed. I remind myself that like Elyse learned in self-defense class, my body's preparing itself to fight or flee. I fought Graham the other night, and I'm going to keep fighting.

"Hi." I smile at him with faux warmth. "It's good to see you." I gesture toward the seat recently vacated by Albie.

As soon as he's across from me, he says, "I've been thinking a lot, Cheyenne. My feelings got the best of me the other night. I really like you. I thought that you liked me, and I just—it got out of hand."

So that's the narrative he's going with. It wasn't anger the other night, it was passion.

My breath is deepening; my arms and legs aren't as cold as they were. I just need to play my part. I can hate him later. I will hate him later. "I understand. I do sometimes send mixed signals."

His face practically liquefies with gratitude. "Sometimes I'm not great at reading women. I didn't get a lot of practice when I was younger." No shit. "Being where I am at INN, it can go to your head. I have to really work to stay grounded. I just want us to be friends again." That's how he treats his friends? I don't want to know how he treats enemies. "Could we do that?"

"Absolutely." I smile. "I would love to be your friend." *But I will never forget that you're my enemy.*

He smiles back. I've just absolved him. Or so he thinks. "I'll make sure I help you however I can. The Until story didn't have the legs we'd hoped, but you do. In more ways than one."

He is so vile. "I know it was my fault. The Until story. I couldn't carry it off. I let you, Ty, and Edwin down. But I'm going to do better."

He makes a move as if to place a comforting hand on me and then thinks better of it. Fortunately, he doesn't seem to see me flinch. "You will," he agrees. "You'll do better."

So the prick is actually agreeing that it's my fault. *He's* absolving me.

But I focus on the most salient point: he believes me. The apology tour has gotten off to a fine start. Graham, Edwin, Ty—the unholy trinity. I'll express remorse that I failed to deliver, I'll let the big men around me provide solace, and I'll vow to never disappoint them again, if they'll only give me another chance. I'll play the broken woman, a good soldier, and they can think that they've put me in my place, wherever it is they want me to be. I'm their Broadcast Barbie. I will thoroughly and completely snow them, so when the knife plunges into their backs, they'll never see it coming.

CHAPTER 33

August 14, 1991

Last night, B.N. found out that I'd met with R.G. He wasn't even mad, just sad, which made me feel terrible. He's such a good person, and sometimes I wonder if I am. I spend so much time thinking about myself, and what I want, and what I'm afraid of. I lose sight of people.

"You were in love with him," he said. "Are you, still?"

Our conversation was happening in the dark, as usual. That meant I had to control only my voice, not my face. "No, I don't love him anymore."

If I don't love him, why am I looking over my shoulder for him every time I'm on the street, both relieved and disappointed when I don't see him?

But I was telling the truth when I said, "I want you, B.N."

We'd been lying back to back, and I could feel B.N. rolling toward me, close but not touching. It was my move, and my chance to prove that I really am over R.G., to myself as much as to B.N.

I hadn't had a drop of alcohol, but I kissed him anyway. Tentatively at first, and then with abandon, like I'd been caged for years. His response was surprisingly swift. He yanked my shirt off and pulled down my sweats and underpants, rounding the bases as fast as he could. I would have expected him to be gentler, but it had been a long time for him too.

Then he was in just his boxers, and I hesitated. "I don't have a condom," I said. I hoped he didn't either.

No such luck. He fumbled in his wallet on the nightstand, pulling out a foil wrapper.

I got that old feeling. Two old feelings, actually: the first that I was losing contact with my own passion and desires, that I was hijacked by the worry that I wouldn't be what he—any he—wants. I thought maybe I could sneak out and have some vodka, and it would get me over the hump, so to speak.

The second feeling was about a different kind of spectator. It used to be Lyndon, though I know he's dead. What I don't know is if there's Someone Else. Not Lyndon, and not Trish. Just Someone. Always Someone.

"Are you okay?" B.N. asked.

I could feel what he wanted, and I wanted to give it to him. That's what you're supposed to do once you've worked a guy up to this state. "No, you go ahead."

"Did I do something wrong?"

"It's not you, it's me."

"Are we already breaking up? We never even got together, exactly." His joke fell flat.

"I'm kind of scarred by everything that happened. With Lyndon, and whoever else."

"Like R.G."

I had the impulse to defend R.G. and our relationship, to pretend we never had any problems other than the stalking, but that would be a lie, and it only hurts me to tell it. In moments like this, R.G. never stopped to see how I was. He never cared whether I really wanted him, and I learned not to care either.

"R.G. too," I said.

"Let's wait for a better time, then. There's no rush. You didn't say no tonight, but I want you to say yes."

Somehow, we were okay. He made it okay. We even managed to fall asleep, his arm loosely around my waist.

Then today, after the show, I was looking across at him as the staff gathered on-set for the meeting Dennis had called. I watched him push his glasses up his nose, thinking that's the man who'll be in my bed tonight, who I want in my bed, who'll wait until it's right. I started to smile.

Then I realized: Trish was the only person who wasn't there. She'd raced out of the studio the second the show ended. Even Scott and Conrad were in attendance.

Dennis said, "I'll get right to the point. Trish will be leaving us. It's for personal reasons that she prefers not to disclose."

Everyone looked shocked, even Conrad. Only Scott was taking it in stride.

Dennis told us that Friday is her final show—as in, two days away. He talked about putting together a tribute montage, bearing in mind what kind of send-off would help the viewer get ready for the new coanchor.

He didn't say who that would be, and my mind was whirling as the meeting concluded. Dennis gestured for me to come over and told me we'd meet in his office in twenty minutes.

In the elevator, I was light-headed. I want this, yes, but am I really ready for it? I've anchored before, but that was a half-hour broadcast in a small market. This is <u>Morning Sunrise</u>. "Have a seat." He gestured, unsmiling, toward the black chair across from his. His manner was arctic. "I've been debating between a series of guest hosts and letting you have the spot—temporarily, as a tryout. The 'Safety First!' segments are performing well, but that doesn't mean viewers want to spend two hours with you every weekday morning."

"I will devote every waking hour to this job," I said.

"If you give me this chance, I won't let you down. I promise you that."

He narrowed his eyes. "You'll have a week's tryout. After that, we either extend, or we bring in guest hosts."

"I just want you to know, I'm not going to give you any trouble. If you promote me, if you let me have this opportunity, I wouldn't even need a raise. I'd stay at my newsreader salary."

"This isn't a financial decision." His lip curled. "You heard that Trish gave me trouble?"

"No, no"—I was stumbling over my words—"I didn't mean anything by it."

"We don't have much time to get ready for your debut. I want you here every day, every night, prepping."

"Of course. Thank you so much, Dennis."

"Get a good night's sleep. Tomorrow, it all begins." He put on a pair of reading glasses and looked down at a sheaf of papers on his desk. It was my cue to leave.

"Thank you so much! See you tomorrow!" Too perky. Not even Katie Couric could have pulled that off and sounded genuine.

As I was about to open the door, he said, "B.N.? That's the best you could do?"

I pretended not to hear.

Down on the lower floor, I gathered my things, talking to no one. I was shaken up. It's just an audition, not a job offer, and now I have to win Dennis back. I'd wanted him to know about B.N., but now it seems like a miscalculation that could have cost me a permanent contract.

I looked over at B.N., and he gave me this smile, like we're in it together, but really, I might need to be on my own.

I can't blow this for a romance that might not go anywhere. Men always say they'll stand by you. R.G. did, once upon a time. He said the same thing a few days ago. Now where is he?

The rumor mill has already started: management is reaching out to a number of high-profile women, including Connie Chung, though they're not sure if America is ready to wake up to an ethnic woman. If it's true, it might not matter how well I perform next week. Depending on who's available, I might be forced to step aside. If it's not Connie Chung, it could be a blonde with a higher profile and a better rack.

I hurried home, not even saying goodbye to B.N.

I just wanted Dennis to leave me alone. Now I might have gotten my wish.

On Monday, though, I get my shot. If the viewers respond to me the way they've responded to my safety segments, Dennis will have to hire me, regardless of his personal feelings. I'll make it so that if he doesn't offer me the job, he'll have to do some explaining to his bosses. He does have a few. That job is meant to be mine. I've suffered for it.

When I got home, I felt like I'd run a marathon. No, a gauntlet. Yet it hasn't even begun.

I was famished. I went into the kitchen and opened the refrigerator to find that the food on every shelf had been rearranged. I hadn't told the People writer that Lyndon used to do that. But Someone Else knows.

If I called the police and said there had been an intruder, there's no way they'd take me seriously. They'd think I'd rearranged my own refrigerator and forgotten about it; they'd accuse me of sleepwalking.

Police can always find an explanation to keep them from having to do their jobs. They'd laugh about me later. Worse, they might leak to the _Star_ or the _Enquirer_: "Morning Anchor Cracks Up!"

There's nothing funny about it. Someone wants me to know they've been here, that they can get to me in my own home, and that they know everything from my past.

Trish is already out of a job, so the only reason she would do something like this is in retaliation. But how would she know about Lyndon's condiment trick? Also, she's a celebrity. If she came into my building, someone would recognize her.

R.G. knew. For the first time, I'm the one who rejected him. Could he be so angry that he'd terrorize me? I wouldn't think he'd do that, but then, I never thought he'd leave me on the courthouse steps.

B.N. knows about the condiments. I've told him everything, and he has my spare key. But he would never try to frighten me like this. Unless he's angry about R.G. . . . ?

I'm talking crazy. Writing crazy.

Maybe B.N. let some of my history slip to someone

else on the show, someone who's angry that Trish was shafted and blames me.

Or it's Someone Else completely. A viewer I've never met. A fan. An autograph seeker. Anyone on the street.

I'm not safe. I'm never, ever going to be safe.

CHAPTER 34

You think you can fuck your way to the top?
Just see where you wind up.

'm in my chair, stunned, when Reese comes back with lunch. Seeing my expression, she rushes to my side. "What is it? Are you okay?"

I hold out the note. It was left on my desk while I went to the restroom, meaning someone was watching me. Waiting for their moment to strike. Officer Mortimer is still supposed to escort me to and from INN in the morning and at night, but his duty outside my office was a one-day affair. I don't really understand the NYPD's danger determination. It could be based on my social media, which is calming down. They have no way of knowing that within the network, everything's ratcheting up. Unless the police are in on the conspiracy too. How else could they have absolutely no leads on Beth?

Reese is scoffing as she takes the note from my hand. "Don't let this get to you. It's juvenile. Worse, it's banal. This is just what females do to other females who are more successful than them. You have nothing to worry about."

Nothing to worry about? Beth is missing. Graham attacked me. There's a possibility that someone shoved me into oncoming traffic. I'm still getting anonymous diary entries, and I'm no closer to figuring out whether they're from a friend or a foe.

"Every bully's a coward, right?" Reese says. "Your dad tweeted that."

"I know you're trying to make me feel better, but I'm really scared." With the office potentially being surveilled, it's okay to say that. If Edwin knows I'm scared, he'll think I'm more likely to get in line. To do what I'm told.

If my office is being surveilled, then there's evidence of who left the note. I just need to get that video.

"I have an idea," Reese says. "Let's go away this weekend." She pulls out her phone and begins texting. After less than a minute, she looks up triumphantly. "I've got us a place that's totally secure. It's basically a compound in the Hamptons. You couldn't be safer, really. Plus, it's gorgeous."

I don't have to work this weekend, and I've never been to the Hamptons. I've been fantasizing about going to Montana, of standing at the arrivals terminal and seeing Dad coming toward me in his dingy Ford pickup, so old that it has bench seats always covered in potato chip sediment. The idea of just curling up and watching a movie with him at home in Tulip is almost too wonderful to contemplate. But it's just a pipe dream. I can't let him see me like this, and I don't know if my presence would put him in danger.

I nod, and Reese claps. I wish I could feel that type of excitement. My emotional repertoire has narrowed drastically of late. Maybe the Hamptons can widen it.

LATER THAT AFTERNOON, Edwin summons me to his office. It's jarring, having him smile and hand me a lime rickey as if nothing's changed. "How are you, Cheyenne?"

"I'm okay."

"I know you were close to Beth. This can't be easy for you. Her going missing, and now all the questions about her identity."

"What do you know, Edwin?"

He shakes his head slowly. "No one knows who she is or where she is."

"You didn't do a background check when you hired her? You've been so thorough about mine."

"She'd been in the business so long. Since September eleventh. I felt like she'd been vetted by the industry. But I have to tell you honestly, if she shows up again, she won't have a job. This is news. Her credibility will always be in question." He looks into my eyes. "I'm scouting for her replacement."

So all the sucking up has worked. I'm back in his good graces. He might hand me a show. Beth's show. This isn't how I want to get ahead.

"Beth thought so highly of you," he says.

Thought. As in, she is no more. But then, anyone might assume that by now. "I think highly of her too."

"I know you're loyal. I saw how you struggled with the Chase situation. But you need to realize, it's business. It's not a betrayal. You didn't do this. She did."

"She did what?" Edwin might know why Beth was crying the last time I saw her. He might be the reason.

"She fabricated her whole life. I hope she's okay, I really do, but when it comes to news, she dug her own grave." At least he has the decency to seem disturbed by the phrase now that he's

298 ■ HOLLY BROWN

uttered it. We're both quiet for a few beats. "A lot is still up in the air. But I wanted to feel you out, see if you want your hat in the ring."

I want to say no out of basic human decency, but as with the Until story, someone's going to get the opportunity. It could be someone with murky motives, like Ty, instead of someone with integrity, like Khalif. If it were me, I'd get to shape content. I'd be running pitch meetings and having a say. With a platform like *Truthiness*, I could have a significant positive impact.

But I'd be getting in deeper when I don't even know what's going on at this network. When I can no longer trust Edwin.

There, I finally admitted it.

It's hard, though, when he's sitting there looking so sincere and so caring. "I'm committed to you, Cheyenne," he says. "I combed the entire country, the entire cyberworld, for the right girl. The one I could take from obscurity and turn into a broadcast superstar. I still think you're the one."

The right girl. Not the right woman.

That's what this has been about all along. His ego. Maybe the rumor Chase told me was true, and INN was just a dare. I could be a bet.

I'm Edwin's creation, a reflection of him. That's why he was so angry the other day. My failures are his, even when I haven't failed. The president of the United States had to answer questions based on my series, but it wasn't enough. Edwin can't accept half success.

He owns me. I finally read the contract that proves it.

"What do you think, Cheyenne? Do you want to be considered for the job?"

The contract talked about reassignments. But this doesn't sound like an order. It sounds like a question, with only one acceptable answer. Which pretty much makes it an order. "Yes."

He smiles. "Good. I'm proud of you, thinking about your career."

"Being ruthless."

He takes a sip of his drink. "I prefer ambitious."

But whose ambitions are they, really?

CHAPTER 35

Another day, another courier delivery. I open the envelope along with the bottle of Patrón that Reese left the other night, and I say my usual prayer: *Please be from Beth.*

Or should I say Trish?

I'm not sure why more people haven't figured it out, or why I hadn't thought to look up photos of Trish sooner. From what I can tell, she didn't get any plastic surgery. She just waited long enough, ten years, to reemerge from hiding after everything went down. Green-colored contacts, darkened hair, some extra pounds, a new name, and a great reel of interviews from the 9/11 first responders, and she was off and running.

Has she been sending me the diary because she wanted me to figure it out? Is she still sending it from wherever she's hiding? Or could it be from whoever might have harmed her?

If I want to know how I fit into someone else's plan, I have no choice but to keep reading.

August 21, 1991

I've been plenty scared in my life, but I don't know that I've ever been THIS scared.

I don't eat. I've already lost weight, and the wardrobe department has to trade their size 2 for a size 0. I don't sleep. B.N. is still in my bed each night, alone, like right now. I haven't heard anything from R.G. It's a little insulting, really, for him to declare that he's not giving up, he loves me too much for that, and then for him to disappear. It shouldn't hurt, since I already knew I couldn't count on him, since I don't even want to count on him.

But why am I thinking, and writing, about R.G.? I've got a lot more important things on my mind.

It was after the show. My third. They've all gone so well, and the ratings are rising by the day. I would have thought I was a shoo-in except that Dennis hasn't said anything to me. Not one word.

Tom Shales wants me made permanent, and Scott said he does too. But then he added, "I don't know why the network's even talking to anyone else. You were born for this."

"Connie Chung?" I asked.

He shrugged. "To be honest, I'm not as in the loop as I was, now that my contract has been finalized."

So he hadn't used his clout to fight for me and isn't planning to. I felt a little bruised by that, but it was nothing compared to what was waiting for me in my dressing room. Across the white wall, in red spray paint:

I WILL KILL YOU, BITCH

I started screaming.

Janelle was the first in, with B.N. right behind her. He was holding me up, saying over and over, "It's okay. I'm here. It's okay."

"I'll call the police," Janelle said, leaving the room.

"The police will have to take you seriously now." B.N. meant that to be reassuring. But if the police get involved, that could overshadow everything I'm doing on the air. It would become news. Would Dennis like that, this time around, or would he feel like I'm more trouble than I'm worth?

Dennis showed up and pretended to care, but I could see how he looked at B.N., like some kind of bug. And the way he looked at me wasn't much better.

It can't be Trish. There's no way she just waltzed into the studio with a can of spray paint.

The police detectives promised a full investigation. They'll question everyone in the studio and do inquiries throughout the building; they'll examine all the security footage. But it's too late. It's not going to matter. Someone's coming for me, and the police can't help. Self-defense classes can't help.

I know my fate. It's been spelled out, in blood.

CHAPTER 36

I keep seeing those letters too. In lipstick, in blood, superimposed over Graham's face. I see a hand shoving me into
the street, and Beth's arm shooting out to bring me back. A
threatening note. Fingers up my dress. Hate groups coalescing.
A show that could be mine. A chess wizard of a boss.

I'm trying to leave it all behind for the weekend, because
Reese made good on her promise. We're about to be locked
down in a beautiful bunker in the Hamptons. But I'm still on
edge. Can you be a little bit stalked, or is that like a little bit
pregnant? Like Elyse said, just because no one is announcing
themselves doesn't mean no one's there.

Reese and I leave the city in a black Lincoln Navigator with
tinted windows, and its driver looks kind of like The Tank,
intimidating, ready for anything. He only speaks when spoken
to. There's a closed partition between the front and back, so
even as large as our driver is, he becomes unobtrusive quickly.

I'm surprised when Reese tells me that the house—and the
Lincoln Navigator, and its driver—belong to Pietro. "I ran into

him the next week," she says. "Another lounge, another VIP room. He's a great guy."

"Isn't he kind of old to do so much clubbing?"

Reese shrugs. "I like older guys. Don't you?" It's the first time she's even obliquely referenced the feelings that I have for Edwin. Used to have for him.

"No," I say, "I don't."

"Would you want to hook up with Pietro?" Reese says. "He's clearly really into you. And you're single now."

"I thought you wanted to hook up with Pietro."

"I did, but then once I saw how he acted with you and how he talks about you, I lost interest. I don't want anyone who doesn't want me."

Could've fooled me, that first night.

"But he won't be here this weekend. He's just giving us the house."

"After meeting you twice?"

"The funny thing about the really rich is that they're the most trusting. Besides, he knows where to find you. You're on TV. What are you going to do, trash his house like a rock star? I said we needed some girl time. Some R & R."

Just the ride does me good. The city seems a million miles away from Long Island. We drive through a steel gate and then behold the house itself. The manse, as Reese calls it. It's a massive Colonial, ten bedrooms, overlooking a private beach, with an incredibly high-tech security system. Reese knows all the codes, though she says she's never been here before, has only seen the pictures. The pool is Olympic-sized, surrounded by lounge chairs and three separate grill areas, the Atlantic as a shimmering backdrop. All the furniture in the entire house is white, or whitewashed, with pale furniture in beechwood.

I tell Reese I'm unplugging from everything, and when she does check feeds, to do it out of my sight. She can give me information on Beth. Beyond that, I don't want any news at all.

I can't entirely relax, but this is as close as I'm going to get. We're drinking vodka tonics as we alternate between chlorinated water and ocean, traipsing back and forth like a couple of mermaids. I haven't told Reese about the diary. I know, based on the dates I've cross-referenced with Wikipedia, that it must be close to the end, but I'm less than eager to get there. Being away means that I won't have to, not this weekend. I've grown attached to Elyse, and I'm starting to have that "don't go in there" feeling you get in horror movies, though I know the futility. She can't hear me scream.

That makes me think of Graham, and the bathroom. I tense up and have to work to remind myself that I'm safe, for the moment.

I grab a novel from Pietro's library. For a real estate magnate, he's got quite a collection of classics. Since it's pretty much the only color in the room, the decorator must have earned her money curating books. I'm only too happy to immerse myself in the much more distant past.

For dinner, we make a caprese salad with fresh heirloom tomatoes, mozzarella, and basil. More vodka tonics. Reese dares me to go skinny dipping. We do, running back and forth from the ocean to the pool to the hot tub, laughing like kids. Then we drink champagne out of crystal flutes as we float on rafts in the pool. I forget I'm naked, forget that there's any other state in which to exist. It's the first perfect moment I've had since this whole adventure started. The sun is setting, and Reese and I have our longest conversation of the weekend, trading anecdotes about where we grew up, what we meant to be, and how close we've come to those visions.

"I used to report live from the kitchen when I was six years old," Reese says.

"So you're sure you want to be in front of the camera."

"Completely sure."

"Even after seeing my 'fan' mail and my feeds? Are you ready to be threatened with every implement in the kitchen and tool in the shed?" Those aren't even the most pressing threats; they're practically hypothetical compared to what's INN-side.

I must be really drunk if I'm making puns like that. But I didn't say it out loud. At least, I'm pretty sure I didn't.

"That's just what fame is now," Reese says.

"To tell you the truth," I say, draining the last of my champagne, "I don't think I want it enough."

"How can you not want what you're so good at? What you work so hard to be good at?"

"Serena Williams said she hates to lose more than she loves to win. I think that describes me these days."

I used to want a mission. I wanted to help the country. I wanted independence. It's hard to believe that not even two months ago, I could have been so naive. Now I'm just trying not to lose.

"See, I love to win," Reese says. "And I'm going to."

I laugh, but it's serrated. "A natural optimist. You sound like Elyse."

"Like who?"

I'm debating whether to answer that question when what looks like a searchlight starts roaming the pool area. I leap off the raft, stroking toward the side of the pool with one arm, the other across my breasts. Reese, using two arms, is much quicker, halfway to the house already. I want to grab a towel to cover myself, but I can't take the time to find it. Instead, I run into the house, heart pounding, like I've just been through an air raid. I turn off the floodlights outside and the lights inside.

In the darkness, I can't see Reese's face, but I can hear that she's breathing as heavily as I am.

"What the hell was that?" I say.

"I don't know. Security, maybe?"

"Didn't Pietro tell them that we're here?" I'm trying to cover myself with the white drapes, but it's too late. I've already been exposed.

Again.

CHAPTER 37

When I get home at three A.M., I'm not surprised by what's waiting for me. I am surprised that I tear into it, like I'm starving.

August 22, 1991

I got it. I got the job. And I don't even care.

Whether I stay in front of the camera or not, someone's coming for me. They're going to kill me. I can feel it. I just know.

I could barely hold it together as Dennis sat there behind his enormous black desk in his enormous black chair in his enormous windowed office, lecturing me. Telling me that while some advertisers like the idea of a demographic of younger career women, he needs an anchor who can hold on to their bread and butter, the housewives.

"Then there's the vandalism in your dressing room. I let the police know they better be discreet, but it'll get out. It'll be a distraction. 'Safety First!' was one thing, but having your victimization be the whole focus of Morning Sunrise is something else."

I couldn't believe it. He was actually blaming me for getting a death threat.

I almost walked out right then. But I've worked so hard. I'm just so fucking deserving.

"So far," he said, "the ratings are good. The audience seems to be responding to you. What I worry about, though, is that they could change their minds. They could start to see through you."

"Excuse me?"

"They could start to see in you what I do. That you're a manipulative whore."

It took all I had not to storm out. But the fact is, I still want this. I'm so close I can taste it. Once I'm a household name, I can take care of him.

"Don't give me that look," he said. "You know exactly what I'm talking about."

"I'm sorry but, no, I really don't."

"That night at your apartment. I told you how I really felt, and I thought you'd done the same. Then it turned out you were using me, feeding me that stalker story."

"I think you know very well that it's no story." I was fighting to keep my voice even. "That night at my apartment, I was telling you about the worst thing that's ever happened to me. I lived in fear. I'm still living in fear."

"That night at your apartment, I opened up to you, Elyse, and you didn't care."

"What do you mean, I didn't care?"

"You led me on."

Oh, if I'd cared, I would have slept with him by now. He thinks I promised him something and didn't deliver. He's hurt, and now he has the chance to hurt me back, to take away something that should rightfully be mine.

Tears were running down my face.

He slammed his hand down on the desk. "Do not cry your crocodile tears in my office!" he thundered.

I was glad his secretary was out in the hall. If I hadn't known better, I'd think he was about to hit me.

I didn't speak, didn't move. I had to let it blow over, let his anger flame out.

"So if you want the job," he said, his voice more controlled now, "it's yours. I can offer you a year contract. Shorter than that, it's too much uncertainty for the viewers. But I don't want to go longer than that for, well, obvious reasons." He slid a folder across the desk. "That's our best and final offer. Don't bring some hotshot in here and try to negotiate. I have big names that are more than happy to take your place if you get any delusions of grandeur."

I took the folder. "Thank you," I whispered. My legs could barely carry me out.

He shouldn't be allowed to get away with what he just did; he should lose his job for that.

But who would I report him to? Human Resources? The head of the network? If I did report him, if I tried to take him on, I'd be finished at _Morning Sunrise_ before I'd even really begun. It could put the kibosh on my whole broadcasting career. I'd be a troublemaker. Damaged goods. A liability.

I could go back to _People_ and see if they're interested in a follow-up. Tell them what he just did. Take the story public and see if that would provide a measure of protection.

No, it would never work. Women are hard on one another. They'll remember _A Current Affair_. They'll decide I put myself in this position, that I tried to use my looks and sexuality for professional gain and it backfired. They'll hold my ambition against me.

But can I work under a vindictive man who seemingly hates me? Who drove my predecessor to drink, and then drove her out?

It's the decision of my life, and I have to make it with a gun to my head—not just Dennis's, but someone else's.

I see those lipstick red letters in my mind, all the time:

I WILL KILL YOU, BITCH.

CHAPTER 38

Different time period, same accusations: Manipulator. Whore.

How far we've come.

I learn soon enough what really happened in the Hamptons. TMZ sent a helicopter that recorded footage of Reese and me in the pool naked. Of course the wily folks at TMZ knew whose house it was, though they didn't see fit to mention that Pietro wasn't actually there. Instead, they intimated that the newest INN superstar had destroyed her longtime boyfriend's life and then celebrated by having an orgy with her assistant and a wealthy playboy developer while a beloved anchor remained missing.

I'm avoiding even reading the social media. Reese is going to handle all the "fans." If there's anything threatening enough, Officer Mortimer will be posted outside my door.

The staff of Beth's show won't look at me at all. It feels like everyone else is staring: the women (and some men) with expressions of mockery, mirth, or judgment; other men (not just

Luke anymore) with a hint of a leer. I keep expecting some dude to ask me if I want to go party, like I'm in high school again. I guess I should feel grateful that it's taken so long for me to get those kinds of looks. It's not like it's the first time they're seeing me naked.

But somehow, it's different, worse, to have it be a video. To have it be contemporary. To have it happen again, when I thought it couldn't because there were no more photos to find. I would never take and send those kinds of pictures to anyone, ever again, but they still managed to get me. I wasn't smart enough.

Last time, my photos were stolen. My dignity was stolen. My right to make the rules when it comes to my own body, to decide who has access, was stolen. And they just keep right on taking.

I haven't seen Graham yet. He might think this gives him even more license than he already had. Any of them might feel that way. I'm surrounded by Someone Else.

Edwin's in his office, and when he opens the door, his face is as closed off as I've ever seen it. I wonder if he's reached the same conclusion that Dennis did about Elyse. I wonder if he—and INN—will want to cut ties and if all this is about to come to an end.

A small part of me would welcome a firing. Then I could walk away without feeling like a quitter. I could be (more or less) safe again. Sure, my internet footprint would dog me forever, but if I get a job in some unassuming industry, far from the spotlight, no one would care. I could stay quiet, and eventually I'll be forgotten.

The only problem is, I'm actually good at this. As Elyse said, I'm just so fucking deserving.

Edwin steps away from the door wordlessly, and I follow him inside, taking a seat on the couch without waiting to be asked. He remains standing, his arms crossed.

Elyse had *A Current Affair*; I have TMZ (again). Elyse's brush with tabloid fame worked in her favor, as she then sat in for Trish. I need to take a page from Elyse's playbook (again) and turn this to my advantage. Sure, I'm humiliated, but this will not break me.

Not again.

"So you saw it?" I ask, not even needing to specify what "it" is. Edwin does the slightest of nods. "The truth is—"

"No one cares about truth, Cheyenne. You haven't noticed that by now?"

"I don't believe that. I think you really do care." He doesn't disagree, so I rush on. "Pietro wasn't even there. Reese got him to loan us the house. We were just a couple of girls having fun, playing in the pool. She's my friend, nothing more. I'm not like that."

"All girls your age are like that."

I can feel his contempt, but something else too. Jealousy. So it wasn't a fluke, the way he behaved during that Chase conversation. If Reese is right, if Edwin really does have feelings for me, that could be the biggest advantage of all. "I'm not like that," I repeat.

"You realize that according to your contract, I could fire you for this. You're representing my brand. You're representing INN."

"I didn't know a helicopter was going to swoop in. You think I wanted this to happen?"

"I don't know. Some people get addicted to fame."

"That's not me. I hate this. I hate that it's happening again."

I will not cry. "I'm trying so hard to become a real broadcaster, someone people will respect. When I made the video that went viral, when I made all my videos, it was because I wanted to show everyone at Stanford that I have a brain. That I care about issues. Then someone hacked my phone and my pictures got out—"

"I know all this." But he sounds less steely than he did. My vulnerability is eating at him. That means he has empathy, maybe even a conscience. At the very least, it confirms his feelings for me.

"Is there some kind of damage control INN can do now? Anything legal, maybe? I had the expectation of privacy. I was inside what's basically a compound."

He shakes his head. "We go after TMZ and we're just calling more attention to the footage. That benefits them, not us."

I'm glad he said "us." I look at him imploringly. Men love a damsel in distress. "What can we do then?"

He scans my face slowly, and while his gaze is far from entirely professional, he has to be thinking that if I fail, he does too. I'm his creation, his reflection. He wants to fall in love with me, like Narcissus.

But he might be getting pressure from someone (Daphne?) to cut me loose. My series didn't do what they'd hoped, and now I've been filmed in a way that only diminishes my credibility further.

I can exert pressure too. I stand up and walk toward him, not stopping until we're less than a foot away from each other. I feel him catch his breath. I feel my power.

"Look at me, Edwin, please. You know I'm not like that." He's having trouble meeting my eyes, and I have the distinct impression he's turned on. If it were even a week earlier, I might have been, too, being in his space like this. In his orbit. But it's not last week, and this is a means to an end. "I don't blame you for being upset, but please don't fire me. I want to make you proud. I've always wanted that."

"I just don't know, Cheyenne." He takes a step backward and runs his hand through his hair. It's like he can't think when he's that close to me. I'm scrambling him. Good.

"Please, Edwin. You saw something in me, and it's still there. You can feel it, right?" He's clearly struggling with himself. Good. "I'm begging you. Don't cut me now. There's so much we can still do together."

He searches my face. I hold his gaze.

It scares me a little that I can act this way. That I can snow someone so convincingly, so ruthlessly.

But he did it first.

"I'm begging you," I say. "Let me turn this into something positive, for us."

"What do you mean?"

"Let me anchor Beth's show tonight. The audience needs to see me in a fuller way, like they did when you first introduced me, when I talked about cyberbullying and about Tulip. That was the real me. I'm not some topless nymph in a millionaire's mansion."

He's considering. "So what's your plan?"

It's kind of cool, having Edwin ask me that, instead of the other way around. "We could make it a riff against fake news—those other networks' fake news, since CNN and MSNBC and Fox have run with TMZ's footage. It's just high-end cyber-bullying. We can say we know people care about the truth, which is that I've been under extreme stress with Beth missing and being a new correspondent and being a small-town girl handed this huge opportunity. Then I do the rest of the show, and I promise you, I'll kill it."

My pitch was carefully crafted. I know he wants to take a stab at those other networks, the ones who didn't hold the president's feet to the fire, who left INN out in the cold. He wants to call them out for their spineless hypocrisy, for letting go of the major story and then treating my naked body like it's news.

But he isn't speaking. So I take a risk. "Graham could write it with me."

"You want Graham?" His voice is hard. He's still jealous, only with a new object. Good.

"He's the best writer here, and I need to connect with the public. We can transform this TMZ thing into a win."

He fixes me with another stare. "You really want to stay at INN?"

"Of course." What I know is that I don't want to retreat like I did after the naked pictures. And I don't want to be fired. If I'm leaving, it should be with a golden parachute like Megyn Kelly's. Or a settlement like Gretchen Carlson's.

"I have some terms," he says. "Any time you're in public, you've got your clothes and your game face on. You don't give the media anything they can use against you." I nod. "We're going to start your media training soon, and you do what you're told." Another nod. "There are some benefit dinners coming up that I want you to attend. We've bought tables, and we need to do some strategic seating where you're next to heads of corporations—the ones with shiny reputations, eco and all that shit—and you're going to schmooze within an inch of your life. We're going to use this new perception of availability. You're good at that, right?"

I'm pretty sure he's referring to that last conversation I had with Chase where he accused me of getting higher grades through the appearance of availability. Isn't that how he phrased it? I can't exactly remember. But I know he called me a cocktease, and Graham quoted him. So Graham and Edwin were both listening in, or Graham told Edwin what he needed to know. My weaknesses, my vulnerabilities. How best to control me.

I nod, a good little girl who won't step out of line, who'll follow instructions to the letter. I'm Elyse, preattack.

"You flirt, you talk up INN, you get them to consider underwriting a broadcast." He gives me a meaningful look. "Maybe your broadcast."

So despite TMZ, I'm still in contention for Beth's show. "I can do that."

"I'll be the one to talk to Graham and see about him writing a script for you."

"I need to be involved with the script, at least a little. You know, for authenticity." I'm going to be a source on my own life this time.

"We'll see," is all he'll give me. Then he asks, "Who do you think tipped off TMZ?"

I just assumed they had their ways, their spies, their tracking devices, something. "I don't know."

"Take a guess."

"Pietro, maybe." It's the opposite of what he said in that VIP room, but then, you can't trust people who proclaim their trustworthiness. "Or it could have been his driver, who took us out there."

"Or it could be the more obvious suspect."

He must mean Reese. "You're the one who hired her."

"Even I make mistakes." His smile is grim.

He said I couldn't trust Beth; now he's saying I can't trust Reese. Could he be telling the truth this time? Or will Reese be the next to disappear?

Finally I say, "I'll go back to work and await my marching orders."

Reese is in my office. "So how did it go?" she asks eagerly.

Too eagerly.

It's strange that in all the time Reese has supposedly had her ear to the ground, she's delivered no real data. She's also managed to miss key moments, like when that note was left in my office. Yet when the teleprompter was erased, Reese was there. When TMZ sent the helicopter, Reese was there.

"It went fine," I say.

"This is all going to blow over. You have nothing to worry about."

I'm not just waiting for it to blow over, I'm capitalizing on it. But I'm not going to tell Reese that.

I'm not going to describe the humiliation of throwing myself on Edwin's mercy, of using my feminine wiles to stay in the running for a job that I shouldn't even want. Maybe I need to be fired. To be saved from INN, and from myself. Saved from the manipulator I'm becoming.

My competitive spirit has been engaged since coming to INN in a way it never was before, and like I told Reese, I hate to lose. If they sack me after all they've done to me, if I'm the one who leaves in disgrace, then they win. I can't have that. I want to write my own ticket and take them down. Let them see how it feels to be humiliated.

Reese can't know any of that. Because Reese most certainly knows what she wants; she's known since she was six years old.

It's possible that she's here to undermine me and steal the

correspondent job. It would make sense, wouldn't it? Reese could have been setting me up this whole time. Means, motive, and opportunity, as Elyse said about Trish.

But is Reese working for herself, or is she working for someone else? Is she a source for Graham and Edwin? She has a key to my apartment. I don't think there's anything to be found there, nothing incriminating that can be used against me. But then, I'm not a trained journalist. It could be that Reese has no intel for me because she's too busy doing the reverse: feeding information about me up the food chain.

If that's the case, though, why is Edwin casting aspersions against her?

Maybe Reese has gone rogue. Or maybe she really is my friend and has been all along. I just have no way of knowing, and I can't afford trust right now.

Wait, there is something to be found in the apartment. Elyse's diary. Which means that the diary could very well have been sent by someone who wants to protect me, but Edwin and Graham and whoever else are using its contents against me. Keeping me off-balance so that I'm easier to control.

Where's Beth? And who's R.G.? My life might depend on finding out.

CHAPTER 39

He actually went for it.

He made me sweat a little, but by early afternoon, Edwin called me for a meeting with him and Graham to put the finishing touches on my "authentic" speech for Beth's broadcast tonight. The competition between them was apparent. It was like that old saying about how pretty girls want to be told they're smart, and smart girls want to be told they're pretty. Edwin's the pretty girl in this scenario.

I wanted to laugh at times as they basically jostled and elbowed each other like a couple of siblings. I like seeing the tensions between them and will subtly stoke that as much as I can. Divide and conquer. I made sure to bat my eyelashes at each when the other wasn't looking. Beth would have been proud. Or should I say Trish?

I just can't think of her as Trish. From what I read, and what I saw, it's like they're entirely different people, like the re-creation went far beyond the cosmetic.

Unless Beth had me and her whole staff fooled.

But I still care for her. That makes it hard to sit in her chair knowing what she doesn't: that it'll never belong to her again, even if she resurfaces.

Resurfacing seems increasingly unlikely. The coverage of her disappearance has died down, since there are no leads. It's nothing but dead ends. That, alone, seems forbidding, like there are some professionals behind it, the kind who are adept at scrubbing away all evidence. Everyone knows the first forty-eight hours are critical, and it's well past that now.

If Beth can be erased, so can I. I'm playing with very dangerous men. And maybe women too.

Despite that awareness, I just have to stay the course. Retreat is not an option, and there's a show to do.

My monologue is first that night, and I can feel that it's magic. That's because it's true: I am just a small-town girl, and it is all too much, and I am under siege by evil network forces. I just couldn't say that INN is the biggest evil of them all. Not yet anyway.

After that first segment, it goes downhill a bit. Beth's show was built around her interviewing skills, and while Albie and I did a crash course, I'm no Beth. The guests were warned not to deviate from their talking points, and thankfully, they don't. But as I discreetly read questions off the teleprompter, the effect is less than electric.

Fortunately, the initial speech draws the bulk of the attention. By the next morning, I discover that people believe in my right to skinny-dip without fear of a helicopter invasion. It's good old-fashioned American values at work.

During the weekly review of fan mail, there's a big HAS pile, as usual, and a small pile of general crazies with veiled threats, and a pile of women ACTUALLY SUPPORTING ME! As they share their own stories of objectification and harassment, I feel tears in my eyes—because of all they've been through and because they finally recognize me as a kindred spirit, an ally.

Reese is too distracted and distant to notice. I can't entirely blame her. After all, I've been freezing her out for the past few days, and it's not like I'm looking to hug it out.

Then I see that Reese's eyes are red, as if she's been crying herself.

I care, but I won't ask. I can't risk softening toward her in case Edwin was telling the truth and she really is behind at least some of what's been going on. I have to pull away. I'm on my own, and so is she.

With Graham, though, I have to risk getting a little closer, or rather, making him think we're closer. Well past midnight, I'm the one calling him from my balcony, hoping he'll be drunk, that his loose lips will be the ones to sink INN's ship.

"I can't get involved with anyone right now; I have to focus on my career," I purr, just above a whisper. "But that doesn't mean I don't have needs, you know?"

"I know."

I can practically hear his erection through the phone. I have to fight my gag reflex to continue. "We have to keep our distance physically right now, okay? It's smarter that way, for both of us."

"That's probably true."

"Do you want to know what I'm wearing?"

I start talking, and he starts doing what I want him to do so that he can wind up in an unguarded postcoital state. I have to let him think he's using me in order to use him.

"That felt so good," I say.

"Amazing."

"I'm so wound up all the time, you know? Wondering where I stand with INN, and the viewers. With Edwin. It's exhausting."

"Don't worry so much about Edwin, okay? He's not what you think."

This is just what I was hoping for. "What do you mean?" Play stupid. That's the only reason he's telling me anything at all—because he thinks there's nothing I can do with it; I'm just his little sex toy. After all, he attacked me in a bathroom and I apologized to him. He's in total control. That's what he has to think.

"INN is barely in the black, and there were a lot of start-up costs. He wanted to be independent himself, but he had to bring in Daphne." He laughs snidely, as if at Edwin's predicament.

"So Edwin has good intentions but he's kind of lost his way?"

"I get it. You've got a thing for Edwin. But you've got to stop being so naive."

"You don't think he's really looking out for me?"

"I don't know what he's doing these days." So the right hand no longer knows what the left is up to.

I'm starting to enjoy myself a little. It's a rush, like what an undercover cop must feel. I don't even have to prompt Graham much. He wants to turn on Edwin. He's looking for the opening.

"I'm the only one at INN doing real journalism because Edwin's too cheap to pay for it. Not to mention, Edwin doesn't even know the difference between good and bad journalism. He doesn't know anything about how you build a story, what's really involved behind the scenes. He believes his own mission statement. His own hype."

If my phone is bugged—and I'm pretty sure that it is—then it's clearly not going straight to Edwin. It must go through Graham, who can erase this later.

This is almost too easy. I've turned him into a source, and he doesn't even know it.

I learn that INN is basically the emperor's new clothes. I already knew that it didn't have many correspondents or news bureaus compared to the other major news networks; Edwin had humble-bragged about it during my tour. But he hadn't stressed what was getting lost, which is original journalism. It's possible he doesn't even get just how much is lost. He thinks you can fire up the viewers and the electorate by stroking their egos and stoking their rage. That's how low his opinion is of real people. He could stand to spend some time in Tulip.

According to Graham, the INN staff isn't finding their stories; they aren't tracking down primary sources. They call other journalists, ones who do actual muckraking for small print publications and online media, and they convince those journalists to feed their investigations to INN. Sometimes the journalists get exposure themselves as guests; sometimes they're quoted, or the anchors plug their websites. Ty might put a link on Twitter or solicit donations for a nonprofit here or there. But more often, their work is unattributed and uncompensated.

The VJs and producers at INN are taught to sweet-talk and cajole the investigative journalists, telling them how important their work is and that it needs to see the light of day. If they want to reach a broad audience, INN is their only hope.

Graham is describing a network built on exploitation. INN steals other people's labor, keeps its own operations cheap, and then, ideally, breaks stories big enough to go all the way to the top, where CNN, MSNBC, or major newspapers have no choice but to use their resources to follow it down. Meanwhile, INN promotes itself to viewers as the only voice they can trust.

It's working, to a point. INN's ratings are growing, while other news organizations stagnate or lose viewers. But it's not fast enough for Edwin. That must be where I come in. Millennial men = advertising dollars. It's like he didn't think hard enough about what I would mean to the network's credibility, with my naked pictures and, now, TMZ. I could be hurting INN's ability to get the other networks to run with stories, which is why the president could wiggle out of the Until debacle with so little discomfort.

That brings back how angry Edwin was after the Until story, how he blamed me. But I'd been set up. There was no other way it could have turned out, based on what Graham is saying.

Graham's been angry too. I flash back to that night in the bathroom. With the way he's confiding in me, you'd think it had never happened.

Maybe he hadn't even been mad at me; he'd been mad at Edwin. But he couldn't shove Edwin into a bathroom stall, so he did the next best thing.

I'm glad he can't see me. I'm clenching and unclenching my fists, trying to calm my breathing.

"Edwin has to do something soon," Graham says. "I have a feeling Daphne is losing her patience. She spent big money on Ty's pay-to-play story, and on Until, and neither of them panned out. She doesn't have a mission; she just wants a return on her investment."

"You think she's going to stage a hostile takeover or something?"

"Something. But she better not mess with my stories . . ." He goes on a rant where, reading between the lines, I can tell that his only real interest is that his stories are well funded, and that he remains the only true journalist at INN. He wants to stay at the top of the pecking order among the staff, feasting on their admiration.

So Graham isn't feeling so secure, either, these days.

Is it possible he's not really as inner circle as he likes to portray? If that's the case, he might not know what happened to Beth. I might need to cultivate another source, someone higher. I think of Edwin's recent jealous streak. I'm not sure if I can dance that close to the fire. But then, I already am.

From what Graham said, INN is a house of cards just waiting for a stiff breeze to knock it down. Desperate people do desperate things. Were those things done to Beth? And who's next?

CHAPTER 40

D on't worry, Reese texted, you won't have to see me around anymore.

 So she didn't even have the guts, or the decency, to quit to my face. That doesn't necessarily tell me whether she's a spy or a saboteur, but it does tell me all I need to know about our supposed friendship.

I'm too busy to respond. I'm hard at work with Albie on my interviewing skills in preparation for what could be a regular anchor stint on *Truthiness*. Albie is tutoring me in Beth's signature move. I have to learn to lull my subjects into a false sense of security before going in for the kill. Could come in handy off-air as well.

That's my morning. In the afternoon, I'll be cramming for a correspondent gig on Khalif's show. I'm definitely not sidelined anymore.

First, though, I cram in lunch. Not even an hour later, when I'm back in the studio with Albie, I get shooting pains in my abdomen, so intense that I actually fall to my knees. He rushes to my side, with a concern you just can't fake. There's no time to get to a bathroom before I'm vomiting with a violence I've never experienced before. My body is determined to expel something.

This is no ordinary food poisoning. It feels more like actual poisoning. Beth had told me to keep my drink in my hand at all times. I should have extrapolated to lunch.

I insist on going to the hospital, and Albie accompanies me in the ambulance and into the ER. I'm seen right away, the celebrity treatment. On my way out of the INN building on the stretcher, I saw Nan, so stories must be circulating by now. I don't even care. I've been avoiding the newsroom, and no one's sought me out either.

Albie seems genuinely worried, but I can't help recalling the events earlier in the day. Lunch was delivered for Albie and me to his office. If someone spiked my food, then it happened there. I have no idea if he stepped out for some reason and someone could have snuck in. If, for instance, he was lured out for a conversation and that's when it happened. But I can't ask him without tipping my hand. I don't want anyone to know I suspect. I have to keep playing dumb like my life depends on it.

There's little curiosity or suspicion on the part of the medical team as to what caused my sudden illness. Did someone from INN call ahead? Could the hospital be in cahoots with INN, the same way the police might be?

I would never say any of these thoughts out loud. I'm sane enough to know how insane I'd sound. But that doesn't mean it didn't happen.

I'M RELEASED BY nightfall, but my appearance on Khalif's show has been canceled. Was that the intent? It would have made more sense for someone to sabotage me before my big speech the day before on *Truthiness*. Reese had been the one who brought me a sandwich then.

Maybe I was wrong about her.

I just don't know anymore, about anything or anyone, past or present. I'm not in any pain, but I'm still weak. It's so hard to think.

Albie asks if there's anyone he can call, who I'd want by my side just in case, and I'm embarrassed to say I have no one. Back in my apartment, I feel emptied from all the vomiting, but from sadness too. It aches, being this alone.

I call Dad to say how bad I feel. I'm not only talking about the "food poisoning"; it's everything, only I can't say any of it. The line isn't secure, and there's nothing he can do. The days of thinking my father's omnipotent are long gone. I'm not his little girl, anymore, much as I wish I could be.

But he still has his parental sixth sense. He tells me, "You can always come home, baby. No questions asked."

"I have a job to do." It's a strategic response. The line is bugged.

"We'll figure something out. You've already done so much."

I begin to cry softly. "It's not nearly enough, Daddy."

"You had the president on the run, Cheyenne! And you're twenty-four years old. I couldn't be prouder."

"You didn't feel that way at first."

"You're right, I didn't. You know how important loyalty is. But I watched your next two reports, and I'm glad you put a stop to Until. I've always known you to do the right thing, and I know you always will."

But the right thing seems to involve so many wrong things along the way. I would never want Dad to know how I got information out of Graham and the way I'm interacting with Edwin—like the cocktease Chase accused me of being. Does the end always justify the means?

I can't ask, not on an insecure line.

"I love you, Daddy," I say.

"I couldn't love you more, baby."

I'm drifting off when security calls up to say I have a visitor. It's Graham.

My heart starts to thump. "I'm too sick to see anyone," I say. "Please thank him for stopping by."

I hear a muffled conversation, and then, "Your friend here says he doesn't mind some puke. He just wants to make sure you're okay."

I need to keep Graham on my side. That means I have no choice but to let him up. What's the worst that could happen?

He could finish what he started the other night in the bathroom. Or finish what someone did with my food. And right now, I'm too weak to fight him off.

But I need him to think he's my friend. It's a calculated risk. "Send him up," I say.

I knot my robe over my pajamas as tight as I can. I'm glad my breath is truly foul, my hair's a mess, and my pallor is still jaundiced. Just before I open the door, I make sure my cell phone is recording.

When Graham sees me, the expression on his face is one of profound relief. He makes a move as if to hug me and then plunges his hand back in his pocket. He's apparently on his best behavior.

"I just wanted to see you," he says. I'm pretty sure he didn't do this to me, but he might know who did.

It couldn't have been Reese. That leaves Albie, Edwin, Ty,

Luke, Daphne, Rayna, the entire female population of the newsroom, the entire male population of the newsroom . . .

I feel faint. Graham reaches out to steady me. "Let me help you get back in bed," he says.

I absolutely don't want him in my bedroom. I gesture toward the couch. Once we're settled, his gaze is so solicitous and tender that it's unnerving.

"Is there anything I can do for you?" he asks. "Could I run to the store and get you ginger ale or anything? That's what my mom did for me when I had an upset stomach."

It bugs me that Graham got to have a doting mother and still turned out to be a date rapist. I shake my head. No ginger ale; just information, please.

"I didn't think you had anyone to take care of you," he says. "I heard about Reese quitting." I get the sense that he was pleased with that news. "I was against hiring her." What doesn't he have his finger in?

That's not an expression I should ever use again when it comes to him. The images of the bathroom flood back.

But Graham keeps talking. Apparently, on the subject of Reese, he has a lot to say. Just like he did with Edwin. "She was always running interference for you. Getting in your way, really. It's never a good idea to have some sycophantic mini-me swelling your head, you know?"

What he's saying is, Reese was looking out for me. She was a friend. A loyal friend, and I betrayed her.

CHAPTER 41

August 23, 1991. The day all Elyse's fears came true.

My fingers are shaking as I hold the pages. I know how it turns out, but still, reading what Elyse was thinking in the immediate hours before . . .

It makes me wonder if those are the same thoughts Beth had the day she was crying by the curb. If they're the same thoughts I might have someday.

But I'm going to read it. I've been with Elyse this long, and I need to see it through. Regardless of the intent of the person giving these to me, Elyse and I are comrades in arms.

August 23, 1991

I fought with B.N.

I walked into my apartment to find him sitting in front of the television, drinking a beer and watching the game. "You're home early," he said.

I showed him my contract, and then I made a mistake. I told him what happened in Dennis's office, which meant I had to explain Dennis's visit to my apartment, which shames me even now. I hear how it sounds. How I sound.

But B.N. wasn't thinking about how I acted; he wanted to talk about Dennis. He said I'm worth more than this contract. I'm putting myself at the mercy of a psychopath.

He thinks Dennis is the only one at fault. I wish I agreed, but I know that it's tawdry to want something as much as I've wanted this job. Of course now that it's coming my way, there are strings attached. I was upset in Dennis's office, but I get it now. I have tried to manipulate him. I've flirted. I've feigned interest in his stories. I've looked up at him like he's the big strong man who's going to save poor little me.

I told B.N. I need to be smart. Beggars can't be choosers. I'm just starting out. Dennis has hurt feelings and a wounded ego, that's all. With time, he'll see who I really am. The viewers will.

B.N. stared into my eyes. "Don't sign this, Elyse. There will be other opportunities. Better ones."

We should have been celebrating. I was holding the winning lottery ticket, and he was telling me not to cash it in, that I should gamble on a bigger jackpot that won't ever come. "You know Dennis is bluffing," he said. "He doesn't want Connie Chung. He doesn't want anyone more established because he couldn't do to them what he's about to do to you. He's going to make you pay, every day, for turning him down."

"He's just hurt, that's all. I know him better than you. I know he really loves his son—"

"You can't do this," he implored. "You accept his terms, and you're condoning his behavior."

"I'm so sorry I can't live up to your standards." I was seething now. "I actually live in the real world."

"Well, that's not a world I want to live in."

"You don't have to! You're a man."

He stood up. "I'm going to take a walk. I need some air."

"Are you coming back tonight?"

"You can't be alone, not after . . ." By silent mutual agreement, we don't talk about red paint.

"You don't need to babysit me. Take the night off."

He hesitated at the door, his shoes on. His conscience was telling him not to go, but I could see he really wanted to. He wants to get away from me. He doesn't respect me anymore.

"Please go," I said.

Now that I'm alone, the terror has set in. I call Dennis. I call The Tank. I call R.G. I even call York. (He wants to represent me, not kill me.) I leave messages to say I need help. I don't care which one shows up.

Fight or flight. I'm not going to run away. I'm going to keep on fighting.

I write my own ending.

CHAPTER 42

The night Elyse was attacked, she called R.G. And on her Wikipedia page, "R.G." made edits today. This section has been added:

Quotes

"In a world where the news is often scary, you want it to be told to you by a friend. I try to be that friend."

"I wish there was room at the top, or on the couch, for two women."

"The more appalling the perpetrator's actions, the greater the victim's crime must have been, because otherwise, why would this have happened to her?"

"I had never thought of fear as motivation, as something I could use. Well, I've got plenty of motivation stored up."

"I've had it with men trying to overrule me and make their desires mine."

"Maybe this isn't about insanity at all. Maybe all this has been entirely strategic."

"That job is meant to be mine. I've suffered for it."

"I write my own ending."

There are footnotes citing each date, but I don't need to cross-reference. They're from the diary I've been receiving. The cumulative effect is one of encouragement, an assortment to confirm that the diary has been from a friend, just like the first letter said. It's from someone who wanted me to educate myself, to see how far women have come and how far they have to go. Someone who wants me to write my own ending, like Elyse did.

It has to be Beth. She used to be Trish, which means she's a survivor. She had to run away from INN, but she's somewhere safe, communicating. She's saying that I need to continue the fight.

I will. I have no choice.

THE BUILDING SECURITY hails a cab and sees me into it. I give the driver the address of one of the downtown boutiques I thought I'd make it back to but haven't until now. If I'm being followed, it looks like I'm milking my sick day for a shopping trip, which would hopefully only make me seem more unthreatening to the powers that be. What a silly, superficial girl I am.

I go into several stores before I find what I'm looking for: a back entrance. I wave off assistance, picking out the most shapeless clothing I can find. It's a pair of slouchy pants with some inexplicable zippers and an oversized T-shirt with Andy Warhol's soup cans emblazoned on it. It comes to a ridiculous sum that

I pay gladly. The saleswomen, in classic New York style, have given no indication that they recognize me, but when I ask to use the back entrance, I get a quick nod and no questions. Before I slip out, I don the blond wig Reese bought me weeks ago.

I walk down the street, concealed by people. It's not impossible to tail me, but I've at least raised the level of difficulty. I take the subway for the first time, and I feel the thrill of everyone's lack of interest. Anonymity, I've missed you.

The Milstein Microform Reading Room inside the New York Public Library is stately and beautiful, with grainy wood and brass accent lamps and massive wrought-iron chandeliers hanging from high ceilings. I lap up the silence and the air-conditioning. It's hot under my wig.

The librarian finds nothing odd in my request. It occurs to me that librarians are a little like priests or prostitutes in that way: they must have heard it all. She gives no hint of recognizing me, though I realize five minutes after our interaction that my wig is askew.

After a brief tutorial in the microfiche arts, I'm left to my own devices. A few hours later, I've found what I'm looking for. More than I dared hope for, actually. Now I've got more information about the past. I just need to make the connection to the present.

I could really use some help from a journalist. From a friend.

I get into a cab, fairly certain no one's following me, and give the driver Reese's address in Brooklyn. I pay in cash, in case INN is monitoring my credit cards. Other than the trip to the Hamptons, it's my first time leaving the island of Manhattan. At a glance, Williamsburg is a lot more my speed than my current neighborhood, but right now, I'm not looking at real estate; I'm recruiting.

Reese's roommate answers the door. I met her that night at the club with Pietro, so she recognizes me and my wig. The reception is not exactly warm.

It might help if I could remember her name, but no such luck. "It's good to see you again," I say, smiling. She remains stony, one hip thrust outward to effectively block the doorframe. "Is Reese here?"

"Nope."

"You don't happen to know where she is, do you? It's really important that I talk to her." She stares me down. "I need to apologize. I feel awful about everything." Still nothing. "Edwin agreed that she can have her job back at double the salary. It wasn't easy to convince him."

She gives a nasty smile. "I bet it wasn't." A pause. "She's near the Williamsburg Bridge. She likes to sit on a bench there and think."

"Do you know which bench?"

"If you really want to be forgiven, you've got to work for it."

That's how I find myself walking up and down the promenade along the river by the Williamsburg suspension bridge, not even knowing what river it is. It's a sort of brown gray, not nearly as beautiful as the Hudson was the night I walked with Chase, and I'm sweating profusely in the heat. Beneath the wig, my scalp itches, but I don't dare remove it.

I'm about to give up, thinking this was all just retaliation, when I notice someone who, despite the heat, is in a sweatshirt, the hood pulled up. While she's hunched over in a very un-Reese-like posture, I move closer. The bench is one of the least popular as it has a clear view of what could be a belching toxic waste plant.

"Hey," I say. "I'm so glad to see you."

Reese gives a sideways glance, then repositions her hood.

"Your roommate said I could find you here."

"Yeah? What's her name?" When I can't answer, she says, "That's what I thought. She texted me. I thought about leaving, but then I wanted to hear this great offer of yours. Double the salary, right? And let's throw in the Williamsburg Bridge."

I'm struck by the anger and bitterness radiating from Reese. It's like she's had a personality transplant. "I was lying. There's no job offer."

"What a shocker. Cheyenne's a liar."

"I've never lied to you before. I'm here because I owe you a big apology."

"That's all? There's nothing in it for you?"

So this is what Reese thinks of me. That I'm all about myself, that I use other people.

I wasn't that way before INN, I know that. But now, I can see Reese's point. I'm not sure I have shown personal interest in her throughout our relationship. I've been trying to get information and support. That was Reese's job, but it's not friendship.

"I'm sorry," I say. "I'm hoping you'll forgive me, and we can be real friends going forward."

Reese shakes her head. "Priceless."

"I know I didn't treat you the way I should have."

"I tried to help you. I got Pietro to give us that place because you needed to get out of town. And then you turned on me. You said you never betray a friend, but you just abandoned me when I needed you."

Reese needed me?

The last time I saw her. The red-rimmed eyes.

"I know I've been self-involved," I say. "And paranoid. When someone suggested that you called TMZ, I went back over everything that's happened, and it seemed to make sense that it would be you."

"Someone suggested me?"

"Edwin."

Reese shakes her head again. "And it just made sense, huh?"

"It's been a minefield for me since I started at INN. That's not an excuse; it's just my head space. Please. Can I explain?" Reese still isn't looking at me, but maybe that's better. It lets me detail everything that's happened, all I've chosen not to share with Reese, or anyone else, including Graham attacking me and what I've learned about Edwin and INN.

I can feel that Reese is looking at me, but I can't look back. I'm so ashamed. I jumped into this with both feet, thinking I could trust my instincts and my initial read on Edwin. A lot of this is my own fault.

Reese reaches over and takes my hand. Despite how moist her palm is, I'm grateful for the touch.

"Laxatives," Reese says. "They put a shitload of laxatives in your lunch. No pun intended."

"How do you know?"

"It's what they do, along with that teleprompter trick, and the note on your chair. I'm pretty sure all that is Nan and Belinda, securing their places with Rayna. That's just jockeying for position. But there is something evil at that place, and I don't use that word lightly. And now, with Beth . . ." She trails off, turning her brimming eyes to the water.

I feel my chest tightening. "What about Beth?"

"You don't know yet? It's all over the news." She pauses, searching for the best way to say it, and then just plunges in. "They found her body. She drowned, more than a week ago."

They got to her. The sorrow is a gut punch. Maybe I didn't really know her, maybe she was just a figment of my imagination, of my longing for the mother I never had. But the loss sure feels real.

Reese and I sit in silence for a while, absorbing. Then I ask, "Have they figured out who she was?"

"I don't think so." Reese meets my eyes. "You have?"

"It's a long story. Do you know who Elyse Rohrbach is?"

"Obviously. She's a feminist broadcasting icon, and pretty much a superhero."

When Elyse was attacked in her apartment, she managed to fight and then flee, her self-defense training kicking in. She got down the hall, banging on every door and screaming for help.

She later identified her assailant as York Diamond, but just as she'd suspected, it was a made-up name. The man in question was actually Trish's husband, Vince Malick. Vince had hatched a plan to get rid of Trish's competition. He needed Trish to keep her job, since she was the only one working. He wanted to drive Elyse crazy so that she'd blow her shot.

Unfortunately for him, Elyse didn't crack. Trish did. She was drinking heavily due to the stress, and she was caught under the influence at work. Dennis gleefully gave her the choice to resign or be fired. She resigned, thinking then she could still salvage her career.

Vince decided that Elyse needed to be punished. He shouldn't have had continued access to the studio, but somehow, security was lax enough that he was able to get in and spray paint the death threat on the wall of Elyse's dressing room. That was going to be the end of it, according to him.

Then he found out that Elyse would be taking over Trish's job permanently. He went to her apartment and tried to make good on his threat. According to his lawyer, he was temporarily insane.

The jury didn't buy it. Not when there was this clear sign of premeditation:

Vince learned that Elyse was accepting the job and that she was home alone, without any security, because she left it on the answering machine that he'd set up under the alias York Diamond. In that message, she asked if he could come over to talk about how he might be able to negotiate on her behalf. She was never planning to be his client, but somehow, she had decided that he wasn't to be feared, that Someone Else was the true danger. She had unwittingly asked for protection from the man who had threatened to kill her. She was so terrified of being alone that she lured her attacker right to her.

Elyse fought Vince off, but the side of her face was slashed, leaving a raised scar, paler than the surrounding skin. Elyse refused to hide it on-air. She called it her badge of courage. Her popularity skyrocketed, and she could go anywhere. She took another morning show gig, and within the year, *Morning Sunrise* was canceled amid an ocean of bad publicity. Dennis lost his job.

Elyse remained a force in broadcast journalism for the next twenty years. She received some of the biggest contracts in network history and was instrumental in getting New York's anti-stalking law passed, as well as being an advocate for victims' rights. She married Barry Nadler, the writer from *Morning Sunrise*, and had three children with him.

Meanwhile, Trish claimed that she never encouraged or knew about her husband's actions, and there was evidence to suggest domestic violence at home, yet the public reaction was harsh. She received death threats, and with two little girls to raise, she needed to get out of the public eye. There are still people who believe she had to have colluded with her husband, that she'd set him up and walked away scot-free, though they've never been able to support the contention. There's a Free York Diamond website, which features lots of comments like, "You know she was in on it. All bitches are evil." That's part of why the Wikipedia entry has undergone so much editing.

"Eventually, Trish wanted back in," I say. "She emerged on-air after September eleventh as Beth Linford, with dark hair and colored contacts. No one was combing headshots from 1991, so she got away with it."

"Or she just thought she did," Reese says. "Do you think someone from her past came back to get revenge? Someone who thought that she was complicit in what happened to Elyse?"

"I don't know yet. But I know that someone from Elyse's past is at INN. Rich Garrett." Ty's executive producer, the suck-up. R.G.

The diary never said what R.G. did for a living. It didn't say that he'd worked as a producer at a different network. He and Elyse had met while they were both at the campus TV station.

Somehow, in all the parsing of the case, the internet never seized on his role in what happened to Elyse. It was practically a footnote in the trial coverage; I'd had to go through with a fine-tooth comb to find it. York Diamond learned all the details about the stalker's MO—the things he couldn't have gleaned from *People* magazine—from Rich. They met in a bar across the street from the *Morning Sunrise* studio and became friends, of sorts. Or Rich thought they were. It turned out that while he was crying in his beer about the one that got away, York Diamond (i.e., Vince Malick) was taking notes on how to send Elyse over the edge.

What I don't know yet, what I'm hoping Reese can help me figure out, is how Rich fits into my story, and into what's going on at INN now. Did he repent and become a feminist, and now he's the one giving me the diary entries and posting on Wikipedia, sending me a message I haven't yet been able to decode?

"No," Reese says firmly. "If Rich is involved, in the present, there's no way he's trying to help you. He doesn't give a shit about women. He acts as Ty's pimp."

It's clear she knows from experience. "What happened?" I ask softly.

"It was going on for a little while. I didn't want you to think less of me. That's why I didn't tell you."

"What was going on?"

Now it's her turn to avert her eyes while she tells her story. They do this to us, and then we're the ones who feel ashamed.

"I was hooking up with Luke," she says. "It was really casual, and there was a lot of alcohol involved. It's not like I wanted him for my boyfriend or anything."

"What did he do to you?"

"It wasn't him. Not exactly. It was . . ." She lets out a shuddering breath before being able to continue. "Rich kind of orchestrated this whole thing with Ty, so Ty wouldn't have to hit on me directly, and instead of me thinking how creepy that was, I was flattered. I mean, Ty's married, and he's more than twenty years older than me, and I'm *flattered*?"

"Don't do that," I say. "Don't blame yourself. That's how they keep us powerless, worrying about our mixed signals and our mistakes. We're allowed to make mistakes, and it shouldn't cost us like it does."

She nods, slowly, before continuing. "So Ty and I were, you

know, together a few times. Luke just disappeared from the scene, like there'd been some prearrangement. Or like Luke had been auditioning me for Ty, because one time, Ty said, 'I know you like this; I saw you.' It barely registered because I was so drunk.

"The last time, Ty met me in our usual spot. He seemed really aggressive. He was grumbling about you, about how he could barely get a meeting with Edwin anymore and meanwhile you're up on the Jumbotron and going after the president. I was uncomfortable and said I needed to leave, but he"—her eyes well up—"he forced my head down and wouldn't let me back up until I did what he wanted."

"It's okay."

"No, it's not."

"You're right, it's not. But you're out of there now, and we're not going to let them get away with it."

"I don't think we can stop them."

"The usual place you met," I say. "Was it a bathroom? On the same floor as the studio?"

Reese nods.

"Then we can stop them."

CHAPTER 43

I walk into my apartment building with a complicated brew of emotions. A part of me is grieving for Beth, and the other part of me feels more hopeful than I have in a while, like I have a true teammate and a real mission.

I stop in my tracks. Edwin is sitting in the lobby. Thankfully, my wig is back in my bag.

"You look a lot better," he says, with a note of accusation.

"You know how food poisoning is," I say. "Quick recovery."

"So you could have come in to work."

"I wanted to rest."

This is the kind of conversation some girls had with their fathers when they came home past curfew. I never did.

"Do you want to come upstairs?" I say. I have to think fast. I have to get out of this, whatever this is.

I've been trying so hard not to leave any traces, not saying anything in my apartment or on my phone, slipping out back doors, wearing my wig, using cash everywhere. I'm pretty sure no one's been following me. But there's something about Edwin's countenance, like he already knows.

The phone itself is probably tracking me. I'm such an amateur.

I do know that it was turned off during my talk with Reese, because I didn't want any interruptions, so I don't think anyone could have actually heard what was said. But I have to proceed as if Edwin knows where I was, and I have to hope that I haven't put my friend in danger.

In the elevator, Edwin and I stand far away from each other. "Nice outfit," he says.

"Thanks. I did a little shopping." He must know that. "Then I took my first trip to the library."

"What books did you get?"

Think fast, think fast. "I just read a bunch of magazines."

Don't ask which ones. Don't ask who was on the cover.

The elevator door opens, a welcome interruption. Once inside my apartment, his manner changes. "I like what you've done with the place," he jokes, badly. He's nervous.

"I haven't had a ton of free time."

"Your office looks pretty good." It has the feel of an accusation. A reference to Reese, maybe? To where I've just been?

"Reese did the decorating. I actually just saw her." Best to come out and say it. Come clean—well, give the appearance of coming clean. "I'd never been to Brooklyn before."

"What did you think?"

I keep moving so he can't see my face, busying myself in the tiny kitchen, looking in the refrigerator as if to see what I have to offer him when I know it's just bottled water and Red Bull. "I liked it," I say, emerging with one in each hand. "Sorry, it's all I have. I never have company."

He glares at me.

Graham. He knows Graham was here.

So there's no camera in the apartment then? Otherwise, he would know that he has nothing to worry about. The visit ended prematurely with another bout of puking. It makes me think of the diary, and the self-defense advice: if someone wants what you don't, do something disgusting. That definitely fit the bill. Graham was out of there fast after that.

But if it's just jealousy about Graham, then that's good for me. That I can handle.

Edwin doesn't take either drink. I put the Red Bull back and open the bottle of water, chugging it. I'm thirsty, having sweat a lot from the heat, and now from the pressure.

"So are you and Reese still friends?" Edwin asks. "I didn't have that impression when she quit."

"I had to do damage control. I didn't want her to bash me on social media."

"What did she say?"

"She made it perfectly clear that now that she's not being paid, she doesn't want to talk to me or about me."

"It's a tough lesson. Finding out who your friends really are."

I'm not touching that one. I guzzle the water, stalling.

"I wanted to check and see how you're taking the news about Beth."

I head for the couch. I hope he'll come sit beside me. I'm not my prettiest at the moment, but proximity might work in my favor. We've always had chemistry.

He sits beside me, and I hate to admit it, but I still feel it. Those damned pheromones. A hint of attraction, despite every-thing.

"I can't believe Beth's really gone," I say.

"I can't either. I had a lot of respect for her, and what she was trying to do." He does look a little sad, actually, but it could just be an act.

"What was she trying to do?"

"What we were all trying to do. Make a difference."

I'm not used to him sounding so facile. I study his face, but I can't get a read. I can't tell what he knows. What he's done. Or what he's had done on his—on INN's—behalf.

I sink deeper in the couch. I should use this opportunity, but I'm not only tired; I'm weary.

Edwin moves a little closer and starts to massage my shoulders. It feels good, though it's totally inappropriate. Very Harvey Weinstein. Have these titans learned nothing?

Still, my eyes close, almost involuntarily. I've missed touch. I've missed sex. Despite all I know about Edwin . . . what do I really know, for sure, about Edwin? It's all so murky, and this feels so good.

"You seem like you could use a friend," he murmurs. "You and I have been friends right from the start. From that first plane ride." His hands slip just a little lower and pause. He's waiting for a signal. So he's not like Graham, or Harvey. He wants me to want him.

The truth is, I do. Which is convenient, because it's also my best move to save myself. I remember in the diary when Elyse said that whatever happened, it would never come to her sleeping with Dennis. But Elyse had never felt this way about Dennis. Her life never depended on him.

Then Edwin and I are kissing, and maybe because it's so bad, it feels especially good. I haven't been with anyone besides Chase in years, and I like the differences in weight and pressure and urgency, and I like the things I know I shouldn't, like that

Edwin's a billionaire and he's my boss and I can bend him to my will, for the moment at least. So I'm going to take advantage of it, and him, and I'm not going to think about whether it's actually the other way around.

Then he's inside me, and we're both gasping because we've waited so long for this, and because I need the release. I've been holding on to so much these past weeks, and I'm letting it go, right now, with a cry.

We fall against each other and I don't know what's next, I don't know how low I'll sink, but this has bought me more time, and hopefully, it'll be enough.

CHAPTER 44

Inside a Manhattan skyscraper, more than a hundred floors up, in an elegant office of cream and pale gold, I'm sitting opposite Elyse Rohrbach. *The* Elyse Rohrbach.

Or should I call her R.G.?

People could be awestruck for any number of reasons: because of how Elyse not only survived but thrived; because of the broadcasting career she went on to have; and her impact on women's issues, to name just a few. For me, it's the diary.

It's been my companion since the beginning of this ride. It's helped me see the world as it was and as it is and what it should (and could) be. It's enabled me to think on my feet in ways I wouldn't have been able to do otherwise. It caused me to realize that there's nothing shameful about female ambition, and that making it seem so is just a tool to deter women from embracing their true power. It's kept me going; it's kept me fighting. It's led me here, to the headquarters of Elyse's nonprofit, and now, I'm the one doing the interviewing.

Reese helped make contact with R.G. initially through the

Talk section of Wikipedia (I could only do so much when I'm being surveilled). She got me a burner phone so R.G. and I could text each other, so I could cultivate my first source.

And what a source it's turned out to be. *The* Elyse Rohrbach, who actually helped Beth to reinvent herself in 2001 and re-enter the world of broadcasting. Elyse was the one who vouched for Beth, which gave this no-name journalist immediate credibility and kept anyone from asking too many questions. No one would have imagined that Elyse would be on Trish's side, so they accepted Beth as an entirely new face and voice on the broadcasting scene.

Elyse and Beth remained close. There are photos online of Beth emceeing Elyse's charity event last year. So I'm holding out hope that Beth went to her old pal Elyse about whatever was going on at INN, and that Elyse might have a good idea what got Beth killed.

I left my own cell phone at home so I couldn't be tracked. I've told no one. I made sure to take the subway and then catch a cab and then the subway again so I couldn't be followed. I wore my wig. But I'm no spy. There are so many ways this could still blow up. The INN clan could be two steps ahead of me.

Still, I've gotten sweet texts from Edwin today, and I continue to string Graham along, so their collective googly eyes might not be seeing straight. Unless they're both playing me; unless they're the ones playing dumb, and getting phone sex and actual sex to boot.

I can't control any of that now. I just have to focus on the icon in front of me.

Elyse is in a coral pantsuit, her blond hair close-cropped, her curls long gone, her badge of courage on display whenever she turns her head. "It's good to meet you," she says. "Beth told me wonderful things. I only wish this was under different circumstances."

"I do too. I really looked up to Beth."

"I know she wanted to help guide you. After she returned to television, one of her goals was to create a different climate for women."

"Did you want to help guide me too? Is that why you were sending me the diary?"

"If I'd known how everything was going to play out, I would never have started that. Beth and I had that idea before—" She breaks off, looking upset. "Beth told me you were coming to INN, and we thought the diary would make you see that no matter what you encounter, you can use it as fuel. You don't have to play their game, you can play your own."

"Why send it anonymously?" Hadn't it occurred to someone as smart as Elyse, who'd been stalked and harassed, that receiving the diary like that could feel, in itself, threatening?

"I thought that it would be a journalistic test. See if you could follow the trail of breadcrumbs, and if you could, then I'd know you're someone who could go far in this business."

"So you were making me play your game."

Elyse colors. "It was never meant to be mean-spirited. But now I can see how it might have felt that way. It's funny how sometimes you can only see your own intentions, and if you know they're good, you presume others know that too. I didn't take your perspective as much as I should have. And then once I learned more about what was going on at INN, and what you were experiencing, I could see it quite clearly. I considered stopping, but that seemed like abandoning you. Then I had the idea of reaching out through the Talk section. I put in the question about what those three things had in common to remind you that just because people don't know something, or don't believe it, doesn't mean it's not real. You need to trust yourself. Adding the quotes was meant to spur you on."

"It did. But why pretend to be R.G., after the way he treated you?"

"I needed some kind of code, and there were only two sets of initials in the diary. Everyone knows B.N. is my husband, so that left R.G. And Rich isn't evil, he's just always been gutless. He doesn't knowingly perpetrate evil, he's just one of the silent bystanders."

"Which lets evil flourish."

"Yes, it does." Elyse brushes her hair back from her face, and I see her peekaboo scar. "I truly apologize, Cheyenne, if I've made your life harder. That wasn't my intention."

It did make my life harder. And it made it easier. "My relationship to the diary is complicated, but on the whole, I'm very glad I read it."

Elyse looks relieved. "Thank you."

"Thank *you*." But enough about me. I have a job to do. "How did you and Trish become friends after everything that happened with her husband?" And after everything I read in the diary, where Elyse was hardly a Trish fan, and vice versa.

"It didn't happen right away, that's for sure. At first, I couldn't believe she didn't know what her husband was doing. But then I learned more about her problems with alcohol, and I came to feel she was a victim herself: of her husband's abuse and mind games, of Dennis Graver, and of network politics. She told me that she had her suspicions and confronted Vince but that he gaslighted her. She started to doubt and blame herself. Vince had put her up to sleeping with Dennis, by the way, and when the affair didn't save her job, he was even angrier.

"In the years after Vince was locked up, Trish saw that she wasn't to blame for his abuse, and that alcohol wasn't solving any of her problems. She went into recovery, and while she was doing the Twelve Steps, she reached out to me to make amends for what she should have known about her husband, and how she should have protected me." Elyse wipes at her eyes. "She was so sincerely remorseful and so determined to be a better person. She'd moved away from New York, changed her name, and started over. She was doing a great job raising her girls with grace and humility." The tears begin to flow. "I just spoke with one of them. It's a huge blow, losing their mother this way."

"I can't even imagine. I never knew my mother."

"I'm sorry. That must make this journey you're on even harder, not having a female role model."

"My father's amazing."

"But he's still a man. They're living in a different world." Her eyes become faraway. "When Trish worked on *Morning Sunrise*, she wasn't much of an interviewer; she was always waiting for her turn to talk. But after all she went through with the speculation and the death threats, and after all the work she did on herself, she developed so much empathy. When she was ready to be back in the limelight, I was glad to help her. She became a great interviewer, which she exhibited after September eleventh. That's why I made sure I got those tapes in the hands of the right people in order to jump-start her career. She deserved that."

"What was your friendship like?"

"We understood things no one else could. We'd both dealt

with sexism and sexual harassment. We were both deeply impacted by Dennis, the network culture, and of course the overall mainstream culture for women. That was all playing out in the morning show wars: the insistence that women be everything but not too much of anything. We could have it all, but we needed to be really careful how we defined 'all,' and in pursuing it, we had to be especially careful that we didn't step on men's toes, or their egos. Our female viewers were going to hold us to those standards that they'd internalized, the ones that support a power structure with men at the top. We do it to one another. That's the worst part.

"Sorry to get up on my soapbox. That's my life's work—addressing the status quo as it impacts women. Trish might have seen through her husband if she hadn't been driven crazy by the rivalry, the who's-blonder-who's-younger-who's-relatable-who's-an-ambitious-bitch competition. The line we had to walk was so narrow, we all fall off sometimes." Elyse looks at me with true curiosity. "Has the line gotten much wider, do you think?"

"I thought it had, but now . . ." I trail off. "That's a conversation for another time. When there's less urgency."

"Every time is urgent." Elyse's smile is faint. "Part of why Beth wanted her own show was to be a force for good, behind the scenes. She wanted to promote respect, kindness, and equality, to hire deserving women, to listen without interruption. To be a haven. She wanted to inspire other women to take back their power, but in a feminine way."

"She led by example. I could feel that in her pitch meeting." Though with the way her staffers have glared at me or ignored me altogether since the TMZ footage, it's not clear that what Beth tried to create will outlive her.

"Beth thought that if she changed the boys' club starting

with her show, if she succeeded in creating a more nurturing and less cutthroat environment, it could extend beyond and soften the entire network. She initially believed in Edwin and his good intentions."

"Did she stop believing?"

"As time went on, she had her doubts. Nothing she could point to definitively, just little inklings. But recently, she told me that she'd uncovered something at INN, something about how the female staffers were being treated by some more powerful men, and that she was investigating further. She started to think that maybe the culture of INN wasn't much better than the culture created by Roger Ailes at Fox, that the highest levels weren't necessarily involved but were looking the other way, with a 'boys will be boys' attitude. You know, the silent bystander syndrome."

The bathroom.

"In the last communication I had with Beth, she texted, 'They know.'"

"Know what?"

"That's what I wrote back, but she didn't respond. They might have known she was really Trish and they were trying to blackmail her, or maybe they knew she was digging into things that could sink their reputation. INN depends so much on looking different from the other networks. If it was revealed that behind the scenes, they're just the same, that could kill their image, and their advertising support. Beth must have gotten in someone's way." Elyse is tearing up again. "I admired her so much. She didn't start out a great human being, but she became one. She worked at it. For her to come to an end like this, it's just heartbreaking."

"The coroner's report is inconclusive. There were no bruises or signs of struggle, and she wasn't a very good swimmer. That's what INN will say."

"I don't put much stock in what they say. Do you?" She gives me a meaningful look. "If only women were the ones doing the taping."

CHAPTER 45

'll never juggle men again. It's too much work.

First Graham needs reassurance. He waylays me as I'm leaving hair and makeup, telling me that the first segment in the show is some of his best work and he can't wait to see me do it justice. I say, yes, it's incredible, I'm honored, yada, yada. I'm not about to tell him that it won't see the light of day.

Then he runs his hand up my arm and asks if we can celebrate later. I manage, barely, to keep the smile on my face as I say yes again. I just have to keep saying yes a while longer, keep from rocking the boat until I tip it over.

My stomach's in knots. It doesn't feel like it did after my food was spiked, but it's close. I haven't been able to eat all day (and haven't wanted to, because I can't let anyone derail me today). The upside is that in wardrobe, they don't have to spend as much time pinning me into that night's scuba dress. Black. How fitting. It's INN's funeral.

Or mine.

Next I run into Edwin. He pretends it's accidental, but I can tell he's been lying in wait in the hallway. It's almost sweet, like he's a high schooler with a crush. A wave of guilt hits me. He isn't going to see this coming.

"Hey," he says in a low voice. "You look beautiful."

"Thanks."

He leans up against the wall, and I lean next to him. It's not long until showtime, and that's what I tell him, though I add that I wish I could talk to him all night.

I'm laying it on a little thick, but he's falling for it. Falling for me. Maybe it's the sex. It *was* good.

I've been trying not to think about that. It clearly can't go anywhere. Not just because he's my boss but because soon, he won't be my boss. It's a no-win situation.

"I'm crazy about you," he says, and I can see the effort it's taking for him not to reach out and touch me. "But I don't know if I can trust you."

I want to laugh out loud. He doesn't know about me? That washes away all the guilt instantly.

I manage to keep a straight face though. "You can trust me. You might not understand everything I do exactly when I do it, but I'm always doing the right thing."

He smiles. "My sweet little girl from Tulip."

So condescending. He's underestimated me this whole time, and he won't be smiling for long.

"See you after the show?" he says. "Your place?"

"Definitely."

"I'll be watching from the booth."

"Perfect. I might be ad-libbing a little tonight. Graham thinks his script is genius, that no one should change a word." I roll my eyes, and he laughs way too hard.

I've enlisted Albie's help. Elyse seemed confident he could be trusted, based on knowing him previously in the industry. She says he's an avowed feminist. So the Hillary Clinton talk was no fluke, and since he's a hired gun, he has less to lose. He must have known when he agreed to this, it would mean the end of his job. But then, when I'm done, so's he.

Graham and Edwin are both in the control room, assiduously avoiding each other. Albie is settled in front and center, next to the technical guys.

Albie gives me the thumbs-up. So he did it. He switched the footage. My heart is threatening to leap out of my chest.

I can still back out. I could just read the teleprompter like I'm supposed to; I could be a good little soldier, and with the way it's looking, this really could become my show. *Truthiness with Cheyenne Florian.* It's got a good ring. I could run it like Beth did, be a beacon for the network, and for women.

If I chicken out, Albie and Reese will know, but no one else will have to. I could show Chase and Lydia and everyone else what I'm really made of. Crusading for justice on my own show, not even a year after graduation.

Elyse is going to be watching too. She'll know.

"We're still on?" Albie says in my ear.

I take a deep breath.

I can't stay at INN, not with what I know. I might not even want to stay in journalism. But that's not the point. This is bigger than me. This is about Beth. Not just what I believe is her murder, but her mission. It's about the public good, and standing up for women. It's about telling the truth and mounting a challenge with the means I have at my disposal. I'll likely never get this kind of chance again.

"Still on," I tell Albie.

The director begins the countdown, and then I'm live, in front of millions.

"Good evening," I say. "I'm Cheyenne Florian. I want to start with a moment of silence for Beth Linford." I bow my head, and when I raise it, there are tears in my eyes. But that's as far as they'll go. Emotion suppressed is always better. "Beth was an amazing woman, and she's been taken from us far too soon. Beth was transforming newsroom culture. Not by being brash or loud or making grand statements, but by quietly doing the work and by recognizing other people's contributions. She made people feel seen, heard, and valued."

I glance quickly into the booth. Graham and Edwin recognize that that's not the beginning as written, but they're not unduly alarmed either. Just wait.

"I want to talk about the newsroom culture and corporate culture. Think about Fox News under Roger Ailes. People were being surveilled, everywhere. It was a fiefdom, and the top personalities, like Bill O'Reilly, were given a pass. Sure, Roger Ailes was finally fired, and so, eventually, was Bill O'Reilly, but they'd already gotten rich. They'd been given a bully pulpit, the operative word being 'bully.' They'd already stunted the potential of many women, subjecting them to harassment and humiliation, causing them to feel that their value was about how slowly they could cross their legs. Or uncross them, as the case may be."

Another glance upward. They're a little more concerned, but still. I'm talking about Fox. That's INN's bread and butter—the demeaning of other networks.

"At the other end of the political spectrum, we have Miramax under Harvey Weinstein. What's the same is not just the coercive behavior of the men at the top, that they feel entitled to degrade and even assault women, but that it's an open secret. Everyone else in the organization looks the other way, and one man's value trumps every woman's right to feel safe in her workplace."

I look up again, hoping that Graham and Edwin are continuing to underestimate me, that they don't think I have the courage or the brains to go where this story is leading.

"Then there's the everyday sexism that's alive and well in corporate America. Women are still pitted against one another, still used for how they look and not for how they think. They're interrupted more. Their competence has to be proven more often, again and again. Their performance reviews reference their 'attitudes' far more than men's do. When we disagree, we have to make sure we don't sound 'bitchy' or 'shrill.' We're not promoted as often. We're pigeonholed more. We're left out of certain conversations that would make it easier for us to ascend."

Edwin and Graham are at opposite ends of the booth, but they're both leaning as close as they can to the glass. Graham is gaining in fury; Edwin is . . . well, I can't quite tell what that expression means.

"We're in an amazing cultural moment, with women finally free to speak out publicly and powerful abusers toppling. But notice that's in glamorous industries like Hollywood, where famous names grab attention and headlines. In the real, everyday world, many women are still afraid to speak up. They're afraid they'll be labeled as too sensitive, and too thin-skinned to hack it. They're afraid they won't be believed. Afraid they'll be blackballed. Afraid that the process of seeking justice will be nearly as brutal as the crime itself, that they'll be told they were somehow to blame for what was done to them. HR is there to protect the powerful, to protect the company, not the accusers, and forced arbitration clauses—common in employment contracts—mean matters have to get settled in-house, which further stacks the deck in favor of the accused. Women often feel they have two options: say nothing and be a team player, or slink away and hope the next workplace will be better."

Now Graham is gesticulating wildly. He wants Edwin to pull the plug. Edwin is looking back and forth, between Graham and then down to me.

"Go fast," Albie warns. "They might cut you off."

"Yes, some bad apples have been stripped from their trees, but in most cases, powerful men continue to assume that their power is absolute and insulating. Despite all the cathartic sharing of stories that catalyzed the #metoo movement, it's still an open question as to whether true change is happening, and what new protections are being put in place to level the playing field between the accusers and the accused. Until now, all the advantages have gone to the home team. But that's where tape can be our friend, just like it was with Gretchen Carlson, who was instrumental in bringing down Roger Ailes. She had the proof."

Graham is about to leap through the glass. But Edwin isn't moving a muscle. He's still watching, almost like he's looking forward to what's coming.

"I'm about to show a video with graphic sexual content," I say. Once the video airs, I'm home free. Every network will run with it, and then no one can do to me what they did to Beth. You can't kill a whistleblower once the whistle's been blown. "These videos were taken in the bathroom at INN. You'll see at least one familiar face."

Speaking of faces, why does Edwin's have a hint of a smile?

After I told Elyse about the bathroom and about how, according to Reese, multiple men seem to know what was going on there, Elyse had the resources to hack into INN's email. The men involved were so sure of themselves that they were circulating their conquests through their work emails. Unbelievable! But fortuitous.

There it is, on the screen: a video montage that Elyse had spliced together, and it shows coercion and in one case, outright violence, as well as sexual contact with women too drunk to stand, let alone give consent. Elyse made sure that the women's identities were protected, their faces smudged out, but the perpetrators' faces were visible: Ty, Luke, and Graham.

There were a few other VJs and producers whose names had been listed on the email chain, including Rich Garrett, but Elyse's tech people hadn't found any videos featuring them. Edwin never appeared, on camera or on the list of names receiving and circulating the videos. Still, it was hard to imagine he didn't know what was happening on his watch, that there's basically a rape ring operating in his midst. Yet the question of "What does he know and when did he know it?" remains outstanding. He has plausible deniability.

Is that why he's smiling?

In the booth, Graham has gone still.

"These images speak for themselves," I say. "But don't make the mistake of thinking that it's just a few bad actors, a few bad apples. Women are being harassed, abused, and assaulted in workplaces everywhere. We have to look at the larger cultures that spawn and enable this horrifying behavior, and how corporations continue to have the means to intimidate and silence victims. But the onus falls to all of us, every one of us, to demand justice. To demand true change.

"Yes, of late, the floodgates have opened, and some of the accused have been punished. But it's a very small percentage of those who are out there abusing their power. Far more victims suffer in silence than speak out. And the status quo relies on us mistaking catharsis and storytelling for change, when the fact is, a movement is only as strong as the corporate and legislative policies that are enacted and the true protections that are put in place. Additionally, we have to address the ways our society dehumanizes and objectifies women, and the men who benefit by maintaining their power and privilege.

"What about industries that are a whole lot less sexy than entertainment and broadcasting? What about when the coverage dies down? When the appetite for the stories inevitably diminishes? We have to seize this moment and make real and lasting change now. Open dialogue is necessary but insufficient. Let's not confuse talk with justice.

"As Americans, we have a long, long way to go. But I hope that we take another step forward tonight."

CHAPTER 46

Silence has fallen. I've been so preoccupied with what's going on in the booth that I've paid little mind to the fact that it's Beth's former show, the one with a nearly all-female crew. We've gone to commercial, and I'm still at Beth's desk, frozen. The crew appears frozen too. We're in uncharted territory.

I've given no thought to this moment, to the "what now" of it. I haven't thought of an escape route, of how I'm going to make it out of this studio and this building, and where I'll go. I've been living in an apartment paid for by INN. Do I go straight to the airport? I'll be recognized, of course. Exposed. Defenseless.

Two officers are positioned around the set, and one is Officer Mortimer. Neither of them are looking at me kindly. Did they already know what was in that report? Have they been covering for INN all this time? I'm not sure if I'm going to get a police escort out of here, or if I'd be better off taking my chances on the street.

I'm starting to panic, when I hear it. The first clap. Then the whole crew is applauding wildly.

I don't know how many of them had already known what was in my report, if any of them were victims whose footage I simply haven't seen. But I do know that it's the proudest moment of my life.

When the applause finally dies down, I look back up at the booth. I see that Albie's gone. So's Graham.

Edwin speaks to me through my earpiece. "You're going to finish tonight's show, because that's what's best for INN. Meanwhile, I'll figure out what I'm going to do with you."

I feel my knees shaking under the anchor desk. I can't speak back to him, not without the whole studio hearing me. I don't even know what I want to say.

I assumed that I would be in no danger once I'd told the world what was going on behind the scenes, that INN wouldn't harm me once the heat was on the network, but that's only if Edwin behaves in a rational manner. Edwin must have realized I was using him, and his vengeance might have no bounds.

I'll figure out what I'm going to do with you.

Has a more terrifying sentence ever been uttered?

"You created television history," he says. "A cultural moment. Only on INN."

Is he crazy? Everyone knows his network is full of rapists!

As if he can see my thoughts—has he managed to obtain Until's technology? I wouldn't put anything past him, at this point—he says, "You were talking about a small rogue element. We'll clean house and move on. So thank you."

That's why he was smiling. He wanted Graham out of there. Perhaps Graham already is out. He could have already been arrested, for all I know.

But Ty, the network's cash cow?

I think of what Ty said to Reese, how angry he's been at Edwin and how Ty sabotaged my first Until report. Yes, Ty too.

The chess master outsmarted me. I've taken care of his enemies for him, and he gets to come out smelling like a rose. He's independent even of the most powerful man on his own network, Ty.

Now I'm supposed to finish the show because that makes it look like my report had been planned, like it was sanctioned by the network. INN is so morally upright that its leadership chose to expose the villainy of its own staff, live.

If I stalk off, if I refuse to be his puppet, then what?

I'm in breach of contract. There's that clause about how I have to not only forfeit my salary but pay back the money they've spent on me. *Boilerplate*, that's what he said. Standard, my ass.

I've outed his staff, and somehow, he's won. My triumph has receded, the applause is no longer in my ears, and I'm filled with a terrible impotent rage.

I've been doing so much thinking, and writing, and rehearsing. I was a real VJ: I wrote and produced my own story, and it was good. It was muckraking at its finest. But I'm spent. I can't think anymore.

So I do as I've been told. I finish out the show. Albie's still gone, and Edwin leaves too. I don't know if that's more frightening or less.

I think of Elyse, then and now. The Elyse who said she would write her own ending and who's gone on to author her story. I don't have to channel the Elyse of 1991; I can channel the one I met the other day, the one who believes I can carry the torch.

The show is over. I take in the congratulations of the staff, and the booth clears. The lights are dimmed, and still I remain at the anchor desk like I've sprouted roots. It's just me and the two police officers. I'm not going anywhere, not without some assurances. This game isn't over yet.

When Edwin reenters the studio, Daphne is with him. She speaks to the officers quietly, and I'm not surprised to see them vacate the premises, without so much as a backward glance at me.

Daphne stands in front of me, impeccable in a power suit. "Thank you for bringing this to our attention. Obviously, I wish you would have given us the footage ahead of time so we could have found the best way to handle it."

"So you could have had me killed too?"

Daphne shakes her head. "You millennials do like your conspiracy theories, don't you?"

I can't tell what Edwin is feeling. What he's decided to do with me.

"There's no Roger Ailes here," she says.

"Unless it's you," I say. "I've learned more about your theory of management." Elyse filled me in. "Give your employees enough rope to hang themselves. Know all the skeletons in their closets, and bring them out when it suits you. You were the one who put in the surveillance, and you gave Graham and Ty access. That way, you could always have the goods on them. You'd always be in control. The women who were sexually assaulted were just collateral damage."

"That's a hilarious theory," Daphne says, without a hint of laughter.

The fact is, it's just a theory. Given enough time, perhaps Elyse could prove something about Daphne's role, but there wasn't time. It could very well be that Edwin had the surveillance installed and has been in the know all along. But despite everything, I don't like thinking that. I want him to be at least a little innocent. To have genuinely cared about me, like I used to care about him.

I force myself to stay focused on Daphne. "Boys will be boys, right? Well, those boys are going to be arrested, and someone will talk."

"I wouldn't be so sure about that." Daphne levels her gaze at me. "Speaking of talking, do you know about your ex's memoir?"

"Chase?"

"He's writing a tell-all. About Until, and about you. How he fell under the spell of a charismatic mission and a charismatic woman. About his subsequent redemption. It's just the kind of story people love. You know, the golden boy tarnished by the femme fatale with the low GPA and a suspicious amount of opportunity."

I look at Edwin. Was he in on this too? He's looking at Daphne. Either he's a very good actor, which is certainly possible, or he's genuinely surprised.

Daphne might not have had anything on me when I started at INN, but she made sure to have something for when I'm finished. Daphne's turned Chase into ammunition.

Chase doesn't have anything on me, not really, but he might think he does. He's probably recast me in the role of an ambitious man-eater, and now every scene will be written from that perspective, every moment we shared. Memory is fragile and suggestible. I imagine Chase writing feverishly each day, becoming more convinced of his own victimhood, believing that this really is a redemption story that needs to be shared to protect others. I thought naked photos and video were mortifying, but the picture Chase will paint will be worse. INN has its hands all over this, but as with Beth, there will be no finger-prints.

Edwin hasn't said a word since he and Daphne came into the studio together.

Daphne smiles. "So some overgrown frat boys were having a high-tech circle jerk. A few bad apples aren't going to bring down a network. Look at Fox. But if I were you, I wouldn't worry about us. I'd worry about yourself."

I can't help it, I turn to Edwin. Some part of me thought he would try to come to my rescue, even though I know full well that I've betrayed him. Still, I thought he cared about the country, if nothing else. At least, I can hope so.

"You're better than this," I tell him. "I know how INN oper-ates and that you're exploiting real journalists. You don't need to do it this way. You have ideals. You're a patriot. This is your chance to overthrow her."

Now's the time. When he gets rid of Ty, Graham, and the other bad apples, he can wipe out Daphne too. Blame her for all the surveillance and prove she was an accessory to sexual assault. Turn against her; send her to prison with the rest of them; purge the network. With her at the helm, nothing will ever change.

He says nothing. I can see by the look on his face that he's no better than this. He has wiles but no courage. I'm not a reflec-tion of him, but INN is.

I don't know if he'll get rid of Daphne or not, but I do know that he'll turn this to his advantage. He'll take to the AstroTurf and be the one who found out about the corruption and eradi-cated it. The hero. He doesn't know news, but he knows spin.

"I don't give a fuck what you do anymore," I say, "but you'll do it without me."

"You still have a lot of time on your contract," Daphne says. "That gives us plenty of options."

"No. Because I have more tapes. Tonight was the tip of the iceberg."

"You're bluffing." But Daphne doesn't look so sure. What else could she have done?

"They're hidden. They're my insurance policy. Let me out of my contract, and you never have to know what's on them."

"Blackmail? Really?" Daphne looks at Edwin with something like admiration. "She's a quick study."

"My father's taken a turn for the worse. I need to get back to Montana."

"Cheyenne has left the network for personal reasons, we've so enjoyed her time here, she has a bright future . . . something like that?" Daphne muses. "And that's all you want? We pay out the rest of your contract and call it even?"

"Works for me."

After a long pause, Daphne says, "Done."

"No. Not done," Edwin says, his voice tight with anger. With Daphne? Or with me? My heart's in my throat waiting to find out.

He comes around the anchor desk, and I'm paralyzed. I couldn't move if I wanted to.

He squats beside me, like he's about to propose. "I want you to stay. You don't have to take Beth's show, just her time slot. We'll build a new show around you. You can work the young feminist angle. Scoop up the female millennials along with the males. You'll be an inspiration. I was thinking too small for you. You're so much more. I saw that tonight."

Daphne gives him a look like he's a puppy that's just gone off-leash. "That's not a decision we can make lightly—"

He ignores her. "Your own show. I want you here."

For perhaps the first time, Daphne sees that Edwin's interest in me isn't strictly (or even primarily) professional, and she doesn't like it. But she isn't sure what to do about it, and that's not a position she's used to. Her mouth clamps shut, in a tight and aging line.

"We'll capitalize on what you did tonight," Edwin tells me. "You can change things for young women everywhere. You're a role model. Continue what Beth started."

"Edwin!" Daphne snaps. "We don't think with our cocks at INN."

I'm glad Daphne said that. It's pulled me out of the reverie, from under Edwin's spell. INN is the network where powerful men have been sexually assaulting young women under management's noses, and if I stay to host the show Edwin is describing, then I'm a part of whitewashing it. I'd be helping to rehab INN's reputation.

"My father's dying," I say. "I'm out."

"After tonight," Edwin says, "you're going to be at the top of the misogynist hit list. INN can protect you. You walk away, and you're on your own."

I stare at him, a million thoughts stampeding through my mind in less than thirty seconds. It's true, I don't know what's waiting for me out there. But you can't always submit to the devil you know. We're a country of risk-takers. "Then I guess I'm on my own."

Edwin has the gall to look hurt. Daphne is relieved. "Done," she says again. "We wish you all the best in your future endeavors. Far away from the media. Make sure you reread your contract." She stands up and offers her hand. She's clearly referencing the gag order.

I stand up, too, ignoring Daphne's hand, which Daphne then lets drift gracefully back to her side. "I have one more condition. Stop impersonating me on social media. You're not the real Cheyenne Florian, even if you stick the @ sign in front."

I'll go silent after tonight and let the story speak for itself. But I won't be silent forever. I'll be the one to decide when and where to use my voice.

Article | Talk   Read | Edit | View history

Independent News Network

From Wikipedia, the free encyclopedia

Independent News Network (commonly abbreviated to INN) is an American basic cable and satellite television news channel. It is owned by the Gordon Entertainment Group, a subsidiary of Gordon Enterprises.

The network launched with the slogan "Because independent thinking is the only way out." It was the brainchild of controversial billionaire Edwin Gordon . . .

Among the controversies is how he actually funds the network . . .

. . . the lack of transparency, when the network blasts opacity in government and at competing networks . . .

Recently, three different women who worked for Gordon earlier in his career have come forward with sexual harassment claims. They all ended their employment more than five years ago, and their attorney has stated that "the climate wasn't right until now" to go public. The change in climate may relate to BathroomGate, and to #metoo. All three women claim the seduction started from their first meeting with Edwin Gordon, on his private jet . . .

INN, pre-BathroomGate

Edwin Gordon has spoken publicly about his influences: the early days of CNN, and the HBO/Aaron Sorkin show *The Newsroom* . . .

BathroomGate

During her brief but explosive tenure at the network, comely correspondent Cheyenne Florian presented a story of rampant sexual harassment and sexual assault occurring within INN. She broke the story on INN's own television show *Truthiness*. *Truthiness* had been hosted by Beth Linford, who disappeared and was later found dead and had been living under an alias . . .

INN, post-BathroomGate

INN cooperated fully with the police investigation, which led to the indictment of six male staffers, some for sexual assault and others for accessory to sexual assault, including popular anchor Ty Fordham and two of his producers (Graham Edelman and Rich Garrett).

Edwin Gordon released public statements of contrition for his "unforgivable ignorance." A legal team was brought in to do an independent investigation, and Gordon has complied with all recommendations. Those recommendations did not include him stepping down, though he has stated that he would if that's in the best interest of INN and the country . . .

Many female staffers have spoken out in defense of Edwin Gordon and the network . . .

INN has brought in new anchors and correspondents, who are notably younger, reviving the old slogan "You can't trust anyone over thirty." *Truthiness* has become the first overtly feminist news show . . .

While Edwin Gordon has largely garnered kudos for his response to BathroomGate, some feminists have criticized him for stage-managing the crisis. At *Salon*, it's been called a "well-orchestrated PR stunt, another way that he uses naive young women like Cheyenne Florian."

Among the new staff is Reese Benson, a correspondent who was previously the personal assistant to Cheyenne Florian . . .

Ratings are up in all demographics, including the coveted eighteen- to thirty-five-year-olds . . .

CHAPTER 47

Though I've met Elyse before, somehow it's different seeing her on the porch of Dad's ranch house. She cuts an even more imposing figure.

"Who's at the door?" Dad calls from inside.

"Elyse Rohrbach," I call back.

"Well, damn! Invite her in!"

Elyse and I both laugh. "Do you want to come in?"

"Why don't we just sit out here for a while? I love porch swings."

I'm going to sit on a porch swing with *the* Elyse Rohrbach. Broadcasting legend, feminist icon, diary writer.

We sit next to each other companionably, rocking in tandem, in sync.

"Thank you again for all you did to bring down INN," I say. "I wish it had worked."

"No, thank *you*. You were the brave one. Besides, we did all right for our first time out."

It doesn't feel all right. Edwin's gotten his controversy, as well as plenty of kudos for his supposed personal integrity; Daphne hasn't been indicted; the ratings are way up, particularly among millennials. Reese had a long meeting with Edwin and decided to drink the Kool-Aid.

"People—and networks—can change," she said. Maybe I would have done the same thing if this had been my dream since I was six years old.

But it's not. And I'm not a public figure anymore; I'm a denizen of Tulip. While there's a lot of internet talk about what people would like to do to me, I feel safe here. The residents protect their own, and many of them are packing heat.

Edwin's been calling. Changing my number does no good; blocking his number doesn't work. At first, his messages attempted to woo me back to the network, promising escalating sums of money. In his last voice mail, he tried a new angle: Now that I don't work for him, we could really make a go of it. Once the dust settles, we could be a great power couple.

As if my power will ever come through him again. I almost responded to that, but I realized that's probably what he was going for. He was trying to make me angry enough to engage him.

Never again.

"Justice didn't go far enough," Elyse says, "but then, it never does. There are incremental steps forward, which is why you have to keep pushing. They want you to get frustrated and give up." She looks at me intently. "You seem like a natural."

"I worked hard, but I don't know if journalism—"

"I meant you seem like a natural activist."

I smile. Considering the source, it might be the best compliment I've ever gotten.

"Did INN just release you from your contract?" Elyse raises an eyebrow. "Generous of them."

I don't say anything. I can't.

"I already know some things. For example, I know that it might be a little while before you feel like speaking up. Five years, maybe." Elyse winks. "For the purposes of this conversation, is it okay if I talk and you just listen? That doesn't violate any agreements, does it?"

"Not that I know of."

"I've heard that some media organizations have gag orders. Can you imagine what must be going on to need a gag order? It boggles the mind."

I don't respond.

"Gag orders should be unconstitutional, just like forced arbitration. And we're making inroads on the forced arbitration front, so I figure might as well tackle this next. We're looking for a test case."

I could never take on INN by myself, but Elyse's backing could be a game changer. I'm just not sure I want to play anymore.

"I'm not only about women's issues, Cheyenne. I'm about human issues. I believe, firmly, that the ends do not justify all means. INN did some good stories, but how it got them matters. People need to get creative enough to find means that are worthy of the ends. They also need to remember there are cameras everywhere."

I was bluffing when I talked about more video, but could Elyse actually have some?

"I'm starting a new foundation, and I need a few good women. It's going to be a revolution. A *well-funded* revolution." The penalties on the gag order are trump change for Elyse Rohrbach.

But I believe in full disclosure. "You should know that my

ex, Chase, is writing a book. It's going to paint me in a pretty negative light."

Elyse laughs. "You mean the man you dumped because he wanted to make mind control mainstream?" I laugh too. "Now that we've got that idiot out of the way, are you with me?"

We're looking into each other's eyes. An electric current travels between us, a bond across the generations. I want to say yes, but I've gotten into trouble this way before.

"Let me think about it," I say. "I need to do my research."

"Good answer."

"I'm sure I'll have a lot more questions soon, but I do have one right now. Could I pass your diary along? I know someone who could use it." Maybe networks really can change. But just in case, Reese could benefit from a history lesson.

"Be my guest." Elyse smiles, stands up, and says she'll be in touch. As she turns to go, I see the lily-white etching on the side of her face, blade-thin.

I wouldn't mind being scarred like that.

About the author

About the book

Insights,
Interviews
& More . . .

Meet Holly Brown

Yanina Gotsulsky

HOLLY BROWN lives with her husband and daughter in the San Francisco Bay Area, where she's a practicing marriage and family therapist. She is the author of the novels *Don't Try to Find Me*, *A Necessary End*, and *This Is Not Over*. ∾

Story Behind the Book

I suppose you could say *How Far She's Come* was inspired by the 2016 election, though it was arguably the least inspirational election in history. It might be more accurate to say that the election provoked a series of incredibly strong emotions in me, waves upon waves, much like grief, and I felt the desire to channel them creatively. At first, I was in a state of shocked outrage over having a president who'd bragged— *on tape!!!!*—about grabbing women "by the pussy." But stopping with outrage serves no one. It's far better to step back and reflect on the larger culture that made this election result conceivable, to consider how far women and society have come, and how far we still have to go. Because psychological suspense is my métier, I decided to do it with a workplace thriller. Since Gretchen Carlson had gotten Roger Ailes ousted from Fox around the time I began, the setting of a cable news network just felt right.

Much like Cheyenne, I had a lot to learn. I've included my bibliography on the following pages, and you'll notice that it's bipartisan. Independent, if you will, just like my news network.

I started writing How Far She's Come in November 2016, not so long ago, but so much hadn't yet happened. Bill O'Reilly still had his job. So did ▶

Story Behind the Book *(continued)*

Harvey Weinstein and Kevin Spacey and Louis C.K. and Charlie Rose and Matt Lauer and . . . the list goes on. (I'm writing this at the end of 2017, and I fully expect that by the time of publication, many other famous men will have been swept up in the tsunami of allegations.) In November 2016, #metoo hadn't yet become a revolutionary Twitter meme, let alone a galvanizing movement. While sexism, harassment, and assault are, sadly, nothing new, what is new is the critical mass of women speaking up and organizing to take down some of the most powerful men in myriad industries. But we can't stop there. It's not about sniper fire, one by one. It's about a much-needed shift in gender relations.

At least, that's what I'm hoping for, that the empowerment is contagious, but it is still in its infancy. What still needs to change is a larger culture where perpetrators are protected, rather than victims. No longer will powerful men have their crimes covered up and their open secrets kept. #metoo will join with #nomore, and everyone will be treated with decency, respect, and equality.

Now that's a virus I'm proud to spread.

Reading Group Guide

1. The opportunity at INN has "too good to be true" written all over it. If you were Cheyenne, would you have been able to turn it down? Or would you have placed different conditions that might have altered the outcome?

2. What do you think about INN's mission? Was it worthwhile, and was anyone (including Edwin, Beth, and Cheyenne) sincere in its pursuit?

3. Elyse's diary is set in 1991; Cheyenne's story is present day. What parallels do you see? For example, now the term "rape culture" is in wide use; did rape culture exist in 1991, by another name?

4. Would you have reported the Until story, despite being in a relationship with Chase? Was this a turning point for Cheyenne, the moment she became ruthless, just as Graham said she would?

5. Was Edwin Gordon sexually harassing Cheyenne? Do you see him as similar to Roger Ailes or Harvey Weinstein? Because Cheyenne is attracted to Edwin, does that mean he's not abusing his position of power? ▶

Reading Group Guide (*continued*)

6. Is female ambition stigmatized in a way that male ambition isn't?

7. Do you have knowledge or personal experience with cyberbullying/ cyberstalking, or with any form of real-life harassment or abuse? Were there any times when the book hit close to home?

8. There are a lot of layers of seduction and manipulation, right from the first meeting between Cheyenne and Edwin, with questions of who's really being used. When Cheyenne turns the tables, her sexuality is a main strategy. Are these means justified by the ends?

9. In the novel, there are multiple times when either Cheyenne or Elyse wonder about the trade-off of anonymity for safety, that making their lives less public might mean they'll be protected. Victims are often given the advice by police of getting off-line or staying home. Is that a fair bargain? And is it true safety?

10. In what ways are Cheyenne and Elyse shaped by their scars, for better and for worse? Do you believe the adage "What doesn't kill you makes you stronger"? ∾

Bibliography

Attkisson, Sharyl. *Stonewalled: My Fight for Truth Against the Forces of Obstruction, Intimidation, and Harassment in Obama's Washington.* New York: Harper Paperbacks, 2015.

Brock, David, Ari Rabin-Havt, and Media Matters. *The Fox Effect: How Roger Ailes Turned a Network into a Propaganda Machine.* New York: Anchor Books, 2012.

Carlson, Gretchen. *Be Fierce: Stop Harassment and Take Your Power Back.* New York: Center Street, 2017.

Carter, Bill. *Desperate Networks.* New York: Doubleday, 2006.

Cohen, Jeff. *Cable News Confidential: My Misadventures in Corporate Media.* Sausalito, CA: Polipoint Press, 2006.

Collins, Scott. *Crazy Like a Fox: The Inside Story of How Fox News Beat CNN.* New York: Portfolio, 2004.

Klein, Edward. *Katie: The Real Story.* New York: Crown Archetype, 2007.

Muto, Joe. *An Atheist in the FOXhole: A Liberal's Eight-Year Odyssey Inside the Heart of the Right-Wing Media.* New York: Dutton, 2013. ▸

Bibliography *(continued)*

Pao, Ellen. *Reset: My Fight for Inclusion and Lasting Change.* New York: Spiegel & Grau, 2017.

Quinn, Zoe. *Crash Override: How Gamergate (Nearly) Destroyed My Life, and How We Can Win the Fight Against Online Hate.* New York: Public Affairs, 2017.

Schofeld, Reese. *Me and Ted Against the World: The Unauthorized Story of the Founding of CNN.* New York: HarperCollins, 2001.

Sherman, Gabriel. *The Loudest Voice in the Room: How the Brilliant, Bombastic Roger Ailes Built Fox News—and Divided a Country.* New York: Random House, 2014.

Stelter, Brian. *Top of the Morning: Inside the Cutthroat World of Morning TV.* New York: Grand Central, 2013.

Tur, Katy. *Unbelievable.* New York: HarperCollins, 2017.

Weller, Sheila. *The News Sorority: Diane Sawyer, Katie Couric, Christiane Amanpour—and the (Ongoing, Imperfect, Complicated) Triumph of Women in TV News.* New York: Penguin Books, 2014.

West, Lindy. *Shrill*. New York: Hachette Books, 2016.

Whittemore, Hank. *CNN: The Inside Story: How a Band of Mavericks Changed the Face of Television News.* New York: Little Brown, 1990. ◢